IRRESISTIBLY PERFECT

J. SAMAN

1

A noise stirs me awake and I groan, rolling over on the bed, and stuffing my head back under the pillow. It's too early to wake up. I don't even know what time it is, I just know it's too damn early. Fallon flew into Chicago for my concert and then we spent all last night talking, not going to bed until about four in the morning.

Even then I didn't want to go to bed.

Sleep feels like such a waste of precious minutes when I get so few with her.

That thought has me groaning again, flopping over onto my back, and reluctantly blinking my eyes open. My hotel suite is painfully bright, and I immediately snap my eyes shut against the blinding morning rays of sunshine flowing through the open curtains.

"Fall Girl?" I call out because that noise had to be her. She refused to sleep in the bed with me, even when I told her I'd be good and not touch her. It's not the first time we've seen each other and not fucked, and despite what she thinks, I am capable of controlling myself.

Barely.

Wanting Fallon Lark and not being able to have her has been the story of my life since I was fourteen. She was the girl next door. Her family moving in without having any clue about the fucked-up nightmare that lived beside them in the pretty old mansion. One night, I was sitting on my rooftop, staring across the Charles River at the twinkling lights of Boston while strumming on my guitar when she climbed up and joined me, introducing herself to me as a girl I can never be friends with, but that she'll always regret not getting to know me.

That's what she said, and I was instantly intrigued.

Plus, she was fucking beautiful.

There was no denying that part of it. I looked at her and my heart spun wildly in my chest. She sat there with me for hours that summer night, listening to me play and sing, talking to me about the books she loved to read and how one day she wanted to see the world country by country by getting lost in each one. She wanted to be a doctor, she wanted to save lives and make a difference—the one thing she did manage to do for herself since she's now officially a doctor, starting her residency in Miami as a pediatrician.

It wasn't until the next day that I realized the reality of our situation.

I met her twin brother Dillon and instantly became best friends with him—well, at least until a life-changing accident made us enemies. He, I could talk to. He, I could be friends with because every guy has that one friend that your parents hate but overlook because they know you will outgrow him soon enough.

Her, not so much.

The daughter of an extremely wealthy and influential senator and an old money heiress, her life had already been mapped out for her. A good girl who was not allowed to spend time with let alone get wrapped up in the bad boy filled with rock star dreams.

That hasn't stopped us from being friends all these years and it hasn't stopped us from meeting up, usually with her coming to watch my shows like she did last night.

As long as it's all in secret, of course.

Her family can still never know about our friendship. Certainly not how our friendship occasionally blurs lines and becomes more.

"Fall?" I try again when I don't get a response and I don't hear her moving about. Maybe she left to go get coffee or breakfast? I hate that she forced me into the bed when she took the couch. She probably slept like crap on that thing. Dragging myself up and out of bed, I go into the bathroom to wash my face and brush my teeth. My next show is in Indiana tomorrow night and I'm grateful for the night off tonight. I've been touring for six straight months, and it's been night after night after night.

Maybe I can convince Fall to stay with me tonight.

This might be my last chance to spend time with her for a while. I have to imagine being a resident will eat up all of her time. Still, I couldn't be prouder of her.

Heading back into the bedroom, I pull on a pair of joggers and then go in search of Fallon. The living room is empty, the couch where she slept all made up, blankets folded with pillows placed neatly on top.

But that's not what's stopping my breath.

Her stuff is gone. The small suitcase she had with her is nowhere to be found. Neither is her purse. Did she leave without saying goodbye?

No. It can't be. Fall wouldn't do that. She'd never do that.

I stare at the pillow she used, running my hands through my hair only to grip it at the roots. Is this why she was adamant about sleeping on the couch and having me sleep in the bed? So she could run out on me?

I spin, ready to grab my phone from my nightstand and call

her when something catches my eye. My name. Scrawled at the top of a piece of hotel stationary sitting in the center of the desk. No, not just one piece of paper. There are several. My heart starts pounding, a merciless, vicious storm banging painfully against my ribs. I lick my lips, my hands shaking as I snatch the note off the desk.

For a moment, I can't make myself read it.

She's gone without even having said goodbye. This note is her fucking goodbye, and I can't... shit. I just...

Blowing out an uneven breath, I sink down onto the couch she slept on last night, my elbows digging into my parted thighs. It's wet. The pages are wet, stained in her teardrops. Jesus, Fall Girl. What are you doing?

Wiping at my mouth, I pull the note up and begin reading.

Grey,

I stood in the doorway of the bedroom and watched you sleep for entirely too long this morning. I haven't slept. Not a wink. I listened as you fell asleep and that's when my tears started. We've been dancing around this thing between us for years. Years of a friendship no one in my life could know about. Years of coming together the way lovers do when that was never a possibility for us.

Even before Dillon's accident, my parents made it clear they thought you were trouble and that I needed to stay away from you. I tried. Sort of. I wasn't very good at it. I'd go all day long ignoring you in the halls at school and then I'd get home and stare out my window at yours and wonder what you were doing. If you were playing music or doing your homework or messing around with a girl. I'd miss you. I'd miss you like crazy.

I'd sneak into your room at night, and we'd talk for hours, and then sometimes, I'd fall asleep beside you. I'd climb up onto your roof when it was warm out and you'd play for me. We'd call or text whenever we could, using secret aliases in our phones so my parents wouldn't know. I never laughed with anyone the way I laughed with you. I never talked to or shared my secrets with anyone other than you. You were my person.

The only one in my life who ever listened to me. No one cared about the thoughts in my head. No one, except for you.

We were two lost and lonely souls who found each other. Who saw each other. Who understood each other. Your friendship was everything to me. Sometimes it felt like the only real thing in my life. The only thing that was true and just for me.

Then Dillon's accident happened, and everything got worse. My parents blamed you. You blamed yourself. It went from us not being able to be friends to me not being able to even know you or speak to you. Your friendship became even more forbidden to me than it already was.

That didn't stop me from holding on to you

when you left to become a huge rock star with Central Square and it didn't stop me when you became a solo artist after. Until now. Until I stand here like a coward writing you a letter because I don't have the guts to say any of this to your face. I knew I'd never be able to do it and I have to do it. I have to.

Even though it breaks my heart, I have to say goodbye. To you. To our friendship. To all of it. Last night was the last time you'll see me. I won't randomly show up at any more of your concerts. I won't call or text. I won't seek you out. It has to be like this. A clean break. A severing of my heart.

Always know your worth. Always know how incredible you are, not just as an artist but as you. The best person I've ever known. I'm so, so proud of you and all you've accomplished. You're forever in my heart and eternally my best friend. Even if our time together ends like this. In another life, you're everything I'd ever want.

Take care of yourself.

All my love,

Your Fall Girl

With my heart in my throat, I ball up the pages in my fist. I'm sick. Furious. Suffocating under the crushing weight of this blow.

Why? Why now? Why after all these years?

Yes, we were impossible. As friends. As lovers. As anything. A perfect Lark princess, she'd never go against her family for me.

I knew that. I always knew that.

She's right. We were secret friends. Friends who had fake names on each other's phones but would still call and text each other constantly. Friends who would only hang out at night after she'd sneak out of her house and into mine. But that friendship was constant and everywhere. A vital source that got me through the hardest moments of my life.

It's why I never told her how much I love her. How in love with her I've always been. There was no shot at us, and I protected my heart from that level of rejection. But that didn't exactly keep me away.

Her either.

For her it was friendship. For me, it was always something else. Especially as we've gotten older and had our stolen moments.

What the fuck, Fallon? She didn't have to do this. She didn't have to fucking do this.

"What the fuck, Fallon?!" I repeat aloud, my voice shredded. *In another life, you're everything I'd ever want.* "Dammit! No!"

Why can't it be this life? Why can't we have each other? Why can't it be us?

I can't lose her. I love her, and I've already lost so much. No. Not gonna happen.

Shooting off the couch, I fly into the bedroom, tearing through my clothes and throwing on a shirt and sneakers. I find my wallet and phone and stuff both into the pockets of my joggers and then I sprint out the door, down the elevator, onto the street, and into the hotel car.

The drive to the airport through Chicago traffic takes forever and I can't handle it. I'm restless. Edgy. Needing to move instead of sitting still and being patient, I call her phone, but it instantly goes to voice mail, and I hang up. I can't leave a message. I can't do this over the phone. I have to find her, and I have to tell her.

Years and years of loving and pining for her.

After an eternity, we reach the airport and then I'm waiting in line and dodging curious glances from people wondering what I'm doing waiting in line at the airport or questioning if it is in fact me. One of the eternal downfalls of being a celebrity is being recognized, and right now I'm in no mood for any of it.

I just want to catch her plane. I just want to get my girl back.

Finally, I reach the counter only to learn I've missed her flight. "The next flight to Miami leaves in three hours," the woman behind the podium says to me.

"I can't wait three hours. Is there another airline?"

"Let me check."

Click, click, click, her nails on the keyboard drive my already frazzled nerves straight to the edge. "Yes, there's a flight that leaves in thirty minutes."

"Put me on it."

"You won't have enough time—"

"Put. Me. On. It. Please," I tack on at the end.

She scowls at my shitty tone and attitude but does as I ask. More clicking and then I hand her my black Amex and license and then a minute later, she's handing me a first-class ticket. I didn't even ask her for that. I would have sat in the fucking bathroom to get on that flight.

"Thank you."

"You'll have to run."

"I plan on it."

And I do. I race through security, apologizing to everyone in the PreCheck line I blow past. With nothing on me, I get through quickly and then I'm going as fast as my legs will carry me through the airport until I reach the gate, sweating and panting for my life, my lungs burning.

I make the flight, just barely, but I'm here and I sag into the leather seat, my eyes closing. My mind drifts, replaying everything from last night. Everything we talked about. I can't pinpoint it. Other than her refusing to get physical, I can't pinpoint a moment where I felt like something was off or that this was a goodbye visit.

She laughed with me. She smiled. We touched and flirted and talked. Hell, we talked about everything and anything. The way we always have.

Not having sex was disappointing, but not out of the ordinary.

In all the years and times we've met up, sometimes we didn't have sex. Sometimes she was just there, holding me and keeping me together when my life was falling apart. Sex was always a byproduct of our friendship. Of our bond and connection.

Her note crinkles in my hand, the sharp edges digging into my fist. I sigh, dragging a restless hand through my hair as I stare out the window at nothing. I'm offered food and drinks from interested flight attendants and I decline everything.

I'm too wound up. Too close to losing my absolute fucking mind.

Why? That's the one thing I don't understand. The one thing that was not explained in the note.

Unfurling it, I read through it again and again, analyzing it. Memorizing it. Every word and swirl of ink I imprint into my brain.

What will I do when she tells me no?

When she looks at me with pity and remorse in her eyes and tells me there is no way we could ever be together?

The plane tracks southeast through the air and by the time we start our descent over Miami, I feel like I'm going down along with us. I created a hundred speeches in my head. Hell, I'd move to Miami if I had to. But as I step off the plane and exit the airport into the blinding hot and humid sun, in my gut I know that won't make a difference.

I power on my phone and stare at it, debating.

It wouldn't be difficult to find her here. A few phone calls at most.

My gut twists painfully, my chest locked in a vise. I slide into the back of a cab, telling the driver to take me to the beach. He recognizes me, instantly chatting me up about my music and a hundred other things I half listen to.

My heart is too exposed, and I duck my head to catch my breath. I left everything behind and impulsively jumped on an airplane and for what? So I can get my heart broken in live action instead of in privacy? So I can demand answers that won't change the outcome of our story and watch as she falls apart?

I know she's hurting. I saw her tears.

This wasn't easy for her, which makes it all the more permanent.

He drops me in front of some posh hotel I never enter. Instead, I head out to the beach, gaze locked on the turbulent water and waves that match my insides. I sink down into the scalding-hot sand, already sweating, and just stare out at the endless ocean.

Her residency, her life, her future, it's all planned out for her. Everything with her family is a strategy. An equation I never fit into. They hate me. They hate my family.

She won't pick me, and I can't ask her to choose me over them. I already know she won't.

That's our reality.

If I love her, I have to let her go. I'm not who she needs. I'm not who anyone needs. A fucked-up bad boy rock star to her perfect princess. I don't deserve her, and I'd only ruin her. Isn't that what Dillon said to me that night so long ago when I confessed everything to him?

In another life, you're everything I'd ever want.

In another life. Just not in this one.

So instead of tracking her down, I sit here. I mourn. I break. And by the time I drag my miserable, sorry ass up and out of the sand and head back to the airport, I vow to let her have the life she's supposed to have. Even if that life isn't with me.

Three years later

"CAN I HAVE YOUR AUTOGRAPH?" the waitress who unsnapped the top two buttons of her uniform after recognizing both me and my older brother asks with a smile that tells me she'd give me anything she could, including her body, if we wanted.

"Sure," I say with a tight grin, mournfully setting down my coffee mug and casting a longing glance at my breakfast. I'm starving, having woken up at 5:00 a.m. with the hope of writing a song this morning. As with every other morning this week I tried to do that, but I came up with nothing. First time in my life this has happened and it's weighing on me.

"Great!" She jumps up and down, practically screaming. "You're my absolute favorite artist. I have all your albums including the Central Square ones." She laughs, batting her eyelashes. "Which I guess means I have your albums too." She points to my brother, Zax with her pen.

"Thank you for that," I tell her genuinely. Hungry or not, a fan is a fan and I fucking love my fans. "That's very sweet of you." I take the pen from her outstretched hand. "What would you like me to sign?"

"My cleavage for sure so I can show my boyfriend later and well..." She searches around as if something is going to materialize before her eyes. "I guess my guest check pad?"

"Um." I have no judgment that she wants me to sign her tits for her boyfriend—that's between them—but we're in a public restaurant, not an after-party or a club. "You're sure about this?"

"Absolutely," she exclaims with a fierce head bob. I shrug and do as the lady asks before handing her pen back. She eyes my handiwork. "Thank you so much. This is amazing. It reminds me of this one time when I came to—"

"We'd like to enjoy our breakfast now," Zax asserts with a gruff yet somehow slightly polite tone.

"Oh." She blushes like a virgin on her wedding night. "Of course. Sure. Enjoy." She shakes her head in a self-deprecating way and then skulks off.

"Thank you," I say to him, finally slicing into my omelet and shoveling a piece into my mouth, stifling my satisfied moan. My stomach was about to start a revolution if I didn't eat in the next ten seconds.

"You have to be harder on them, or they'll think you're easy pickings and drape themselves all over you."

I nod as I chew. "I know," I garble around a mouthful of eggs, spinach, and bacon, washing it down with a sip of my coffee. "But I'm not good at it. Suzie used to tell me that fans are fans and without them, you're nothing—which is true—and that if you start blowing them off or making them feel unimportant, word spreads faster than chlamydia at a frat party that you're a dick."

Zax chokes on his benedict. "Did you have to use the word *chlamydia* while I'm eating?"

I give him an amused look and then continue to devour my eggs.

"You know, if you had a steady girlfriend, women would back off you."

I laugh because truly, that's funny. "You know that's not true. You were a rock star once and had women all over you even though you were with Suzie at the time. It was even worse after she died, and you were mourning. The women who want to fuck a rock star for the sake of fucking a rock star don't care if you or even they are coupled up already. That waitress just had me sign her tits and she has a boyfriend. Besides, there is no one out there I'd want to date."

"You sure about that?"

"Which part?" I retort cheekily and he rolls his eyes at me. "Yes, matchmaker Jane, I'm sure. What is this? Because you've found someone again you must make sure the rest of us do too? Monogamy doesn't fit with my lifestyle right now," I tell my brother, chowing down on toast this time. "I'm coming off my most successful album yet. Eden Dawson, my producer, and Lyric Rose, my record company exec told me it's also my *best* yet. I have to follow that up, make the next album even better." I subdue the rising panic with that thought. "I have to tour to promote my music, which means I'm traveling for weeks or months all the time. Dating doesn't jive well with that. As it is, I spend too much time getting hit on for simply being Greyson Monroe. That's not what I want in a woman and until I meet the perfect one, it's a big fat hard pass on dating."

Zax laughs. A real laugh, which for Zax is saying a lot. He lost Suzie who was his girlfriend, the woman he was going to propose to when she had a stroke in the shower. A stroke at the age of twenty-two. It was freak and gut-wrenching. Losing her, especially like that destroyed him for over eight years. Zax eventually took over for our father as the CEO of Monroe Fashion, our family's luxury fashion label, when our piece of shit father did some unscrupulous things. Last year our ex-step-sister Aurelia became his design intern and after some serious drama, they fell in love. Now it's a lot of smiles and laughs, which seriously make me smile and laugh in return.

He was the grumpiest fucker on the planet before she came into his life.

Suzie was like a big sister to me. We were as close as close could be. Our band Central Square was our love child. It was the dream we both shared, her our manager and me the front man.

"Except we both know there already is one perfect woman out there for you."

And just like that, my world shuts down.

"You could look her up," he continues casually as if he's not scrambling my insides and frying them in searing hot butter like the eggs I'm eating.

"Fuck you." I practically snarl the words at him, my hand fisting around my butter knife. He knows better than to bring her up to me like this. It's one thing when our friend and former bandmate Asher jokes around, but Zax? No. Not cool.

A nonchalant sip of his coffee. "I'm serious. You could."

I glare, and I do it hard, so he knows just what level of a dick he's being—it's a twelve out of ten, in case you are curious. "I can't. You know I can't." I've forced myself not to hundreds of times. There is no win for me if I do. Nothing changes except reopening ancient wounds. No thanks. I'd just as soon dodge those for the rest of my life.

Zax's eyes cast over my shoulder toward the exit of the restaurant in a contemplative wander. But there is no contemplation with this. With her. My best friend or I guess she was. She's an obsession I haven't been able to shake in the sixteen years since I first laid eyes on her.

But the last time I saw her...

"Where is she living now?"

"Fuck. You!" I repeat, not even bothering to temper the octave of my voice. We're getting looks, I'm positive about it, but right now I don't care. "Stop, Zax. I'm not kidding around with this. Not her, brother."

The one woman I will *never* have as mine and he knows it.

He sighs. Then he stands, wiping his mouth with his napkin before dropping it onto his half-finished plate. "I have to make a call. Then I likely have to go. So..." His eyes up high toward the exit. "Yep. See ya. Call me. I'm here for you and I love you. Remember that."

With a crinkle in my brow and a what-the-fuck expression, my brother waltzes out of the restaurant with a meager pat on my shoulder, leaving me here alone. Only, it takes less than two seconds to realize why he did that.

A woman takes the bench seat diagonal from me at the table beside mine. I stare. My breath gone. My lungs empty. My mind frazzled. My heart a rave...

Then I blow out a breath. Even and slow. Warmth creeps slowly through me like drugs and I smile like the devil I have occasionally been known to be.

I haven't seen her since that night three or so years ago when she came to my concert in Chicago. We spent the night talking because she told me nothing else could happen, and in that talking, the woman whom I considered to be my best friend, the person to whom I told all my darkest secrets, who knew me inside and out, who I was insanely, disruptively, terminally in love with left me a Dear John note.

Except now here she is, back home in Boston sitting across from me in a random café.

Without hesitation, I climb out of my seat, toss some cash on the table, and then drop down onto the bench directly beside her.

She jumps, her head snapping in my direction, caught off guard by some random weirdo creeping in on her personal space until recognition lights her features. Purple eyes—the most insanely beautiful eyes in the world—grow wider than Fenway Park, her pink glossy lips parting on a surprised breath. Her hair, much shorter than the last time I saw it, flows like ribbons of black ink around her shoulders.

"Hi," I say. "This seat taken?"

"Greyson."

"Fallon," I mock her exaggeration of my name, especially when we never use each other's full names. "Shocker of shockers seeing you here. You don't even like breakfast food."

She swallows audibly. "I... I do now."

"Really?"

She lets out a remorseful laugh, her gaze flickering over to me briefly before it playfully bounces around the restaurant. "No. Not really. Eggs are the slimy food of the devil and pancakes make me feel like I'm eating a loaf of bread doused in sugar. The only thing redeeming about breakfast is bacon. And toast. But that has to stay our little secret."

"We're good at that," I chide, nudging her. "Having our little secrets and even some bigger ones. It's been a thousand years, Fall. You good? I'm good," I say to her since that's always been our thing. Whether we're saying goodbye or hello. "You look beautiful."

Her eyes sparkle and a smile curls up the corner of her lips as we fall back into our old routine. "I'm good. How are you, Grey? Handsome as ever I see."

I wink at her and take her hand from her lap, trying not to think about how smooth and soft it is, and set it down on the seat between us. Then I loop our pinkies together.

"When did you get into town?"

That question does something unexpected to her and suddenly she's staring at me so intently I can see all the flecks of purple and lavender and even touches of blue in her eyes. It pains me that I've gone so long without looking directly into them. I squeeze her finger, but I can feel her resistance, her need to pull away.

She blinks and then blinks again. And in those blinks, I catch her oh shit moment and it hurts. It hurts a lot.

"I... um." She licks her lips, her head bowing slightly, her voice strained with genuine regret. "I've been here, Grey."

"Here?"

She sags further while breathing out the word "Boston."

"For how long, Fall Girl?"

Her pinky clings to mine as her gaze plummets to the empty place setting before her. "Since I finished med school."

Sucker. Punch. Everything inside me freezes over. Like holding an ice cube in your fist, it hurts and it's brutally cold all the while numbing you from within. "Wow."

"I know."

"Do you, babe? You told me you were doing your residency in Miami. You lied to me."

"Yes. I lied," she admits, shame consuming her features even as she leans ever so slightly against me, shoulder to shoulder now. "I did my residency at Boston Children's Hospital and at Hughes Healthcare."

"Jesus." I run my free hand across my face. "I don't even know what to say to that. All this time? Why? Why didn't you tell me?"

Vulnerability and dismay drip from her voice as she says, "I'm sorry. I hated myself for the lie and I hated myself for being back in Boston and not telling you, especially anytime I knew you were here." Her gaze climbs back up to mine. "It hurt like hell. Not seeing you, not telling you, keeping something like that from you. I didn't have a choice though, Grey. I didn't."

"You could have told me the truth."

"No. I couldn't have," she says adamantly, but her fierceness crumbles before me. Suddenly she looks wrecked, exhausted, her weight falling heavily against me, her head on my shoulder, and fuck it if anyone is taking pictures or not. She squeezes my pinky again and tilts her head, staring ruefully up at me. "If you knew I was here, we would have seen each other, and I couldn't see you. It was difficult enough for me to hold back." A hard swallow and then her gaze lands on our joined pinkies. "I told you the last time I saw you..."

"No, you left me a note that never told me why," I accuse. "I woke up in that hotel room and found the couch you were supposed to be sleeping on empty. A fucking note on hotel stationary saying goodbye."

A note I've since burned because reading it over and over again was nothing short of self-destructive. Not that I needed the actual note. I had memorized it. Examined every dark scrawl of her inked words.

I ran after her. She doesn't even know it. I hopped on that flight to Miami, and she wasn't even ever in Miami. Fuck. Just fuck!

"I'm engaged," she blurts out, righting her body. I stare at her, positive I did not just hear those words from her sweet lips. "Engaged? Since when?"

"Two weeks. The notice is going out publicly this week. We waited for political reasons since the mid-term elections are coming up and both of our fathers are running for senatorial reelection." She emits a mournful sigh. "I should have told you. I know this. I've thought about it so many times, but I..."

She trails off just as the door of the restaurant swings open, and in walks a dude who screams aristocrat. His blue eyes sparkle, his short blond hair is expensively cut and perfectly coiffed, and his Monroe suit—which inherently makes me want to kill him since it's my family's brand—is expertly tailored. He does a sweep of the restaurant, not immediately finding Fallon, but I know that's who he's searching for.

I know it the same way I know how to play any song I hear once without sheet music.

"To him?" I point incredulously. Fallon's other hand covers mine, lowering it back to my lap and I take her hand, holding it firmly, touching the ring on her finger. My stomach sinks like lead. It's a big diamond, I'll give the prick that much.

"Yes. Grey... I..."

Finally, he locates Fallon and the smile that erupts across his face has my jaw clenching. Why didn't Zax drag me out of here when he saw her enter? Why didn't he save me from this? I should—could—get up and walk away. Walk right out of the damn restaurant, but I can't seem to make my legs move. *Engaged?* How in the fuck did that happen?

She's going to marry this guy? *Marry him?* No. She can't.

"Bacchus," she murmurs, her hands releasing both of mine as she slips around the other side of the table and stands.

I choke on a laugh. *Bacchus?!* For real?

"Dumpling!"

"Dumpling?" I repeat and she kicks my shin under the table before she rounds it and greets him with a kiss on the cheek—not the lips, I note—and then sits back down beside me.

"And who is this?" he asks, taking the chair opposite us and setting his napkin down on his lap. Eyeing me with a look I'm all too familiar with. One that says he knows exactly who I am, and he doesn't like it one bit.

"Greyson, this is my fiancé, Bacchus Hastings Astley the fourth. Bacchus, this is Greyson Monroe—"

"The original," I cut her off. Fallon coughs out a laugh but quickly stifles it. Bacchus Astley. Son of a senator. Naturally. I stretch out my hand and he grips it, but it's limp compared to the death grip I'm giving him. I smile. It isn't friendly. He returns it, and for a few moments, we do the male sizing-each-other-up thing.

He releases my hand first and I win, though there is no victory to be had for me.

"It's nice to meet you, Greyson. Fallon never mentioned you

before. How long have you two known each other since I assume you didn't just meet now?"

"Funny, she never mentioned you to me either."

He makes a displeased noise in the back of his throat and Fallon pinches my thigh.

I redirect. "I imagine she wouldn't have told you about me. Her family doesn't like me too much. Fallon and I used to be neighbors growing up. I was friends with her brother Dillon before the accident."

Fallon shifts beside me, her foot rubbing mine. She hates it when I blame myself for the accident with Dillon. I want to throw my arm around her shoulder or retake her hand, but I restrain myself. Just barely.

"How long have you two been together?" I toss back at him, though I'm pretty positive I already know the answer. I never looked her up. I never had the stomach for it, but now I feel foolish for that.

"Three years," he tells me arrogantly, and yep, it's all coming together now.

"Interesting. That's exactly how long it's been since I saw her last."

Another pinch, this one harder, and yeah, I likely shouldn't have said that. Or still, be here since her family can't know we kept in touch after I left when we were teenagers.

"Hmmm," he says, appraising me with a tilt of his head and narrowing of his eyes. After a beat, a smug smile twists his lips, and he snaps his fingers in that "aha" way as if he's just figured out who I am and didn't already know. Douche. "You're one of those boy banders, right? From that band that broke up all those years ago after that girl died." Fallon stiffens beside me at the mention of Suzie's death, but her dirtbag fiancé doesn't catch it before he continues with, "What was it called again... Harvard Square?"

"Central Square," she corrects for me.

His gaze snaps sharply over to hers. "You're a fan?"

"You know I am, Bacchus. I have his concert T-shirt in my closet and his music on my phone. You've caught me listening to it several times."

That shouldn't give me as much satisfaction as it does.

"Well, now I know why."

"It's good music," I cut in to take the heat off her. "You should give it a listen too. Though technically we were never considered a boy band. Now I play as a solo artist. What do you do?"

He squares his shoulders and sets his folded hands on the edge of the table. "I'm a partner in a law firm, but one day I hope to follow in my father's footsteps and run for office."

I grin. "Of course you do. The Larks wouldn't have set their daughter up with anyone else."

"How did you know they set us up?"

"Greyson," Fallon hisses under her breath, and I need to stop this before it ends badly for her.

"Lucky guess, but what a small world that I ran into Fallon here." I turn and take her in, wanting to continue to be angry and hostile, but it's impossible. I know Fallon. A hell of a lot better than this douchebag does or ever will. I know why she didn't tell me she was doing her residency here and I know why she's engaged to this guy.

I want to ask her if she actually loves him. If he's the guy for her and if she's happy. If she's happy, well, at least then this would be easier to swallow. I always swore I wouldn't be another person in her life to demand things of her. Especially things I know she can't give me.

Like herself. Like her time. Like her heart.

Now... now she's going to marry him and there is nothing I can do to stop it. No matter how much the thought feels like someone is stabbing me with a jagged knife and twisting it around in my chest. I have to protect myself. Unwittingly she tried and now I'm looking at this guy and I'm an open, bleeding mess of a man.

Not something I manage well, so I do what I do best and shut it down. Only this time, it's not working. This feeling. It's refusing to be brushed off or locked away. It's a twenty-ton boulder on my chest, restricting my breathing and making everything hurt like a son of a bitch.

I clear my throat. "Well, I'll let you two enjoy your breakfast." I stand and her eyes follow me, saying so many things to me. Things like I'm sorry and this hurts and I miss you and I wish, I wish, I wish. "Take care of yourself, Fall." I turn to her fiancé who is watching us carefully. "Nice meeting you, man."

I smack his shoulder and head for the exit, my heart in my feet making my steps heavy. I stop short, blinking at the rays of sunshine as they shine through the glass door, thinking. Before I can talk myself out of it, I slip my small notebook and pen I occasionally use to write song lyrics from my back pocket and scribble down a quick message. Then I tear the sheet from the spirals and fold it in quarters and tuck it into my palm.

I'll never get another chance again. Might as well take it. She left me a note and now I'm returning the favor. Though mine is very different from hers.

Turning back around, I realize she's still watching me even as she's speaking to him. I smile because damn, she takes my breath away, and then I return to her table. "How rude of me. I forgot to congratulate you on your engagement. I hope you're as happy as you look."

I lean in and press my lips to her cheek while at the same time, I clasp her hand and slip her the folded piece of paper. She takes it, her brows pinched questioningly even as her breath catches. Her hand closes around the paper and I release her.

Walking away.

This time I don't look back. My message was delivered. It's

hers now and I feel better for her having it. Knowing I'll never see her again after today.

3

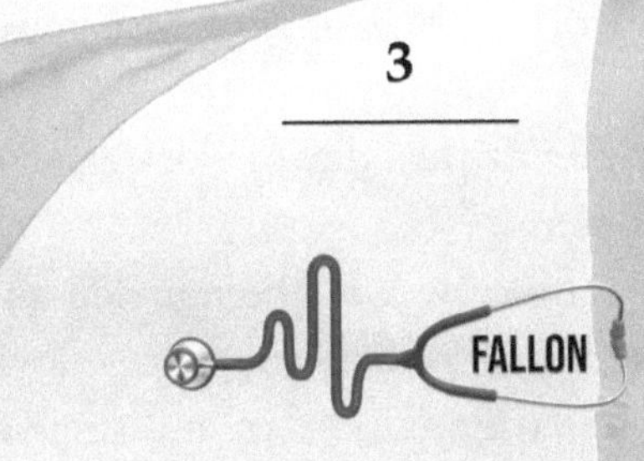

Six Months Later

"JUST HEAR THOSE SLEIGH BELLS RING—"

"It's April," the guy walking beside me clips out, glaring at me in a way that tells me he's not a fan of holiday music.

"So? Bah humbug." It's not my fault the kid I was treating today kept singing that over and over again to calm himself down. Trust me, all you need is to hear it once and then it's stuck in your brain on repeat. Lucky for the kid and unlike the Scrooge who just blew past me, I like Christmas music. Even if it is April.

A cold and rainy April at that.

I huddle into my coat as a wet gust of Boston wind hits me in the face. Still, it does nothing to dampen my spirits or the surprise Japanese takeout I'm carrying that smells out of this world delicious.

Just two more buildings until I reach Bacchus's office and

then he and I can eat. And see each other since we haven't done much of that in the last couple of weeks. I'll admit, my schedule at the hospital has been nuts. A lot of night shifts. It's as if they were piling on the hours the second they found out I was leaving. Plus, Bacchus is working on some big case before he calls it quits too.

But today was finally my last day of work as an attending at Children's Hospital Boston.

Two weeks from tomorrow, we'll be married and then after our two-week honeymoon in Hawaii, we're moving to Philadelphia. It's where he's originally from and since Bacchus has grand plans to take over the world one political move at a time, it's where he wanted us to live.

It's not the first time I've left Boston, but this time it's hitting me hard. I always imagined myself settling down here. Practicing medicine here. That didn't fit in so well with Bacchus. A pediatrician can always find work, he told me, so the choice was sort of removed from me. Not to mention both my parents and Bacchus expect me to give up my profession to be the perfect political wife to my husband.

Except I have zero plans to stop working, whether he's a senator, congressman, or the fucking president. I love being a doctor. I love working with children. Philadelphia Children's Hospital will be incredible. I know it will be.

My phone rings in my pocket, pulling me out of my thoughts. It's Kaplan Fritz. He comes from a family of billionaires here in Boston. He along with his five brothers are all doctors. Rina, the youngest and only daughter is a kick-ass ICU nurse. Our families are friends, so I know them socially as well as professionally. They were like distant, older cousins to me when I was growing up. I also worked with his youngest brother Oliver at Hughes Healthcare. He was one of my attendings when I was a resident.

"Hey," I answer, surprised by the sudden rush of emotion as

it sweeps through me. I'm going to miss this town and these people so much.

"Hey," he says into the phone. "Sorry to bother you on a Friday night, but I wanted to let you know, I saw the patient you referred to me. The little boy with the pathological murmur."

"Oh. Please don't tell me he needs surgery."

"He needs surgery. The regurgitation is too great to treat medically. I have him scheduled for early next week."

Ugh. "Well, I'm glad it's you doing it. You're the only one I allow to fix the tiny broken hearts of my little patients."

He chuckles into the phone. "It's what I do." A pause. "You okay? You sound... funny."

I force a smile to my lips even though he can't see it. "Just feeling a bit melancholy. Today was my last day before I move."

"Shit. I'm sorry. That's rough. We'll miss you here. Let us know if you ever need anything. You're like family and we take care of family."

I puff out a breath, his words hitting me hard. "Thank you. I appreciate that more than you know."

"Anytime. Take care and we'll see you at the wedding in two weeks."

The call ends and I tuck my phone back in my bag just as I reach the door to Bacchus's office building. It swings open with a swoosh, and I throw a wave at the security guard before stepping onto the elevator twenty people just vacated. Everyone else is heading home, anxious to start their weekend, and yet my fiancé is still here, working late on a Friday night.

The ride up is quick and then I'm dumped onto his mostly vacant floor. Only a few stragglers remain, but they're heading out as I meander through to the back where his office is. I hear his voice when I get close and realize he's on the phone. With a deep sigh, because I'm ravenously hungry, I pause, pressing my body against the wall to wait while he finishes up.

At least no one is here to see me do it.

He hates it when I interrupt his work calls and since this is a surprise visit, I know he won't appreciate that.

"Don't jerk me off, Tommy. You know I can't agree to that deal. Not only is it bullshit, but my client won't let it happen. You're the federal prosecutor for this case. I need more than that if you're wanting to make a deal."

He listens and then I hear him move, flipping his phone to the speaker as he gets up. "It's a straight deal, Astley," Tommy says. Tommy is one of Bacchus's closest friends. "More than your fucktwat client deserves in this."

"I can argue that."

"I'm positive you can since that's what you've been doing by dragging this out, but we're both reaching the deadline, and no one wants this to end up in court." He's silent for a beat. "How about we make this in everyone's best interest? Your clients pay thirty million instead of forty, and I sweeten the pot with an extra twenty grand over the top for you."

Ice clinks in Bacchus's glass and I hear him audibly take a sip. "Are you trying to bribe me?"

"Never." Tommy laughs. "Just think of it as doing a favor for your old law school buddy and everyone makes out. Especially you. What do you say? Twenty for you and the deal is signed."

"Fine. But I want it by next Friday or the deal is void."

I cover my gasp with my hand. What he just did is illegal. What Tommy just did is illegal. They could be disbarred for that. They did it so nonchalantly too. Not even a thought in their minds or a second guess or a moment of hesitation where they reconsidered the legality of their actions.

Another laugh. "Because that's your last day of work before you tie the knot?"

Bacchus groans, the leather of his chair crinkling as he retakes his seat. "Don't remind me."

My eyes bolt open wide as silent dread fills my stomach. I strain, listening for each word that comes next.

"What?" Tommy squawks in outright shock. "How can you say that? This is everything you and your old man wanted, right? Are you having cold feet about Fallon?"

"I don't know, man." The glass clatters as he sets it down on his desk. "Not exactly." He falls silent and then I hear him moving around in his chair. "How do you stick to one pussy for the rest of your life? Three and a half years has been hard enough."

My insides run cold, and I stand here, pressed against the wall, frozen through. My pulse flutters angrily in my throat, a painful throb I feel through my skin.

"Who says you have to? I'm shocked you made it this long."

Bacchus clears his throat. "Fallon is very anti-cheating. Her parents have an ugly marriage, and she doesn't want that for us. I've been faithful all this time because I was afraid she'd catch me fucking around on her and I couldn't mess this up. But now that I'm staring down the aisle, it's all I can think about. No way I can keep that promise after we're married."

"Do you love her?"

Bacchus laughs as if that's ridiculous, the sound scrambling my insides making my eyes smart with unshed tears. "Sure, I love her. She's perfect. Sweet and beautiful even if she's a little on the fat side."

"Asshole, women aren't fat anymore. They're curvy."

Bacchus snickers. He takes a sip of his drink and then sets the glass back down. "Really? Her huge ass and hips would disagree with you. Whatever. I don't care about her being fat so much, especially when it comes to her nice tits. The rest can all be fixed with surgery or diet or whatever. Fallon is going to be the perfect political wife and that's exactly what I need from her. She's my ticket to the White House. But she can be so fucking boring sometimes. Both in and out of bed. I have to keep reminding myself, you marry the bitch for her pedigree, not for her bark or her ass. In Fallon's case, both are definitely true."

"I still don't see why you have to keep your dick in your pants. What she doesn't know won't hurt her and you're smart enough to find ways to hide it from her."

"I know. You're right. Plus, there's this woman in the Philadelphia office I'm moving into. Now she's fucking hot. No way I don't fuck her within a week of starting. She wants it too. She told me so."

"Then you should fuck her."

Bacchus laughs. "I should fuck her. You think that's bad form to do the week after your honeymoon?"

More laughter and my mind screams at me. *Run, Fallon. Go. Get away.* But my muscles won't take action. I have to hear him. Every cruel word. I'm not breathing and I'm grateful because I know, if I take a breath, I'll sob. And fuck him, he doesn't deserve my agony. My hand covers my mouth as bile climbs the back of my throat. Outrage and pain slash through me. I can't believe I'm hearing all this. I can't believe the things he's saying about me.

"Fallon would freak if she ever found out."

"Then make it so she doesn't find out. Fuck this woman a few times and get it out of your system if you don't think you can keep a steady mistress a secret. You just have to be careful. Men get caught when they get sloppy."

"I know. I'm all over it. I just can't bring any of it home with me. Fallon can never find out about this woman or any others because if she does... well..." A pause and then he laughs. "Whatever. It's not like she'll divorce me. Bitch is too well-trained for that. Too perfect." He laughs some more and Tommy laughs and *ha, ha, ha*, all I see is red. A haze so thick it's like a flaming fireball before my eyes.

I'm humiliated and ashamed and sick and *enraged*.

Clutching the bag of food in my hand, I fly into his office

and with the force of ten thousand suns chuck it at him. It whirls through the air, the containers fleeing the confines of the brown paper and smashing all over his desk and onto him. Sauce and sushi and wasabi and salmon teriyaki are everywhere. His glass is collateral damage, knocking into his chest and then crashing to the floor spraying tiny bits of crystal and bourbon.

"You son of a bitch!" I rage on an earsplitting scream.

"Shit. Tommy, I gotta go." He slams his fist into his office phone. "What the fuck, Fallon?" He stands, shoving at the hot, sticky, wet mess covering his suit and shirt.

I point my finger at him, raging. "Are you kidding me?! You refer to me as a bitch and talk about how you can't wait to stick your dick in another woman because I'm so fucking boring and you dare to ask me what the fuck?" My voice carries higher with each word. For once, I don't care if someone sees or hears.

Flustered, he abandons the mess. "Listen, dumpling, it's not what you think. I don't know what you think you heard, but—"

My finger jabs through the air. "Don't you *dare* take a condescending tone with me. You know what you said, and you know I heard it. Try again, asshole."

He moves to come at me, and my hands shoot out, stopping him. If he touches me, I might kill him. I don't have a scalpel or a knife or even a pen on me and the chopsticks are now on the floor by his feet, but I'll find something and that will be that for him. "Dumpling, no. I love you. I swear, I do. What you heard..." He growls in frustration, spins in a circle, and kicks his chair. "I'm sorry, okay? I am. Jesus, Fallon, it's been a long day and a long week. It was just guy talk. Just shooting the shit." Another step and I stop him, making him growl in annoyance. "Come on. What are you doing getting so upset about this? You're making this into more than it has to be."

"Are you... are you trying to gaslight me?"

How many times has he done that before and I haven't realized it?

"Fuck! No! That's not... you have to understand me. It wasn't anything. Just bullshit talk. I haven't been unfaithful. I swear to you, I haven't."

I shake my head because that feels like such a ridiculous thing for him to say to me. I don't need his hollow apology or his nonsense explanations. The irony in all this is, I'm not surprised. I mean, I didn't think he was planning to cheat on me the week after we get back from our honeymoon and moved states. That I most definitely *didn't* assume.

But I'm not surprised he is either.

My parents are no different. Their friends are no different. It's a running goddamn joke at political cocktail parties. The men in one room with their brandy and cigars and the women in another, sipping champagne and tittering about their faces and all the injections they want to get. But it's there beneath all the superficiality. This one is fucking this one's nanny and that one is fucking this one's husband. It's all out in the open without being out in the open at all.

Naively, I didn't think it would happen to me.

Bacchus knows what my parents did. How much it bothered me. How much I hated that and the way it felt like we were all living a life based on it. When I told him about it, he held me and promised it would never be us. That we'd be that real couple everyone would be envious of. For three and a half years, we were.

But it was all a lie.

"You want a perfect political bitch to heel at your feet, find her somewhere else. We're over. I can't believe I was about to marry a slimebag like you." I rip my engagement ring from my finger and hurl it at him and then take off at a sprint.

"Fallon! Wait. No." I hear his phone ring and then I hear the motherfucker answer it. He answers his phone instead of chasing after his fiancée. Well, ex-fiancée now. The only saving grace for me is that he hadn't cheated yet. My vagina is grateful. If he had given me an STI, I swear, they never would have found his body.

Mercifully the elevator doors open the second I hit the button and then I ride down, pacing around the car, riled up beyond rational thought. My feet hit the ground floor and then I'm racing out of the building, delighted that it's raining and cold and not warm and perfect. This weather matches my insides, but while my body is soaking wet as I run, my eyes are dry. I'm not crying over this. I just ran and I'm not sure if that makes me a coward or smart. I don't want to look at him and I don't want to hear more of whatever bullshit he'd have to say about it.

The things he said about me...

Wow. I just... I just can't with all of that. How do I wrap my head around any of it? Maybe I'm not crying because I'm so angry? It felt damn good to throw that food at him. It certainly ruined his suit. I laugh. It's not real. It's caustic as hell and it feels oddly good.

What is this... *odd* sensation coursing through me?

I can't place it and I can't name it, but it doesn't matter because right now, I have bigger problems. As I reach our apartment building, a shivering drowned rat, I realize I can't stay here. This is his place. I moved in with him. Hell, it won't even be his place for much longer since he sold it and we're moving to fucking Philadelphia in a month. Right after we were supposed to get back from Hawaii.

I'm homeless. Jobless. Fiancéless.

If I tell my parents, they'll make excuses for it and essentially tell me to deal. That this is modern married life. My mother would tell me he didn't technically cheat and to move past it. I doubt they'd even care that he's a criminal, taking bribes to get a deal done. They'd probably consider that savvy and smart business practice.

I heard it all when we got together, and even more so when we got engaged.

He's the perfect man for you, Fallon. Smart and ambitious. A strong political name from an important swing state. Massachusetts and Pennsylvania. With those states and both your fathers as backing, you'll be living on Pennsylvania Avenue before you know it. Think of the power the two of you will have in this country and throughout the world.

"Fuck them all!" I cry out as I slash through his condo, littered with half-filled boxes.

That's all they ever cared about. Power. Money. The right connections.

I never cared about any of that.

All I wanted was for them to see me. To love me for me when I never felt like they did. To make everyone happy because we were so goddamn miserable, and I couldn't stand it another second.

"Fucking pathetic, Fallon. Look what you've let them reduce you to."

Urgency propels me. Bacchus could be here any second and I don't want to see him, so I find my biggest suitcase and fill it with everything my hands touch from my closet. Everything in my drawers and off my shelves gets stuffed into it. My passport. Oh, I definitely want to hold on to that. Shoes. Yup, can't forget my shoes. Especially that cute pair of sparkly heels I've never worn.

The bathroom is next, and I just swipe along my counter like it's Supermarket Sweep and then I'm zipping the heavy fucker up, pressing my weight into the top so the zipper will close all the way, and then I'm running again. I drop my keys on the floor—hoping he steps on them with bare feet—grab my purse and then I'm back out in the rain.

With nowhere to go.

I have no one.

A few friends, I guess, but I'm embarrassed and I'm not sure I'm ready to talk about anything yet. My only female friends are my work friends and they ask a lot of questions, gossip like crazy, and think the sun rises out of Bacchus's ass.

I'm getting wetter by the second, the rain heavier now, and I'm lost and alone and freaking cold. Mentally I go through hotels close by when I catch sight of Bacchus's car driving down the street. He'll see me standing out here for sure. My head whips around and two buildings up on my left is a bar that has my name written all over it.

A drink or twenty sounds pretty damn good right about now.

Ducking my head, I shoot straight for the bar. Bacchus is at the light a couple blocks up, the glow of the streetlights illuminating his car. It's dark out, so hopefully, he hasn't seen me yet. A warm blast of air and the scent of stale beer and fried food hit me as I enter the pub. It's crowded, filled with Friday night after-work drinkers, but I manage to drag my suitcase behind me and snag a lone bar seat in the corner.

People are eyeing me, no doubt because I look like the people who didn't make it on Noah's ark. I push my hair back and wipe the excess water from my face. I can't do anything about my clothes, but they'll dry. It's my insides that feel like they've been wrung through.

"What'll ye have?" A cute bartender with an Irish brogue asks, leaning his elbows on the counter and staring straight into my eyes with a furrowed brow. It's not new, so I don't return his puzzled look. My eyes. No one can make sense of them. They're not blue and they're not silver and they're not green and certainly not brown. They're purple, lighter or darker depending on the lighting.

My patients think I'm a superhero because of them and I never dissuade that assumption.

"A dirty martini, please," I politely request. He nods, but before he can get far, I hold up my hand stopping him. "And a double shot of tequila. Good tequila. Not well tequila."

"Ye want a double of tequila and a dirty martini?"

"Please," I say with a smile that hopefully makes me appear less unstable than I clearly am.

He takes in what he can see of me since I'm mostly hidden by the bar. "Yer a bit small for all that alcohol."

Short, yes. Small, well, Bacchus certainly doesn't think so.

"Can't we just pretend I have the liver of a gold medal alcoholic? I don't want to tell you my sad story and I seriously doubt you want to hear it. I'm not driving. I'm twenty-nine years old. And I have plenty of money."

"Just give the lass her drinks, Seamus. Stop mother-henning her."

I glance to my right and find a tall man with blazing red hair and a matching beard. He's Scottish. I think. I might be mixing my accents, but they're all delicious.

Seamus gives me a wary nod and then goes about making my drinks.

"Thank you," I tell the tall fellow.

He smacks the bar top in front of me and mercifully leaves me to myself. The last thing I want right now is small talk with anyone. My phone buzzes in my purse and I'm so tempted not to do it, but curiosity is a nefarious wench, and she always, *always* wins out with me.

> Bacchus: Call me. I want to make sure you're safe. I know you packed a bag, and I'll give you a day or two to think about this, but we need to talk.

Bacchus: Or you can come back now. Did you eat? I can pick you up something to eat. I know you must be hungry.

Bacchus: Please, Dumpling. I'm so sorry for what you overheard. I didn't mean it. I swear I didn't. It's just stress. Just stupid stress that means nothing. I won't cheat on you. I swear to you that I won't. Just come back to me.

Bacchus: Where are you and why aren't you returning my calls or texts?

I stare at his texts, reading them over and over just as he calls, interrupting me. I send him to voice mail immediately. Part of me wants to believe him. Part of me wonders if maybe I overreacted. He hasn't actually cheated on me. Maybe guys do that. Talk shit about their women as a way to blow off steam or stress or to work it out of their systems so they don't cheat or do the wrong thing. The bartender slides my drinks in front of me and I note his wedding band.

"Can I ask you something?"

Reluctantly he agrees. "Aye."

"Have you ever cheated on your wife?"

"Oh, bloody Jesus." He wipes at his forehead, grimacing.

"Wait, I'm not done with my questions. Have you ever cheated on your wife or talked to your friends about how you want to cheat on her?" Because she's fat and boring in and out of bed. That stung.

The look he gives me is nothing short of revulsion. "Em. No. My wife would string me up by my balls if I ever did that."

Good woman. "Okay. Have you ever, I don't know, said some disparaging or quite frankly hurtful things about her to your friends then? You know, maybe said you marry the bitch for her pedigree and not her bark or her ass. And speaking of asses, would you ever tell your friends that your wife is fat and has a fat ass?"

He sighs, dropping his elbows on the counter again and leveling me with a pitying look I'd quickly brush off if I wasn't so interested in his answer. "A real man who loves his lady would never do that. He'd know she's the most precious and valuable possession he has. We might complain she doesn't have sex with us enough or that she's naggin' or whatever, but we never speak down about our women. It makes us look bad to do that. Complaining isn't disparaging. There is grumblin' with yer mates and then there is being an unrepentant disrespectful arse, and there is a difference. If yer man disrespected ye like that and ye left the bastard, ye did right."

"Thank you, Seamus." I offer him a weak smile that feels more like a twisted frown and then go for my shot. I've never actually taken a tequila shot before, but it always looks so cool and easy in the movies. I shoot it straight down the back of my throat and wheeze a sputtering hack of a cough. He slides the limes to me, and I quickly snatch one, shoving it into my mouth and sucking on it for dear life.

Then I wave my finger around in the air before pointing at my empty shot glass.

He does the sign for the cross over his chest. "Blessed Mary, this is going to be a long night. I'll get ye some water too."

I give him a thumbs-up as I remove the now dehydrated lime from my mouth. "That's likely a good idea. Hydration is key," I tell him as I sip on my martini that doesn't go all that well with tequila but who cares? I have to come up with a plan. I have to think, only that seems so difficult to do right now.

My stupid phone buzzes again.

> Bacchus: Just text me back so I know you're somewhere safe.

My fingers linger over the keyboard on my phone, debating what, if anything, I should write back and if I should let him have it again. Probably not something I should do in my current state of tequila and vodka inebriation. I want to remember it when I eviscerate him.

Me: I'm safe.

With Don Julio. I snicker to myself.

Me: Stop texting and calling me. I'll call you tomorrow.

I set my phone down, only it is too close to the edge and it slips off the counter and clatters to the floor.

"Crap," I hiss, bending to pick it up, only the case came partially off, and now I drop to my knees. My hands start to tremble, my body along with it, my heart galloping in my chest because it's behind my phone case. I didn't want to lose it and I couldn't leave it any place Bacchus could find it, so I stuck it there.

Greyson's note.

If I take it out, if I read it again for the thousandth time, if I give in to that temptation...

My family *hates* him. Hates the Monroes. Dillon's accident is why they hate Greyson in particular, but they didn't like him all that much before that when he and Dillon were best friends. The latter is more my mother's doing. She caught my father in bed with his mistress—not that it was his first—and used Mr. Monroe to take a bad situation and turn it into the stuff of Lifetime movies.

I retake my seat, gripping my phone, and squinting at the half-on case, trying to ignore it as I take another sip of my martini. I could call Dillon. He's a congressman now—the youngest one ever from Massachusetts—living in DC and rarely makes time for me. But he's also my twin brother and I don't have anyone else I feel like I can call about this who will understand.

My chin drops toward the chipped bar top, and that's when the tears officially start because that's not true. I had someone else. Someone who stuck with me without asking for anything in return other than what small pieces of myself I could give him. A guy I could call at three in the morning and he'd always pick up. He'd always make time for me even when he had no time to spare for anything.

I threw him away. My best friend. For them.

I'm crying over Greyson and not my horrible fiancé.

Though that's nothing new. I've shed millions of tears over Greyson throughout the years. Some of them with him. Most of them alone. I've missed him terribly. Like a missing appendage, he's always been a part of me, and his absence has been felt even after he was gone.

Five guys from Central Square, Cambridge hit it huge on a YouTube video gone viral and overnight everything changed. Grey was the lead singer and main talent, but together they scored a record contract and were leaving Boston to be the opening act for Wild Minds which was the world's biggest rock band at the time. It was a dream come true for all of them.

Except for me.

I was left behind with parents who swayed between indifference and volatility with each other and a brother who was angry and nasty to anyone who dared to look at him because all he saw was the accident and what it did to him. I was the perfect one. It was both a survival skill and what was expected of me. The one who tried to sew all our torn pieces back together and make everyone happy.

When Greyson left, I had no one. No other friends I connected with the same way. No one I trusted. My life turned superficial as it was always destined to be as Fallon Lark. Parties and clothes and smiles and tittering of girlfriends who talked shit behind my back and sloppy kisses by half-interested social climbing boys. Perfect grades, perfect extracurriculars, perfect schools. I was the show pony my father could parade around when needed to demonstrate how perfect our family was.

Grey was the only thing real in my life.

To him, I was just his best friend. The substitute for my brother after the accident. Someone who would listen, and he could talk to without judgment. To me, he was a lifeline to a world beyond the one I was stuck in. But that's all we were. Friends. Friends who occasionally fucked, but that's where it stopped, and it wasn't every time we saw each other. We both knew the score and never thought of or attempted for more.

After Central Square broke up when Suzie died, Grey continued as a solo artist while the other guys went off and did other things. Zax an entrepreneur turned fashion mogul, Asher Reyes a quarterback in the NFL, Callan a doctor—and yes, I know people he works with, and Lenox... well, I'm not sure what you'd call what Lenox does.

At first, after Suzie's death, Grey and I clung to each other a bit tighter. Her loss destroyed all the guys, but it did something different to Grey. He was a little more lost. A little more out of sorts. Central Square was his and Suzie's baby and then that was gone, and he was scared it was all over for him.

It wasn't.

His first solo album took off like a rocket and he never looked back. I was in college and then med school and had little time for anything else. I'd break away here or there, go see him play, and we'd slip back into our old habits because it was easy and comfortable, and I missed him and craved that connection. He did too, I think. Our chaotic worlds always stood still for just a little while when we were together.

But it was all a secret.

Always had to stay a secret. Our friendship was too forbidden for the light of day to touch. Even if my parents didn't hate him and his family, it still wouldn't have been accepted. Not the right blood. Not the right kind of money. A rock star.

Which is why I had to stop seeing him. It's why I didn't tell him I was living in Boston. I'd have wanted to see him. I'd have wanted to be near him and that wasn't fair to anyone. Bacchus could never know about our friendship because my parents could never know. Bacchus wouldn't have understood it. He didn't even like that I listened to his music and had his concert shirt.

I had to let Greyson go.

That's what I told myself. I had to. I couldn't sneak off and see him. That felt duplicitous. Like cheating, even if I wouldn't have. Writing that note and saying goodbye was the hardest thing I've ever done. Certainly the most painful. Though that night as I walked out the door, casting one last glance back at his sleeping form, for the first time, a strange thought hit me. What if Grey had shown any sort of an inkling that he wanted me beyond friendship? Would I have given up everything for him?

"Coward," I accuse myself. "Ugh!"

"Pardon?"

I shake my head at poor Seamus as he places my second double in front of me. "Nothing. Just trying to figure out my life now that it feels like it's over."

"Ah, shite."

"No. It's fine." It's so not fine. I give him a watery smile. "Did you ever have a dream?"

"Fuck," he mutters, scrubbing a hand along his bristly jaw.

I wave him away. "You don't have to answer that. I'm sorry. But once upon a time, I had a lot of dreams. Dreams I knew would never become my reality because of what my reality was. My parents are wealthy and powerful, and my life was planned out for me before I was even born. Still, I always felt... I always wanted..." I shake my head. I don't even know what I'm saying.

I let those thoughts die out forever ago. "Never mind." I pick up my double and drink it down in one giant gulp and surprisingly it goes down a lot smoother. "I'm good. You go on."

"Ye sure?"

"Positive."

He walks away and I sag against the bar, my mind growing fuzzy and my body growing warm, no longer cold or noticing the wetness of my clothes and hair.

"Fallon Lark, this is your life. And it kind of sucks at the moment." I sigh, finishing off my martini, and how did that happen so fast? I should have asked Seamus for a refill.

A wet hiccup pops out of my mouth, and I slap my hand over it, giggling brokenly. I'm a mess. A hot fucking mess. What the hell am I going to do about Bacchus? Ending it with him isn't as easy as it sounds. But how can I marry a man who speaks about me that way? Who plans on fucking another woman the first chance he gets.

I can't.

That's one sacrifice I won't make, and I've already made too many. I just don't know how to get out of it. It will mean severing things in my life. It will mean publicly ruining a marriage-to-be that both our families are very keen on happening.

I'm sitting alone, drunk in a bar, and I have no idea what to do next.

My gaze snaps back down to my phone. To the case. To Greyson's face when he slipped me the note. Peeling off the case, the worn paper falls to the counter. I don't even have to open it or read it to know what it says. I've memorized it. But it's the action of it that's dangerous.

Carefully unfolding it, I read it aloud.

"You're irresistibly perfect as you are and not

as who they say you have to be. Never forget to live your life for yourself and no one else. If you ever need someone to remind you how you know where to find me. Love,

Your Grey."

Did the man have a crystal ball when he wrote this?

The first time I read it, I didn't understand it. I was even a little hurt by it. Who was he to tell me I wasn't living my life for myself? Greyson was fun. Greyson was an adventure. Greyson was my friend, but only in our stolen moments, and those ended three years prior. Greyson wasn't tangible in my real life.

So what the hell did he know about it at that point? About me?

I'm a doctor—that was all my doing. Like when I snuck out to his concerts or spent a night in his bed or even reading deliciously smutty romance novels—I still love to read those—that was all me too. I was engaged to Bacchus because I loved him—the fact that my parents set us up only made it better because I was pleasing everyone.

But that last thought was the clincher.

For the last six months, anytime I read Greyson's note or replayed it in my head, something inside of me would fragment. A piece of myself I couldn't name or fully grasp, but was there, hidden, tucked away like a dirty truth would break apart.

I pushed it away time and time again, convincing myself I was happy. That pleasing my parents—being their perfect Lark princess—was what brought me joy. Praise and recognition from my parents I needed the way I needed oxygen. I never even pretended otherwise. It was easy to tell myself that Bacchus was the man for me—the man I was always supposed to marry and be with because that's what I had been told. Why wouldn't I believe it when I felt that way too?

The reality is, Greyson was right. I was always living my life for someone else. Modeling their form of what they deemed perfect and making it my own.

A deep frown slashes at my face as I reread the note. "I don't want to be this woman anymore." The one who is engaged to the asshole to please her parents because he has the right résumé and pedigree. The woman who allows others to dictate how she lives her life. I'm drowning and I've been deprived of oxygen for so long, I didn't even realize I could still come up for air and take a breath for myself.

I stare around the crowded bar. Then down at my suitcase. The first night I met Greyson, sitting up on his rooftop at the age of fourteen, I told him how I wanted to explore the world by getting lost in it. All these years later, I chalked that up to a child's dream. But as I stare at my filled suitcase with nowhere to go and no job or fiancé holding me down, dawn rises from within me, bringing with it something else. Something I maybe hadn't fully killed after all, and I smile.

I know now what that feeling was. That one I couldn't quantify.

Relief.

It's relief I've been feeling all night. Dread too, but not at losing Bacchus, I don't think. It was dread at knowing how messy climbing out of this life I've been trapped in is going to be. But I'm no longer trapped. I mean, at least I don't have to be. I can be brave. I can say fuck you to my life and my family and I can make this bitch mine. I can. I can do it.

Stand up, Fallon, and do it. Now. As in right now!

"This is it, Fallon, it's now or never."

A psychotic sort of laugh flees my lungs as I rise to my feet and with shaky hands, drop some cash on the bar. I head for the door and do the thing I likely should not do but can't seem to find my fucks to give at this moment to second-guess it.

I make the call, because yes, I do know how to find him.

5

"**G**rey, your phone is ringing, man," Asher calls out to me as I'm washing my hands in the kitchen sink since they were covered in more buffalo sauce than any amount of paper towels could handle.

"Who is it?" I yell back over the sound of the running water.

"Oh shit." He starts cackling. Then I hear Callan and Zax say the same thing. Even Lenox grunts and since he doesn't speak much, that's his equivalent.

"What? Who is it?"

"It's no one." Then I hear Asher drawl, "Hey baby doll, it's Asher Reyes answering Grey's phone."

My eyebrows pinch together, but I smirk. It's probably some chick I hooked up with once calling me for a repeat though for the life of me, I can't think of who it could be. It's been a while and I'm not exactly known for exchanging digits.

"It's good to hear your voice too. How are you, honey? It's been... hell, it's been a long-ass time since I've seen you. Since Suzie's funeral, I think."

"Huh?" I shut off the faucet and dry my hands on a dish towel. "Ash, who is it, man?"

"Dude," Callan calls out. "You need to get in here and take your phone back unless you want Asher talking to your girl."

The fuck? "My girl?" I murmur under my breath and start for the media room as my brain works overtime.

"It's Fallon," Callan yells as if he is able to hear my musing. "Ash is talking to Fallon. This is a code red."

"Fallon?!" Shit, I sure as hell do not want Asher talking to Fallon. He's a flirt. A harmless and loyal flirt, but a flirt nonetheless. I race across Zax's penthouse, wishing it were a lot smaller than it is. A door opens and Aurelia steps into the hall, but I don't have time to make the last-second adjustment and I slam not only into her but into the door, stubbing my big toe on it through my sock.

"Ow!" Aurelia rubs her shoulder, glaring daggers at me. "What the hell, Greyson?" She smacks my shoulder as I hop up and down, my toe stinging like a bastard.

"Sorry, Reils," I murmur, hopping past her in the direction of the game room, anxious to get to my phone. "You okay?"

"What did you do?" Zax pops his head out, finding his fiancée still rubbing her shoulder.

"He smashed into me. Before you go all caveman on your brother, it was an accident."

"Normally I would anyway, but he has a very important phone call to get."

Aurelia's blue eyes light up. "Oh, who is it? A lady friend? Grey, are you holding out on me?"

I roll my eyes at my soon-to-be sister-in-law and hobble into the room, only Aurelia isn't having that. She's in hot pursuit.

"Who is it that has him like this?" she whispers to Zax, her eyes sparkling with intrigue and excitement.

"Do you remember Fallon Lark? She lived next door to our house when we were growing up."

Considering Aurelia is our ex-stepsister and was living with us at the time right before Central Square hit it big and we all left, I have no doubt she does. A point she proves when she squeals in delight.

"Wait, *that's* who Asher is talking to?"

"Yup," Callan tells her, all grins.

"You let him pick up the phone when Fallon is calling!" Aurelia chastises Callan and then Lenox. Even my brother isn't without reprimand. "What is wrong with you men?"

"What were they supposed to do?" Asher mocks. "Tackle me?"

She points at Asher who is standing by the window, two hands protectively holding my phone that he has pressed to his ear. "Can't be that difficult. I've seen you play."

"Ohhhh," the guys all start crowing at her dig.

"No way we were letting this call go to voice mail. Even if Asher did pick up before I could."

"You're supposed to help me out here, Doc," I admonish. "You're the nice one of us."

"No way. This is Fallon."

I flip Callan off and then go for Asher only he quickly side-steps away from me. "Ash, give me my phone."

Asher is holding my phone up to his ear, mumbling something to Fallon I can't fully hear, and staring at me as he dances around the furniture, trying to dodge my advances. He's a championship-winning NFL quarterback for the Boston Rebels, so he's better at it than most, I'll give him that.

"Aw, thanks. You're the sweetest," he coos to her. Then he laughs, winking at me. "You sound it, but I think it's sexy, just like you. I saw a picture of you a few months back. I like your hair shorter like that. Really frames your face." He laughs a little harder. "No, I'm serious. It totally fits you. My mama taught me to never tease a woman about her hair. She's a nice Southern lady, you know. I'm sure our boy Grey would agree. He's always had a thing for your hair. And eyes for that matter."

Callan and Lenox and even my traitor brother are laughing their asses off.

"Speaking of, can you imagine what color eyes and hair our babies would have? They'd be stunning."

"Come on, dickhead. Phone."

He shakes his head. "Nah, bro. I'm having a scintillating conversation with my girl, Fallon."

"It's truly her?" I'm skeptical, even as I dive at him—and miss—from around the sectional. First, because until I saw her in that café, I hadn't heard from her in three years. Second, because last I checked she was still engaged and about to be married in a couple of weeks. Incidentally, I've also scheduled myself to be out of the country then. Here's hoping European tabloids don't care about Fallon Lark marrying Bacchus Astley.

Their engagement announcement was a special form of hell.

"It is," Zax confirms with a frown that tells me he's not at all happy that she's calling me.

Honestly, I'm not sure how I feel about it myself. There is only so much a man can take.

"Asher, can I have the phone?" Aurelia sweetly blinks her huge blue eyes at him. "Please?" she tacks on with a dazzling smile. Aurelia was a famous fashion model who now owns her own design house as part of Monroe, but it's the first time I've seen her use her charms on Asher and it throws him off because he's not sure what to make of it. "I'd love to say a quick hello before you finish your conversation with her."

"Uh. Sure, doll. Here."

He hands her the phone and then she quickly tosses it to me. I catch it, holding my hand up in the air in victory.

"What the hell?" Asher yells with a pout. "You played me."

"I did," she tells him without an ounce of remorse. "Played the player. Now get out of here. All of you. Give the man some privacy to talk." Aurelia starts pushing all the guys one by one toward the door as they gripe and moan like small children. "Come on. I'll go bake brownies. You want brownies, don't you?"

"Yes," they grumble. But do as they're told because Aurelia makes fantastic brownies. Once she has that accomplished, she turns back to me with a wink and then shuts the door behind her.

"Thank you," I call out.

"No problem," she replies distantly and then I stare at my phone for a second. Sure as death and taxes, it says Fall Girl. I bring it to my ear.

"Fall?"

"Hey, Grey. Yes, it's me." Then she laughs. "Wow, that was a bit intense. Asher Reyes is still a flirt and charmer, isn't he?"

I smile but quickly wipe it from my lips. "He is. What's up? Everything okay?" She sounds... I don't know, drunk maybe?

"Um. No. Not exactly."

"Are you going to leave me in suspense?" I push when she doesn't follow that up. I start orbiting around the room, unable to sit still, one hand gripping the back of my neck, my other holding my phone to my ear.

"Sorry. No. I was thinking. And the car I'm sitting in the back of was spinning a little, so I had to close my eyes." A sound I can't make out. "No, I'm not going to throw up. I promise." She clears her throat, her voice growing louder into the phone again. "Anyway, do you remember in *My Best Friend's Wedding* when the hot guy whose name I can't remember calls Julia Roberts and tells her he's engaged and asks her to be his best man/woman?"

"Uh." I blink. "No. I don't think I've ever seen that movie." Nor will I be her best man. Again, there is only so much a man can take.

"Right. Well. Good thing because this isn't that. This is *so* not that. This is the opposite of that."

"Huh? Fall, what are you talking about?"

"I can't ask you to be my best man because we're technically not even supposed to be friends. But, well." A heavy breath crackles in my ear. "I was all going to the mattresses like two seconds ago but now all my mafia-style bravado is failing me."

I pause, my brows scrunched tighter than they've ever been "What? How much have you had to drink?"

"Oh. I don't know. I think it came out to the equivalent of four shots and a martini. On an empty stomach, which for the record, I know isn't smart. I didn't even end up sipping my water."

I blink and then walk over toward the sectional. That's more alcohol than I think Fallon has ever had in her life. "Do you want me to pretend to be patient while you're quoting *The Godfather* to me and talking about chick flicks?"

"You? That's asking a lot."

"Fall Girl..."

"Ugh. Fine. Sorry." A deep breath and then a loud exhale. "Do you remember the note you gave me?"

"Yes," I say slowly, falling onto the sofa and sitting with my thighs spread and my elbows digging into them. My toe is bleeding through my sock, but I don't care so much about that right now.

"Well, I read it again tonight and that's why I'm calling even though I'm not sure I should be. My life sort of imploded tonight and I didn't know who else to call, but more importantly, there was no one else I *wanted* to call. I'm doing it. I'm doing it and I'm determined, and yes, drunk, which means I'll follow through. You were my best friend, Grey. I've missed you so much and I'm so sorry for cutting you out of my life. It was cowardly, but I felt like I had to. I think you understood that since you didn't try to talk me out of it. I realize that might be wrong or inappropriate of me to say. I haven't been nearly as good of a friend to you as you've been to me."

"That's not true," I immediately interject. "After the accident with Dillon, you were the only thing that kept me from jumping off a bridge. You have no idea what your words to me that night meant. Then there was when Suzie died, and you flew out to see me and held my hand when I was falling apart once again. I did understand it. I've always understood, Fall. I didn't like it, but I wanted what was best for you and I knew I wasn't it."

A heavier breath into the phone. "He's a scoundrel," she says on a venomous half-whisper. "A dirtbag low-life piece of shit slimy-ass buttmuncher whose feet smell and he has the worst morning breath on record. It's like necrotic tissue and a GI bleed had a love child in his mouth."

I start to throw up in mine because that's about as gross of a description as you can get. I'm also about to say I could have told you that—minus the feet and morning breath part—but this doesn't seem like the moment.

"Not holding back or giving me the polite Lark language. What did he do?"

My fist clenches before she even says the words, already assuming the worst.

"I overheard him laughing on the phone with his friend about how I'm nothing more than a bitch with a good pedigree and how I'm fat with a fat ass and that he wants to fuck other women because I'm boring in and out of bed and he doesn't think he can be married to my pussy for the rest of his life. Or something along those lines. The exact language is a little fuzzy right now. I was delivering him a surprise dinner because I'd barely seen him in two weeks. Pathetic. He doesn't love me. He was using me because I'm a Lark. What do you do when you realize you've wasted years of your life on someone for all the wrong reasons?"

I fall back against the cushion of the couch and throw my forearm over my eyes. I don't want to be happy about this. She's hurting and he hurt her, and I hate all of that. The things he said about her... she's right about him. Every name she called him and worse. He's lucky I wasn't there to hear any of it or he'd have been dead. The urge to find him and dangle him by his toenails off the side of a building while he cries and begs for his life is compelling.

Still... I can't fucking help the ill-fated bubble of hope in my stomach.

"I'm sorry, Fallon."

"No, you're not. You didn't like him."

I grin at her tone. "I didn't like him. But I'm sorry for you. You deserve infinitely better and maybe that's a cliché and trite and dickish to say, but it's true all the same. He's wrong. Did I mention that? Everything he said about you is wrong. I can attest to that better than anyone. Your ass is fucking fantastic and there is nothing boring about you, babe."

"Be that as it may, it seems given who he is, I dodged a bullet. I threw our dinner and my engagement ring at him. It's over."

My arm falls to the couch in a heavy heap. I blink up at the ceiling. "You mean that or is this the alcohol talking?"

"He's a wannabe cheater and an asshole. Yes, I mean that." She emits a deep resonating sigh. "It's going to be awful, you know. Telling my parents. Dealing with that fallout. But I don't want to be this person anymore. I realized it tonight. I'm twenty-nine years old and as you wrote in the note, I've been living nearly every day of my life for someone other than myself and for all the wrong reasons. It's a horrendous realization to come to and I... I'm not sure I like the woman I've become."

Fuck. "Oh, Fall Girl. It's not you who you don't like. It's what they've turned you into. You just have to find yourself. Who *you* truly are outside of the confines of everyone else who wants to mold you into something else."

"I want to find that woman. I'm worried I killed her or most of her."

"So let's do it. Let's find her. Resurrect her hot ass from the dead."

She giggles. "I am already. That's the thing. I'm in an Uber on my way to the airport. That's why I had to call you. To tell you that your note set me into action."

I bolt upright, my eyes blinking wide as I stare at the dark television across from me. "What? You're serious? The airport? Where the fuck are you going, Fall Girl?"

"I don't know," she proclaims, all excited. "That's the coolest part. I don't know yet. I'm going to get to the airport and have them put me on the soonest flight out. I'm thinking Europe though. Remember I told you I wanted to get lost in the world and experience it all? I'm doing that. It's time. I'm crazy, I know, but what the fuck, right? A week or two away is exactly what I need to clear my head a bit."

"Jesus, babe. You can't just do that by yourself."

"Why the hell not?" she snaps indignantly. "I can and I am, and you better not try to talk me out of it, Greyson Monroe. I called you for a reason. But I also called you because you're the only person I know who truly gets me. Who sees *me* and not Fallon Lark. Please, you have to be on my team."

"I do see you and I always have and always will be on your team." *Fuck.*

A pause. A bitter laugh. "I didn't have any place to go. In four weeks, we were moving to Philadelphia and the place we were living in was his."

"Philadelphia? Why there?"

"His father is planning to run one more time and then retire in four years before that next election. Bacchus was going to run in his place. I was going to get married in two weeks and then go on my honeymoon for two weeks and then move. Today was my last day of work. I have no job. No apartment. I'm trashing my shitty fiancé. I'm drunk like a sad country song. I'm a mess."

"You're a mess," I agree, but I'm smiling like a bastard because I have the absolute best idea in the history of ideas. "But I think you're right. I think going to Europe tonight is the best thing you've ever done for yourself. I'm proud of you for leaving Bacchus and reclaiming your life. You're the one who has to live with it. Not Bacchus and not your parents."

"Yeah? You mean that?" The self-doubt and hope in her voice slay me. "God. Ugh. I'm so scared, but I'm trying not to be. Or maybe I'm trying to turn scared into excitement."

"That's great. You do it. Call me when you land, okay?"

"O-oh, u-um," she stutters, taken aback by my abrupt change in tone and how I'm suddenly blowing her off. "Yeah. Sure. I guess. Right." Then she hangs up on me. Likely because I just embarrassed her without meaning to, but I can't sit here and idly chitchat. I had to get her off the phone, so I can get the hell out of here, and do it quickly.

The airport. I need more time.

"Aurelia," I cry out, scrambling off the couch and opening the door.

"Yeah?" She's somewhere in the apartment but still manages to hear me.

"I need a Band-Aid."

She mutters something I can't make out, but I follow the trail of her voice. She's in the kitchen, the guys all at the counter watching her because yeah, she's making them brownies. We were supposed to have a poker night tonight. Now, who cares?

"They're in the cabinet above the sink," she tells me. "Help yourself."

"Then sit down and tell us what Fallon wanted," Zax commands, still frowning at me.

"You're the one who left me alone with her in that café."

"That was before I knew she was engaged. What did she

want?" he persists, ever the protective big brother. "Sit down, you're going to fall."

"Don't worry, Mom. I'll be okay," I mock. "Besides, I can't sit. I don't have time. I'm on the clock." I take out the Band-Aids and after I remove my sock, I start to clean off my toe with the antiseptic wipes I found beside them.

"On the clock?" Asher asks. "What does that mean?"

"It means that she overheard her fiancé as he trashed talked her while plotting how he was going to screw around on her."

"Sounds like a good guy," Callan says sardonically, sipping on his scotch. "She dump him and beg for you to take his place?"

"Ha." I point at him. "You're very funny."

"If not, then why do you have that look in your eye?" Callan maintains.

"Because she *did* dump him and is on her way to the airport to randomly fly to Europe, thinking that will help her rediscover who she is. Only I'm going to race to the airport and meet her there."

Silence. Everyone is frozen staring at me.

"What? Bad idea?"

"Her parents?" That's Lenox and it's a serious question, which is why he voiced it. Fallon has never gone against her parents. Well, I mean, she has, but not on anything major. I don't consider sneaking out of your room and into the boy next door's room or running off to a concert or two signifies any major rebellion.

"She said she's done living her life for other people." I throw the wrappers in the trash and then lean against the opposite side of the giant island from the guys while I put back on my sock.

Zax grunts in dismay. "She's saying that now, Grey. She's hurt. But she's not a stranger to cheating couples. Her parents perfected the art. With our father, no less. She might be singing this tune now, but I doubt it will last. You know how her parents are. You know how manipulative and domineering they are with her. Especially when it comes to something they deem as vital as this union. They want a kid in the White House and feel she's their best shot."

"Dillon is a congressman."

"Dillon isn't Fallon. Fallon's the princess. The golden child. She always has been even if her parents treat her like shit."

"Okay, so say she's serious and she's done with people running her life and is actually running away to Europe," Aurelia cuts in, bringing us back to the task. "What are your plans with this?"

I grin like the devil. "Meet her at the airport, travel with her, and make her fall in love with me, of course." I'm met with crickets again. "What? The timing is perfect. I'm supposed to be in Paris on Friday for the spring festival that starts that night and goes through the weekend. It's as if it's all meant to be."

"But..." Callan holds up his hand. "And I'm saying this with love, brother, but you don't exactly, well, put yourself out there like that."

"Ever," Asher agrees.

My shoulders hunch. It's true. I don't. I'm not a big lover of feelings or emotions because they haven't always been the kindest to me. Or ever. If you don't put yourself out there, then you can't risk getting hurt or losing someone you care about. Ninety-nine-point-eight percent of the time I cover all my anxiety and fear and sadness with smiles and deflective teasing because it's always served me well.

I also acknowledge I'm likely insane to try this again and expect a different outcome.

But ever since I saw Fallon in the café with that guy and felt that ring on her finger, I don't know, I can't explain it. It's as if something inside of me has cracked open and everything I've battled to keep locked away has been spilling out. Some days it's a slow drip. Others, it's a tsunami. I've been burning with jealousy and disappointment and fury. Not my standard operating procedure by any stretch. In my head, I had already lost her, but that seemed to seal the deal, and I've been wrecked by it since.

Not to mention, I've been stuck in a worst-ever case of writer's block.

I have no music. No lyrics.

My last album was my most successful and loved yet, and I can't help but feel that was my peak and the only place to go from there was down, and then I saw Fall with that guy, and now…

Now I'm a fucking mess. Just like my girl is a fucking mess. We're a match made in disaster. All this has had me in a tailspin for the last six months despite my patented Greyson Monroe mask of cool confidence.

I look at my brother. "You said it yourself that morning in the café before you dropped me like a bad habit. There is only one girl out there for me. She's it. She's always been it whether I like it or not. This is my shot."

"I don't know." Zax runs a contemplative finger across his bottom lip. "Maybe."

"I agree with the maybe, because all you ever were to her was a best friend."

I snort at that. Callan. So cute. So fluffy. "Trust me, we were more than just friends."

"But that was friends with benefits and fleeting. You were never more than that and you haven't had sex with her in more than half a decade."

Straight facts and not my favorites. "You saying I can't do it?" I toss back at him with a tilt of my head.

"He's saying it's one hell of a challenge," Asher jumps in, angling the bottom of his drink at me before he tosses the rest down and sets his empty glass on the counter with a clink.

"Especially given her propensity for doing everything her parents command of her. They hate you. Right or wrong, they blame you for Dillon's accident and will *never* agree to let their princess openly be with you."

Also true. I shrug. "I just have my work cut out for me is all." I'm not sure they're buying my feigned nonchalance though.

"Well, I think it's insanely romantic." Aurelia smiles reassuringly at me as she pours the batter into the square glass dish. "White knight sorta thing, right?"

I wink and shoot her with my finger. "That's what I'm planning."

"Love it. We totally swoon over that. And Europe?" She sighs, her hand going to her chest. "So romantic. I say go for it. Just be careful and protect your heart if you feel it's not going the way you want it to."

"Yes," Asher shoots out of his chair as if he's about to jump into the game and QB this session. "You can do it, Grey. You totally can and we'll help because we're all fucking awesome at wooing women. But Aurelia is right. Have an exit strategy."

"I always do." Sorta. My exit strategy has always been that after she leaves, I get drunk for about a day or so and wallow in misery and then force myself to get back up again and breathe while pretending it doesn't feel like someone hit me in the chest with a tire iron. That's not new for me, though. That was my daily life as a kid, and then after Dillon's accident, and then after Suzie died. I had perfected the art of emotional evasion, only that hasn't been working so well for me lately.

I followed her once. After she had left me that note saying I couldn't see her again, I ran after her to the airport and got on a plane since I missed her flight, and when I landed, I realized I was only going to get rejected. I was never good enough to be her guy. I had accepted that for the most part and was smart enough not to try and be more, but knowing she was walking away for good was the last blow I could stand.

She liked the sex and she cared about me as her friend, but she would never tell her family to fuck off and take a chance on me. Maybe I'm delusional for thinking this time is different, but I have to. I can't keep going around in this never-ending loop where the girl I want is always just out of reach. I have to give this everything I've got and if I still end up alone after, well, at least I won't die with regrets.

"Wait," Asher grabs my arm. "How the hell are you going to catch what flight she's taking if she's already on her way there? You have to go home and pack and get there. No way you'll be able to do all that."

I point at Lenox. "Help a friend out?" He's strictly a "just the facts, ma'am" kind of guy, but his hacking skills are unrivaled. He also plays the hell out of piano and keyboard, which is why our band, Central Square, was so awesome. His inking talents are pretty stellar as well and he's the only one I'll go to for my tattoos. But right now, I need his handiwork with a computer.

He nods, his eyes already on his phone. "I'll text you when I know what flight she's taking, and I'll have the airline delay the flight if I need to."

"You can do that?" Asher stares incredulously at him.

He grins like the devil, his huge, tatted arms on full display making him look menacing. "I can do anything."

"Okay then. Awesome. Do everything, and thanks." I blow him a kiss that he catches and plants on his cheek. Love that man.

"You'll call me if you need anything?"

"Yes, big brother, I'll call you," I say to Zax, blowing him a kiss of his own that he ignores because he's Zax. "Or more likely your woman, but I'll be in touch. I gotta jet. There's a lady who doesn't know it yet, but she's waiting for me at the airport."

6

____

It's like déjà vu. The worst kind. Only this time, I haven't missed her flight yet.

The next hour of my life is a blur of panic and uncertainty. I race home and pack up everything I'm going to need for the next week. My assistant will pack my stuff for the show I have scheduled after that and bring it when he meets up with me in Paris. That's easy.

The panic and uncertainty come from the fact that I'm dropping everything and running to the airport to try and catch Fallon who is drunk, just broke up with her fiancé, and doesn't know I'm crashing her impromptu trip to Europe that might end before it even begins if her family gets wind of her plans.

Or if she chickens out which is also a real possibility.

I've chased her to an airport once before and missed her flight then. I can't miss it this time. I can't.

Zax's driver Ashley takes me to the airport, and I send around the required texts and emails. I inform my manager I'm going off the grid for the next week before the festival starts. I let my assistant know the same and tell him he's on standby for random things that I might need during the trip. Lenox calls and informs me she booked a 9:30 p.m. flight to Rome and that he booked me on the same flight with a seat beside hers in first class.

"You have an hour to make it through security," he tells me. "Do you want me to delay the flight?"

"No. I'll make it." I hope.

"Do you want me to start monitoring her fiancé and family?"

I think about that for a moment. "You realize hacking someone like Astley and a senator who likely has top secret classified clearance is a felony?" I point out.

"Hacking is a felony, Grey. Everything I've done tonight is a felony."

"I know, but this seems worse given who he is and pretty invasive. I'm not sure Fall Girl would appreciate that. Not to mention, right now, it's an unnecessary risk. She dumped him. People do it all the time. Let's hold off on that for now until I get a better sense of what's going on."

Zax says something in the background and then I hear his voice come through the speaker. "Are you sure this is the kind of heat you want to bring on yourself? A guy like Astley with his money and family connections and the Larks with theirs won't go easy on this."

"Would you have run from that if it were you and Aurelia?" I counter.

Zax doesn't even have to hesitate when saying no. Our father pulled some true dirtbag stuff, using Aurelia to get at Zax. We knew about it but that didn't stop Zax from falling for her, even when he wasn't sure he could trust her.

"We'll be in Europe," I tell them. "What the hell can they do to us there?"

"I'm not worried about what they'll do to *her*," Zax growls. "I'm worried about what they'll do to you when they realize you're with her and given who they are and how much they dislike you, I wouldn't put anything past them."

"Then we'll just have to make sure they don't know I'm with her until I win her over and it's too late for them to do anything about it."

Still, I take that little nugget of unwelcome information and tuck it into the back of my head because right now, I have more important things to focus on. Like running through an airport on a Friday night to try and catch an international flight to Rome. And of course, whatever can go wrong, does. It's as if the fates are trying to keep us apart and I'm wishing I had told Lenox to have them hold the flight.

As it is, it's too late for that now. I don't have time to go for my phone much less slow down to catch my breath. At first, they give me crap at the desk because they don't understand how I have a ticket when the flight is set to take off so soon and I am not on their manifest before that. Then I get heat for my acoustic guitar in its hard case for reasons I don't quite understand until the woman behind the desk asks me for my autograph and digits.

This is why I tend to fly private, as elitist and obnoxious as it is.

Because after I sign something for her and politely decline to give her my digits, and I'm heading for security, it's as if everyone on the planet takes this exact moment to recognize me. And I can't be a dick. I can never be a dick, especially in public. So I have to smile, take quick selfies, scribble my name on random things, and make apologies for being abrupt.

I scoot through the PreCheck line, but then my belt goes off in the metal detector. Then my watch, which isn't even supposed to light up metal detectors, but that's just how my night seems to be going. By the time I make it through and I'm on the other side with my backpack smacking against my back, I have to haul ass down to the gate, which is naturally the farthest gate in the terminal. Sweat runs down my temples and the back of my neck, and I hear them call final boarding on my flight over the loudspeaker.

As I get close, finding the gate empty, I wave my phone at the flight attendant, yelling for her to hold the plane.

"It's okay, Mr. Monroe," she says with an indulgent smile. "They called ahead from ticketing to tell us you were coming. We were holding the plane for you."

I slow to a jog, gasping for air as I hand her my phone with my boarding pass on it. "Thank you," I tell her, my hands planting themselves on my thighs as I catch my breath. "My girl is on there. I'd hate to miss it."

"Oh," she exclaims, and I mentally chastise myself for saying something like that so offhand.

I laugh, trying to play the blunder off and hoping it doesn't come back to bite me in the ass later. "She's my best friend. It's not like that."

I get a wink and brush it off as I head down the jetway. Stepping on the plane with my right foot—always the right foot—I grab one of the cold towels from a tray and wipe my face and neck off.

"Good evening, Mr. Monroe. We're so pleased to have you flying with us tonight. Let us know if there is anything we can do to make your trip more comfortable. Your seat is just over here."

I nod in gratitude at the flight attendant and then turn the corner into the first-class cabin, scanning the sleeping bays until I see the one directly beside mine. I practically collapse at the sight of her. Her hair is a little wet, the black strands hanging with a soft wave around her face and dusting her shoulders. She's wearing one of my concert T-shirts—a T-shirt I'm nearly positive I gave her to sleep in when I saw her in Chicago—and black yoga pants. By all means, it shouldn't be sexy. But that shirt. Her wet hair. Her pretty face.

She's immersed in her e-reader, so she hasn't noticed me yet as I walk through the narrow aisle, unable to remove my eyes from her.

"This seat taken?" I asked her the same question the last time I saw her six months ago in the café. Her head snaps up, her amethyst eyes wide only to instantly brim with tears when she registers it's me.

If this were a rom-com, it would be the scene at the end of the movie where the guy moves heaven and hell to get to his girl after some strange misunderstanding broke them apart. It'd be where he races onto the plane, drops to his knees, and kisses the girl crazy. Only this isn't a rom-com, I'm not that guy for her, and chances are, there isn't a happily ever after for us.

Her chin trembles as she watches me slide into the bay next to her, the partition between the seats already open. "Hey, Fall Girl."

"Hey, Grey." The first of her tears hit her cheeks.

"Aw, babe. Don't cry." I'm dying to kiss them away, but I hold firm and use my thumbs instead.

She sniffles. "I'm not."

I lean in and kiss the tip of her nose. "Good. You good? I'm good," I say to her, looping my pinky with hers that's sitting on the armrest. I shake my head in dismay at her. "I can't believe you were going to do this alone."

"I... I've been trying to talk myself out of second thoughts."

"Excellent. Keep that up. Second thoughts aren't happening. I won't allow them."

She nibbles on her lip. "I'm twenty-nine years old and I'm running away from my life. I can't decide if that makes me brave or a coward."

"Brave. Ask yourself this. Are you running away from your life or are you running toward a new one?"

"Can I get you a beverage before takeoff?" the flight attendant asks, interrupting us as she pops her head into our row.

"Two glasses of champagne, please."

With that Fallon emits a wet laugh. "More alcohol?"

"You're safe. I won't let anything bad happen to you." I buckle up and settle in, stuffing my backpack under the seat in front of me.

"Can you promise my stomach and head the same?" she quips as she accepts the glass and stares at it as if the woman just gave her poison.

"Probably not, but we've got a long flight ahead of us and I never travel without Advil and rehydration packets."

Fallon stares at me, blinking in rapid fire, but it's useless. More tears fall and I reach out to brush those away as well before she has the chance. I wonder if she'd notice if I popped the finger in my mouth and tasted them.

"You're here? You're really here? You're sitting beside me on this plane flying to Rome with me?"

My gut twists and I smile softly, angling my head so it's as close to hers as I can get in these larger, sleeping berths. "I'm here. You didn't think I'd let you run off to Europe alone, did you?"

"Yes," she answers frankly with a wry smile. "I did. Especially after the way you—"

"I had to get you off the phone," I interject. "I'm sorry if that hurt you, but I was in a bit of a rush."

She shakes her head. "I deserved it. I walked away from you and I'm so sorry. I should have never done that, but I... No one could know about our friendship Grey, and I was with Bacchus and..."

"I know."

She shakes her head again, harder this time, and wipes at her face, blowing out heavy, uneven breaths. "Thank you. Thank you for coming and..." She trails off, tilting her head and squinting at me as if something just occurred to her. "Wait.

How did you find me? I didn't even know what flight I was going on when I called you."

I smirk, giving her a wink as I take a sip of my champagne. I fucking hate champagne, but I know she loves it and I wanted to have a drink with her. "I have my ways. Don't question them."

She rolls her eyes, sinking back into her seat as the plane goes through its checks and we pull away from the gate. "Let me guess. Lenox." A small incredulous giggle. "Do you remember when you got a D in Spanish our freshman year, and he hacked the school's server and changed it to a B-plus so your dad wouldn't find out and yell at you?"

Just thinking about the way my father used to yell at me, the things he used to say and call me, makes me inwardly shudder and I quickly push it away as I always do.

"Yes. Lenox's dad taught him how to do it. He had the coolest parents on the planet."

"I remember." She laughs. "Speaking of the guys, I ran into Asher's dad at a conference where he was a motivational speaker."

"The Reyes and their championship-winning football legacy. I swear that's the only reason Alabama took a shot with Asher as a walk-on. He was a freaking junior when he finally made it to in-person college, and it's not as if we had a lot of playing time when we were traveling as Central Square, though that didn't stop him from practicing and doing drills and working out whenever he could. I still can't believe his father was okay with him doing that. We were only sixteen when we left, and he gave up his shot at being scouted."

"Seems to have worked out for him. Even if he was a seventh-round draft pick instead of a first-round like his brothers and father were."

"Do you ever run into Callan? If you do, he never tells me about it."

Her expression falls a bit. "No, but I know he finished his residency at MGH last summer because I worked with Oliver Fritz at Hughes Healthcare and his good friend Drew Albright was Callan's attending."

We're handed another cold towel and thank God because I'm still fucking sweating. So much for being in good shape.

I practically shower with it, Fallon's curious eyes all over me. "You look like you just had sex. Did you run here?"

"I did as a matter of fact. Run, not have sex. Which was not nearly as much fun as having sex, but it brought me to you, so I have zero complaints." I set the cloth down on the small table attached to the armrest. "So. Rome?"

"It was either that or Amsterdam. I flipped a coin. The woman behind the counter thought I was nuts. *I* think I'm nuts."

"You can talk to me about it," I finally say, regarding her with a steady look.

She shrugs as she takes a deep pull of the champagne. "I don't know what to say. I'm still processing it all. How do you spend three and half years of your life with someone only to discover you didn't know them the way you thought you did? I was going to marry him. Now I'm sitting here on a plane, half-drunk and out of my mind."

"Are you regretting that?"

She studies me, contemplating my question. "No. I don't think so." She tosses her hand up and lets out a harrumph. "I don't know. I reacted and then I got drunk and reacted some more. I was… hurt. I felt stupid. I felt duped. It was like he took every soft spot and vulnerability I have and threw them out there as truths. I didn't matter to him beyond what I could do for him and that's how it's always been. For my entire life, that's how it's always been for me. Naively, I thought it was different with him. I thought what we had was real despite how we got together. I thought he loved me. It was all a lie."

"Do you love him?" I have to ask. I have to know.

She glances down, staring at her half-empty champagne. At the bubbles as they undulate to the top of the gold liquid. "I've been asking myself that question a lot tonight. The answer isn't so easy to come by. Or admit. I tried to. I knew why my parents introduced us. They were candid about letting me know how he was the man I should be with." She meets my eyes briefly and frowns, only to cover it with a sip of champagne. "I guess the best answer I can come up with is I thought I did. We had some good times. Some happy times. But in learning it was all a lie, I think a larger part of me had been lying to myself about him. About all of it. The problem is, now I have no job and no apartment. My family won't take this well. I have a lot to work out."

"But that can wait, can't it?" I toss out, inching in closer to her as the plane takes off into the Boston night sky. A jolt of nerves hits me, and I lick my lips. Here goes nothing. "You're already here and so am I. You told me you weren't going to be working for a while anyway. And as luck would have it, I'm expected to be in Paris next Friday for a festival that weekend. We can even continue on after the festival if you'd like. Stay with me, Fall Girl. Do Europe with me. Find that wild, adventurous side of you again."

"You're serious?" she practically squawks the words.

I hit her with a rogue smile and then lean into her, my mouth by her ear. Chills race up her arms and neck and I feel her shudder ever so slightly when I whisper, "Give me this week to change your life. I promise you'll never look back and regret it."

7

The scariest part of Grey's proposal? I'm tempted to say yes despite its impracticality and recklessness. Or maybe that's the main reason I'm into it. I do genuinely need to try and get my jobs back and find a new place to live and somehow convince my parents that I'm serious about not marrying Bacchus.

But it's like my brain is screaming, yeah, that *can* wait.

And why not?

I had this whole plan in my head. A week to find myself. To be alone and get my head on straight as I get lost in ancient cities. Like *Eat, Pray, Love*, only my version of it. But now Grey is here. Freaking ran through the airport to make that happen. And he's offering me a week with *him*. And he forgives me. I don't deserve his forgiveness. Leaving him that note and cutting him out of my life was unforgivable. But he's here. With me.

Trying to make what could possibly be the worst day slash situation of my life so much better. That's what he's always done for me. He's the best person I know.

The alcohol making my brain fuzzy and my inhibitions nonexistent aside, it's insanely romantic and whimsical and fantasy-like. Which is why I need to say no. The words don't come out, though, and he must see that somehow I'm unable to answer because he finishes off his champagne, wipes the excess drop from his bottom lip with his finger in an insanely sexy move, and then says, "I'm going to find the bathroom."

A kiss on my cheek and then he's up, moving past me and out into the aisle. Everyone around is staring at him. Greyson Monroe is nothing short of recognizable even if you're not a fan, but his gorgeous face and fearless confidence make him impossible not to stare at.

He's tall and muscular without being overly built or bulky and has thick, dark hair—longer on top and shorter on the sides—that you can't help but want to drag your hands through. His face is art. Smoldering dark eyes that are always a little hooded and a lot seductive, straight nose, and full, soft lips. A sculpted jaw handcrafted by Greek gods is perpetually lined in two days' worth of stubble and he has a sexy dimple right in the middle of his chin.

Gorgeous doesn't even begin to cover him.

Holy fuck. What have I done?

A desperate feeling sours the champagne in my stomach.

I'm drunk on an airplane flying to Rome with a hot rock star and he's asking me to spend the week with him.

No way. Can't be done. It's one thing to buy hot clothes or occasionally fly across the country to a concert and then get drunk and sleep with said hot rock star since he was also your best friend. It's another to light your dumpster of a life on fire and not try to put out the flames. When I called him wanting to find a better version of me again, I didn't mean for that to trans-late into hopping continents and getting lost for a week or more with him, and yet here I am.

I've missed him. I've missed him terribly during the years we've been apart.

He's the craziest thing I've ever done, but he never felt that way. He felt safe and comfortable and like mine. Always like mine. A secret the world would never be clued in on. My parents especially. They would have flipped if they knew.

I'm pragmatic and responsible and a good girl. Possibly to a fault, I admit.

So... no. I can't.

Then again...

I slurp down the rest of the champagne because I think I need it. Because I think I'm about to say yes to this. It's one week. Ten days really, including the festival, but that's just semantics. I gnaw on my lip, my finger swirling along the rim of my now-empty glass.

What do I have left to lose?

He returns, his hair wet and brushed back from his face. The man gives tall, dark, and impossibly handsome a run for its money. The freaking Monroe chin dimple doesn't hurt either. The sleeves on his black long-sleeved shirt are pushed up his forearms and I can tell he has some new ink on them since the last I saw him.

"Hi," he says as he buckles up. "You look like you've got a lot on your mind."

It's easy to forget his godlike beauty when you're not continuously immersed in it, but it's been a while, and wow, how this man's face can dazzle and disarm. He doesn't even have to smile, though it has a power all on its own. And he's all too aware of it.

With my breath stuck in my throat and my heart beats choking my lungs, I meet his steady gaze and throw caution to the tailwinds. "I'm in."

"Excellent," he says plainly, giving nothing away.

"I have some rules."

Now he cracks a smile. "Great. I have some of my own too."

"You go first," I counter with a smirk, because I've never known Grey to be a man of a lot of rules.

He chuckles as if reading my mind. The very attentive flight attendant comes over to us. "Can I get you another drink? We'll be serving dinner soon or we have your sleep kits if you prefer."

"I'd love a bourbon and I know my lovely friend here would like another champagne. And dinner for sure."

"Oh, wonderful," she exclaims. "I'll be right back with that."

I inwardly roll my eyes and then twist on my side to face Greyson. "Does that ever get old?"

"What?"

Now I outwardly roll my eyes at him. "Don't play coy. I'm shocked she didn't ask if she could be your latest mile-high conquest."

"My *latest*?" His eyebrows hit his hairline.

I lean conspiratorially over the armrest, angling my head at him. "I've heard the rumors, Greyson Monroe. Sexy, bad-boy rock star with a different woman in his bed every night. The tatted-up god with the velvet voice who makes panties melt with a wink and a smirk and a song." I huff before I can stop it. "Does it ever get old having women fawn all over you?"

"There is way too much to focus on there. Like how you think I'm a sexy bad boy and a tatted-up god, and that I can make your panties melt."

"I didn't say *my* panties."

"You said women and last I checked that's you."

"Whatever. Is it not true?"

He gives me that rogue smirk he's famous for. "Depends. Sometimes. Especially when the one woman I want fawning over me with melted panties never does."

I find myself sucking in a breath and holding it there for reasons I can't quite explain. I never thought of Greyson with a serious girlfriend. I've never known him to have one, serious or otherwise. Still, it... I don't know, rubs me strangely, which he clearly reads.

He laughs, reaching over and tucking a strand of hair

behind my ear. "Ah, Fall Girl. You're so damn cute. You, my babe, are the only woman I ever want fawning over me. But since you never do, I have to settle for fans."

I sigh. If the man is ever serious about anything it'll be a first.

A tug on my hair brings me back. "My rules are you can't question me," he demands, literally yanking us back to the task and away from rough pastures. "Where I take you. The things I have us do. You can't say no. You picked Rome. The rest is up to me until we get to Paris. And you have to stay through the festival that ends that Sunday night."

"I have veto power."

"I'll think about that, but I'll have veto-veto power."

"Whatever the hell that means."

A wicked smirk makes my toes curl. "It means I run the show. I have control."

I pat his shoulder. "Sure. I'll give you that illusion for now."

He loops the lock of hair he had been playing with around his finger until it's in a tight coil. "You can pretend all you like, but you never had a problem when I was in control in the past."

I risk glancing at him, and the hunger in his eyes has a pleasure curling deep in my chest. Yes, I liked his control. And I liked it when we played and were silly. He made it so damn easy to melt into him and forget everything else around us. He's doing it now too because look where I am and look at what we're discussing.

He clears the gravel from his throat. "Your turn. What are your rules?"

I grow apprehensive, but my rules are nonnegotiable if I'm going to survive ten days with this man. He all but proved that to me just now. My head is a mess. The last thing I need is anything physical toying with my already dented parts.

"Separate bedrooms."

He tilts his head, scrutinizing me with his sinfully dark eyes and devastatingly handsome face. It sends a frizzle of heat straight through me as if he's already trying to shake my resolve with this rule. He's pure sultry seduction, even when he's not trying to be.

"That's your rule?"

"That's my rule," I say quietly.

For a moment, the air holds still between us. A palpable pressure that makes my mouth go dry and my vagina screams at me to change my mind before it's too late. She's saying it's been a while since we've had the full undivided and eager attention of a worthy male counterpart. But remembering how good the sex was between us is exactly why I need this rule. Sex leads to confusion and confusion leads to the dark side. Or however that goes.

He looks like he's ready to argue, but instead sits up straight and runs his hands through his hair.

"That might not always be possible if we go off the beaten path," he slowly remarks.

"As much as possible then."

He takes the drink from the flight attendant and pulls out his tray. I do the same and she sets some kind of dish in front of us that looks like it could be beef, and likely not chicken, over what I believe to be mashed potatoes. The bread and butter look safe and that's where I head first.

"Fine," he relents, his expression tight. "Anything else?"

Self-preservation has me blurting out, "No sex." And because I blurt it out, I have no filter on the volume of my voice. It carries and garners the curious and amused looks and head swivels of the entire first-class cabin.

"Yes, that's the name of the movie I never want to watch," he says loudly as if that will throw everyone off.

I snort out a small laugh under my breath, ignoring the blush staining my cheeks. "You need to work on your cover-ups."

His eyes lift to mine, a smile curling the edge of his words. "You need to work on not being so loud about the S-E-X. Or the non-S-E-X, which incidentally doesn't sound nearly as fun as having the S—"

"You can stop spelling it now. Everyone within earshot is older than eight."

"But that doesn't change the not-fun part of not having it with each other. As I recall we do it quite well."

Yep, full-on blush once again. This man. Did he have to say that? Because yes, we did it quite well. Greyson Monroe had me doing things I never thought I was capable of doing and loving every second of it. Things I will deny to my dying breath and never tell my grandchildren about. Things I never even thought to do with Bacchus, and I don't like my explanation for that when I dig deeper.

I trust Grey with myself in a way I never trusted Bacchus. Not that he ever attempted anything beyond the standard of s-e-x. The man called me boring in bed and yet sex was always on his power structure and always the way he liked it. And yes, boring. If it lasted more than five minutes and came with fore-play and a pre-sex orgasm, I considered it hot.

Reliving how good the sex was with Greyson and being physically intimate with him will only complicate things between us and this is already complicated enough. My mind is a muddled-up mess of a thing and sex, for all its benefits and fun, has a tendency to toy with your emotions when it finds the opportunity. The last thing I need right now is for my mind to start playing games it has no business playing simply because it's butthurt and needs a little reassurance that we're still fuck-able and lovable.

I can't just fall into a man's bed, no matter how sexy, good-looking, smart, or charming he is. I need to protect my heart. Keep it locked up tight and safe. And Grey is the perfect storm to disrupt that plan.

"Be that as it may, it's not happening again," I assert, taking a bite of my roll.

"I'm only messing with you. I assumed that came with the separate bedrooms rule," he deadpans, his gaze on his food as he bravely cuts into whatever this is and takes an unconcerned bite. "Doesn't mean I like the terms."

"It's not because I don't—"

He shakes his head, silencing me. "I get it."

I frown, feeling shitty. But also a bit relieved if he felt this trip was just going to be a romp in each other's pants through Europe. I momentarily close my eyes and try to force my mind to clear. Tomorrow is going to be an interesting day. I haven't told my parents yet. I haven't spoken to Bacchus since I ran out on him. But all of that is overshadowed by the knowledge that I'll wake up in a completely different country, ready to embark on who knows what with my former best friend who has always been the most forbidden part of my life.

"You're okay with that though?" I check but feel the need to explain my thoughts out loud to him. "Just friends? I'm not sure I can do this any other way. I don't want to start confusing things between us that shouldn't be confused all in the name of sex."

"You don't have to worry about things ever being confusing between us when you set rules like that." He drops his fork and knife and blows out a harsh breath. His eyes close for a beat before they reopen and he twists his head, giving me a look that's both frustrated and vulnerable. "I'm not here to fuck up your mind. I'm not here to throw expectations at you or pile on bullshit to your already full pile. This is meant to be fun. It is most definitely meant to be *freeing*. If you want me to behave myself, I will. If that's what you need to say yes, you've got it. I'll be your best friend like I always have been, and we'll go explore the world together. I just want to spend time with you. It's been too long, Fall."

"I know. It has been and I'm looking forward to this time with you too."

We let it drop and after we sort of eat dinner and they clear away our trays and give us our sleep kit with sleep masks, a blanket, and a pillow, I flatten out my seat and he does the same. I haven't closed the partition yet and somehow we find ourselves on our sides facing each other in the darkness of the plane with only the thick armrests between us.

"Do you want to read to me for a bit?"

I hear him tap the e-reader on the armrest on my side.

I laugh, the tension cracking along with it. "Sure. Were you thinking Jane Austen or Shakespeare?"

"I was more thinking one of the other books you hide on there."

"I most definitely cannot read those books aloud to you. Especially on an airplane. Besides, you're not supposed to know about those."

"Ah. But I do." He chuckles, but it's shaky. "No reading then. Sleep?"

"Sleep," I agree, rolling onto my other side so I'm facing away from him. "Good night, Grey."

"Good night, Fall Girl. See you in Rome."

A smile hikes up my face, a giddy burst of excitement bubbling up through me. "See you in Rome."

8

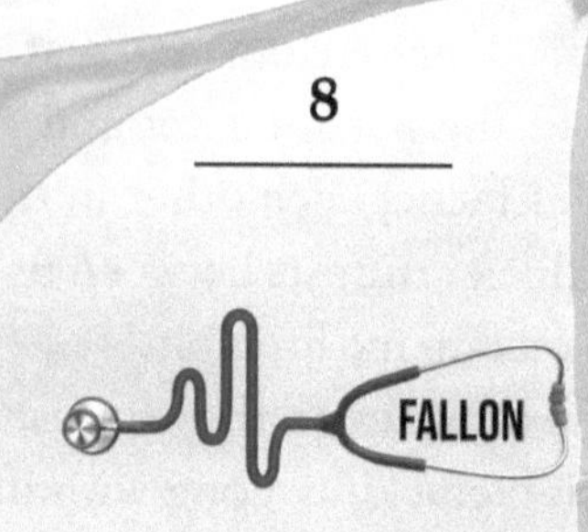

hat began as madness has turned into a mess of one event after another. We land after being woken for breakfast by the flight attendants an hour before landing that neither Grey nor I touched except for the coffee. We didn't get a lot of sleep, barely four or five hours, and it's showing as Grey and I silently gather our things and trudge our way through customs.

The customs officer immediately recognizes Greyson and I can tell this could become a problem. Especially if we're planning to travel under the radar, which we both said we wanted as we sipped on our coffee. Still, we make it through relatively quickly and with no issues, but all that changes the second we get to the baggage carousel. My suitcase comes off quickly, and Greyson's guitar thankfully made the journey.

His suitcase is another story.

The last bag is picked up and then there's a loud buzzing and the carousel stops. I look over at Greyson and he looks over at me and then we both look back to the empty carousel.

"I guess I should find someone and report this."

I deflate. "I'm sorry."

"For what? I should have expected this. I had to run for the plane. I'm just grateful Aurora made it."

"Aurora?"

"My guitar. Suzie named each of our instruments. Zax's bass is Belle, my favorite acoustic lady is Aurora, Lenox's keyboard was Cinderella, Asher's electric was Rapunzel, and Callan's drums were Ariel."

"Suzie named your instruments after Disney princesses? How did I not know this?"

"She sure did and we didn't exactly share that around."

I love that way too much. "Okay. Then I'm especially glad Aurora made it. But your bag could be anywhere."

He gives me a grim look and with a defeated sigh we make our way to the lost luggage desk, and all the while he's doing something on his phone. I haven't turned mine on yet, too afraid to see what I shut off from yesterday. Yesterday. I nearly laugh out loud. Yesterday I was still engaged to Bacchus. I was still in Boston with an apartment and a job waiting for me in Philadelphia when we moved there in a month.

Today I'm in Rome with a famous rock star and I have no idea what he has in store for us next. I should care about this, about all of this, but I can't force myself to work up the effort that will take. I could blame it on jet lag or being slightly hungover, but that's bullshit, and I think we all know it.

I'm not sad I broke up with Bacchus. I don't miss him. I don't feel pained nostalgia for the life we'll never have together. I'm still rolling around in relief like it's glitter, glad that I got out when I did. I'd question why I was ever engaged to him in the first place if this is how I'm feeling now, but I already know the answer to that.

My family.

Who would I be if I wasn't forced to always be Fallon Lark?

The man behind the counter who is nothing but smiles and sunshine tells us in very broken English that Grey's suitcase will arrive later today on another flight and that they'll deliver it to our hotel at some point tomorrow. That seems to mollify Grey enough, but when he turns to me, I can see there is something he's apprehensive about telling me.

"How hard and fast is your separate bedroom rule?"

I blink, and it's a slow blink because I'm not sure how to answer him.

"My assistant booked us a room," he starts since clearly I'm incapable of coming up with anything. "The problem is, it's the last hotel room available in Rome."

"How is that possible?"

"Do you know what tomorrow is?"

"Um. The ninth?"

"Yes. The ninth of April. It also happens to be Easter Sunday and we're in the capital of the Roman Catholic Church."

My face falls. "Oh."

"Yes. Oh. Because you picked one hell of a weekend to visit this city. It's going to be packed with people, which may or may not be to our advantage since sometimes it's easier to blend in with the crowd than it is in smaller spaces, but legit, this is the best I can do and since my suitcase is being delivered there tomorrow, we're stuck here for at least the night."

"Okay."

He squints at me. "Okay? Just like that after all your rules?"

I shrug because I'm trying to be this Fallon. The one who goes with the flow and isn't afraid of a little adventure rocking her orderly, pristine life. It's why I'm here in the first place, right? Sleeping in the same bed doesn't mean sex.

"Afraid if you sleep beside me you won't be able to keep your hands to yourself?" I tease.

Without warning, he steps into me and suddenly his hands are up in my hair, tugging the strands from my face as his dark, almost sinister eyes hold mine. "It was your rule," he whispers, his face inches from mine, his lips so close I can practically taste them. "Maybe I should be the one asking you that."

My breath whooshes from my body in a gust as my mouth goes dry. His fingers release my hair and find my upper arms beneath the hem of his concert tee that I'm wearing. Drawing circles on my skin, a shiver races up my body as heat flares in the opposite direction, hardening my nipples and causing my empty core to clench.

Gulp.

"Just trying to make it easier on you, is all." My voice is all husky shake and zero cool.

He steps closer, his chest practically touching mine now, and I have to crane my neck to meet his dark hooded eyes as he peers down at me through his lashes. "So that's why you made that rule? To make it easier for me and my hands that will be oh so tempted to touch every inch of your body?"

He smirks. It's not necessarily a friendly smirk either and I get the impression I'm not going to like what he has to say next.

"If that was your main concern, let me put you at ease by saying I have no problems sharing a bed and a room with you and keeping my hands to myself. Despite the notion you have of me and my supposed reputation, I don't fuck every woman I encounter." His nose brushes along mine and I tremble. "Even the ones I'm dying to."

Oh shit. What did I just do? *This is what happens when you try to be coy, Fallon!*

"So now that we've sorted out one of your rules and you know I won't touch you or fuck you tonight," he rasps, "do you think you can manage one bed with me?"

Double gulp. "Yes." I might have squeaked that.

His dirty smirk makes my belly flutter as he stares at me for another long second, his eyes dipping to my lips where they hold. He sucks in a breath and then steps back, all the sex and heat evaporating in a flash, throwing me for a loop. I forgot how good he is at that.

"Fantastic. Let's go to the hotel. Incidentally, I think you'll love the room I was able to get us. We were lucky it was available all things considered."

He takes my hand, adjusts his guitar case on his back, hands me his backpack to take, and then grabs my suitcase with his other hand, leading me toward the exit of the airport. It's bright out here and impossibly crowded with tourists as he said, but he's unconcerned as he guides us through, down the sidewalk, and around the corner to where there is a sleek black car waiting for us along with a tall, surlylooking dude in a black livery outfit and dark sunglasses.

"Signor McQueen?"

"Si. Sono oi. Grazie," Grey says when the driver takes our stuff and loads it into the back of the car. Still holding my hand, Greyson tugs me into the back seat beside him and then we're being whisked up through one of the seven hills of Rome to an exclusive hotel high up above the city with sweeping views, air that smells of jasmine, and promises of a large suite with LED lights overhead meant to look like the stars and a private rooftop balcony with a hot tub.

Our driver checks us in, the staff giving us the full-on celebrity treatment of a private butler, concierge, and hostess even though we're checked in under the name Mr. Steve McQueen—Greyson thinks old Hollywood actors are cool and it's a lot easier than picking random aliases. Our suite is magnificent, filled with gold and tan ornate furnishings, a giant bathroom with a huge soaking tub, and a gorgeous king-sized bed and stairs that lead up to the balcony.

I'll be honest. I hadn't given accommodations much consideration when I drunkenly got on the plane. I was more focused on my exodus than my arrival. It's so unlike me to go anywhere without a plan and a backup plan, but Grey seems to be all over it and after looking at this place, it's not something I intend to challenge.

"I need a shower. And breakfast." Stretching, I twist my body this way and that to work out the stiffness of sleeping on an airplane.

"But not eggs," he teases with a sparkle in his eyes.

"You mean chicken fetuses?" My nose scrunches up. "No. Not those. Definitely more coffee though."

"That for sure." He glances down at himself. "I have nothing to change into."

"Sorry."

With an exasperated headshake, he takes my hand. "Stop apologizing. I wasn't blaming you, nor did I expect you to fix it for me. You are not responsible for me, my situation, or my happiness. Got it?"

I fight my grin, rolling up onto the balls of my feet and bouncing lightly. "Not yet, but I'm working on it."

"Good." A smile and a kiss to my forehead. "Keep on that."

"I plan to. Incidentally, I have nothing you'll fit into either." Now it's my turn to glance down because, well... "Do you want the shirt I'm wearing? I know it's not the cleanest, but it's all I've got."

He freezes. "Like, you'll take it off here?"

The alarm on his face makes me giggle. "No. I would change into something else without your peeping eyes on my tits."

A hard swallow. "Shame."

Then his dark gaze drops to my shirt. His shirt. Grey keeps a T-shirt from every concert he's ever done. He gave me this to sleep in years ago and it sat in my closet since I never felt comfortable wearing it around Bacchus. But it's also the only thing I own that I know will fit him.

"I can't decide if I want to wear that shirt because you've

been wearing it or if I love the way it looks on you too much for you to change out of it."

I blush. Stupidly. "Either way I'm changing out of it. I've been wearing it since I changed into it at the airport last night."

"I think I want you to keep it. I gave it to you and if I wear the shirt you slept in... yeah. Not smart. You go shower and I'll be back with coffee and whatever I can find downstairs in the hotel shop. Then we'll hit up the city together like tourists."

"Sounds great."

He heads for the door, snatching a room key off the desk by the door. "And Fallon?"

"Yeah?"

"Don't turn on your phone." The door clicks shut behind him and I frown. Don't turn on my phone. Except I need to. I need to face this and be done with it so I can go into this week without my ex-fiancé and my family hanging over my head. At the very least I need to let my parents know where I am. And why I won't be at the house on Sunday for Easter. I giggle a little at that. How did I not remember that before picking Rome of all places?

Though, from what I could see on our drive up here, there are tons of festivals and fairs for it that will be amazing to explore.

Opening up my suitcase, I grab the first thing my hands touch—ripped jeans and a white blouse—along with my toiletries and things and head into the bathroom. My phone comes with me, and I turn on the water in the huge walk-in shower and start to pace, staring at my phone. Why did Grey have to say that? Does he not know me at all?

I'm here and I'm being reckless for the first time in my life, but...

"Argh!" I turn on my phone and once it sets to the fact that I'm in Rome, it goes berserk. A zillion texts and voice messages light up my screen and I don't want to read or listen to any of them. Instead, I call my mother, checking my watch, which tells me it's 5:00 a.m. in Boston. She's up. The woman rises with the birds.

She picks up instantly, having no clue I'm in Rome and not somewhere in Boston.

"Hello, Mother." I start to pace again, reaching in and shutting off the shower, flicking my hand to remove the excess water as I go.

"I received a troubling call last night from Bacchus informing me of things that I know cannot possibly be true. Then I don't hear from you until now?"

"He's planning on cheating on me the first chance he gets after we say I do. Did he tell you that?"

"Yes. He told me you overheard him speaking privately with a friend. Did he explain to you that he was simply expelling normal pre-wedding jitters?"

I stare around the bathroom and drop onto the edge of the jetted tub. "Is that supposed to be a joke? He was telling his friend how he couldn't imagine being married to me and staying faithful for his entire life. He's been pretending to be a loving, doting fiancé all the while I bore him and am nothing more than a bitch with the right pedigree. You should have heard the things he said about me, Mother. The way he spoke about me."

A huff. "Fallon, don't be ridiculous. He's a man. It's what they do. He's assured me he will be faithful to you since that seems to be so important to you."

The way she says that. So condescending. Like I'm ridiculous to expect my partner to not screw around behind my back or speak poorly of me.

"Wow, Mother. All romance and poetry."

"Don't patronize me. The only purpose romance serves is to disappoint. This is marriage, not a fairy tale. Grow up and get over your adolescent fantasies of love and romance."

"You want me to grow up?" I spit at her. "He's a con artist and a criminal."

"He's everything he needs to be to get ahead in this world. Just like your father and grandfathers. This is your duty. To your family. To your name. It is who you were born and raised to become. This is why we never told you about him. Even from an early age, we knew you were too romantic for your own good."

I sit up straight, unblinking. She said that last part under her breath, almost dismissively as if she were speaking to herself. "What? What does that mean? You never told me about him."

She ignores my questions completely. "You have an opportunity to sit as the wife of a man who at the very least will be a United States senator. One day, he could very well be the most powerful man in the world. You've always claimed to want to make a difference. This is your chance to make the biggest difference of all. Don't throw away everything we've built for you simply because you don't like the way he spoke about you and things he hasn't even done yet."

"Jesus, Mother, you really are drinking his Kool-Aid."

"No, I'm doing what needs to be said and done. You're the one who has been living this life through rose-colored glasses. Wake up, Fallon. This is the life that has been set before you."

Painfully, she might have a point in that. Delusion has been my boyfriend, my best friend, and my most intimate lover. I believed in its power and used it accordingly. I believe Bacchus loved me for me. I believed he was a good and honest man. I believed he was going to stay faithful because that was the promise he made me. I believed that by doing everything my family asked of me I'd make everyone happy and in return, they'd love me or at the very least appreciate me.

And look where it's gotten you. What did Greyson just say? *You are not responsible for me, my situation, or my happiness.* But that's exactly the role I've taken on since as far back as I can remember. And with it, I became weak, passive, and blind.

All of which I allowed to happen.

I deluded myself and in doing so I lost myself. Bending forward, my elbow drops to my thigh, my hand covering my forehead as I stare down at the plush white bathmat beneath my bare feet.

"Why did he call you?" I ask after a long moment of silence.

"Because he knew I'd be the voice of reason in all this and that you'd listen to me."

My stomach twists painfully as I utter the next words. "If I don't?"

"You will," she tells me in no uncertain terms. "Put your petty emotions aside and think like a Lark. I realize it's distressing to discover something like that, but you're smart enough to learn how to manage it and what your role in this relationship is meant to be. Bacchus is going to be your husband, Fallon. Men make mistakes. He promised to change. You'll forgive him and take him back. Simple as that and it's final. You will marry him."

Her voice. Her voice has always been so cold and sharp with me. I can't remember a time in my life when my mother was warm and tender. Was she always like this or have the years of a loveless marriage, of being forced to live a life she might not have desired hardened her irrevocably?

"Did you ever love him?" She knows I'm not asking about Bacchus. My parents hate each other and live separately as much as possible.

My hand slips from my forehead to cover my eyes. I'm not sure it matters for anything more than what it is. My father is far from a prince in her story. He was always too busy. A senator, he lived mostly in Washington DC while we lived in Boston. I saw him on sporadic weekends and holidays and during those times he was in his study doing work. He never played tea party or dress-up or took me to ballet class. He never tossed a ball with Dillon or sat and helped him with his math homework. There were no quintessential childhood clichés that memories and family are built on.

I tried. Lord knows I tried to manufacture smiles and love for everyone but to no avail.

Hell, he missed my medical school graduation and made no apologies for it. Not even the empty ones I used to get as a child.

My mother was the same. Constantly out and about with friends or at charity events, and even when she was there, she wasn't. Her parenting skills consisted of telling the nanny to make sure we did what we needed to and dismissing us whenever we begged for her attention.

They had no interest in parenting. We weren't a burden because they didn't bother with us. We fell in line and were the perfect obedient Lark children they expected us to be.

I gave them everything I could.

I've sacrificed so much of myself to be that perfect image of the daughter they wanted without ever receiving anything in return. No matter how hard I tried and begged and pleaded for their love and attention, I was never more than a puppet to them. It's a fucking cruel realization. One I wish I had come to sooner, or maybe accepted is better because I think part of me always knew it was like this.

I just didn't want to admit it to myself—back to that delusion.

How does one accept that their parents likely never gave a shit about them beyond what they could do for them and that their fiancé is no better?

"Did you ever love us?" I switch it up because she didn't answer that question, not that she needed to. The answer was glaringly obvious.

I get the perfunctory, "Of course, I love my children." But there is no affection in her tone.

She's lying, but I use that lie against her. "Then why don't you care about me?"

"Who do you think I'm doing all this for?"

For yourself, for appearances, I want to say, but I can't make the words leave my lips. It's futile. She'll never hear me.

"Come over tomorrow for Easter supper. Bacchus will be here. The two of you can talk and work everything out. All couples go through this. They call it cold feet for a reason."

My hand falls to my thigh and I sit up, discovering Grey stoically watching me, casually leaning against the doorjamb of the bathroom, arms folded, one foot crossed over the other.

I stare at him, my insides tumbling around like clothes in a dryer. My hand trembles against my cheek as I press my phone harder to my ear and say, "I can't do that."

"Fallon—"

"No, Mother," I interject before she can start on me and weaken my resolve. "No. For twenty-nine years, I have lived my life for you and Dad and I'm done with it. I don't want to marry a man like Bacchus. A man who claims to love me while he says and does the opposite. A man who only sees me as a foothold to some political future I want no part of. I don't want to end up in an empty marriage living an empty life simply because that's what is expected of me. I don't want to smile on the outside and feel dead on the inside. Fuck, Mom, I don't want to be you!"

She doesn't make a sound. Not a gasp or a cry or anything else. In fact, her voice is as calm and composed as it has been this entire time. "If you don't marry Bacchus, you're betraying your family," she finally says as if my speech didn't mean anything to her. Her heart is as frozen as her face.

A deep breath.

"And if I do, I'm betraying myself. I'm sorry, but I'm not

going to marry him. In fact, you can officially call the wedding off. It won't be happening."

I press end, and my arm falls to my side. I'm half ready to throw up and half ready to streak through the center of Rome naked. I'm sick and exhilarated all at the same time.

"I turned on my phone."

He briefly eyes the device hanging limply at my side. "I see that. You okay?"

"Not at the moment." Deep breath. "But I will be. Originally, I couldn't help but wonder if I overreacted since he didn't technically cheat, but then I reminded myself that I shouldn't have to wait until he actually did something for me to react. I deserve better and I know it. But the truth is, regardless of what he's done or not done, I don't want to marry him."

Grey crosses the room and sits beside me, matching my pose. "Then it's a good thing you're not."

"It's a good thing I'm not," I agree, still feeling pale and clammy. "My family being unsupportive and shitty aside, I'm insanely happy that we're in Rome." My head falls to his shoulder. "Thank you for dropping everything and coming with me. Thank you for being here and being a constant person in my life who cares. You're the only one, you know. I can't even say that about Dillon."

His lips plant themselves in my hair, but then his hand is beneath my chin and he's tilting my face up to his. "In case you missed it, there isn't anything in the world I wouldn't do for you. Including traveling through it with you."

He smiles and I get light-headed from it. It holds and then his gaze dips to my lips, his face dipping in along with it as if magnetized. His sweet breath fans my lips and I'm painfully aware of how close our bodies are. The heat of him is exquisite against me, luring.

Dangerous.

For a panicked moment, I think he's going to kiss me, and I

debate what I'll do if he does, only his lips meet my forehead instead. And they hold there, firm against my skin.

He blows out a breath and then releases me. "I'll shower when you're done."

With that he gets up and walks out, shutting the door behind him, leaving me here to wonder if the next week will continue to be like this between us. Tense as we toe the line. And how long can I stave off something that already feels so inevitable?

9

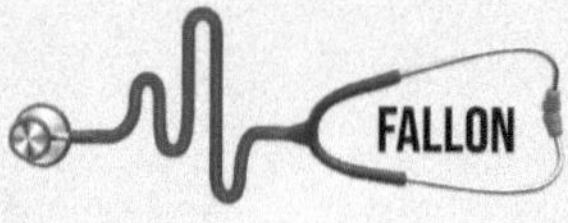

I can't shake the feeling of panic. It's that one where you feel like you forgot something or forgot to do something. Only I'm in Rome. Anything I forgot is at Bacchus's and I seriously don't care if I left the stove on, which I obviously know I didn't. It could be that I don't have a job. That's weighing on me. Or that I have no way to get the rest of my stuff without dealing with my ex.

But even as I think that I know that's not what this feeling is.

All through my shower, I can't shake it and I can't figure out what it is.

It isn't until I get out and wrap a towel around my chest and find my phone on the edge of the bathtub where I left it after hanging up on my mother that I realize what it is.

Bacchus.

I tossed my ring at him, and I ran. I packed a bag and I fled.

But I never had the closure that's supposed to come with a breakup. Unless my mother told him, which I highly doubt. Knowing him, he likely still thinks I'm throwing a temper tantrum and this will all blow over.

I dry off and get dressed, do a quick swipe of makeup across my face, run a brush through my hair, and call it a day. I'm tired from the flight and yet oddly wound up with all that's happening. And happened.

Exiting the bathroom, I find Grey sitting on one of the cushioned chairs in the living area strumming on his guitar. His head is angled and bent toward it, keeping his ear as close to the sound as he can. He's singing something I can't make out the words to, but just hearing his voice gives me chills.

I never told anyone in college or medical school or even residency that I knew Greyson Monroe or any of the other guys from Central Square. I'd get teased for being so obsessed. For having concert shirts and always playing his music. I know every lyric to every song he's ever written.

It was my way of staying close to him when I couldn't.

He was always destined for more than I was. A larger-than-life presence the world loved and devoured. For me, he was part of my blood, my heart, the beat of me.

I was that for him too and I'm dying to know what the years apart have been like for him. The first night I met him, it took me over an hour to work up the courage to climb up onto his roof and introduce myself. I told him I was the girl he'd always regret not knowing and at the time, I was half-serious and half-joking. I knew nothing could ever form between us and I also knew the regret of us not knowing each other would be mine.

I watched him from my bedroom window and even at the age of fourteen, I couldn't tear myself away. He was doing exactly what he's doing now, and all these years later, I'm no less captivated.

"You don't have to stand there. You can come sit."

"I'm enjoying the show."

He twists his head without missing a chord as he continues to play. His dark chocolate brown eyes meet mine, staring at me with a crooked grin that makes his chin dimple appear practically edible and a smoldering gaze that promises all the mischief and sweat my body craves.

For a delirious moment, I contemplate walking across the room, putting his guitar on the couch, and straddling him. The way he's watching me tells me he wouldn't object to that, but I know I need to hold firm to my rules if I'm ever going to be the phoenix rising from the ashes.

Until then, I'm still the damn bird risking being burned alive and turning into a pile of dust.

"This show ain't much. I've been having a little... trouble coming up with new stuff that I don't hate."

My eyebrows shoot up. "Really?" I'm shocked. Grey was always scribbling things down and plucking out cords. He was never far from his guitar or a piece of paper or his phone even.

He gives me a wry grin. "Yeah. First time. Zax called it burnout and told me a few weeks ago to take a vacation and chill out from it. I guess that's what I'm doing now."

"Then it's a good thing you made my flight."

That crooked grin slays right through me as he says, "Definitely a good thing."

"When was the last time you had a vacation?" I ask, slowly making my way over to him.

"A vacation for me involves hiding away in my house and doing nothing, but I don't do that well and I get restless too quickly. So... never."

My arms fold over my stomach as I stand before him, peering down at him. "Me neither. College, med school, residency. My honeymoon was going to be my first vacation. We never even went on them as kids because my parents couldn't stand to be that close to each other for that long. It was worse after my mother and your father had their affair. You're lucky you were already out of the house by that point. It wasn't pretty. My mom used your dad as revenge and your father was only too happy to oblige. So yeah, no vacations for us as a family. Before or after that."

"We should live this up then," he muses, half-focused on me and half-hearing his music. I can only imagine much his writer's block is weighing on him. Music is the biggest part of him, larger than anything else. It's beyond passion. It's infused in his soul. Struggling at it must be eating him alive.

He needs this as much as I do.

"We should." I laugh lightly, toying with the end of my blouse. "Only I have no idea what that means. I'm hoping you do. I'm not sure I've ever lived anything up."

"Until now." He winks at me. "I know how to get into trouble and fun in foreign countries. Don't worry, I won't get us arrested," he promises when he catches my oh shit face.

He continues to watch me, strumming a little more. It's something I haven't heard before and he plays louder. I like it. It's restless. A little manic even.

"What's this one called?"

He smirks at me and plays a few more chords before his hands rest and then he's standing and pulling his guitar over his head and putting it back in its case. He drops a kiss to the side of my head and then heads into the bathroom.

"I'm going to shower," is all he says, shutting the door behind him.

I'm tempted to run after him and hug him, so instead, I walk up the stairs and out onto the large balcony, soaking in the sunlight and the breathtaking view of Rome including St. Peter's Dome. Rome. Wow, it's almost surreal. We're far enough up that I can't hear the street noise, even as I lean against the railing by the whirlpool.

With a sigh, I start scrolling through my missed texts and then decide I don't want to read his messages that swing from furious to contrite, so I hit his number instead.

It rings and rings, the hour still early in Boston, but finally his gravelly, sleepy voice fills my ear.

"Where are you? I haven't heard from you all night."

"I told you I'd call you today. I don't know why you kept calling and texting."

He sighs heavily into the phone and then I hear him moving around, likely sitting up in bed. "Because I didn't know what else to do. I'm glad you called. We have to talk."

"You're right. We do." I start to pace along the edge of the large balcony, my skin prickling with nervous adrenaline, my heart feeling the strain of it as it picks up two beats for every breath I take.

"Can I go first?" he asks.

"Okay."

I start to nibble on my lip, my steps quickening.

"I fucked up. I know I did. The wedding is in two weeks and there is so much in our lives that's changing and changing quickly and I... I got scared. I panicked. And I took all that out on you. I was blowing off shit with Tommy and you heard stuff I never intended for you to hear."

"No kidding. And all this time I thought you liked my ass."

He growls at my sarcastic tone. "You're beautiful, Fallon. And fucking perfect. You've always been perfect and none of this stuff fazed you. You were all, oh, okay, let's move and sure, I can find a new job, no problem. I'm already getting pressure from my dad about my image and how I have to step it up if I want to take over his senate seat. This new firm has a lot of big names who aren't so thrilled I'm coming on. It was just pressure and I'm sorry."

I sigh.

"And the woman in your new Philadelphia office? The one who wants to fuck you and who you want to fuck?"

"I won't touch her. Or anyone else."

His resolute tone, his heartfelt apology... it's everything I need to hear. Everything that would have me forgiving him and moving on. But...

"But that's not what you want," I challenge.

Silence fills my ear for a deafening second before he says, "I only want you."

I know immediately it's a lie. He can make me all these promises, say whatever he wants to get me to walk down the aisle because at the end of the day, he needs me more than I need him. I don't give a shit about politics and have no desire to be part of the game. I'm a pediatrician. But if his dad is already giving him pressure to step up his image, marrying good girl Fallon Lark is the first step.

His father will go ballistic if this union doesn't happen. Mine too.

"Can we do something?" I ask. "Can we be honest with each other? Like actually honest?"

"What do you want me to say?" he asks quietly, remorsefully. "You want honesty? Fine. I was never raised to believe monogamy in marriage was a real thing. Both of my parents had other lovers. Just as yours did. Marriage is a business arrangement."

I nod absently, pausing and resting my hand on the railing. I know this. My introduction to Bacchus was as planned out as everything else in my life. Maybe that's what my mother was hinting at. How long has my union to him been arranged as business without my knowing? That hits me hard. Probably harder than it should, because I likely should have known this all along, but I didn't. How stupid do I feel?

"I'm not interested in business or arrangements."

"I know. We all know that." Another breath and some more rustling. He's agitated. "Listen, Fallon. Please listen because this is the truth, business or not. I care about you. A lot. I want to be married to you."

"With the perks of other women."

He grows agitated. "I'm a man and men like to fuck around. It's in our DNA. It doesn't mean you're not my wife, my priority, and it doesn't mean I don't love you."

I fall onto one of the deck chairs, the wood warm on my back from the sun's rays. Beyond the glass balcony is Rome. Adventure. A new life waiting for me if I'm willing and brave enough to reach out and take it.

"Do you love me? Since we're being honest. Do you actually love me as in you're in love with me or has this been business for you all along?" How long has he kept up this ruse?

"Fallon."

I swing my arm behind me, gripping the back of the chair. "No. Don't Fallon me. And don't lie to me. Respect me enough to give me honesty and I'll do the same in return."

"Fine. I love you. That's the truth."

I grin. "But you're not in love with me."

"Christ. I already told you I love you. What else do you need? Why isn't that good enough for you? I'm trying so hard here Fallon and you're splitting hairs over trivialities that aren't as important as what we have with each other."

I sit up and then stand, walking to the railing once more, my nerves gone, the adrenaline now a welcome shot of courage. "I feel sorry for you, Bacchus, and relieved for myself. I can't marry a man who isn't in love with me or doesn't respect me, but more importantly, I can't marry a man I don't love or respect in return. I don't want this to be angry and I don't want it to be volatile. It just wasn't the right fit and that's all. I'm sorry. Or not. Anyway, it's over and we can both move on with our lives."

"That's not an option and you know it."

"Actually I don't know that. Last I checked humans were divined—or ruined, however you want to look at it—with free will. For the first time in my life, I'm exercising mine. Go find yourself a better business partner and do yourself a favor and be honest with her from the start. You and my parents can go fuck yourselves for all your lying and manipulation."

"It won't end this way, Fallon. Don't fool yourself into thinking it will. I'll give you a few days to come to your senses, but after that, we both know how this goes."

"Not this time. Don't waste your time, Bacchus, it's over."

I hit end and a satisfied smile sweeps across my face just as a brush of warm wind does the same, kicking up my hair and tickling my skin. I don't think I've ever felt this exhilarated and light in my life. My life is finally mine.

I shoot Jonah Hughes, my boss from Hughes Healthcare, along with my attending at Boston Children's Hospital each an email, letting them know that the move to Philadelphia fell through, and asking if they still have an opening I can refill starting in two weeks. I know they have been interviewing people, so it's far from a guarantee, but for now, it'll have to do.

Shutting off my phone, I slip it into my back pocket just as two hands land on the railing on either side of mine. Grey's chest meets my back and his chin lands on my shoulder putting us nearly cheek to cheek. He smells of shampoo and body wash —and Greyson—and my chest flutters with all of it.

Being attracted to your best friend sucks sometimes.

He must have purchased something downstairs in the shop because the shirt he's wearing is black and has cuffs that he's rolled up to his elbows revealing the colorful ink on his forearms. Some of it is old, but he's definitely added to his sleeves in the last three and a half years since I've seen them.

"Ready to go out and do Rome?"

"Absolutely." The reality of what I'm about to embark on hits me, rolling through my veins like a shot of dopamine. I'm smiling so wide right now I'm positive all my teeth are showing. I'm a geyser, getting ready to explode. A rocket about to launch into space.

I'm free and it's nothing short of magnificent.

"Do you remember my rule?"

I snicker. "We already broke one of mine. Why do you get to keep yours?"

"Because you get to keep your second rule, so I get to keep my one. Besides, mine is way more fun than yours. You don't question me."

"I won't question you," I promise.

Frankly, I'm far too curious and excited about whatever he has in store for us that I couldn't care less. I trust Grey. I trust him with this as I trust him with all of me. He's my white freaking knight, swooping in and taking what could have been a failed attempt or a disaster of a try and turning it into something magical.

"Then let's go."

10

I did two things I'm already partially regretting. One, I rented a motorcycle to get us through Rome instead of a driver. I wanted to push Fall beyond her comfort zone, and I didn't want to have to rely on a driver and call attention to myself. This is vacation as we both said, and on vacation, I think we're both entitled to a break from our daily lives and that means I'm not Greyson Monroe here.

I'm just Grey and Grey likes to ride motorcycles.

But Fallon screamed at me about the dangers of motorcycles for a solid five minutes before I was able to convince her to put on the helmet and my leather jacket.

Things didn't get any better from there because drivers in Rome are fucking fearless and believe accidents will never happen to them. We had two very close calls, and we don't speak the language all that well, so even I'm a bit frazzled riding through the city streets on this thing. Fallon clung to me like a monkey, screaming and whimpering and terrified out of her mind and this was not how I wanted to start this.

The second thing I'm only sorta regretting is that I—or more likely my assistant—did use some of my Greyson Monroe celebrity status to get us into things we wouldn't typically be able to get into. Vacation or not, I didn't want us going through tourist traps without the buffer of private tours. Asher and I tried that once when we went to the Art Institute of Chicago—he was playing against Chicago that weekend and I met him there. We barely made it through the door before we were surrounded by fans. We figured no one would know us in an art museum, but that wasn't the case.

Fall doesn't seem to mind or even question it. I think she's just relieved not to be on the motorcycle anymore. We go through the Colosseum with a private guide who tells us all about the history of the building and the games that took place here. We meander through ancient ruins not too far from there. We race each other up the Spanish Steps—she wins because I'm too busy watching her ass to care about beating her.

We eat a quick lunch at a food stand near the Colosseum but Fall hems and haws over what to order, her face scrunched up as she attempts to read the menu plastered to the top of the stand. Eventually she orders a slice of cheese pizza and then refuses to take a bite of my mortazza panini.

"What gives?" I ask, ducking my head so I can look at her downturned face.

"I only eat food I can trust from trusted places."

I blink at her about ten thousand times as I take a bite of my sandwich. "I'm not sure I understand what that means," I tell her as I chew.

She makes a face, clearly not wanting to elaborate. "You'll make fun of me. Bacchus always did."

"Do I look like Bacchus?" I tease, needing to say something because the flat line of her lips with their slight downward curve at the corners makes me want to kiss them.

"Definitely not. Kind of the opposite of him actually."

We start to walk along the Arch of Constantine, milling

away from several groups of tourists. "Exactly. I won't make fun. Try me."

"You will. It's sort of ridiculous. Even I know this. In med school during my emergency medicine rotation, I had a patient with the worst case of food poisoning I've ever seen from bad sushi. He ended up in the ICU for a week with it and I vowed I'd never eat raw fish again. Certain things you can't unknow or unsee. Trust me on that. Meat is another thing that scares me for that same reason, and I only eat it in certain places I trust won't make me sick."

"Huh," I muse as I take another bite, thinking that over.

I can feel Fallon watching me, waiting for my reaction. "That's it? Just huh?"

I shrug. "I get it. I do. It doesn't surprise me, Fall Girl. You're cautious and a bit of a rule follower." I suppress my grin as I throw her a side-eye. "But we're also here breaking some rules, right?"

"Um. Not that rule."

I take the last bite of my sandwich and toss the paper into the trash. I decide to let it drop for now. She's pushing herself and I'm pushing her too, so now isn't the time for more of that. But on this trip, I will get her to eat something she'd never otherwise eat.

"Ready for the next adventure?"

She loops her arm through my elbow. "Sure. Let's do it."

Neither of us is all that excited to get back on the bike, but there is no way I'm missing this tour my assistant no doubt had to pull a million strings to get us. I ride us through the traffic of Rome out to Vatican City, weaving around cars. I can hear the GPS through my AirPods, but that doesn't make the drive easy.

Especially as a car comes so close if I tilted my shoe just a little, I'd touch the side of it. Fall starts screaming, clinging tighter to me. "Don't tilt your body weight. Hold still."

"I'm trying! Oh my God! We're going to die!"

"We're not going to die," I assure her though I'm silently praying I don't make a liar out of myself. This isn't a moped. It's a fucking Ducati, sleek, black, and fast. But also sensitive to body movement and Fall is terrified out of her mind and throwing our balance off.

If we were on the open road, this bike would be the hottest ride she'd let me give her—you know, since we have the whole no sex rule. But this is not an open road. This is congestion and rotaries and piazzas and Rome during Easter.

Horns blare as I pop the clutch and unleash the throttle, zipping us around two cars because there is no other way I'll be able to get us over and we have to get over because I cannot go through the roundabout again. I can't.

"I'm going to throw up my pizza."

"No, you won't." *Please don't let her throw up her pizza on me.* "Just breathe, baby. I'll get us there. I promise. Try to relax."

"Relaxing is not possible!"

We reach a small clearing and I take it, flying us through. The bike vibrates beneath us, the handling smooth and powerful. It's one hell of a high and despite the fact that Fallon is freaking out and I hate that I'm the cause of that, I love the feel of her pressed against me like this. Thighs and arms and chest.

If I ever manage this, if I ever get this woman to be mine, I'll take us out to Cape Cod, and we can ride on one of my bikes there and it will be a completely different experience for her than this. So I can't kill us before that can happen.

Finally, we make it, weaving through and parking in a spot after showing no less than five guards the pass on my phone that was emailed to me.

"Oh hell, Grey. We're never doing that again," Fall exclaims, climbing off the bike and removing her helmet. She points menacingly at the motorcycle. "I don't care if you have to ditch this death trap here or what, but I'm never getting back on that donor-cycle again. Look at my hands. I'm shaking like a freaking leaf." She holds her hands out in front of me and yes, they're trembling like leaves. I take them in mine, squeezing some life back into them.

"Donor-cycle?"

"Yes! As in the people who ride it become organ donors. Because they're dead! That was the most terrifying half an hour of my life. I tried to be brave, but I'm not that brave. That was worse than the drive into the city this morning and I didn't think I'd survive *that*. I'm invoking my veto power."

"Okay." I won't argue it because yeah, that was a bit much for even me. "No more bikes in the city. I promise. Happy?"

She looks so hot like this that I can hardly stand it. Her black hair is windswept, helmet-mashed, and wild. Her face is flushed—likely from the fear of the ride or yelling at me, but whatever. She's wearing my leather jacket and jeans and Vans, and I want to kiss her so fucking bad I have to look away from her, or I'll act on it and ruin everything.

"Very." She takes a deep, calming breath and then swivels around to face the buildings behind her. "What are we doing and where exactly are we?"

"You didn't think we'd hit up Rome without checking out the hand of God, did you?"

Her violet eyes brighten as her head turns over her shoulder to me. "You're kidding me. On the day before Easter, we're going into the Vatican and the Sistine Chapel?"

"We will have exactly twenty minutes of alone time once we get inside. That's all I was given and I'm pretty sure I made a huge donation to the Catholic Church even though I'm not Catholic."

Fallon giggles. "Then let's not waste a second out here."

I take her hand because she lets me, and our harried-looking guide meets us off to the side of the main entrance. St. Peter's Square is absolutely packed full of people, many of them praying, many of them waiting in lines, or part of tours anxious to enter the basilica.

"I give you ten minutes in the basilica and ten minutes in the chapel. Si?"

I give the guy a nod and then we follow after him. I wish we had more time to do this, but it is what it is, and Fallon doesn't seem to care that we're practically sprinting in. The basilica is massive and ornate with its towering arches and curved gold ceiling and larger-than-life stone statues, many of them so tragic and lifelike you can't help but feel the majesty and awe of this building whether you're Catholic, religious, or not.

We reach the dome, both of us staring up, but we don't get a second to appreciate any of it before we're whisked away, down long art-filled hallways with a few twists and turns. The entrance to the Sistine Chapel is quiet, with only a few other private tours and small groups lingering around.

"Ten minutes. Do not touch and no video or photography. You exit on the other side and go. Yes?"

"Si. Grazie."

He gives us a nod and then we're set free into the chapel. Fallon gasps and I might do the same as we take in the rectangular room that is smaller than I would have thought. I've never been here. In all the times I've visited Rome, I never made it here. Touring for work doesn't leave you with a lot of downtime. It's moving from one city to the next, playing one show after another.

Maybe Zax and Fall are right.

Maybe a vacation is exactly what I need to get my mind back on track. I hadn't had any words in the longest time and then I hopped on a plane with my girl and this morning my head was filled with notes from the second I opened my eyes.

I retake Fallon's hand, having lost it somewhere in the basil-ica, and walk us to the center of the room. We're both silent, staring around the room at the art adorning all the walls and the ceiling. I have no idea if this is breaking the rules or not, but he didn't say we couldn't lie down. So I give her a tug and both of us lower to the floor. Our heads resting on our hands as we stare up at all the different scenes and images that comprise the ceiling.

"Incredible," Fallon whispers, her voice filled with awe. "Ninety percent of our lives are spent going about our days and routines and then you see something like this, and you're reminded that magic does exist, that humans are capable of extraordinary things, and that beauty should never be taken for granted."

Her words hit me in the best and worst of ways. "I could live to be a thousand and I will never write a song as masterful as all this."

Her hand snakes out and tugs mine from behind my head, looping our pinkies together between us. She gives me a squeeze. "Your music got me through more lonely nights than the image of this chapel in my mind ever could. That's the incredible thing about music. It's visceral. You experience it in multiple parts of your brain because it's not just sound, it's words with sound and both evoke feeling and emotion." Her head tilts and her eyes meet mine. "You're an artist, Greyson Monroe. Same as Michelangelo if not better."

My chest explodes, open and exposed, full of such love and longing and fucking gratitude. I squeeze her finger back, so she knows.

Other than the guys, no one in my real life has ever thought much of me. My father hated my guts and made sure I knew it on a daily basis. His favorite pastime was to remind me I was stupid and useless and would never amount to anything he could be proud of. I've been adored by fans, won awards, and fed words of praise, but I never believed I was anything special to anyone until this moment.

My heart twinges, shifting painfully in my chest. Emotion

clogs my throat and I manage to scratch out a "Thank you." Then I blow out a silent breath, ignoring my quivering insides and festering need for this woman to be mine and do what I do best: deflect. "Is it me or are all the dicks up there tiny?"

She chokes out a guffaw, slapping her other hand over her mouth to stifle the sound before it carries around and bounces off the walls and ceiling. "Oh my God. Did you just say that in here?"

"You're the one who just took the Lord's name in vain in his chapel."

"I totally did." She's smiling so hard, her voice full of it.

"Tell me I'm wrong though," I challenge, smiling along with her.

I can practically feel her eyes squinting. "You're not wrong. You'd think Michelangelo would have been more complimentary considering the muscled physiques of Adam and Moses. Adam's is sort of a small, flaccid thing resting on his thigh. Utterly unimpressive. No wonder Eve went on to find temptation elsewhere."

Now it's my turn to laugh. "Maybe Michelangelo didn't want to distract the popes or patrons with large penises during their services."

"Oh, so you think it was a kindness he was bestowing instead of an insult."

"Maybe a bit of both."

"You realize I'll never think about this ceiling the same way again."

I sit up and Fallon does too since we're just about out of time. I twist to face her, giving her a toothy grin. "But I made it better, right?"

She rolls her eyes playfully, her tone mocking. "Most definitely." She stands, wiping the dust from her pants and blouse. "Let's get out of here before you decide to make something else better."

11

By the time I manage to deal with the bike, and we make it back into the city and then walk for a while only to end up near the Trevi Fountain, we're fried. Like dragging ass, jetlagged, utterly indifferent to the beauty and splendor around us fried.

"Food. Wine," is all Fallon can manage only it's like 5:00 p.m. and not nearly time for dinner since we're in Italy and not ninety years old, but I'm sort of agreeing with her. That said, it's insanely crowded here, and I don't want to risk going into a restaurant and being recognized. I also don't have the energy to keep walking to find another piazza or even a quieter space.

Scanning the street, I spot a gelato place attached to a restaurant not even a hundred yards away. "What about gelato and wine?"

She sways, staring across the street at the gorgeous fountain three rows deep with tourists. "Totally sold. One hundred percent sold. In fact, I'll take an IV of alcohol while Roman gods shovel gelato down my throat." She moans. "Fuck, that sounds like heaven."

I snicker. "How about a bottle of wine we sip from without

glasses because we're classy like that and if you really want, I'll feed you gelato and lift my shirt to flex my abs, so you get the same Roman god effect. Plus—and you can't deny this because you know from personal experience—my dick is way bigger than what these guys are packing."

She throws me a side-eye and then returns to the fountain. "I'm not going to feed your adorable rock star ego about your abs or your dick though yours is bigger than Sistine Chapel Adam's—because I've seen toddler peens bigger than his—so use that however you will. But I'm down for whatever you think will give me all the sugar and alcohol my blood and stomach require."

"Cool. You wait here and I'll find us sustenance until we have dinner somewhere other than here. Tourist traps give me hives, but before we leave, we have to make a wish into the fountain because I won't live the rest of my life without knowing I was this close to getting all my wishes granted."

She sags against me, leaning heavily on my shoulder. She really is wiped. "Agreed on the wishes, but you don't have to pay for everything, you know," she challenges, raising a tired eyebrow at me. "I can go buy the wine and gelato."

"You mean because you have a trust fund that could likely run this entire country?"

She scrunches up her nose, tilting her head up to meet my eyes. "That makes me sound like a princess."

"You're a Lark princess."

"Not anymore." She gives me a smarmy smirk. "I'm a jobless, homeless vagabond mooching off a hot rock star in Europe." She snorts. "Wow, that sounds way cooler when I hear it aloud than it actually feels. Minus the hot rock star part. You're aces and I wouldn't trade you."

She's practically delirious. And fucking adorable. "You think I'm hot?"

She rolls her eyes at me. "Again with not feeding your ego."

"But you said it, not me."

A puff of air flees her lungs. "Touché. You're hot and you know it, so there is no point in pretending otherwise. I digress. What I was trying to say with all this is I'm a doctor and I didn't pay for medical school or much after that when I was living with Bacchus, so I have plenty of savings. Trust fund notwithstanding."

My arms wrap around her waist, and I shift her until her chest is pressed to mine. Her neck cranes up to meet my eyes even though we're both wearing sunglasses and it bothers me I can't see her pretty eyes. I remove mine and prop them on top of my Boston Rebel's hat and then swish hers up so they're resting on top of her head, nestled in her dark hair.

I stare into her eyes, holding her close. "Does it bother you if I pay for stuff?" I question. "Because I like paying for stuff for you. For this. Like you, I have plenty of money and I've never had anyone special to spend it on. It's all just sitting wherever it's sitting accruing interest. The only money I spend is what I earn from tours and shows and it's more than enough to pay for all my staff and my expenses and then still have too much left over, and that's not talking album sales or endorsements or the trust fund my grandfather left me into consideration *or* the money I earned with Central Square. Simply put I'm too loaded for my own good."

"Do you always brag about how rich you are? I have to tell you, it's a total turnoff. No wonder you're single."

I pinch her side and she yelps in my arms, but my thumb is there, rubbing that spot and the nonexistent sting away.

"I don't trust anyone enough to tell them stuff like that. You're the first and the only." That's the definition of Fallon Lark to me. My first. My only.

Her hands land on my chest and she blinks up at me. "Greyson, stop being so damn perfect. It's annoying how you always say and do the perfect thing time after time. You're going to make me fall in love with you and then what the hell will you do?"

A smile overtakes my face even though I fully appreciate her words are in jest. "Do you want me to answer that honestly?"

She giggles lightly at my teasing tone and never have I seen Fallon laugh or smile so much. I hadn't realized it. And maybe she's spent the last three years like this with Bacchus, but somehow I doubt it. I think this is Fallon finding a different sort of happiness than any she's ever known.

Before it was smiling through and being happy despite.

This is different and I doubt she's even aware of the shift yet.

"You'll have to run for your life to escape me because I'll turn into a stage three clinger," she tells me. "But it'll be too late for me, and you'll be screwed because you're my best friend and inherently a good guy, so you won't run too far." She squints. "I'm not even sure I'm making sense anymore, but you'll have to be the one to explain to my parents and Dillon why I'm a pathetic mess and following you around like a lost, besotted puppy."

"So they can hate me more than they already do?"

She nods exaggeratedly, her expression mockingly grim. "Yes. Exactly. My father placing a hit on you is the only way you'll escape me."

I plant a kiss on the tip of her nose. "I'll risk it. Plus, I have a feeling when your father and Dillon find out you're here with me, there will be a hit placed on my head anyway."

She worries her lip between her teeth at that, and I reach up and tug it free even though I want to do that with my teeth and not my fingers.

"Chocolate?"

"Chocolate," she confirms. "But if they have Nutella, even

better. And some fantastic Italian wine that's suspiciously missing a cork."

"You got it. Stay here. Don't run off on me."

"Never again," she promises and the potency of that promise hits me square in the chest, altering my breathing. My instinct is to shake it all off. To fight it away. After we lost Suzie, after I lost my absolute fucking mind and watched my brother and my best friends do the same, I decided that was it. I was done. I couldn't take anymore.

My life had been a lot of pain interspersed with periods of elation. But no matter what, it never lasted, and the fall was all the more painful for it. It was easy to detach after that. I have my guys, but that's it. No other attachments in my life.

Here, now, I'm opening myself up to hurt again. Just as agonizing if not more so.

I can't stop it, but more importantly, I don't want to. She's worth the risk.

You'd think all these years apart would have changed that. That I would have grown dispassionate and indifferent and moved on. One thing I've learned from her is that love isn't a decision. It's not a choice your heart gives you the benefit of having. It is predestined and predetermined and you're nothing more than a helpless victim to its premeditation.

If it were a choice, I'd have gotten over her a decade ago.

Forcing myself to get my shit together, I go and purchase our gelato and bottle of wine sans cork and return to find her missing. Only it doesn't take me long to find her. Somehow she's managed to get herself wrapped up in an Easter parade. Mesmerized, I stand, smiling and I realize she's not the only one who hasn't smiled like this and certainly not this often in... I don't even know how long. I make my way over to her and hand her a huge waffle cone overflowing with two different kinds of gelato.

"Chocolate and Nutella," I explain when she stares curiously at it. "I got brownie and salted caramel, so we're going to share, spit-swapping be damned. But what is all this?"

"Some sort of religious parade for Easter, I'm assuming. It's incredible." She beams, bouncing on the balls of her feet.

All around us are floats overflowing with flowers and statues as young girls in white gauzy gowns twirl red ribbons through the air. People are singing and clapping and kissing their fingers and then touching the statues or the floats.

After a few moments, we're both lost in it, watching the parade and eating our gelato. I pass her the bottle that's wrapped in brown paper because we're hard like that and she takes a hearty gulp and then hands it back to me. But then something catches my eye. Something that has me calling out her name and telling her to move out of the way. She doesn't acknowledge me directly, just nods her head in my general direction.

"It's beautiful, right?" she comments airily.

"No. Yes. Shit." I shake my head. "That's not what I said. I said we have to move." I take a step back, but she doesn't follow, oblivious to what's headed our way. My hands are full of ice cream and wine, so I can't grab her, but fuck. "Jesus! Watch out!"

"What?" Her head spins to me. "What is it?" Her brows furrow as she yells over the noise of the parade.

I point with my gelato. "Jesus. Watch. Out!" I repeat, louder and far more urgent this time.

Her head whips back the other way, but it's too late and I panic. Reaching across her body, I yank her back just in time to avoid getting trampled by a human re-creation of Jesus on the cross in full relief. White loin cloth, fake blood, thorn crown, and everything. Wine splashes all around, and my gelato is I don't even care where.

We both go tumbling, staggering back, and barely catching

ourselves before we fall to the ground or into the other spectators who are standing around us.

"Holy crap!" She gasps, falling against me as she pants. "My life just flashed before my eyes and it was alarmingly pathetic. I was two seconds from getting plowed over by him." She points after the float. "How did I not see him?"

"I don't know!" I yell because my heart still hasn't slowed. "How did you not see him?!"

She shakes her head in total bewilderment, her eyes wide as saucers. "I'm sorry. I couldn't hear you and I was a bit lost watching the girls twirling their ribbons in the air. It reminded me of one of the *Twilight* books for some reason and I was thinking about that scene when Bella ends up in Italy to save Edward and there is a parade about exiling vampires from the city and I think there were girls like that and—"

"What? I have no idea what you're talking about."

She waves me away. "It's nothing. I was just lost in my thoughts. I'm sorry. Truly. I'm good. You good?"

I blow out a breath, gripping the bottle of wine and chugging half of it down. "I'm good. Sorta. I didn't see him till the last second either."

She grabs the bottle from me and finishes it off. We're both breathing hard and fighting our laughter because she was almost run over by Jesus.

She shifts and then glances down at herself. "Oh. Now I'm feeling that."

I follow her gaze and that's when we see it. There's a huge smear of chocolate right across her chest along with large splatters of wine staining her white blouse.

"Hell. I didn't mean to get you like that. I panicked when I saw him and grabbed you without thinking." I chuck the now empty bottle—since it appears most of it ended up on her—and then take some of the napkins in my hands and begin rubbing urgently at the mess on her shirt.

"Grey! Give me the napkins."

"No, I made the mess. I've got it." I push her hand away as she tries to take them from me because she's making the mess so much worse. I keep wiping and wiping, but it's smearing everywhere, seeping into her shirt and I can't tell if now *I'm* making it better or worse.

She goes for the napkins again, trying to take them from me. "Do you have any clue what you're doing?" she demands.

I throw her an irritated look before returning to her shirt. "You mean other than trying to clean you up?"

"Yes! I mean other than trying to clean me up!"

I press again, this time a little harder, and in the process, my thumb brushes something hard. Something hard that suspiciously feels like a nipple. A breathy whimper slips free from her lips, and I freeze, eyes wide as they climb back up to hers.

"Did you just—"

She grows redder than I've ever seen her. "No. Shut up."

I lick my lips, all the blood flow in my body instantly traveling south. But still, I can't fight it. I'm laughing. And hard. And I'm starting to realize *exactly* where my hand is.

"Don't laugh."

My vision casts down and yep. "Why didn't you say anything? I've been groping your tits and didn't even realize it!" Now I'm dying. Like hard. Laughing hysterically. "I should lose my official man card for this. It's not exactly like your tits are small."

"I tried to push your hand away, asshole. How did you not realize you were rubbing my tits?"

A hiss has both of our heads popping up to find three nuns in full habits standing there, glaring at us.

"Oh! I'm so sorry," Fall murmurs, her face is redder than it was seconds ago if that's even possible, burning hotter than the fires of Hades where we're both clearly headed.

I straighten and remove my hands. "Yes. We're sorry." I give them my most charming smile. "We had a small mishap with gelato and wine." I gesture to Fall's blouse. "As you can see. I was helping my foul-mouthed friend clean up."

Fall covertly elbows me for that only the head nun sees it and crosses herself while muttering something neither of us can understand. Could be Latin. Could be Italian. My guess is it's a prayer for our heathen souls, which I'll gladly take because frankly, at least for me, I could use it.

One of the younger nuns giggles lightly while batting her eyelashes at me. I smirk in return and toss her a wink because that always seems to win when I need it to but not tonight. I get a pointed finger from the head nun that might in fact put me in places I don't want to be in the afterlife.

"Non è fatto con Dio."

"Si. Grazie." I press my hands in supplication and bow in their direction. The head nun scowls but they all move on along with the parade and I take a relieved breath.

"What did she say?' Fall murmurs in my ear, but I'm still busy smiling at the nun.

"I have no clue," I reply. "But I'm thinking whatever it was, it wasn't good. But that has nothing on you. You're the damned one."

Her free hand covers her eyes. "Oh my God! I just said asshole and tits in front of nuns while you were visibly touching them."

"You just took the Lord's name in vain. Again. Did you learn nothing in the Sistine Chapel?"

She elbows me in the arm. "Shut it. Not my fault. Who rubs someone else's breasts in public?"

"I also made you moan. Don't forget that." I sure as hell won't. That sound and the feel of her hard nipple against my thumb will keep me hard all night now.

"I told you not to mention that. It never happened. Got it?"

I throw my hands in the air and my gelato nearly goes

flying. Fucking gelato. I quickly dump it in the nearest trash can and do the same with hers.

"Hey! I wasn't done with that!"

I spin to her. "Oh, we're done with that. If you want some more, you can lick your shirt."

"Ha. You're very funny."

"We haven't even made our wish yet and we were almost run over by Jesus and cursed by nuns. I think this wish is our last chance at salvation. Fuck the gelato." I hold up two coins.

She cocks a hip and an eyebrow. "I cure sick children. I'm straight with the big Lady up there. You're the boob-rubbing bad boy rock star."

"Fine. You win. Come on." I grab her hand and cross the crowded street, moving us until we're in front of the fountain. "Come here, babe." I spin us, hold up my phone and then take a selfie of us. I haven't gotten a lot of pictures yet and I decide I need to remedy that.

She grabs my phone, shifting it so she can see the picture. "That came out cute. Text it to me."

"I will. Here." I hand her the coin and she immediately closes her eyes, holding the coin in a tight fist. I watch her for a moment, how serious she is with this wish, and then turn to the fountain. It's noisy, the sound of rushing water slapping over stone, of tourists shouting and bumping into us as they try to get closer to the fountain.

It's all distracting, but I force myself to concentrate. To think.

I don't make a lot of wishes.

Not on stars or in fountains. Anything I ever wish for is for my family and friends to be happy, healthy, and safe. Everything else for me is gravy and I feel like I have no right to ask for anything extra. For a half beat, I'm tempted to ask for my musical mojo back, but that seems selfish and like it could backfire on me.

Or maybe I'm still nervous about the nuns damming me to hell and I don't want to risk it right now.

But as I squeeze my coin against my palm and look back over at the woman standing beside me, I wish for her. I don't plan it and I don't question it.

The wish is there, and it can't be stopped.

I wish for her to have the life she wants for herself. I wish that I can be a part of it. I wish for this to all go according to plan.

I wish for her to fall and fall hard for me.

Because I have no idea what I'll do if she doesn't.

12

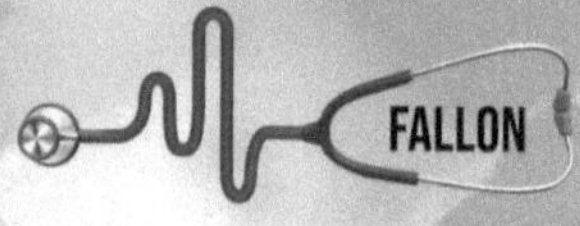

Shutting the bathroom door behind me I burst out laughing the second I catch my reflection. Chocolate and red wine smears streak through my white blouse like a kid's finger painting. Shaking my head at myself, I rip the shirt over my head and chuck it in the trash.

At least my jeans were spared thank God because I only have one other pair. I packed the weirdest things when I tore through the condo before fleeing. That's definitely not something I'm looking forward to dealing with when I get home.

Getting my stuff from Bacchus.

As if hearing my thoughts, my phone pings on the counter, and without looking at it, I immediately shut it off. My curiosity isn't so great anymore.

Stripping out of the rest of my clothes, I turn on the shower and walk under the heavenly hot spray. I moan as I think of the day spent nearly dying on a motorcycle, lying on an ancient church floor, nearly getting run over by Jesus, and then getting slathered in sticky, cold, and wet gelato and wine only to have Grey rub my boobs and turn me on in front of a bunch of nuns.

I smile as I lather my hair in shampoo. It's already been an incredible day and though I have no real clue what or where tomorrow will bring me, for the first time in my life, I don't care, and I don't want to question it.

But before tomorrow comes tonight.

I've slept in a bed with Grey before. He knows my hard limits. Nothing is going to happen between us. It's no big deal to break this rule because we have no choice. I could make him sleep on the couch, but the truth is, if I'm brutally honest with myself, I want to sleep in the bed with him.

Just this once. Just for this night.

I've missed him and though I know I shouldn't, I want to be close to him. To hear him breathing and know he's here, beside me. Even if it's just in this way. I can also ignore the not-so-small corner of my mind that wants to feel his hands on me. All over me. That wants to get lost, wrapped up in his arms as he possesses my body.

Finishing up in the shower, I dry off and slide into a pair of leggings and Grey's concert T-shirt. I brush my hair and moisturize my face and pace around a few times, but all too soon, the lure is there, and I've run out of things to keep me occupied.

I open the door and walk through the bedroom to find Grey sitting in a chair at the ornate, antique-looking desk with his guitar strap slung over his shoulder, resting on his lap. His eyes are closed and he's playing but there's a pained expression on his face. One I've never seen before while he's playing.

"Fall Girl, you can stop lingering," Grey says to me with a crooked smirk as his eyes blink open and his head swivels in my direction. He waves his hand for me to join him. "Get your adorable ass over here."

Oomph. Busted.

Grey watches as I cross the room to him. His eyes are saying something. Something I've been trying desperately to ignore. I don't even think it's conscious. Just the look he naturally gives me, but it never fails to heat my body from the inside out.

He pats his thigh for me to sit and for the first time in my life, a rush of something awful hits me. It freezes me and I hate it and yet, I can't stop the self-consciousness of it. Fucking Bacchus. I never gave a second thought to my weight before last night. Before I can let it consume me, he grabs my hips and plants me down on him, shifting me so I don't bang into his guitar.

"There. Much better. Right where I want you."

"Ha. Nice one." I move to stand, but he stops me, keeping me firmly rooted on his thighs.

"No. Don't. Stay with me like this."

"You sure? I thought you'd want to work, and I don't think you can play with me sitting on you like this."

"Oh, I beg to differ with that. But unfortunately, work still isn't coming all that easily to me right now. Better, but not great."

His hand slides up my back, rubbing, caressing, lightly tickling. His eyes are on me, watching my expression, possibly waiting for me to stop him and I should. I seriously should, but I also don't. Instead, I run my fingers along his face, smoothing the crease between his slightly furrowed brows and along his cheeks and across the softer-than-I-expected bristles of his two-day-old scruff.

My body starts to hum, a fluttering vibration pulsing through my lower belly. A warning I don't heed, but I also know I won't allow this to go beyond what we're doing now.

"Play for me," I tell him because I'm dying to hear him. It's been so freaking long and that is one of the things I've missed the most.

"What do you want me to play?" he whispers, his eyes closing as I continue to explore his face and hair.

"Whatever you're trying to work on."

A heavy, frustrated breath. "I have nothing good to give you on that."

"You mentioned you're having some trouble. Tell me about it. Maybe I can help."

My hands fall to my lap, and I twist so that I'm sitting sideways, perched on one leg, my knees between his parted thighs.

His eyes spring open and he looks curiously at me for a moment. Almost as if he's not sure what to do with my request and then he says, "My last album was my biggest success. Had the most singles on it I've ever had. It's easily considered my best work to date." His hand starts to move on my back again, his fingers tickling the line where my leggings meet skin. "I'm not sure how to follow that up."

"Meaning?"

"Meaning what if my next album isn't as good? What if fans hate it?"

I frown, diving my hand into his hair again. We can't seem to stop touching each other and it's not strange or strained, it's natural and comfortable. And more, but I'm not going there or thinking about it.

"Why would that ever be?"

Distressed, he glances away, staring out into the expansive living room of the hotel. We came back shortly after the Trevi Fountain. Exhausted, we said we were going to order room service and relax on our terrace.

That has yet to happen.

"Central Square's third album was our most successful by far. We were big, but that made us huge. I was the songwriter. The one who wrote all our lyrics and music. I was working on the fourth album, trying to keep everything together and us on top of everything. It was starting to fall apart, and I felt it, and I... I was being selfish. I knew Asher and Callan wanted to leave. They both wanted to go to college in person instead of online. Zax didn't care. He was there with Suzie and Suzie wanted Central Square. Same with Lenox. But I felt nothing but guilt over Asher and Callan, and I kept thinking, 'If I can make this next album even better...'" He trails off and I already know what's coming next and my heart cracks open in my chest. "I was halfway through writing that album when Suzie died, and everything fell apart."

Ah. "So it feels like that's where you are again?" I surmise.

"I don't know. I released that album a few weeks before I saw you in the café and then I—" He shakes his head, cutting himself off drastically.

"You saw me and what?"

His eyes bore into mine. "Knew I lost you for good. The album was everywhere. It hit number one on the charts and eight of my singles hit the top ten and stayed there for months. I was already a mess with that and then after I saw you, I was even more of one. I haven't been able to write anything since the album was released."

"I'm sorry." Shame cuts my heart up into tiny pieces. My forehead meets his and I close my eyes as anguish takes hold.

"No. That's why I didn't want to tell you. I was struggling before I saw you, babe. I was. It was just a lot all at once is all. Please." His hand cups the side of my head and he holds me to him. "Please don't feel bad about anything. I mean it. I understood your situation. I just didn't like it and I missed you."

I've never wanted to kiss Greyson Monroe more than I want to kiss him at this moment.

The need is so pervasive, so compelling that I press my lips to his cheek. Then the other, forcing myself to skip over his lips and ignore it when I feel him inch in, trying to catch me. My kisses are an apology.

A selfish need for forgiveness I haven't earned.

But more than that, I want to erase every piece of heartache he owns because fuck, this man has owned plenty. He has all these hooks tethered in his soul, ones he's never been able to free himself from. His father. The accident with Dillon. Suzie. Then he lost me too. But this is more than that. Or perhaps different is the right word. For him, it's never been about the fame or the money. It's always been about the music. His fans.

I understand his fear. I understand his strife. He's not a big one for effusive feelings. Those he strictly unleashes in his songs. Outwardly, he goes to great lengths to either hide them or shove them away. And I think that's why he's so stuck now. He's feeling and he doesn't like it because in his mind, it's all bad, and he doesn't know how to tap into his usual coping mechanism of forced indifference and is now stuck.

"Can I tell you a secret?" My hands brush the strands of his hair back from his forehead and I tilt his head back as I do.

His brown eyes sparkle at me. "Always."

I chew on the corner of my lip. "I didn't love your third Central Square album as much as your second and though I do love your latest album as a solo artist, it's not my favorite of yours."

"No?" he asks, his voice rising an octave his eyes widening.

I shake my head. "Nope. I like the one you released before it the most."

He chuckles. "Seriously?"

"Yes. It felt the most authentic to you somehow. I still listen to that one on repeat. More than any of the others."

"Can I tell you a secret?"

I grin. "Always."

"That's my favorite too."

"Okay then," I say after a moment. "Play something from that album for me."

"Which song?"

"Whatever you want. Like how you used to when were sitting on your roof or even hanging out with Dillon. You always had your guitar in your hands and most of the time you weren't playing anything specific. Do that."

"I can try." He gives me a lopsided grin. "Do you want me to sing?"

Yes! "Not necessarily. Whatever comes naturally to you."

"Huh. I don't know."

"What's your favorite song you've ever written? Play that one for me."

I climb off his lap and perch myself on the edge of the desk because I don't want to go far.

Grey gazes at his guitar, his face downcast toward it. He blows out a breath and then another and closes his eyes and starts strumming away. A smile erupts across my face because somehow, I knew he'd pick this song. It's fast. Fun. Sorta flirty and sexy without being sexual. Any time I had a bad day or needed a pick-me-up, I'd put on this song because it always, *always* made me feel like I was catching a piece of his sunshine and smile.

He starts singing and chills instantly erupt along my skin. Greyson Monroe can fucking sing. And when he does it just for you? There is nothing better in this world. Or sexier.

I get the female groupie cliché.

I always have.

Musicians are sexy as fuck and it's not just because the man is gorgeous and shredded like lettuce. It's not just because he has the most incredible smile or the most beautiful, *sincere* heart.

Though all those certainly don't hurt. Or help in this instance.

He plays through the song and immediately goes into another. It's fluid and simple and he's smiling instead of frowning as he sings. His eyes open and we beam at each other, and I see as some of the clouds looming in the back of his mind start to clear.

My heart swells and if it grows any fuller, it'll burst.

After the song finishes, he has me ordering us room service

and then he takes me up onto the terrace and he plays more for me. And without meaning to, as I do every time I see him play, and purely in a fan-girl way that isn't anything more or real, I fall just the tiniest bit in love with Greyson Monroe.

Stupid. I know.

13

Asmall, soft hand runs along my chest, and I groan at the feel of it. I'd know that touch anywhere even though I've never felt it on my bare skin before.

"Grey," she whispers, but I don't dare open my eyes. I'm leaving tomorrow for what will likely be forever and if this is a dream, I don't want to wake up. I want to keep sleeping, keep dreaming that Fallon is in my bedroom, touching me, whispering my name in my ear. "Grey, I have to ask you something."

I groan again, this time in dismay. "What is it?"

"I'm afraid," she says, and I blink my eyes open, staring across the room at my wall because that was not a question. Then I tilt my head down and find tiny Fallon on her side, in my bed, gazing up at me. It's not the first time she's been here. She's crawled in my window too many times for me to count, but this feels different. Her touching me is different. Her eyes... her eyes are telling me I'm not imagining that either.

"What are you afraid of, Fall Girl?"

"You'll leave and I'll never see you again."

Hell, she has no idea I'm afraid of that too. Tomorrow my brother, my band, and I leave for New York and after that, we start a *fifteen-month world tour. I'm praying this is the beginning. That our album continues to soar, and the follow-up does even better. I need this. I need to get away from my old man. Away from his verbal abuse and blatant hatred of me. Away from the man who has never, not once, given a shit about me or Zax. He only cares about himself. The man has only ever cared about himself. I hate him. I hate him for the father he's never been and the asshole he always is to me. I need this dream to become my reality because it's all I've ever dreamed of.*

With one exception. Her.

The girl I'm not allowed to touch. The girl who isn't allowed to be my friend but is even though her brother tells me he'll kill me if he catches me with her. He's serious too. Painfully, I know this all too well. The guy hates me. He wishes I were the fucked-up one instead of him and most days, I'm right there with him, so I granted him that demand.

I've kept my hands to myself, but now here she is and tomorrow I'm gone.

I don't know what to say to her. I have no promises with that. I don't want to come back. My father... he's horrible. He doesn't hit me, but his words pack more of a punch than his fist ever could.

I just want her, and I can't have her.

My hands slide around her body, and I tug her into me, ignoring how unbelievable her large tits feel against my chest. How sweet her curves that drive me crazy are beneath my hands. She's in a tank top and no bra and fuck. I'm already hard and I have no clue how to hide it this time.

We've slept in the same bed before when she's snuck over and fallen asleep beside me, but always with space between us. She's never been like this with me, so close.

"Will you do something for me?" she asks softly, her finger swirling on my shoulder in dizzying circles.

"Anything," I swear, my hand running through her thick inky hair and then down her back. A mind of its own, I can't stop my

hand from exploring. I've never touched her before and it's so much better than anything my mind has imagined.

And trust me, my mind loves to imagine Fallon.

She pulls back, her amethyst eyes on mine. "Have sex with me."

I choke. "Fall Girl—"

"Please, Grey. Please. I know you don't see me that way. That you only see me as your friend and Dillon's sister, but you're leaving and I... please. I know it won't be more than this. Maybe that's why I'm asking for it. But I want my first time to be with someone I trust. Someone who cares about me. You're the only one I can picture doing this with."

Jesus. Does she not have any clue that what she's offering me is nothing short of all my greatest fantasies? I haven't had sex with any other girl because she's all I see when I close my eyes and my dick grows hard.

"How can I do that and then leave you? How can I do that and then not be with you?" How can I have you once but never again after this? The thought is like death. Like my insides are being pulverized.

"Because it's us. Because even if you stayed, we couldn't be more than this. A secret we'll never be able to share. That's why I need this." She rips her tank top up and over her head, revealing her perfect tits to me for the first time. Hell. No hiding my hard dick now, I'm a goddamn steel pipe.

I can't stop staring. I've seen tits. I've fooled around.

None of those girls have been Fallon.

"I... you're sure. You're absolutely positive you want this? With me? Knowing what happens tomorrow morning?"

"Yes." Those eyes. Her body. The feel of her. The goddamn smell of her.

In a flash my lips attack hers, kissing her for the first time. Tasting her, and hell, I'm drugged. My mouth is all over hers, our tongues swirling, and I have to mentally shout at myself to slow down. It's our first time and I don't want to hurt her, and I want this to last for as long as it possibly can. Until dawn comes and steals us away from each other.

I want it to be a night she remembers always with a smile on her lips.

I roll us until I have her pinned beneath me, my hand on her face, my lips pecking along her jaw, face, and neck. "Keep your eyes on me, Fall Girl. I need to see them the first time I taste you. The first time I feel you around me and all the way through."

"O-Okay."

"Are you nervous?"

A shaky nod and I run my hand up along her jaw. "Me too. This is my first time too. I've got you. I've got us."

I kiss her again, softer, sweeter this time. I hold her and start to play with her breasts, squeezing and lifting their heavy weight in my hands. She moans, arching into me, anxious for us to be closer, and I lower my mouth, sucking one pretty nipple into my mouth. She tastes so good. Her skin is so sweet.

I'm trembling, unable to catch my breath. Especially when I kiss my way down her belly and remove her shorts. She's quivering, her hands ripping at me, and I shush her with my mouth licking and nipping up her inner thighs.

"I've got you," I assure her again and close my mouth over her pussy. Eating her. Tasting her. Worshiping her. Fucking her with my fingers and lips and tongue. I build her up, getting her as wet as I possibly can. So wet she's dripping and sighing and moaning and murmuring my name over and over and over.

And just before she comes, when she's so worked up and needy and soaked for me, I roll a condom on, take her hands in mine, and slowly slide myself inside her. Stars dance across my vision because fuck, she feels so good. So damn tight and hot.

She feels like everything.

Tears spring to her eyes and I kiss them away, rocking as gently as I can, whispering words in her ear about how beautiful and perfect she is, about how she feels so incredible. How I don't want to *let her go. Ever. I'm leaving tomorrow. We're being torn apart, just as it feels like we're coming together.*

It's brutal as it slams into me. I hold her hands and kiss her lips and pump in and out of her. Moving her, adjusting her, shifting positions. We're deep, staring into each other's eyes, and I fall hard. So much harder than I already was. We keep going, clinging to each other, loving each other, just breathing. I touch her and play with her clit until she comes around me. The feel of it pushes me into nirvana along with her.

"Grey."

"Yes, baby. Again."

"Grey."

"Fall."

I'm shaking.

"Grey. Wake up. You're moaning."

My eyes flash open, staring straight up at the LED lights meant to look like the night sky on the ceiling of the hotel, sweat coating my body in a cool, tacky blanket. A hand on my face and it's like I'm dreaming all over again. I roll on my side to find Fallon there, dressed in my concert T-shirt once again and not that tank top.

"Hi."

She grins, running her finger along my eyebrows, smoothing the disoriented furrow between them. "Hi. You okay? Did you have a nightmare?"

The best night of my life was that night and the random nights scattered throughout the years after that. "Not quite."

She's quiet, staring at my chest, swirling her finger over my shoulders just as she did that night, across the ink I now have there. She didn't see me when I got into bed. We did the awkward friends who are sharing a bed dance of she used the bathroom first and then climbed into bed and then I used it after her and had the lights off and she was on her side facing away from me as I climbed in, both of us on opposite sides of the large bed, but now that's not the case.

Not at all.

And just like in my dream, my cock thickens in my boxer briefs because she's touching me, and she looks so fucking pretty right now. Sleep-mussed hair, dark eyes, pink lips, and my shirt on her body. I touched her boobs yesterday in the piazza—it was an accident, because truly, how did I not realize what I was doing—but damn, the feel of them is wired into my brain.

If she's touching me, I'm going to return the favor, and I do, finding her shoulder beneath the sleeve of the shirt. I scrawl swirls of cursive, lyrics to songs I've written that she'll never know are about her. I want to tell her. I'm dying to. I have so many things to say, but at the same time, I can't make the words come out.

I never could with her.

Right now, it's too soon. I know this.

She's far from ready for the wild things going through my head. For all I know, she could go back to Bacchus tomorrow and all this will be for nothing. No public announcement has been made about the cancelation of their wedding, which leads me to believe Bacchus and her parents either believe Fallon will come to her senses and crawl home or they have something planned to make that happen. Either way, I have to protect myself here too.

"Is holding each other and touching crossing the line?"

"I wasn't going to say anything since you didn't."

Her eyes sparkle at me as she gives me a wry grin. "Am I being ridiculous with my rules?"

Yes! Absolutely, one hundred percent, unequivocally yes. My cock agrees with me, jerking in her direction as if to say, remember me, we're awesome together.

"What are you worried about?"

Her hand on my arm stills. "I've been telling myself that walking away from a bad situation is brave, only what if I'm leading myself directly into another?"

"How could you possibly be doing that if you're with me?" I'll keep her safe with my life. "This is all meant to be fun, Fall. Not stressful, but fun. A vacation. And when you get back to Boston, you'll get your old jobs back or something new. You're a freaking amazing pediatrician and I have to believe you'll have no trouble finding a job or an apartment. Until you do, you can stay at my place for however long you want." Forever.

Only Lenox's and Zax's warnings tickle the corners of my mind and I wonder if being with me will cause her more harm than good.

"You're right," she says as if I'm making ultimate sense. "Yes, I guess when you put it that way, you're right. It's me, I'm the problem, it's me."

"What?"

"Nothing. Taylor gets me. Anyway, we have a little less than a week in Europe before your festival. Greyson Monroe, with this newfound freedom, what do you want to do with it? Where will it take us next?"

She's teasing me, but my mind doesn't catch up because my answers are easy. I want to make love to her on a sleeper train across Italy. I want to go to a nude beach and watch her blush as she removes her top. I want to fall asleep under the real stars with her beneath me or above me—I'm not picky about which. I want to feed her gelato—that was my plan for yesterday and it didn't work out—and lick the excess off her lips. I want to fuck her all the ways and all the places I can until she realizes the only place she's meant to be is in my arms.

Like she is now.

"This trip is about you. Not me."

"No, this trip is about both of us."

"Well, hopefully my suitcase comes today, and then, I was

thinking maybe we'd rent a car—not a motorcycle—and drive up the coast a bit. See what trouble we can get into."

"All right. Let's do it."

I laugh at her enthusiasm. "You realize I said trouble, right?"

"Oh yes. Trouble is my new name. Didn't I tell you that on the plane? I'm a runaway fiancée who hopped on a random flight to Europe with a famous rock star. I'm some kind of romance book awesomeness right about now."

"You mean the smutty, dirty ones you like to read?"

My hands are on her back. Under her shirt. I have no idea how that happened, but it did and I'm touching her skin and she has no bra on and it's like I'm sixteen all over again.

"I have no idea what you're talking about." She gives me a coquettish smirk. One of her hands is on my arm and the other is on my chest and I'm dying. To kiss her. To touch her. To watch as I make her come on my fingers. On my tongue. On my cock.

"You know anything those guys in your books do, I can do better." It comes out as a husky rasp because now her hand is trickling down my chest, skating over my abs that tighten reflexively until she's swirling that goddamn finger around my belly button, playing with the thin patch of hair beneath that leads straight down.

"Oh, is that so?" she taunts, and I fully take the bait.

"Yes. A hell of a lot better."

My hands are roaming now too. The one pinned beneath her finds the dip of her waist. The free one on top is on her soft belly, tickling back and forth. Her breath hitches. Mine is nowhere to be found. My cock is ready to explode, angry with me for holding him back from her.

"I remember." Her voice is breathy. A little uncertain because I know her brain is trying to force reason back into her. She doesn't know how we got to this point and frankly, I'm right there with her, but I can't stop now.

It's been so long since I've had her. So long without her.

Her. The one woman I could never get over. The one woman who always fucking held my heart in her hand.

"You know, part of this adventure while discovering who you are again can be exploring your fantasies."

My hand goes south and *fuck me* she's not wearing anything but her underwear beneath my concert shirt. And Fallon loves the hell out of sexy panties. Lacy or satin, all thongs, pretty fucking things that men dream about and drool over. My finger slides along the thin string on her hip, swishing back and forth and her hips cant toward me, though I don't think it was a conscious move.

She nibbles on her lip, debating, deciding, and I know enough not to push too far too fast. I scoot closer to her, though, dragging her in a little tighter to remind her how perfectly she fits against me. Her fiancé is fucking insane and I'm so thankful he is. How could anyone be bored with her? How could anyone think her curves aren't the most lusciously delicious things ever? She's a rose that only opens to the right touch, but when she does, there is nothing more stunning in the world.

"Fall Girl," I whisper because she feels me now. I know she does. She shudders and shakes and emits the tiniest of gasps. Her eyes are wide, her pupils matching them. The hand beneath her squeezes her hip and my other one abandons her panties in favor of her face. I cup her cheek and stare into those wide, beautiful eyes.

"Grey—"

I cut off her words with the swipe of my thumb along her bottom lip. It's too soon for any of this. She might be trying to tell me that. Didn't I say that before? I think I did. I don't know. All the blood that once resided in my brain is in my dick so I'm not sure about anything right now other than her.

My head dives in to close the gap between us just as her

motherfucking phone rings. At three motherfucking in the morning. She freezes. I freeze. But I don't let her go. Even when she tries to pull away.

"Don't answer it."

"I have to."

"Stay with me instead."

"I can't." Her breath hitches. "Please, I can't. Let me take care of this first and then..."

"And then?" I prod when I see the turmoil in her eyes, refusing to release her.

"I can't." She scoots away from me, and I fall onto my back, my forearm over my eyes, breathing hard. I hear her say that asshole's name and my insides wring like a wet towel.

She's different than she was the last time she snuck over to my concert and we spent the night talking. There is so much uncertainty and second-guessing and nerves that weren't there before. It's as if she's trapped in a shell, the exterior walls fragile, but she's terrified of what happens if she fully cracks them open.

I'm going to have to be the one to help her smash them.

I'm going to have to erase everything being with him has done to her.

I just hope she gives me the chance to try.

14

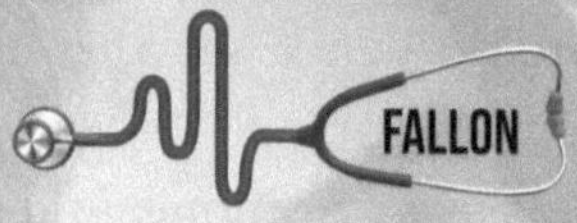

When my eyes open, with the bed empty and cold beside me, I'm stricken with a real, physical deprivation. Part of me is relieved. A larger part of me isn't and it's that part that's plaguing me the most. Two nights with the man and things already got out of control between us. My eyes close and I roll back over onto my side. Europe seemed like the most brilliant of ideas when I was drunk and looking to find myself while picking up the pieces of my bruised heart.

Marriage to Bacchus was set to have been a lifelong business deal and both he and my parents knew how to play me to their best advantage. Pathetically, I both wanted and expected love from my partner—doesn't take a shrink to know it's because that's what's been lacking in my life. Bacchus was sweet and contrite and pleading on the phone with me. He had no clue it was 3:00 a.m. since he has no clue I'm in Italy.

He swore a million times over that what I heard isn't how his heart feels. "It was just cold feet. It was just blowing off steam. It was just lust and fantasy, nothing real because you're real to me." He started feeding me all the lines. Lines like, "I miss you," and "I didn't understand how much I truly do love you until now and I'm so sorry I didn't realize it before." He pulled out all the stops, every word delivered as if he were reading it from a how-to make Fallon forgive you handbook.

Once upon a time, I would have listened to his practiced lies. I maybe would have believed and forgiven them, or at least plunged myself back into the toxic world of denial until I had convinced myself that everything he was saying *was* true. That would have gotten me through until the next event—and there would have been a next event—and then the process would have begun all over again all the while chipping more pieces of myself and my self-esteem away.

Eventually, I'd become an empty shell. A vacant person. Someone who turns to pills or alcohol to numb away any of the lingering pain. I'd turn into my mother.

And for what?

I couldn't think of a solid reason and any lingering angst I had over Bacchus and dealing with my family evaporated.

Bacchus begged me to tell him where I was so he could come to me, and we could talk. I told him it was too late for all that now and we hung up with him telling me it wasn't and that he wasn't accepting this. I don't know what that means, but he's not a man accustomed to losing or not getting what he wants. Regardless, he can't get to me here and he can't touch my life. His power over me is gone.

It feels fucking fantastic, but then there's the other, more present issue, I'm dealing with.

I know Greyson was most likely angry or at the very least disappointed that the phone call interrupted what could have very quickly become something hot and heavy. The ache between my legs was running the show, and he felt and smelled incredible, and he wanted me. I could feel that too, and it was such a turn-on I could hardly think.

When was the last time Bacchus wanted me like that, touched me like that?

But then Bacchus called and by the time I returned to bed, Grey was on his side facing away from me, the blankets up over his shoulders as he pretended to sleep. Bacchus, for once, saved me from making a mistake. I forgot how easy it is to get swept up in Greyson. It's scary how quickly my rules seem to be dissolving one after the other.

I tell myself I'm relieved for the time alone—a girl can really use that when she's blown her life up and is in the process of rebuilding it brick by brick. Grey is nowhere to be found and I don't hear him in the suite, but that's fine. Better even.

I climb out of bed, stretching and yawning as I press the button on the nightstand that lifts the room's darkening shades. The sun is just starting to climb over Rome, bringing with it a new day, and it's a sight and feeling I want to hold on to and remember always. I'm no longer Fallon Lark, perfect blue-blood princess, senator's daughter, or Bacchus Astley's fiancée.

I'm this Fallon Lark and I already like her so much better.

"Grey?" I call out, walking into the living room of the suite, but it's empty and dark and quiet.

Maybe he's at the gym? I bet the time change is messing with him too. It's only six-thirty in the morning—the middle of the night back home in Boston—but we passed out early last night. I mentally shake my head and go for the bathroom, twisting the knob and stepping in. It's dark in here too, the only light coming from the small window that looks out into the bedroom, which is why it takes me a second to register every-thing I'm seeing.

Greyson in the shower.

Naked.

His perfect sinuous profile to me, his wet head bowed, his

hand on the flat of his stomach just beneath his navel as if he's about to touch...

His rock-hard cock.

"Oh my God!" It comes out as a screech and I slam my eyes shut, smashing my head and elbow into the wall as I jump at the same time. "What are you doing?"

"Taking a shower. What are you doing? I locked the door."

"No, you didn't!"

"Yes, I did. It must not have latched all the way."

"You didn't test it?!" I cry, my voice climbing into hysteric decibels with each word.

"Why the hell would I do that? Who tests the bathroom door to make sure it's locked?"

"I don't know. People who are sharing a bathroom and want privacy."

"Well, clearly I didn't and clearly the door didn't lock as I thought it did."

He's not nearly as upset about this as I am. In fact, if I'm not mistaken, there is some serious amusement in his voice.

"No kidding!"

"Why are you shouting?"

I stab a blind finger in the air in what I think is the general direction of the shower. "Because you're naked! In the shower!"

"That's how people usually are when they're in the shower. It's nothing you haven't seen before," he points out flippantly.

"So?! It's been a long time and I wasn't expecting it."

How did I not realize this? It's not steamy in here at all and I didn't register the sound of water because I was lost in my thoughts, but—wait. Why isn't it steamy in here?

A sigh. Not from me, but from him, and I wonder if I voiced my question aloud.

"Because clearly I needed a cold shower after I slept next to you all night, Fall. After we nearly... well, you were there. You know what we nearly did, but then you curled into me this morning with your sweet ass pressed right up against my—"

"Stop!" I shriek. "Don't say the word."

"Which one?" He's laughing at me now, not even bothering to hide it. "Dick? Cock? Penis? Which one do you find the most offensive because that's definitely the one I'll use."

"Oh my God! Shut. Up!"

"You're a doctor. I thought for sure you'd be better able to handle my male anatomy."

"I'm not handling your male anatomy."

"Shame. I happen to know how good you are at it."

I flip him off and he bursts out laughing.

"You're adorable when you're flustered."

"I'm not flustered," I lie.

"Uh-huh. Sure. Anyway, I woke up and my cowboy was ready to fire his six-shooter and since I didn't think you'd appreciate that coating your ass as your wake-up call, I'm in here."

I snort out a laugh. "Cowboy?"

"I have a lot of names for my big guy, but I'm open to suggestions if you're interested in renaming him."

My head flies left and right and once again, I bang it on the wall, unfamiliar with the layout of this bathroom. "Ow. Ugh." I rub my smarting temple. "I'm not renaming any piece of your anatomy. And you wouldn't have woken me up that way. Right?"

Why is that notion hot? Him coming on me as he jerks himself off to me. Heat flares like an unwelcome guest, making my nipples harden beneath his concert shirt I'm wearing. If he looked, he'd see them for sure.

"I'm not sure you want me to answer that."

"I don't." I totally do.

"Then why are your nipples hard?"

Bastard.

Why isn't he taking a hot shower? Because then the glass would be steamy, and he wouldn't be able to see me so well.

"They are not. It's just... you know. Morning." I roll my eyes behind my closed lids because that was pathetic, even to my ears.

"Well then, babe, if you're not going to join me in my frigid shower and help me take care of my Fallon-induced problem, the least you can do is leave instead of standing there looking like that with your pretty nipples saluting me and your panties likely wet. It's not helping."

"I'm leaving. And they're not wet. Or hard."

"But I am, so this is your final warning."

I'm smiling like crazy, and I can't even hide it because my hands are patting along the wall, searching for the open door. How can one man make me feel so beautiful, sexy, and turned on all at once? And why did he always have to be the last man on the planet I could ever be with? It was random, fun sex with no strings.

That's when a thought hits me, and I pause. "Are you taking a cold shower or are you planning on..." I wave a hand in the air. "You know."

"What?"

"You know."

"Nope. You gotta tell me. I'd hate to make an assumption."

I huff, propping my hand on my hip. "Jerk off," I mumble under my breath and once again feel my face flaming at the image it conjures in my head. I have no idea why I'm so worked up over this. Or maybe I do. Greyson Monroe.

"To you or in general?"

"Grey!"

He laughs. It's kind of loud and full of mirth. "I was taking a cold shower for a reason, but if you'd like to stay and watch a show instead, I'm game. I'm thinking that might be more fun for me anyway than this frigid water."

I would. I totally would. Which is why I have to leave now, or I'll end up not just watching him but joining him so we can pick up where we were last night, and that's not something that can happen.

"Have fun with your cowboy."

"I plan to. I'll even give him a good tug for you."

I laugh and most definitely blush. "You do that, gunslinger."

"Hey, Fall Girl?"

"What?" My eyes pop open now that I'm on the edge of the bathroom, my face pointed toward the bedroom.

"You are entirely too much fun to mess with."

I flip him off and shut the door behind me because I don't want him to catch my frown. He wasn't trying to hurt me, but he succeeded all the same. He was simply messing with me. I know he was. Grey and I are opposites in so many ways. For all the ways he's outgoing and adventurous, I'm quiet and reserved. For all the ways he's wild and unafraid, I'm timid and scared.

That's not the woman I want to be anymore. It's just a learned skill or ingrained habit that feels impossible to break. Though I am trying.

But first I need coffee. And a cold shower. I laugh to myself as I change my clothes, doing my best to listen while telling myself I'm not listening at all. I don't hear him. Not a grunt or a groan or a moan or my name. Maybe he *was* just messing with me. Unable to stand it, I kill five minutes upstairs on the balcony watching the sun brighten the Roman sky and then I head back downstairs, wanting to brush my teeth.

"Grey!" I yell through the door.

"Yes, Fall Girl? Change your mind?"

"I need to brush my teeth." And pee, if we're being honest. This is why separate bedrooms would have been better.

"You can come in. I'm just finishing up."

"Grey!" I reprimand.

A hearty chuckle. "The shower, babe. The shower. I was standing under the frigid water going back and forth with you for too long. Gave my poor soldier frostbite. He was too numb for me to feel much. I'll have to play with him later."

"Such a boy," I grumble as I open the door, catching Grey wrapping a fluffy white towel around his waist in my periphery. I try not to look. I truly do, but when a man who looks like Greyson is standing wearing nothing but a towel and water, it's nearly impossible not to.

I start brushing my teeth, averting my gaze from the mirror when I feel him move in beside me. His mouth dips to my ear. "Does it taste like me?"

I choke, spitting white bubbles and foam all over my sink. I turn on the faucet, rinse my mouth out, clean up the mess, and then glare at my friend. He used my toothbrush last night, and apparently again this morning because he obviously has none of his stuff and we were too lazy and exhausted to go back down to the shop last night and get him one after he forgot to purchase one when he bought himself his new outfit yesterday morning.

"If you're going to do this with me, you have to learn to relax."

I flick the drops of cold water on my hand at him and he screams like a little bitch.

"Evil woman, that's cold and I was already cold."

I find his reflection in the mirror, giving him a mocking pout. "Poor baby. Next time don't make a woman choke on toothpaste."

"Would my cock have been better?"

"Oh my God! You're incorrigible." I cup water in my hand and chuck it at him only he dodges it, and the water hits the floor in the corner. "Stop. No more innuendo. Or blatant sexual teasing."

He laughs, coming in to stand beside me, his hip against the counter as he faces me. "It's like shooting fish in a barrel with you. With my six-shooter." A wink.

I turn off the faucet and wipe my hands on a towel before turning on him. "Friends, Mr. Monroe. You promised. I know we've done some fun and naughty things in the past, but that was a long time ago and only one-nighters. We're spending the next eight days together and I just got you back in my life. I don't want to mess that up. You're too important to me."

He sighs with genuine regret. "You're right and I haven't been very good at sticking to that. It's harder than I thought it would be, and no, that wasn't meant to be a pun. Being with you feels like I'm a kid in a candy store with no adults around to stop me from indulging in every delicious confection I crave." He holds his hand up and then brushes some of my hair back from my shoulder. "I'll stop, though. I will. I want to be the good guy for you. The one you can trust and count on. I'm not trying to make you feel uncomfortable or push boundaries you don't want me pushing."

"Thank you. It's not easy resisting you. I mean, look at all this," I quip, waving my hand up and down his body, my gaze following, and in doing so discover I have a front-row view of his incredible chest and abs and inked arms. Before I can process how it got there, my finger glides over some of the swirls and designs on his arm. He takes in a sharp breath, jerking ever so slightly. I blink and quickly glance up at him. "Should I stop? Did I hurt you somehow?"

"No. You can explore since I know you're curious. It was just a ticklish spot," he says, but there's an undercurrent of something in his voice I can't quite make out that makes me wonder if that's not the whole truth. I decide to let it slide. I have plenty of things to explore and return to his arms.

"You got a lot more in the last few years."

A nod. That's it. But he's breathing hard. Standing close. Smelling like soap and Greyson. Naked under the towel. I'm determined to keep this thing between us platonic and fumble for a way to diffuse this latest round of tension I brought on.

"I like them. They're pretty," I tease, my voice barely above a whisper.

"Pretty?" It's a grunt as I tickle over the new flowers, stars, and moon on his inner biceps. "Manly. They're manly." His voice is gravelly, low and rough as it scratches the air between us.

"Right. That was the word I was missing."

I give him a cheeky grin even as my heart thrashes in my chest and then return to his skin, reaching stuff I've seen before. The scroll of what I know is from the first song he wrote as a solo artist. Suzie's name twisted into a bleeding rose growing out of a dagger on the inside of his forearm.

Suzie's death did things to him. It did things to all the guys, I know it did, but I was closest with Greyson and watched how it burrowed a hole in him, caverning out his heart. It changed him in ways he's never told me. After her funeral and I returned to college, whenever we'd talk, he'd put on a brave front. He'd lie and say everything was fine or great when I knew it wasn't. That's Grey for you though.

Covering his bleeding heart with smiles.

He wasn't fine or great though and the reminder that he knows what it feels like to hit a crossroads in life and feel like it's all falling apart is sharp. His band broke up. His best friends and brother were a mess, all going off in different directions as they tried to pick up the broken pieces of their lives. Music was it for him, but he was twenty then and had only been successful as the lead singer of Central Square.

If there is anyone who can walk this with me it's him, and the rush of comfort I feel in that is overwhelming.

His unrelenting gaze is on me as I touch him, but I can't force myself away from his ink. My fingers are light but cold, making goose bumps erupt across his skin.

"What's this?" I whisper when they reach the hint of black wings on the edge of his left shoulder. He captures my wrist in his hand, holding it firmly so my hand is pressed against his warm skin right above his pounding heart.

His gaze is fierce and vulnerable and once again, we're trapped on this roller coaster. That's all it's been between us since he stepped foot on that airplane.

The bell for the suite rings followed by a loud knocking, pulling us out of this moment.

"Probably my suitcase," he murmurs.

Without another word he walks backward toward the door, eyes on me, and then he's gone. I suck in a shaky breath, meeting my reflection in the mirror. My hands are trembling and the tips of my fingers that were touching him are prickling, so I shake them out. I can demand friendship and nothing more, but there is no denying the sexual tension that's there between us. We're a dormant volcano with searing hot lava simmering just beneath the surface.

He knows it. I know it.

There's only so long we can play this game with each other before we erupt. And when we do, we'll leave nothing but destruction in our wake.

15

y bags showed up just in the nick of time. Where Buttass's phone call overnight stopped us from doing something we couldn't undo, my suitcase stopped me from doing the same.

I had been teasing her about jerking off in the shower, but I went in there, deciding between doing just that or taking a cold shower and praying the problem away. Then she was there. All adorable in my shirt and only wearing panties beneath. Then the vixen went and touched my ink, running her fingers across my skin, and the second she got to the dark angel on my shoulder—the one with purple eyes—all my resistance snapped like a twig.

My mouth was a second away from consuming hers.

Considering she threw the word friends in my face not even five minutes before that, I know she's not ready. I was wrong to push her. I was wrong to tease her the way I'd been teasing her. She's going through a lot and she's vulnerable, and I don't want her to ever feel uncomfortable or that she can't rely on me when she needs me the most.

We will only cross that line once, and once we do, there will be no going back.

Only forward.

But not yet. Pacing, I have to remind myself. It's all about pacing with her.

Am I okay with that? No. Fuck no I'm not okay with that. I've never been okay with that, but it's not the first time someone told me I couldn't touch her, and I was forced to play by the rules. Dillon was my best friend for a year and a half, and he promised he'd break every one of my fingers until they were unfixable if I ever touched his sister.

I kept that promise, even after he was no longer my best friend, until one night, the night before I was set to leave Boston for an indeterminate amount of time to tour the world, and the girl I had been secretly obsessed with begged me to take her virginity.

I gave her mine that night as well and she's owned me since.

Still, part of me wonders if this is already a lost cause.

If all those times I let her go and kept my distance and told myself I wasn't good enough or that she'd never take a real chance on me put me irreparably in the friend zone. There is a very real possibility that nine days isn't nearly enough time to sway her heart, and when this is done, she won't love me back.

Until then, I have to be her good guy. That's what she deserves.

This is why the second my suitcase was delivered, and I got dressed, Fallon and I decided it was time to get the hell out of Rome and continue on our adventure. Today is Easter Sunday and I have to imagine that will present challenges, but we'll figure it out as we go. My assistant managed to score us a car and I'd be lying if I said I wasn't looking forward to driving up the coast and seeing where it takes us.

"Fall Girl?"

"Yes, Mr. Monroe?"

She pops her head out of the bedroom, hitting me with a bright, dazzling smile and I realize just how screwed I am. How much power she unassumingly holds over my head and my heart and my life. I've given her up time and time again because it was torture to try to keep someone you knew couldn't be yours, but now…

I don't know what I'll do if this woman doesn't end up as mine.

Pushing that aside, I scroll through a map of Italy on my phone, trying to figure out our next location. "You're still cool with me picking where we go? You want no say in it?" I ask instead of the hundreds of other words plaguing my mind and battling my tongue for freedom.

She saunters over to me, all black hair and purple eyes and voluptuous curves with that smile still spread across her pretty, full lips. Yeah. I'm totally fucked.

Her hands reach for mine, looping our pinkies together as she gazes up at me. "Second thoughts?"

"No. Definitely not. Just not sure why you're all passive smiles and serenity when you were demanding veto power not too long ago."

"You put me on a motorcycle and nearly killed me on the streets of Rome. I think veto power was warranted."

"Fair. But now?"

She gives a half-shrug that's a lot casual and a bit indiffer-ent. "I was told I'm not allowed to question and since we're now sticking to our preset rules, I feel that's only fair."

Damn her and these fucking rules. "I agree, but I'm not sure you'll love my thoughts on where we head to next." I'm honestly not sure where I want us to go next, I'm more looking for her reaction to that concept.

She rolls her eyes at me, but she's still giving me that look. That same look she's had since early this morning in bed when my hands were on her. The one turning me inside out.

She gives my pinkies a squeeze. "I'm excited. I've been all work and no play for, well, forever. I'm free and it's a foreign sensation, but it's captivating and thrilling as hell, so I plan to ride it like a wave and see where it takes me. You good? You don't look so good."

A laugh bursts from my chest. I want to tell her I'm suddenly worried for myself, but I don't. I've known her most of my life, but in so many ways it's as if I'm learning who she is all over again. There's a lot she doesn't know about me either.

I lean down and plant my lips on her forehead and breathe her in and smile against her skin and say, "I'm great. Let's go."

With our suitcases dragging behind us and my guitar on my back, we make our way outside toward a waiting Ferrari Portofino convertible. Have I mentioned I love my assistant? shockingly, it has a back seat for my guitar and a trunk for our suitcases, which is perfect. The only problem? It's flashy. Cool as fuck, but flashy.

And possibly because of that, or not, as with everything else on this trip, things immediately start to go wrong. First, my phone pings with a text.

Lenox. And considering it's sometime in the wee hours of the morning in Maine where he lives, I know this can't be good.

Lenox: Our friend is actively searching for her and knows she used her credit card to purchase a plane ticket. I'm on top of it, but don't let her use her cards or passport again unless you want an uninvited guest to crash your trip.

That's... not so great.

Me: How did you know he did that? I thought we said not to hack them.

Lenox: I didn't hack them. I'm monitoring specific search activity on both you and Fallon and it popped up.

Me: Anything linking me with her here?

Lenox: Not publicly and the search was only on her, so it doesn't seem that he's aware of your role in anything. Yet.

Me: Good. We have to keep it that way. It won't go well if he discovers she's with me.

Lenox: No. It won't. For either of you.

I haven't been playing it all that safe since we got here. What would happen if Fallon's family or Buttass found out she's here with me before things between us get worked out? What if she was photographed with me in Europe when the world thinks she's still engaged to Bacchus? The last thing I ever want to do is bring unnecessary heat down on her.

I slip my phone back into my pocket just as the valet loads our bags into the trunk and Fallon gets into the passenger seat. I hand him some euros and then right as I'm about to get into the driver's side, a blinding flash goes off right in front of my face. Two adolescent girls are all over me, throwing their arms around my neck and screaming my name and saying things in Italian I don't understand.

Pictures. Clicks of phone cameras and selfies and then other people who are watching this, catch on quickly and come racing over, climbing all over me, taking a million pictures and videos.

Crap. Serious crap.

Because this is almost exactly what I was just worried about in live freaking action.

I wasn't careful. I'm usually so careful, but yesterday was quiet and I went about Rome unrecognized.

Today, I have no baseball hat on. No sunglasses. I have no security with me to help contain the situation. And Fallon is sitting exposed in the passenger seat of the car I was just getting in with an open top.

I do my best to move the crowd away from the car. To push everyone along and smile and pretend like I'm not mentally freaking out. I have no idea what pictures these people got and I have no right to ask to see them or demand they delete any that captured her. Nor do I want to call attention to Fallon in any way because then she'll be a target for sure. With any luck, they missed her completely.

The valet runs over along with a manager of the hotel who bolts out the front of the hotel to help. I take selfies. I sign shit. I hug and kiss cheeks until the two men manage to push the crowd along, speaking in rapid Italian.

"Mr. McQueen. Go."

That's the valet and my head whips around to the car. Fallon is about as low as she can get in the seat, wearing my Boston Rebel's hat, her own large sunglasses, and a grimace. For a moment, I contemplate heading back into the hotel until it's safe, but Fallon waves me on, and with the valet and the manager still speaking to the crowd, I take my shot and jump into the Ferrari, slamming the door shut, and peeling out of the circular driveway.

"I'm sorry," I tell her as I zip us along one street after another, having no clue where I'm going, but just needing to get as far from that as possible. "I'm so sorry." The heel of my hand slams into the steering wheel. "Dammit, Fallon. I wanted to be your person. The one who would show up for you and help you. The one who is always on your team as you said and all I've done since I got on that plane is make things harder for you."

"Stop. That's not true at all and none of that back there was your fault. You're Greyson Monroe and it's easy to forget all that entails when it's just us."

"What if they got a picture of you? I mean, hell. Did the freaking Roman gods read my damn thoughts and decide to spring into action? Jesus, think what this could do to you."

"Pull over, Grey."

I shake my head.

"Pull over and let's talk. You're too worked up."

With a growl, I turn onto a side street and then up against the curb, putting the car in park. She twists on her seat so she's angled at me, her hand on my shoulder as she tries to comfort me when it should be the other way around.

"The second I saw those girls run for you, I went for your backpack because I knew that's where your hat was. My hair is tucked up into it and I have my sunglasses on. Even if they got me in the background, you likely can't tell who I am."

"Astley will know."

She gives me a what can you do shrug. "I'm not his fiancée anymore so he can't exactly have much to say about it."

"Fall, you know that's not how this will play out. He hasn't made any sort of announcement about your engagement ending and neither have your parents. He's looking for you too. Lenox told me he knows you bought a plane ticket to Rome. No more using your cards or passport, babe."

Her hand shoots out, stopping me. "Wait, how does Lenox know Bacchus knows this?"

"Lenox has been monitoring search activity on us for this reason. He saw that someone was looking into your stuff. He's not hacking anyone. Just monitoring us."

She plays with her mouth, pinching her bottom lip between her thumb and forefinger as she thinks about that. "Hmmm. Okay. I suppose it's good to know that. Not that it matters so much anymore."

"What do you mean not that it matters so much anymore?"

Her hand falls onto the leather seat. "Grey, I told him I'm done. I told my mom I'm done. Bacchus doesn't have to like it and neither do my parents, but they will have to announce it at some point because come a week from Saturday, I won't be walking down the aisle. If they realize I'm here with you, then that's that. I'm done seeking their approval."

"You're sure about this?"

"I'm a grown-ass woman and I'm tired of living the way everyone expects me to. That's why I'm here." She pans her hands around as the mild sun shines brightly down on us. "That's why we're doing this. So let's do it and stop worrying about everything else. A scandal is only a scandal until the next one comes along. Then it's yesterday's news and who cares. The world has the attention span of a gnat. My father may be a jerk, but he was right about that. Besides, those girls were far more interested in you than anything else. I doubt they even noticed me."

My head falls to her shoulder, my face screwed up and tense.

"I hope you're right."

Her fingers meet my hair, running through the strands and I sigh because it feels so good and she feels so right, and I want her so badly. Still. It's been years that we've been apart, and we only had brief interludes before that. This very easily could have fizzled out once we started spending all this time together, but so far, it hasn't. It's grown. It's solidified.

I fucking love her. It was love at first sight for me and it hasn't stopped.

What I feel for her is rare. It's unique. It's survived years of starvation and still owns every piece of me.

"Honestly, me too because it won't look favorable for either of us and I'd hate to have the press watching out for us or be all over you, saying things that aren't true. But it's done, and we can't change it."

I nod against her and then sit up, pulling out my phone and texting Lenox about everything that just happened.

"Who are you texting?"

I give her a sideways glance. "Lenox." I shoot out the message and put my phone down. "Just to let him know what happened and to notify us if any of those pictures surface anywhere."

Pulling off my hat, she drops it on my head, adjusting it so it's just right.

"I'm sorry about all of this."

She shrugs dismissively. "I don't want to talk about it or dwell on it anymore. I don't think it will be as big of a deal as you're worried about it being, but yes, clearly it means we should be a bit more careful."

I grab the back of her head and drag her face to me, pressing it into my shoulder. "Agreed, and we will be. Let's hope we dodged a bullet."

"Amen and hallelujah. Now let's go see Italy."

"Right." I release her and then blow up the map of the coast north of Pisa on my phone. "Close your eyes." I pull off her sunglasses to find her eyes already shut and the trust she has in me blows my mind every time.

"What am I doing?" She smirks playfully.

I stare at her, thinking about how easily I could kiss her like this. She looks so kissable right now. Eyes closed and pink glossy lips quirked up into a slight smirk. Before I can stop it, my knuckles graze the line of her cheekbones.

"You're so beautiful. Did he tell you that enough?"

She tilts her head, her brows furrowing a bit, and that smirk slithers down. "Not really."

"If nothing else, that right there should tell you how wrong for you he was. Any man worthy of you will have to tell you every day how beautiful you are because they won't be able to stop themselves."

Her breath catches and her lips part on a silent breath. Now she's seriously fucking kissable, but instead of ruining this moment by pressing my luck and likely getting rejected in return, I get my shit together and take her hand, closing her fingers with the exception of her pointer.

"Touch anywhere on my phone screen, but keep your eyes closed."

I guide her hand to my phone, and she does as I ask. My head angles over the top and I laugh.

"That's the middle of the Mediterranean Sea, so unless you want me to rent us a boat, try again."

"Help a girl out then. Guide me a bit."

I shift her wrist until her finger is hovering over land and then release her.

"Monterosso al Mare. Sounds good to me." I kiss the corner of her mouth and then tap the tip of her nose. "You ready?"

Her eyes pop open and she greets me with a dazzling smile. "I'm ready."

I plug in the small coastal town that's about four hours north of here into the GPS on my phone and set it on the car's interface and we set off. With any luck we can disappear and what happened this morning won't turn into the problem I fear it could.

16

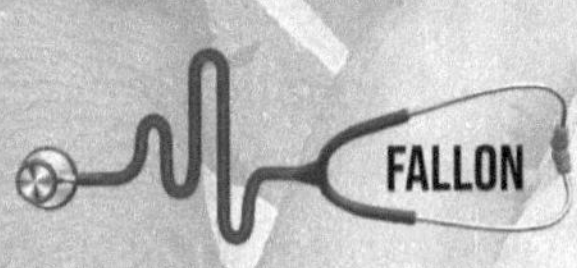

So far, this adventure isn't at all what I was expecting. It's been one event after another—missing suitcases and near-death experiences and close calls with Jesus. Boob play in front of nuns and almost sex and bathroom mishaps—and then this fan-girl thing.

I'm not as worried about that last one like Grey is though.

I don't want any pictures of me to surface for several reasons. The world still thinks I'm engaged, so that's not good right there. But almost worse, I'm not sure what Bacchus and/or my mother will do if they discover I'm here with Greyson. If Bacchus knows I flew to Rome, then I'm even more relieved we're leaving it behind.

No passports. No credit cards.

I'm officially off the grid, traveling through Italy with my rock star best friend. I feel like a rebel for the first time ever and it's the sweetest thing I've ever tasted. I know I'm avoiding reality. I feel its heavy burden on my back and shoulders, even as I try for light and carefree. I'm angry and confused and out of sorts, but I'm doing my best not to let any of that drag me down when it's trying oh so hard to.

All that aside, the drive up the Italian coast was long and splendid. Like a deranged, rabid bat, I was flapping my wings and chirping with glee while wanting to suck all the blood from every ounce of this new life I'm experiencing. Weird or not, that's how all this has felt. I'm free and a bit dangerous and feeling a tad unexpected and I'm loving the hell out of all of it.

We stopped in Pisa and even though we both wanted to go to Florence, we decided we should likely avoid a big city after Rome. Everything also took so much longer than we had anticipated because we stopped constantly to take pictures.

The Italian coast is picturesque to say the least. High, sharp craters of rocky earth dive into the sparkling blue-green ocean, brightly painted houses perched precariously atop. By the time we made it to the village we had decided on, it was late. Dark. And quiet because it was freaking Easter Sunday.

We managed to find a bed and breakfast open that fed us some dinner and then the two of us took to our separate bedrooms and passed out.

Well, I think Grey passed out because he did the majority of the driving. Me? I went to bed with the hope of falling asleep quickly, but my thoughts were on it, and knew what I was trying to do and thwarted my attempt before I could make it.

I spent half the night tossing and turning. Rereading texts from my mother and Bacchus. I've all but stopped responding to them. They bounce between threatening and unkind—my mother—to overly effusive, pleading, and remorseful—Bacchus.

I didn't think Bacchus would care this much.

Especially after all I heard him say about me. He's a handsome, wealthy, successful man. There are plenty of women who would gladly take my place and smile while they ate shit or be indifferent enough to it that they have no issues carving out their own path through it.

I'll be totally honest, there is so much about this that truly sucks. The moment you realize you've been living your life for the wrong people for entirely too long, allowing their toxins to seep into your blood and control your thoughts and actions is gruesome. It's fucking humiliating. I mean, try explaining that to yourself—your own worst critic.

The sad truth though? I don't want to lose my family.

Even if they aren't all that great, they're all I've got. Other than them, it's mostly superficial because I was raised never to let people in or get too close.

I'm afraid I'll hate them by the end of this and then what?

But there's more to this. More I was never aware of until all this began. More that's been sitting on me like a lead blanket. Things my mother said. Things Bacchus said.

I feel like a dock in a hurricane, constantly battered and barraged with water and wind and waves, and I can't stop it. All I can do is try to weather it, but I'm drowning a little too.

I don't want to feel like this. So alone and venomous and torn. I've spent my whole life following one set of rules and within a matter of hours, I've ripped them up and redrafted them. I like this new set. I do. I'm keeping my big girl panties—or in my case thong—pulled up high and my smile bright and my mind open.

But I can't pretend anymore.

I need to know. I need answers.

Climbing out of bed, I grab my phone and stare at my screen for the better part of five minutes. Debating. Thinking. Deciding. With tremulous fingers, I send a crazy text I'm not sure if I should send. Then make a call I'm not sure I should make either and when his voice comes through the phone, groggy yet loaded with surprise, I know this was the right thing to do.

"Hey," I say. "We need to talk."

WE SET OUT EARLY, and I tried to nap a bit on the drive, but the sea is a bright blue today as we climb up into the mountains, reflecting the glorious sun and shining diamond sparkles of light every which way it can. The air is fresh and clean and the rest stops here have wine—wine!—and gourmet food, and that's how we do our brunch since we skipped breakfast. Sitting on a rock overlooking the Mediterranean Sea with wine and coffee and cheese and bread and cured meats that Grey forced me to try, promising me they were cured and therefore won't make me sick.

If someone ever asked me where my happy place is, it's right here. The food. The guy. The wine. The location. The incredible view that goes beyond visual as it seeps into your soul and you change because of it. Never again will I be the Fallon I once was and it's all because of this, and I'm totally and completely chill with that.

Plus, Grey is a complete goofball and I've missed this so much about him.

He doesn't relax with many people. The Central Square crew are a very exclusive club and rarely allow outsiders in. They've been hurt. They've been betrayed. They don't trust all that well. They like their secrets to stay close and I can't blame them for any of it. When you were as famous as they were and still are, trusting outsiders doesn't come easy.

But Grey trusts me.

With that, I get him. This guy.

The one who allows me to blast all his songs, solo and

Central Square ones at top volume. The one who sings along with me and doesn't comment when I sing horribly off-key, which I do. He tells me about some of the songs he has written since their beginning. I know he's struggling with writer's block. I know it's frustrating him, but maybe if he lets go a little and rediscovers his foundation the way we tried in Rome when he played for me, he'll find his way again.

That's what I tell him when he makes a glib comment about it, and he quickly shrugs it off—no shocker there—changing the subject.

"Some of the Central Square songs were handed to us by the studio, especially when we first started out," he tells me as we wind higher up through the Alps, the mild wind tossing my hair about. "They wanted marketable hits and that's what we got. But Zax was smart and negotiated three of our own original songs onto the first album and those were the singles that took off for us. After that, they let me do my thing."

"So what gave you the inspiration for this one?" I ask, angling to face him since he's on the ocean side and I get the benefit of his handsome profile and the water.

It's funny, for as long and as well as I've known him, in some ways, I don't feel like I know him at all.

His head swishes in my direction for a half-beat before turning back to the road since this is the sort of driving that requires two hands and total focus.

"I wrote this song about a girl."

I nod because that's all I can do but in doing so, I swallow dry air that makes me cough. I quickly cover it with a sip of my water and look straight ahead. This is my favorite song of his. It's a ballad and he doesn't do a ton of those. But it's about a girl. A girl who is not me and I shouldn't care at all because it's never been like that between us but that doesn't stop the new, odd twist I feel from that explanation either.

I painted you with a thought and never got it right.
Purple and gray or black and white, all they did was fight.
You came to me once and then once again.
I saw you and knew, time couldn't be our friend.
We were locked in a moment, a moment meant to end.
No matter what I believed, time wouldn't bend.
So we say our goodbyes
and we say them with lies.
Heartbreak is easy
when love has no possibilities.

The song continues and we both listen, no longer singing. I'm filled with questions I won't ask and he's filled with answers he won't share. *Did* he write this for me? We've certainly said our goodbyes and purple and gray...

God, the flutter that takes over my chest makes it hard to breathe. Where the hell did that come from? I mentally catch myself and smack sense back into me. Again. Since that seems to be all I'm doing right now.

This is what I was talking about. The confusion. The muddled brain.

And we haven't fucked or done much more than some petting and neck kisses but nothing since that night in Rome.

Greyson Monroe is quicksand, dragging me under, pulling me in, owning my movements and my body all the while stealing common sense from me.

His presence is summer. Warm, inviting, comforting, glorious. His full attention is no small thing and when he gives it, he gives it in such a way that makes you feel whole and safe and lit from within. You're sparklers on the Fourth of July and he's your match, striking your fuse in the most irresistibly perfect of ways.

His absence is winter. Dark, barren, and cold. Endless. Crushing in its lacking yet no more than what you've come to expect from winter. I've lived through his winters more than once. Most of them were my own creation. I haven't even been single three whole days yet. Which is why I can't allow myself to use him as an emotional crutch or imagine there's more here than there actually is.

We're not love, we're desire. We're not a relationship, we're friends who have fucked.

I'm so lost in my thoughts I don't realize what we're doing or where we're heading until we hit a tunnel, dark and cool and a bit freaky if I'm being honest.

"Where are we going?"

"Monte Carlo. I've never been, and I saw the exit for it and figured, what the fuck."

"Just like that?"

"That's what this trip is, babe. You, me, and what the fuck."

He's right of course, and Monte Carlo is everything you've seen in the movies but so much better. It's a tiny island, no square footage left unused, and we drive along a road that I think the Monaco Grand Prix races along. Grey whips out his phone and hits a button on it and then a guy's voice chirps through the speaker of the car.

"Oh goody, just the man I was hoping to hear from."

Grey snickers. "Morning Jacob. How are things on this lovely Monday?"

"I'm trying to get Lamar to come with me to Paris for the festival this weekend."

A voice in the background says, "And I told him I'm not fucking going."

"Who are Jacob and Lamar?" I whisper near Grey's ear.

"Honey, we can hear you. I have the hearing of a nursing mother. I'm Greyson Monroe's personal assistant and Lamar is my boyfriend who incidentally works as Zaxton Monroe's right-hand man at Monroe Fashion. He's trying to tell me that since he was recently in Paris for fashion week, he doesn't have to go again."

"Which I don't, bitch. Besides, he called you for a reason, so talk to the man. I'll see you for dinner."

"Fine. Love you."

"Love you, too."

There's a kissing noise and then Jacob is back. "Okay. What can I do for you, Grey and Miss Fallon?"

"We're in Monte Carlo—"

"No shit! Oh, fucking fabulous. Say no more. I'm hanging up now and you'll get a text from me with details very soon."

And then he hangs up. I glance over at Grey who only shrugs at me. "That's how he works, but he's the absolute best assistant I've ever had, and I made him sign a blood oath that he'd never leave me. I think Zax did something similar with Lamar."

Within minutes, Grey's phone chimes and then we're heading toward a hotel, pulling the car in front of a beautiful old building that looks like something directly out of the Belle Epoque era with its elegant stonework and beautifully wrought iron balconies. The ocean is steps away and though it's cool today, with the sun shining on us this feels like something straight out of a fantasy or movie.

"Mr. and Mrs. Grant," the valet says, opening the door for me and helping me out. "Your assistant has made arrangements and Sarafian will be here to greet you and take you up to your suite."

"Thank you," Grey says, palming the guy some euros.

I tug on Grey's leather jacket. "What arrangements and why am I Mrs. Grant?"

"I'm not sure," he murmurs back. "But for now, let's go with it and see where it takes us."

I don't have a chance to argue because a posh blonde woman with a sleek chignon is before us, smiling brightly and shaking both our hands. "Please, if you will be so kind as to follow me. I apologize if you had to wait. We were not alerted to your visit with us until just now."

My eyes widen at the fuss, but Grey just places his hand on my lower back, urging me to follow after the woman. She leads us to a private elevator, informing us we're in the penthouse suite named after Princess Grace.

"It is our finest suite, but if you find there is something not to your liking or something else you require, please do not hesitate to call me or your butler, Jacque. Your dining reservation has been made for eight p.m. and your designers should be up within the hour."

"Designers?" Grey questions.

"Yes, sir. Your assistant was very specific that you and Mrs. Grant should purchase a new suit and gown for this evening. Here we are." The elevator doors open, and we're led into an extravagant suite that puts the one in Rome to shame. She shows us around from room to room. Elegant and modern furnishings comprise the two bedrooms—thank God!—dressing rooms, two sitting rooms, a living room, a full kitchen, a study, an exercise room with gym equipment and yoga space, and a lovely terrace with a gorgeous lounge area, outdoor gas fireplace, and one-hundred-and-eighty-degree views of the ocean. "This way, please." She guides us up a set of curved steps to another terrace and I immediately clutch Grey's arm, trying to contain my excitement. "The pool is heated but there is also a Jacuzzi if you prefer. I will leave you two to get settled in. Your luggage will be brought up shortly."

With that she leaves Grey and me standing out here on the pool terrace, stuck in some version of a fairy tale. Or nightmare because suddenly I'm Mr. Grant's wife, only everyone will know he's not Cary Grant the second they see him. He's Greyson Monroe and how long before this sort of thing gets out?

I turn to him, eyebrow quirked. "Mrs. Grant?"

"I know. I'm sorry. I'll take care of it," he promises me, coming in to stand behind me and dropping his chin on my shoulder as we both stare out at the magnificent view of the azure sea. "You have to admit, this is the nicest suite you've ever seen. And there are two bedrooms, so you can't complain that I'm breaking your rules. Besides, I thought you loved Cary Grant."

A deep sigh. "I do. I suppose there are worse dead people to be married to." I shrug out of his leather jacket, tossing it on a nearby chaise.

"For sure, but I think it goes against our trying to keep a low-profile thing, so I'll have your name removed from the room completely. There will be no Mrs. Grant with me, and I'll make sure Jacob knows that for next time. I think he was trying to be cheeky, and I hadn't told him your whole story, just that you were escaping your life for a week, so in fairness to him, he doesn't know we're evading your parents and ex."

"I'm not mad. I was just taken by surprise." I inhale through my nose, breathing in the sweetness of the air. "Your assistant has fabulous taste. A girl could seriously get used to a view like this. Maybe we should just move in here."

He wraps his arms around me, swaying us to whatever beat is going in his head. "We can spend the rest of the week here if you want."

"Tempting. Seriously tempting." We're silent for a moment and then I say, "A gown?"

I can feel his smile against my cheek. "And a suit. Apparently we're going fancy tonight."

"I like it."

"Me too." His hands move to my hips. "But first I think we should test out this pool."

In a flash, he scoops me up and tosses me with all his strength. A scream explodes from my lungs as my body catapults through the air. My limbs flail and then with a hard splash, I go ass-first into the pool, sinking quickly, only to shoot myself up, sputtering out an angry breath as I furiously shove my wet hair from my face.

"Asshole!" I splash water at him. "I can't believe you did that."

"What? You look good wet. Is the pool really heated?"

"Yes." Another splash. "Now help me out!"

"You're no fun."

With an exaggerated roll of his eyes, he sticks his hand out to me and I plant my feet into the side of the pool, latch on to him, and with all my might, give him a hearty yank until his body tumbles into the pool.

He goes in gracefully, far more than I did.

His arms wrap around me, and he tugs me back under the water with him only to push up so we both come up together. He brushes back his wet hair and I do the same with mine.

He dips his head, speaking against my cheek. "I totally knew you were going to do that."

His arms encircle my waist and mine his neck. The pool is not that deep. We're able to stand, but with the air being cooler than the water, we both want to keep our shoulders below the surface. "I figured. Who would be stupid enough to reach their hand out to someone they just tossed in the pool?"

"Certainly not me." He smiles, his brown eyes sparkling. "You really do look insanely hot when I get you wet."

"And you look insanely hot when I dunk you." I climb up his body and use my weight to push him back. He goes under, a look of shock on his face that I take way too much pleasure in. Only he's not going down without a fight and he grabs me behind my legs, stands to his full height, and drops me on his shoulder at the same time.

I squeal as the cool air hits my wet skin. He spins us around in a circle and then intentionally falls backward, forcing me to hold my breath as we dive back into the pool. We attack each other underwater. Tickling and pinching and trying to grab the other. We both break the surface, splashing and screaming, yelling and taunting.

He flies at me, pinning me to the side of the pool. "Do you yield?"

"Is that a joke? I can raise my knee right now and have you crying like a little boy."

His eyes light with amusement and challenge. "Oh, that's how we're going to play this?"

"Definitely."

His body inches in, pressing me deeper into the tile wall. Water clings to his eyelashes and runs down his face making me think about that morning in the bathroom in Rome. My body instantly starts to heat, and he must notice because he licks a trail up my neck. I shudder and gasp, startled by the move and yet unsure of what to do.

"Now do you yield, or would you like me to keep going?"

I open my mouth and no sound comes out. He shifts in closer and I—

"Mr. and Mrs. Grant?" We freeze and spin around to find a woman curiously watching us, unsure what to make of two people fully dressed in the pool. "I'm here with the clothes you requested."

Grey wipes at the smile on his mouth. "Right. We'll be right out." He looks back at me. "Come on, Mrs. Grant. Time to go shopping for a gown."

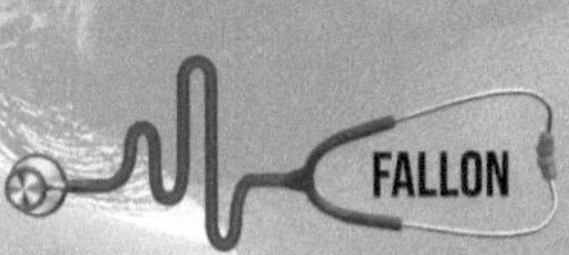

17

Wrapped in plush white bathrobes, Grey and I survey the racks of suits and gowns the woman and her assistant have waiting for us. I won't lie. This feels like something out of *Pretty Woman* or *Cinderella*, only I'm not a prostitute or an indentured servant. I'm a doctor with plenty of my own money I'm no longer able to access without tipping off my ex. Grey has assured me he has plenty of money and then some and is having the best time spoiling me with it.

So here we are.

"Mr. and Mrs. Grant, your assistant specified that these should only be Monroe suits and Lia Sage gowns," the main designer says with her thick French accent.

"Lia Sage?" I question as it sounds vaguely familiar, and I can't fully place why.

Grey is smirking like the devil. "Lia Sage is Aurelia Whitlock," he murmurs to me so only I can hear. "She runs her own design house under her former model name Lia Sage. It's all part of the Monroe umbrella."

"Oh." I giggle lightly. "Your assistant made sure everything was your family's brand?"

He gives me a wry smirk. "Are you surprised?"

"No. Not in the least and these gowns are stunning." My fingers run along the silky fabrics and sparkly beads.

"Excellent. Mr. Grant, if you'd like to follow Sarah, I can help Mrs. Grant—"

"No," he interjects quickly. "I'd like to pick out Mrs. Grant's gown."

My eyebrows hit my hairline.

"Just give me ten minutes," he says, snatching two different suits off the rack and then sauntering away toward his own dressing room slash closet.

I shrug in a what can you do way. "Husbands."

They both give me a look, so I take my phone and find the sitting room. I go to start checking my email, but my eyes are tired and heavy after a nearly sleepless night last night and instead I close them, leaning back on the plush sofa.

I've always been an overachiever—with parents who demand perfection, it tends to lead to that. But with it comes a lot of overthinking and overplanning and not a lot of quiet downtime.

My mind starts to wander, drift, only to rouse at the feel of a hand on my cheek. My eyes blink open and I take in the sight of Greyson Monroe standing tall over me. He's wearing a black tux with a white shirt and bow tie and my mouth instantly dries. This suit was not a custom fit for him, but you'd never know it with how perfectly he fills it out. Tall. Broad shoulders. Trim waist. God, he's so damn sexy.

His still damp hair flops playfully on his forehead, his eyes dark and soft. "Hey, did I wake you?"

"I don't know," I admit.

"You haven't been sleeping well," he notes, swiping at what is likely a purple stain beneath my eyes.

"I have a lot on my mind." I let it end there without explaining further. Sitting up, I give him the full head-to-toe. "I like."

He glances down at his tux and then back at me. "Yeah?"

I nod. "Definitely."

He takes my hand and helps me to stand. "Now it's your turn."

With a yawn, I follow him back to the dressing room. Both women are there, chatting and looking at stuff on their phones. My guess? They're searching for pictures and gossip about Greyson Monroe.

Grey clearly assumes the same because he says, "I'm sorry to ask, but can you please move your phones to the table by the door? We don't allow them in our space." He sells it with his patented charming smile and both women frown but are smart enough to know better than challenge it and do what they're told.

Meanwhile, Grey peruses the rack of gowns. Some short, some long, some loaded with sequins, some with huge, puffy bottoms, and some sleek and sexy. I lean against the far wall, watching him. I know which ones I'd like to try on, but I'm curious which one he'll pick.

He comes up with two different options. A strapless black bustier top with a full skirt and the other is a pale pink and lavender mermaid gown that appears almost sheer as it's layered with what looks like thousands of tiny crystals. It has a plunging neckline and stiff cups to hold my girls in and is easily the most stunning gown I've ever seen with the exception of one problem.

"I'll never fit into that," I tell him, nodding my head in the direction of that dress. "Fat ass and hips, remember." The words were meant to be light. Teasing. But they manage to twist themselves on my tongue and come out sounding bitter and a little scathing.

I've done my best to push off Bacchus's fat ass and hips comment and for the most part, I've succeeded. But hearing the things I heard about myself from a man who was supposed to love me was brutal and clearly, I'm not as okay with it as I thought.

I never gave my body a whole lot of thought before. I had breasts from the moment I hit twelve and my hips and ass grew in similarly. I exercise and I try to eat healthily, but I eat, and I eat without remorse. It's something you learn early on as a medical student because regular meals are rarely guaranteed, and you need fuel and energy to keep going through the perilously grueling hours and demands of work.

Plus, truthfully, as a pediatrician, you learn what a horrifyingly toxic and destructive word fat is by watching adolescent girls, and sometimes boys, mentally and physically torture themselves.

Grey's not having that at all. He's got a look in his eyes, but it's nothing like the one from earlier. This one is something else and I can't quite name it. All I know is that it makes me nervous.

"This is the one I'd like you to try on for me."

He smiles, but it doesn't reach his eyes. His arm bands around my waist and he tugs me toward him. Leaning in, his mouth skirts my cheek, my jaw, my neck to my shoulder, where he places a kiss and then a sharp nip on the dip between my shoulder and neck. Then he releases me, hands me the dress, and walks out of the room. I blow out the breath I hadn't realized I was holding. The tension hovering in the air like a fog is almost too much to bear.

All I know is my failed joke did something to him.

For the first time in my life, I think I just saw Greyson Monroe angry.

I hang up the dress beside the full-length mirror and untie the knot in my bathrobe. I'm naked underneath. I was soaked and these two women were here, so I stripped down and just threw this on. Good thing because this dress would never accommodate a bra or even underwear. I stare at my nude form in the mirror and I'm furious with myself. Why would I allow one man, a man like Bacchus to do that to me?

To allow me to question my self-worth?

Shaking it off, I run my fingers through my water-snarled hair and then slip the delicate dress off the hanger. The next time I see Aurelia, I'm going to tell her how fucking incredibly talented she is. I've never seen a gown like this.

I step into it, sliding the thin satin up my body that hugs me like a second skin. The tiny crystals catch the lighting and reflect off the mirror making the whole thing sparkle. I loop each narrow shoulder on and then reach around to the zipper. The bust slices straight down to the bottom of my sternum, showing a swell of cleavage and hugging each breast tightly.

The zipper goes up slowly, the angle awkward and yes, tight as the fabric stretches across my ass and hips. I sigh, twisting, but then something catches my gaze and I snag on Grey standing by the entrance of the dressing room. He crosses the small space, his fingers instantly latching on to the zipper, and I release it, allowing him to finish this for me.

He slides it up, the nail of his thumb grazing my spine as he does, his hooded eyes unapologetically lustful on mine in the mirror.

Blood pounds through my ears, my insides quivering at his deliberate touch making it impossible to focus or think about anything other than this. My skin zaps with sparks like an electrical current, scrambling my senses. He's changed out of his tux and into dark jeans and a green T-shirt.

Once he has the dress zipped all the way up, I expect him to step back, but instead, his mouth meets the back of my neck and he begins plying it with open-mouthed kisses and sucks and flicks of his tongue. I shudder and gasp, jerking forward into the mirror.

"What are you doing?" My hands plant into the wall on either side of the mirror, not sure what to do.

"Showing you something," he tells me, his voice rough with whatever anger, frustration, and desire is coursing through him. He continues his assault on the lengths of my neck and upper back. The slopes of my shoulders. I haven't stopped him yet and I know I need to, but my eyes, they're closing on their own volition. And my head tilts automatically to the side, allowing him better access.

A whimper escapes and then my teeth clamp down on my lip, declining other sounds their freedom.

"This is the dress you will wear tonight. For me."

His hands come in, gripping my ribs on either side, the tips of his fingers catching the sides of my breasts through the dress and then he slopes down, down, until he reaches the outer curve of my hips. He keeps going until he's gripping the globes of my ass, one in each hand, giving them a hearty squeeze.

"This. Is. Fucking. Delicious."

My voice catches and my eyes snap open. "Grey—"

He thrusts into my backside, so I'm forced to feel every hard inch of him. His mouth comes up to my ear and his eyes pierce mine in the reflection. "Doubt me, Fall Girl. I dare you. Tell me I'm not insanely fucking hard over how hot your body is."

He continues to lick and kiss and suck at my neck while his hands start kneading my ass. I moan, my eyes closing again, my head falling back against his shoulder.

I love this.

I've always loved this. His attention. The way his mouth works my skin. How his hands touch me—knowing exactly how to do it.

This is why it's been impossible to resist him. Why my rules are a must. Yes, my heart, that wicked organ scares me. But it's also more than that.

It's this.

Greyson Monroe has a way of driving me to the point of madness. He makes me crave him with a recklessness that is nothing short of dangerous.

"I didn't mean what I said before."

A hard pinch to my ass. "Except you did. You didn't mean to. I know that. I know that's not who you are. That fucker poisoned your mind. So let me set it straight. His chubby or fat is my fucking delicious. Is my fucking *heaven*." He licks a trail up my neck with the flat of his tongue before blowing cool air over it, making me tremble. "Every inch of you is irresistibly perfect to me. I have *never* been as attracted to anyone as I am to you." He thrusts into me again. "Tell me you don't believe that."

"I do." It's a sigh on the back end of a moan and I can't help but reach around to grasp one of his hands. On a gulp and a mental fuck it—we've already come this far—I take it, sliding it along my belly and then up until he's cupping one full breast.

He groans, thrusting against me again as if he can't stop himself. It makes me squirm, my empty core clenching.

"I am so obsessed with you," he breathes in my ear. "I've been trying to hide it. Trying to give you time. Trying to be your good guy while you come to terms with your situation. But I fucking *want* you, Fallon Lark. I *need* you. I haven't seen the way your eyes sparkle when you come on my mouth or my fingers or my cock in too long."

He nips along the side of my jaw, his hand working my breast, toying with my hard nipple through the thin material of the dress, his other holding firmly on my ass. All the while I watch him in the mirror, a voyeur helplessly and wantonly strung out on the visual and physical stimulation this man is giving me.

I want every wild, wicked inch of him to consume me. I want every perfect stroke of his cock. But...

"Greyson, we shouldn't—"

He bites the soft flesh of my earlobe, cutting off my words. "Do you want me to stop? Is that truly what you want to happen or is this more of the bullshit you're telling yourself you should do?"

"I... I... I don't know." I gulp, my eyes clinging to his in the mirror. "I don't know what I want or what I should do or shouldn't do. This is why I needed rules. Everything is falling apart and coming together all at once and so fast my head is spinning."

"I get that." His hand slides into the long V of my dress, tickling up and down along the skin between my tits. "I do. So how's this? I'm not going to fuck you. You told me that's your rule and I'll stick to it. But I can finger you until you come. I can touch your body and show you all the things I can't get out of my head about you without slipping my cock deep inside you. I won't cross lines I'm not allowed to cross. Not until you beg me to. Not until you can't stand how your pussy feels without my cock in it for another second."

My hands claw at the wall, at the glass, my eyes hold tight, and I... I don't know. I don't know what I want or what I don't want. I just feel and it feels so good and I...

"Your fucking tits, Fall. I can't even with how gorgeous these things are, and I haven't seen them in entirely too long."

"Oh God!" My voice hits the air on a rasp as he slides his hand beneath the fabric, rolling and pinching and kneading and playing with my breast.

"No. Not God. Say it. Say what I need you to say."

"Grey." It slips out and I don't even care right now.

He smirks against my neck. "That's it. Are you good with this? Me touching you and making you come? It's on your terms. All of this is. You're in control, Fall. Not me."

"I like your control," I admit, and that admission is a truth that unlocks a piece of me. A piece I've kept close to my chest and sealed off from all others.

More open-mouth kisses, these ones on my jaw. "I know, but I need to know you're okay with this so there is no confusion. If you want me to stop, I will. You are always safe with me. I will stop and we will once again be Grey and Fall. But if you want this, if you want my fingers in your pussy and my mouth on your neck and my hand on your tits, just moan for me. You don't even have to say yes, just give me that moan or say my name again and it's all yours."

I can let this happen. It doesn't mean I have to give him my heart. He's talking about taking my body, not anything else from me. I can play on those terms. It wouldn't be the first time with him.

I close my eyes. "Greyson."

In the next beat of my heart, he rips the straps of the dress from my shoulders, the material tumbling in silky waves to my waist where it sits. My eyes spring open, my face inches from the glass and I stare mesmerized by the hungry look on him as he takes me in from the waist up.

A shudder rakes my body as he stares at my puckered nipples, his hands coming up, rubbing his palms over the very tips of them. It's agony and bliss. Just that small point of contact without his hands on my breasts, without more pressure. They grow heavy and swollen and needy.

"You want me to make you come?" His dark gaze grabs me in the mirror.

"Yes," I beg without shame. "Please, Grey. Make me come until I see fucking stars. I don't care. Maybe I should, but I don't. That's how badly I want this. It feels so good when you touch me."

"I'll tease it out. Slowly. I'll take my time until you're so wound up, all you can do is pant my name on a heavy breath while I make your pulse race and your pussy wet."

"I'm so wet." I am. I can feel it leaking onto my bare thighs.

A devilish grin. "I'm about to find out just how much and then make you wetter."

Fuck yes.

The shaking in my chest makes me dizzy as I feel the back of my dress slowly slide up my legs. His hand sweeps beneath the skirt and then he's on my thighs, gliding up and up until he reaches my inner thigh and feels the evidence of my arousal. He groans, a rumbling from his chest that vibrates into my back.

"That's my girl," he whispers in my ear as he continues to kiss me. "Eyes on me, baby."

It's impossible to look away when he's staring at me like this. Not when I can watch him play with my breasts and feast on my neck. Not when I can feel his fingers between my soaked flesh as he starts circling my entrance.

He's trembling, same as I am, and I cover his hand on my breast, threading our fingers as we both touch me.

"Fuck that's hot." His mouth continues lower, trickling along my shoulder.

All the while his finger continues to circle me without dipping in, brutal and so pleasurable my toes curl against the carpet. I can already tell standing while he does this will be impossible, but there is no way I'm going to miss a second of his face while he does this to me. His want is etched in every one of his gorgeous features. It's mind-bending, more so than anything he could ever physically do to me.

The heat of his body, the impatient needy thrusts of his hard cock against my ass, as if his need to fuck me is beyond his control, the touch of our hands on my chest, and his fingers exploring me have me panting and whimpering and halfway there already. This is close. This is fierce, unrestrained eye contact. This is sexy and dirty and so intimate I couldn't imagine ever doing this with anyone other than him.

Finally his finger slides inside me and I buck forward, my hand scratching down the glass.

A startling thought hits me. "Grey, where are those women?"

"I got rid of them the second I left you in here to try on this dress. No one gets to hear my wife scream my name, but me."

A breathy laugh. "You want me to call you Mr. Grant?"

"Fuck no."

I smile but it instantly falls as my lips collapse into a heavy moan when his finger starts rubbing my clit. I rock against his hand, and he rocks against my ass, and I'm a half-beat from begging for his cock the way he said I would. My empty core convulses, and I whine.

"What is it, Fall Girl? What do you need? Tell me what this pussy wants."

"More. I need more."

"Cup your breast, Fallon. Show me how you like it while I take care of you."

His hand slips out from beneath mine and then my dress is flung up as his other hand burrows beneath the shimmery fabric. Both of his hands are under the dress now and without warning, he slips two fingers straight into me. I cry out at how exquisite that is. Holy hell, it's just his fingers, but that with his other hand working my clit and his eyes devouring me...

He fucks me like this, slowly at first, but gaining momentum. I continue to play with myself as he continues to play with me. Pumping in and out of me, rubbing circles, working me up higher and higher. My legs shake and I abandon my breast, needing the support as I press my hands into the wall on either side of the mirror. My forehead falls to the glass and it's no longer possible to keep my eyes open.

"You're so close. I can feel it."

"Mmmm."

"Did he ever make you scream?"

My eyes pinch tight. "No."

"Well, you're about to scream for me."

With that he shifts his stance, angling his wrist and crooking his fingers.

"Fuck!" My head flies back as he starts to rub me in earnest, focused on this one magical spot both from the outside and on the inside. It's so much. Almost too much. His mouth is on my shoulder and he's murmuring things to me. Things I can hardly make sense of but still manage to make my clit pulse and my pussy clench.

Warmth spreads through my veins, a tingling heat that builds and builds and builds until it explodes from within me, shooting up and out of me. His name. God's. I scream them both as I clutch onto the wall, spasming and coming so hard flickers of light zap behind my eyes.

He continues to work me, fucking me until I'm boneless tissue, spent muscles, and have a dopey grin on my face. I let out a bemused laugh as I sag fully against the mirror.

When was the last time I came like that?

His fingers slip out from beneath my dress and my eyes slant open in time to watch him lick the evidence of my orgasm clean from them.

"You're dirty."

"Yes, ma'am, I am." We're both smiling stupidly at each other, but then he grabs me and spins me around, not even bothering to adjust my dress as he hauls me against his chest and holds me. "You good?"

"I'm good. You good?" I tilt my head and peek up at him.

"I'm good."

He leans down and I think he's going to kiss me, and then this will all start again. Or continue. Or grow. But instead, his lips land on the tip of my nose and then move up to my forehead, where they press in. He's breathing hard and heavily against me, battling whatever is going on in his head.

"I did something for you," he whispers against me.

"I know. I'm still coming down from it."

He grins, chuckles lightly, and kisses me again. "No, babe. Something else. I set you up with a full spa day. Massage, facial, nails, toes, hair, makeup, the works. Whatever you want, they're going to give it to you."

My heart skips a beat. "Why?"

His hand cups my face. "Because you need a day to be pampered. You deserve it, and I wanted to. That's why. I have some work I want to do, words in my head I need to get out, and then I'll see you for dinner tonight. We'll eat together and then maybe go across the street to the grand casino since we'll be all fancied up."

I blink at him. At the shift. It wouldn't be perceptible to anyone else, but I know him, and I see it. I just can't figure out what it is or what it means.

"All right. I'll leave you to it."

His thumb brushes along my cheek. "And Fall?"

"Yes?"

"Don't let your mind start overthinking this. Okay?"

I fight the urge to frown. "Okay."

He turns and leaves me and even though I'm forcing myself not to overthink, my body reacts anyway, bereft and winded.

Don't overthink this, Fallon. It was what it was and nothing more. You knew that going in. You said you were fine with that.

And I am. It's how we've always been so there's no reason I should suddenly feel different about it. Besides, it's not as if I *want* there to be anything more between us.

My head knows it. Now I just have to force my heart to do the same.

18

I had to get out of there. I was a hairsbreadth from telling her I love her, and I knew she wasn't ready. I could tell her I wanted her. I could tell her I was obsessed. But in love?

Too soon.

The fact that she let me touch her was a miracle in and of itself.

But I couldn't stop myself. I was too charged up. I was either going to make her come, take her over my knee and spank her ass red, or hop on a flight, find that motherfucker of an ex of hers and kill him with my bare hands. I don't get angry often. Actually, it takes a hell of a lot to get me worked up. I'm typically a roll with the punches sort of guy—it's how I survived my childhood with my asshole father. But I could see what Buttass's words did to her, and it made me ballistic.

All women are beautiful, but Fallon is a work of art and her doubting that for even a second... no. Not okay and not cool.

But it's more than that. It's that she's spent all this time, all these years with him and not me. The frustration of this grows instead of dissipating, because still, I can't have her. She's not mine, but worse, she doesn't want to be.

That's what guts me like a fish.

That's what has me questioning everything I'm doing with her here.

What is it about me she's so resistant to? Why did she feel she had to cut me from her life and why does she always walk away? Why is she still so against us that she has to create rules to hold me back?

How can she not know? After all these years, how can she not know the way I burn for her? We fucked, but she never gave me her heart. We talked, but she never gave me her soul.

I'm tired of it.

And time is not on my side. It's ticking away and flowing through my fingers like grains of sand. I have less than a week with her left and I know that once the last day of the festival hits and she returns home, that will be it for me. My shot with her will be gone.

Am I just setting myself up for the heartbreak of a lifetime, or am I propelling myself toward the one thing I've always wanted? I don't know. But I do know a few things... one, I've never been particularly good at following the rules. Two, she was okay with me touching her, and three, I'm not always as nice as I seem.

Fallon went down to the spa shortly after I left her in the dressing room. That's when I practically sprinted from there, grabbed my guitar and phone, and went outside to the main lounge. The moment I saw Fall Girl in that dress, even before I touched her sweet pussy, I had words floating through my head. They were uncoordinated. Choppy. But thank fucking Christ, they were there.

I spend the entire afternoon into the early evening out here playing, writing, and working things out and by the time I go to get ready for dinner I have a solid song I'm feeling very good about. I'm hoping this is my jumping off point away from the land of writer's block and back into the land of writing the fuck out of this album.

But just as I get out of the shower and check my phone, I see a text from Fall.

Fall Girl: Change of plans. Meet me at the casino across the street when you're ready.

I swipe my finger across my bottom lip, smiling.

Me: See you soon.

I leave it at that and slip on my tux. I take a selfie of me in my Monroe digs and send it to the guys and then I head out, taking the private elevator and keeping my head ducked as I exit the hotel. The Grand Casino with its gold façade, green-domed roof, and old-world architecture is surprisingly busy for a Monday night in April. Expensive cars line the front, and people enter wearing gowns and tuxedos similar to mine.

I make my way inside to the main casino floor boasting table games and roulette. The ornate ceiling and sparkle of crystal chandeliers give a warm and elegant vibe I seriously dig but come up empty. No Fallon to be found. It isn't until I make my way to the lounge just off the casino floor, that looks like something straight out of a James Bond film, that I see a vision that makes my breath and my heart come to a screeching halt only to have both instantly restart in double time.

Fallon is sitting with her back partially to me, sipping on what I can guess is a dirty martini. Her shoulder-length black hair is up, twisted and piled messily on the back of her head with a few strands loose, framing her face. She's wearing the gown I picked out, the beads over the sheer lavender fabric sparkling against her alabaster skin making her glow like a firefly in the night sky.

I weave my way through, staying in her blind spot, not wanting to catch her attention just yet. Her face is dusted in shimmers, her long, thick black lashes fan her cheeks as her glossy pink lips take another sip of her drink and then she checks her watch as she sets the glass down.

My girl is waiting on me and I won't disappoint.

I come in behind her, my mouth dipping to her ear. "Monroe. Greyson Monroe."

Her breath hitches and she swivels on her chair as her violet eyes meet mine. "Aplenty. Vagine Aplenty."

I lean in and kiss the corner of her lips, lingering so she knows it's a touch more than friendly. "As delicious as your name." I take the royal blue stool beside her as my gaze roves over every incredibly visible inch of skin, and every curve and swell barely suppressed beneath her dress. "You're stunning, Ms. Aplenty. By far and away the most beautiful woman I've ever seen. May I buy you a drink?"

Her finger rims her nearly finished cocktail. "It's a vodka martini. Shaken, not stirred. And dirty."

Damn this woman is making me hard and this tux won't hide much. "Just how I like it," I order us two and shift my position so that my knees are on either side of her crossed legs. "Why the change in plans?"

"I figured we could get a bite here instead since I was already too dressed up for a regular restaurant. Then a bit of gambling might be fun."

"I like it. Should we order something?" My hand drops to her knee, my finger grazing the inside of it over her gown.

Her hand covers mine on her thigh, stilling my ascent. "We should, but then I'm thinking we need to keep a low profile and some distance. This place is crawling with celebrities and selfie-taking influencers. In the thirty minutes I was sitting here before you arrived, I saw plenty of both. I'm not all that recognizable outside of Boston, but you are."

Dammit. She's right. I get so swept up in being with her that I tend to forget everything else.

I sit back, removing my hand. "Okay. A quick dinner then and then we'll separate."

"Perfect."

An hour later after eating dinner side by side at the bar, we walk toward the main casino floor area. My hand grazes the bare skin of her back and I throw her a wink as I waltz past her, heading toward the Texas Hold'em tables. Fall Girl gives me a returning smirk and then she's headed off to roulette.

She's more relaxed tonight. Less in her head. She's letting me touch her and she's flirting back. She let me make her come today and didn't pull away from me after. She needs to know this is so much more than physical for me.

I just have to find the right time and way to tell her.

"Fold," I tell the dealer, setting my miserable hand down on the felt and sitting back in my seat. The game continues, and I glance up, searching around and instantly finding Fallon over at a new roulette table. She's chatting with another woman as they place their bets. Phones aren't allowed at the table, so I twist in my seat and slip out my phone, making sure I'm angled away from the table completely.

> Me: You having fun?

She feels her phone vibrating in her purse and takes a step back from the table as she searches for it. She smiles when she sees it's from me and looks up, searching around for a moment until she finds me. Her teeth sink into her lip as she returns to her phone.

> Fall Girl: Yes. I'm up. You?

> Me: Same. Bet twelve, twenty-three, and eighteen for me.

> Fall Girl: Why those numbers?

> Me: Twelve and twenty-three are mine and Zax's birthdays and eighteen is Suzie's.

> Fall Girl: You got it.

> Me: I wish you were sitting at the table beside me.

> Fall Girl: Why's that?

> Me: Because if you were, I would sneak my hand beneath your dress and play with the skin of your inner thighs. You'd blush and try to ignore what that was doing to you while you tried to concentrate on the game, but you wouldn't be able to stop how wet it was making you.

A blush instantly stains her cheeks, and her eyes flash up to mine, her expression equally shocked and turned on.

> Me: You have no idea how hard I've been all night knowing you're wearing nothing beneath that sexy as fuck dress. I have half a mind to beg you to bring me another drink just so I can watch you walk toward me in it. Smell your skin as you get close and touch your hand when I take it from you.

I watch her read my text. Watch as her teeth capture her plump pink lip. Watch as she battles whether to reply and what she would say. But then her table erupts in cheers as someone wins, pulling her away. She slides her phone back into her purse, effectively ignoring me, but my message was clear, and it was received.

I put my phone away and return to my table playing a few more rounds as Fall does the same. Just as the betting is heating up on a particular hand, my focus entirely on the table and the other players, the English guy at the far end curses.

"Bloody fuck," he hisses. Absently I ignore him, assuming

he's speaking about his hand until he says, "Look at that stunning creature. If she's not with anyone at this table, she's mine."

I glance up along with everyone else and instantly fall back in my seat, the game forgotten. Fallon is holding a martini in one hand and a glass of champagne in the other, her eyes glued to me as she saunters in my direction.

My mouth dries. My cock turns into a steel pipe. My heart hammers away.

All the men at the table start spouting off, making one comment after another that I only half listen to. I don't even get jealous or feel the need to crack skulls because this woman only has eyes for me. Bringing me a drink because she wants to see just how riled up she can make me.

She comes in and stands beside my chair. "Thought you could use a refill, Mr. Grant," she says in a voice that is pure seduction.

"Thank you, Mrs. Grant." My fingers meet the delicate skin of her wrist, grazing across her fingers until I take the martini from her. I set the glass down but don't let her leave. "You could stay and join us." I cast my hand to the empty chair beside mine.

She gives me a siren's smirk and then leans down, granting me an unholy view of her cleavage through the deep V of her dress, and brings her mouth to my ear. "But isn't it more fun to watch me walk away?" She breathes into my ear and then straightens up and without another glance or word does just that, leaving me and every other man at this table panting.

Fucking vixen. Fucking *mine*.

"I fold." I throw my cards down on the table, grab my money and chase after her. My arm swoops around her waist and I walk us toward the side where the restrooms are. There's a small parlor here, probably once used for men to share a brandy and do business. It's empty, the lights off, and I swish her into it, spinning her around until I have her back pressed against the wall pinned by my body.

Her breath leaves her mouth in a gasp. "What are you doing?"

"I couldn't wait another second."

In a flash I'm on her. My lips melding to hers and instantly opening them, demanding access. My tongue invades, pirates and pillages, dominates and controls, taking what should have always been mine. Her hands twine up into my hair as mine cup her face, tilting her head until I have her exactly how I want her.

I forgot the paradise that is her mouth. The sweet, divine treasure of her kisses. The way her full lips move against mine. The keening little noises she always makes in the back of her throat when my tongue massages hers. The way she tastes, so uniquely Fallon, it makes me ravenous.

"Fall," I whisper against her, sucking her bottom lip into my mouth and then dragging my teeth along the beefy flesh of it. I pull back so I can find her eyes, those violet fucking eyes that are dark and glazed and raw. My forehead falls to hers, her fingertips grazing along my jaw and down my chest.

"What are we doing?" she asks, rephrasing her previous question.

"Everything we should have always done. Everything that should never have been one night or random or here and there. Fuck, Fallon..." *I'm so fucking yours.* "I want you so badly."

My thumb drags down her bottom lip, over her chin, down the front of her throat and through the center of her chest.

"Tell me, Fall Girl. Tell me I can have you. Tell me you're mine and not just for tonight. I fucking need you and that'll never stop."

I force myself to shut up. Terrified I'll say too much and scare her off.

Blood pounds through me propelled by a hunger I'm

battling to keep in check. My feelings for her and the power they wield over me have always terrified me. Feelings in general have never been my favorite commodities and I've done my best to trade them or give them away any chance I got. Mostly they've never been in my favor, and I've always found it easier to push them away than to dwell on them. Even with Fallon, that method of survival got me through her walking away and the absence in between.

This time is different.

I know it is.

She's the only thing I've willingly allowed myself to feel and touching her now, finally kissing her after all these years, I realize just how starved I've been. Starved of her. Starved for her love and affection. I never tried to be with her, always knowing she'd reject me and then I'd lose what little piece of her I had.

Now she's mine and I won't lose her again.

"Take me home, Mr. Grant. Fuck me until I don't know if I'm Mrs. Grant, Fallon Lark, Fall Girl, or even Vagine Aplenty."

I smile against her lips. Her confidence, her newfound freedom, her trust in me are all a heady, euphoric, erotic cocktail I can't get enough of.

"There isn't anything I wouldn't do for you. Anything I wouldn't give you if you asked." My world, my heart, all of it is hers if only she'd ask for it.

I take her hand and run us out of there, back into the night and toward our hotel. I'm about to remind her just how good getting fucked by me feels.

19

My first toxic trait? I have a tendency to be my own worst nightmare. I'm spontaneous. I act without thinking things through. I speak my thoughts without much of a filter. My second toxic trait? I don't typically give a fuck about my first toxic trait, and sometimes, on occasion, that gets me into trouble.

Which is how I got here with Fallon. Ready to devour every perfect inch of her.

And while I acknowledge this could, in so many ways, all lead to trouble, I don't give a fuck.

My hand holds hers as we race out into the cool night. The moon is full and bright and before we reach the road to cross the street, I twirl her into my chest and claim her mouth with mine once more. The way the moonlight glitters off the crystals on her gown makes her look ethereal, like a fairy. Magical.

She hums against my lips, vibrating against me, bouncing on her toes, and playing with the hair at the nape of my neck.

"Missed you," she whispers into me and my chest clenches impossibly tight.

"Missed you more." And God, have I ever. Every single part of her.

I retake her hand, running us across the street, both of us laughing. We reach our private elevator and attack each other as the doors close. I don't understand the sudden change that's happened with her, where all her precious rules have gone, but I'm not about to question it either.

She's here with me. That's all I need.

Pressing her into the elevator wall, my tongue thrashes with hers, my hands groping, claiming, feeling greedy as they slide and grip and squeeze their way across her body. I start to rip at one shoulder strap, my lips following the trail as I slide it down her arm. The curve of the top of her tits peeks out at me and I go in for the kill, licking, nipping, eating at them. I won't reveal her in an elevator. I have no clue what security they have in here.

The second the doors part, I fumble with my key card, my mouth all over her and hers all over me, unable to separate for even a second.

Finally I manage it, scooping her up and twirling her through the entrance only to slam the door shut and then shove us both into the wall right beside the door. Her dress rips from her shoulders, falling once again to her hips, but it's not enough this time. Not nearly enough.

My mouth clasps on one pert nipple while my fingers work behind her, unzipping the remains of her gown. I need her naked. I need to see all of her. I think I must have voiced this because she starts to help me out, our joined fingers running that zipper down until the entire dress falls away.

"Fall—"

My breath dies and I step back, the pool of mystical sparkles now at her feet and standing before me is this woman. This fucking goddess. Naked, in her strappy heels. Violet eyes hazy but locked on mine. I've never been harder in my life. Never knew it was possible to desire one woman this much.

I drop to my knees, my eyes on hers as I inch my way toward her, clasping her hips in my hands and dragging her pelvis toward my face. My nose buries in her pussy, inhaling deeply. She jerks, her hand flying down to my hair, gripping me by the roots as if she's not sure if she wants to pull me away or drag me in closer.

"Greyson!"

"Fallon," I mock her tone, smiling as I kiss her smooth mound, nuzzling against it.

"I-I mean. You. You don't have to." Hard swallow. "Do that."

Fuck. What did that motherfucker do to her? The Fallon I knew went wild any time I did this. I glance up at her, her head is back, and her eyes are scrunched tight. My hand drops to her ankle and slides up, tickling her skin until my finger finds her soaked entrance.

"Look at me, Fallon."

I use her full name deliberately in a tone that is not to be questioned. Her eyes open and her chin drops and reluctantly, she meets my steadfast gaze.

"Do you have any idea how perfect you are to me? How fucking hard the idea of eating this pussy makes me?" My finger swirls around her opening without pushing in. "I've jerked off to memories of eating your pussy more times than I can count. I don't ever have to do anything. I *want* to eat you out. I want to taste you and smell you and I want you to come on my face as you fuck it."

Her eyes turn glassy, and she emits a wounded sound. "He... he never did that. He always said..." A heavy breath. "He made me think... and I..." She shakes her head against the wall, her face screwed up in anguish and disbelief. "God, Grey. What have I been doing all this time? Why did I allow myself to settle for so little when I want so much?"

"Never again," I tell her, swirling my hand on her lower belly. "You are no longer that woman, Fall. Look at you. You are a beguiling force of nature. You have no idea the things you do to me. The things I'm dying to do to you. I need you so much. Please, baby, tell me I can have you. Tell me I can do this with you."

She gulps and then nods. "Yes. Please, yes."

I take a moment to stare in wonder. It's been so long. My hand glides up her belly and captures her breast and I give it a shake and a squeeze. I'm dying to watch them bounce when she rides my cock. I tell her that as I slide one of her knees over my shoulder, her heel scratching at my back.

I'm still in my tux, but I don't care, and Fall doesn't even seem to notice right now. I trace a lazy circle around her opening. She's spread open wide for me and for a girl who has always thrived on inhibitions, she has none now with me.

It's the sexiest thing on the planet and I tell her that too.

"Your pussy is so pretty." My eyes lock on hers as I finally slip the digit that's been ringing her entrance home inside her, pumping in and out. Her lips part on a silent moan, her eyes half-mast and drunk. With her leg wrapped around my neck and her pussy directly in front of my mouth, I use the flat of my tongue to lick her from her ass all the way up to her clit.

She shivers against me as bursts of pleasure flush her skin and force her hips to rock up into my face. Her eyes close and her head slides back against the wall and she lets go. Surrendering completely.

Finally.

I run my teeth along her inner thigh, teasing her skin and watching it mark up since all her blood is resting just beneath.

She starts to squirm, a bit impatient, a lot ticklish, since yes, I remember her spots, and eventually those eyes pop open wide as I've wanted them to.

"There you are," I say, sliding my finger back inside and angling it up.

"Here I am," she replies quietly. Then she slays me with a smile and a small self-deprecating breathy laugh. "All of me."

I smirk. "Don't get shy on me now. It's far too late for that." I stroke her inner thigh and hold her eyes. "You're beautiful and I'll happily stare at every inch of you for as long as you allow me to because for me, it'll never be enough."

I swallow down a noise of pure male satisfaction when she nods her head at me as if to say she won't hide from me. She's nervous though. I can tell that much, and truth be told, so am I. She doesn't know it yet, but this is the moment that changes everything for us and I'm not sure how she's going to take to that.

Her ass fills my palm, firm and yet with a perfect bounce to it, and I use it to drag her into me. She's breathing hard, a flicker of impatience creasing her brow, more than anxious for me to stop talking and playing around. I give her a lick and continue to slowly finger fuck her, working her up, but she needs more, and she needs it now.

Her belly quivers and she inhales as I swirl her clit with my tongue until her heel flexes against my back. I take my time, playing with her soft, silkiness. Licking her, sucking her, sliding my one finger in and out of her. Teasing out every moan and whimper. Building her up higher and higher.

I groan at her clean, feminine taste, at how pretty she looks coming undone at my touch. My tongue replaces my finger, sliding in and swirling around. She bucks in my hand, her legs starting to shake. I thrust my tongue up and use my thumb to play with her needy bundle of nerves, rubbing it without giving her too much pressure yet. I want this to keep going, terrified that when she comes, it all stops. Her sounds echo through the air, soft and subtle and sweet and real.

Everything about Fallon is real and maybe that's my favorite part about her.

I've been with a lot of women over the years. Not as many as you'd think, but enough. A rock star never wants for female companionship, and I've had women put on Oscar-worthy performances for me. Loud screams and wails and flailing and theatrics. Practiced moans and flattering words they think I want to hear.

Not Fallon though, and it only makes me want to coax some of those screams and wails from her more.

I kiss her pussy deeply, tongue fucking it as I increase the pressure of my motions. I'm greedy now. Starving. She tastes so fucking good and smells like my own personal brand of heaven. Like her pussy was designed for me and me alone. It's driving me wild, my cock and hips mindlessly thrusting.

My nose rubs her clit as my tongue plunges inside her. I peek up at her through my lashes and grin against her when I find her watching me, hypnotized. Her eyes are hooded, her pupils blown out, her cheeks stained red, her chest heaving, making her gorgeous tits move with every breath.

"It feels so good," she hums. "The way you lick me like that. Rub my clit like that." A loud moan. "So good. I'm getting so close."

If I was grinning before, I'm fucking smiling like a fool now. My girl.

Listen to how filthy she talks to me. Fallon has always been excellent at following directions. She likes it. She likes me taking her out of her element and stretching her imagination and feeling safe while she does it.

But she's never vocal. Occasionally, she'll pant out my name, but rarely do I get status updates beyond a simple head-shake or a yes.

"Good," I tell her, sliding my fingers back in and increasing their pace. "Because I haven't even started to get my fill of this pussy yet." I give her a wicked grin and then dive back in, pushing two fingers knuckle deep in her, her wetness coating me as I quirk them to rub that spot that will shoot her to the peak of ecstasy. I stroke her from the inside out, sucking her clit into my mouth and flicking the hard bud with the tip of my tongue.

It's a lot all at once and her body reacts accordingly, thrashing against the wall, struggling to remain upright. My hand presses into her belly, holding her up and then I think better of it. Grasping her hips, I remove her leg from my shoulder and bring her down to her knees, moving and adjusting us both until she's straddling my face.

"Ride me, Fall. Fuck my face until you come."

"Oh!" she cries. "Oh, fuck. That. That Grey. Just that."

I keep going, mixing in long licks and flicks of my tongue, my fingers swirling and rubbing and fucking her as deep as they can go. She starts rocking against me, her head completely thrown back, lost in ecstasy. The walls of her pussy convulse, squeezing me and I groan into her, thinking about how that will feel on my cock. Her thighs squeeze my head, her pelvis twisting and writhing, and I have to grab her hip and hold her steady and against me.

She's right there on the edge so I take her entire clit and suck it into my mouth until she detonates against me.

A keening, garbled scream rips from her throat as the first of the waves hits her. Her clit pulses in my mouth, and her body spasms as she comes all over my fingers. On and on her orgasm goes, tearing her apart and leaving her almost stunned when it's over. She laughs incredulously, falling forward and twisting off me until she's on her back, panting, eyes closed.

My hand runs over her face, and she blinks open. "Hey," she says, and I chuckle.

"Hey, babe. You good?"

Her thumb comes up and wipes at the evidence of what I

just did to her from my bottom lip. "I'm more than good. Your mouth is a terrorist. How could I have forgotten that?"

I swoop in and scoop her up in my arms, hugging her body to mine. Her soft breasts squish against my chest and I resist the almost uncontrollable need to thrust my steel pipe of a dick into her.

"Because it's been a seriously long time since I've done that to you. It was like an entirely different lifetime, it was so long ago. I've missed you. So much." Then I clamp my mouth shut, mentally berating myself. Hastily professing my love for her practically ruined my life once. Now is not the time to strike that match again.

Her hand glides down my chest and she frowns in dismay. "You're dressed."

"We should remedy that."

"We absolutely should. Now."

"Here?"

She looks around and then giggles. "Wow, we didn't make it very far, did we?"

"Nope. I couldn't wait."

"So you keep saying. The beds are about a mile from here. How about that couch?"

With her tucked against my chest, I stand, walking us over to the main sitting room and setting her down on the plush sofa. She adjusts herself, staring up at me in the darkness, the only light coming from a lamp on the far side of the room and the moon peering in through the windows. Her dark hair is wild and messy having fallen out of her updo. Her makeup still shimmers, and her cheeks are flushed from her orgasm and arousal.

My knuckles sweep up her cheek. "I've never seen you look more beautiful than you do in this moment."

Her eyelashes flutter and I know part of her doesn't know what to make of this. Of me. I was better at hiding the way I felt for her in the past. I wasn't nearly as effusive. Back then, I knew what our situation was. Now I don't know how to stop.

Her love is all I need. All I'll ever need.

"Strip for me," she commands, calling us back to what this is. Sex. It's only been four nights. I can't expect her to fall in love so quickly. Not so soon after leaving Buttass and working on herself.

"Yes, Mrs. Grant." I shrug out of my tux jacket, tossing it over to the chair. Toeing out of my shoes, I nod to hers. "Yours stay on."

She smirks, crossing her legs and showing off her sparkly heels, completely nude and no longer the least bit reserved. Fucking. Sexiest. Woman. Ever.

I undo my bow tie, letting it hang loosely from my neck, and then go after my buttons, one at a time. She watches with rapt attention, her gaze smoldering and hungry. I get to the last button and then she's there, standing and helping me drag it from my shoulders. It goes in the same direction as my jacket and then her hand is on my arms, swirling over my ink.

I undo my belt, swooshing the leather through the straps, and then my button and zipper are open. Suddenly, I grow impatient, my cock throbbing. In a flash, I spin her around, pushing her over the arm of the couch so her ass is in the air and her swollen pink slit is visible. Her heels give her a better height for me, and I run my hand over each perfect globe, giving one a small smack and loving how it bounces back at me.

She jerks forward, rocking against the arm. I do it again, this time with her other cheek and she squeaks.

"Too hard?"

"No. I want more of it."

I smile so wickedly, the devil himself seeping past my lips. My pants and boxer briefs hit the floor, but not before I fish out a condom from my wallet. I've never gone bare with anyone, not even Fall, not even when I was a teenager and it was our first time. I'm dying to do that with her now, but not before I know she's fully and completely mine. Being inside her like that will own me and I won't risk my heart fully until I know it's the right time.

I take a minute to appreciate the vision before me as I roll the condom on. Pushing her feet together so she'll feel every inch of me, I line my cock up against her slick opening and with my hand on her hip, slide inside of her. Her nails scrape along the couch, and she lets out a wounded hiss through her teeth.

I rub her ass, stilling myself once I'm fully inside her, seeing fucking stars with how goddamn tight she is. "You good?" It's a pant. A wheeze.

"Yes. I forgot how big you are." She sucks in a breath and then pushes back against me. "Give me more of him."

"My soldier?" I tease, and she giggles, clenching around me and ripping a groan from my throat. Sweat is already slicking my brow and if I'm not careful, I'll blow my load like a teenager.

Her head rolls over her shoulder and her eyes meet mine. "Show me how good Greyson Monroe can fuck."

Jesus. My grip on her hip tightens and my eyes scrunch closed for a second as I gather myself. I give her a lazy pump. "You want this cock, Fall Girl?" Another thrust. Deeper. "You want me to fill you up?" Thrust. "Baby, I'm gonna fuck you till you're sore." Thrust. "Till all you feel when you move is how good I gave it to you."

"Yes. God, yes, Grey. Give it to me."

Then I start to pound. Legs spread, feet on either side of hers, I take her hips and unleash myself inside her, making sure I hit her front wall with every driving fuck. I'm squeezing her ass, slapping it in time with my thrusts. My hand pushes into the center of her back and I hold her down, controlling her movements so all she can do is take what I'm giving her.

I struggle to breathe, absorbed and obsessed with the tight, hot sheath of her pussy around me. The slope of her waist and curves of her hips. Her inky hair lost in the fabric of the sofa and the darkness of the room.

I'm burning. She feels so good. Too good.

"Does it feel good?" I demand.

"Yes. So good. Deeper. I want to come on you so badly."

"Christ, Fall Girl. You'll be the death of me." And I'll die a happy man, buried deep inside my girl. Her mouth is an erotic storm and I'm so grateful she's unleashing it on me.

I want to fuck her sweaty and fast. I want to feel her squeeze around me as she screams out my name. That's how this first fuck is going to be. The time to savor fucking her will come, but right now, I'm coiled too tight. I've gone too long without.

"Grind your pussy against the couch, Fall. Rub your clit as I fuck you."

She has me feral, mindless with lust. I can't slow down, and I can't stop. I just keep fucking into her, slapping my hips into her ass, my cock impaling her over and over.

She's not quiet. She's anything but as moans and whimpers and cries and screams penetrate the heavy air. Her body starts squirming and I want to watch. I don't even know how it's possible, but I slide out of her, listening as she protests and then crouch down, staring at her pussy.

Three fingers slide inside of her, and she screams as I start to fuck her with them, jerking myself off through the condom.

"Grey!" She cries and I abandon my cock, loop my hand around her thigh and rub her clit while I continue to finger fuck her.

"Come, Fall. Come like this and then I'm going to fuck you to another orgasm."

Instantly she starts trembling, shaking, convulsing around my fingers and I watch as she comes all over them, wet and hard. And when she's just about finished, I slide my fingers out and my cock back in and holy motherfuck! Her pussy is clamping down on me, aftershocks of her orgasm, and then I'm ramping her back up, demanding more.

She's thrashing, sensitive, overstimulated, and loving every second of what I'm doing to her. I fuck her until she ignites once again, both of us tumbling over that edge in a frenzy of heat, combusting into flames. I smack her ass and then grip it bruisingly, bellowing out a harsh expletive followed by her name as I come and come and come. Waves and spurts shoot from me, my cock impossibly hard, and I jerk in her until there is nothing left of me.

I collapse forward, my mouth on her upper spine and for a second, all I can do is breathe. Subconsciously, I know I have to move. I know I might be hurting her in this position. With all my might, I curl my arm around her waist, my hand on my cock, holding the condom, and I pull out of her. She whimpers and then relaxes.

"Here, baby." I move her to the couch and then remove and tie off the condom, wadding it up in tissues I grab from the end table. I take her in my arms, adjusting us both so that she's on top of me and I'm beneath her, her head resting over my pounding heart.

For a moment I think she's passed out. She's silent, breathing heavily, but then her fingers start to draw a pattern over my heart, and I smile. My fingers run through her snarled hair, and I kiss her forehead.

I love you. "You were incredible," is what I go with instead.

"Mmmm."

Another kiss to her forehead. "You had a lot more to say before."

"That was prior to you scrambling my brain and destroying my body."

"I plan to do that again. Maybe in the shower."

"Shower."

I chuckle, wrapping her up tighter into my chest, feeling so full and content I could die. I never thought I'd get this again and it makes me angry that I allowed myself to go without her for so long. I should have done more. I should have fought for her. I should have told her all those years ago all that she meant to me, and I should have challenged her family over it.

Dillon.

I should have challenged Dillon, but I was young and wracked with guilt and never felt worthy of the princess in my arms.

After all, my loving Fallon is what ruined everything to begin with.

20

GREYSON

The inky water of the Charles River shimmered against the black sky, reflecting the ghostly white of the nearly full moon. Sweat clung to my brow. Alcohol and weed along with the heat and humidity of the day held onto me with fierce determination. I didn't care. Today was the first day of summer break and my father was mercifully out of town. The fucker didn't say anything before he walked out the door for New York. He didn't even spare me a backward glance, which is frankly an improvement compared to our blowout two nights ago over my report card.

Three As and four Bs and one fucking C and the guy lost his shit. Or more aptly, he was looking for an excuse to.

Whatever. Fall Girl crawled through my window and read to me for an hour before we both passed out, pinkies intertwined as our only point of connection. She didn't say anything. Not a word about the shouting she no-doubt overheard from next door. She was there, my angel, and that was all I needed. I didn't even care about the fact that she was reading boring-ass historical romance to me.

The moment she fell asleep, and I was positive she wouldn't hear me, I told her. I told her I loved her and everything inside me felt better for it.

Lighter. Freer.

I had never told anyone that I loved them, and it hadn't occurred to me that's what that feeling was until Suzie started teasing me about it a few months back. It dawned on me that she was right even if the words "in love" felt ridiculous at the time. What the hell did I know about being in love? I was fifteen.

But since that day, I hadn't been able to stop the words from reverberating through my skull like a metronome. So I finally worked up the balls and told her, even if she was asleep.

Because yet now, today, back in reality, she's still not mine.

I can keep her a secret if that's what she needs. Her parents can't find out, I know this, and I'm okay with that. But not having her... it's the fucking worst. It's torture, especially when she falls asleep beside me. Most nights that happens, I have to get up and jerk off twice just to lie beside her and get some sleep.

"What are you doing?" Dillon called out to me, and my head snapped up, away from the water and my thoughts.

"What do you mean?"

He laughed, kinda loud with a drunk slur around the edges of it. "You were humming again, man. You always do that, the same song, when you're deep in thought, yet I never know what the song is about."

I held his gaze, my balance unsteady. I had no idea I did that, let alone that whenever I thought about Fall Girl.

My heart started to pound in my chest. What if I told him that I loved Fallon? Fucker has already threatened my life, told me I couldn't touch her, or he'd kick my ass. But he doesn't know how I feel. It's more in the way guys protect their sisters from their asshole friends, but I'm not an asshole despite what my father says about me, and I'd never be one to her.

What if Dillon was cool with it the way Lenox is cool with Zax dating Suzie? Lenox and Zax are best friends and Suzie is Lenox's twin sister, the same way Fall is twins with Dillon who is my best friend.

"You really want to know what I'm humming about?" I threw out at him, watching his expression as I did. Dillon was a bit of a sloppy drunk when he got wasted and tonight we'd both hit up the bottle of scotch we stole from his dad's liquor cabinet hard. We also scored a joint off a friend and the combination of both was making me bold and reckless. But hopefully it was making him chill and amiable.

"Yeah, dude. Tell me. It's about a chick, right? Are you banging her?"

I laughed awkwardly. "No. I'm not banging her." But I sure as hell want to. "She's different."

He snorted. "Right. Different." The word slithered past his lips at the ridiculousness of such a possibility. The only girl I've seen him not be a total douche to is his sister. Girls read that shit on guys and tend to stay away from him, even if his last name is Lark and his trust fund is bigger than mine.

"She is," I told him in earnest, so he knew. "I..." Gulp. "I love her."

He paused, studying me, staring straight at me while he attempted to read every feature on my face and the exaggerated deep breaths I was taking. My hands trembled terribly.

"Wait," he said, his tone growing as harsh as his expression. "Who the fuck are we talking about here?"

I shook my head and shifted my weight, suddenly losing my nerve. "No one. It's cool. Forget I said anything."

"No," he yelled, not even giving a shit that we weren't supposed to be out here at night or doing the things that we were doing. "Tell me. Who the fuck are you talking about?"

"Calm down." I held my hands out to him, but he saw it all over me and hurled the mostly empty bottle at me. Missing terribly, it splashed in the water with a hard thunk.

"Fuck you!" he screamed. "Fallon?! Is that who you're talking about?"

I took a step back, my hands still out in front of me, shocked by his vehemence. "What? No. I mean, nothing is happening."

He pointed an accusing finger at me, a step in my direction for each one I took in retreat. "But you want it to, right? You want to fuck my sister?"

At my silence, he roared.

"Jesus, Grey. Fuck you. You're supposed to be my friend. You're my best friend."

"I am your best friend," I snapped back defensively, growing closer to the edge of the river. "I love her. Why is that so bad?" My arms flared out wide. "I'll treat her better than anyone."

He laughed caustically. "Bullshit. You'd only taint her. Ruin her. She's meant for better than you. Hell, she's too fucking good for you. You're nothing but a piece of shit, trashy-ass Monroe."

His words sliced straight through me, hitting their intended mark. He knows the things my father says to me. How I'm nothing but a piece of shit.

"You're an asshole!"

"It's true. Your family isn't like mine. Our lives are all mapped out for us. Everything. It's how we work. You know that."

I do. I mean, I guess. Fall told me the first night I met her on my rooftop that she'd be the girl I'd always regret not knowing. She's not allowed to date any of the guys in school. Her parents are wicked strict with that, and she told me it's because she has to be with a certain kind of guy that her parents approve of. But I never took it that seriously, because that's just like the crazy stuff parents like to say. Isn't it?

I shook my head, lost, dazed, and angry. Fucking furious, actually. "Fuck you," I spat at him. "You're no better than I am. Your father is a belligerent drunk and your mom is colder than ice. You don't think we hear your parents fighting? They can't stand each other. Good luck with that shit. Fallon sneaks into my room and falls asleep in my bed practically every night to escape you fuckers."

That was it.

That stupid last line.

That sent him over the edge and in the next second he launched himself at me with a savage roar. I turned to run, but he caught me with his forearm around my throat. Dillon was shorter than I was by a half a foot at least and he dangled, choking me, cutting off my air completely, snarling a million insults right into my ear.

I panicked. I couldn't stop the reaction.

I was high and drunk and angry and scared, and I reacted. Dillon was smaller than me and I used my extra weight and height to my advantage. In a flash, I grasped his forearms and flipped him. His body catapulted toward the water, and I watched in horror as he landed on the shore of the river.

But he didn't just land anywhere. He landed squarely on a rock. A boulder. A no-bullshit piece of earth that instantly broke one of his lumbar vertebrae when he landed on it. He cried out in agony, and I knew that I had just ruined both of our lives.

I bolt upright, covered in sweat with my heart literally attempting to beat itself out of my chest. It's thwacking against my ribs, making it hard for me to catch my breath. All around me it's dark, and quiet, Fall fast asleep beside me as she's been hundreds of times before.

For a moment, I watch her as I get my breathing back under control. She never knew what Dillon and I fought about that night. He made me promise not to tell her and I didn't have any problem at the time keeping that promise. I never understood his reasoning for keeping that secret and he never explained it. He just told me to keep my fucking mouth shut and I did because my guilt was wrapped around me like a lead blanket.

My father didn't even care why or how it happened and whatever passed between Dillon and his parents was between them.

Dillon, despite his flagrant hatred of me after that, never breathed a word about what went down between us.

Not to the cops. Not to our parents. Not to anyone.

I was never charged with anything. His parents never sued. It was ruled an accident, but he and I and likely everyone else knew the truth. I wasn't shy about blaming myself, and I wore the guilt around me like a cloak, visible for all to see.

Sitting up a little straighter, I twist, taking in the sleeping form of the woman—no longer a girl—beside me.

Fall fell asleep tonight contentedly wrapped up in my arms. We fucked again in the shower and then we both climbed into bed, and I took her one more time. Laughing and talking after until we both passed out, utterly spent.

I blow out a breath, scrubbing my hands up and down my face.

There have been three moments in my life that have irrevocably changed me and not for the better. I'd love to say I've walked through the fires of hell and came out stronger on the other side, but I don't think that's true.

More resistant maybe.

More detached definitely.

The first I don't remember. I was a toddler when my mother died, but I was in the back seat of the car and as per police reports, I had likely done something to distract her. They think that's why our car veered into oncoming traffic and why her body was twisted the way it was.

My mother's death is why my father hates me.

A fact he's never been shy about letting me know. His hatred of me is the thing I care about the least. Wherever he is now, he can rot in hell. The best thing that ever happened to me was hitting it big with Central Square and leaving him behind. Plus, I had Zax who always made it clear my father was the problem and not me.

The second event was the accident with Dillon and the third was Suzie's death.

After losing Suzie I did everything I could not to feel anymore. Not anger or frustration or sadness or loss or fear or anxiety. It was too much. All of it. Her death was my breaking point. The guys—Zax and Lenox especially—self-destructed. I was watching my band—my life—fall apart and didn't know what my future would look like. It was a culmination of everything. Growing up with my father and then the accident with Dillon... I'd had enough.

I think that's why I never really went after Fallon until that last time when she left me that note saying goodbye for good. I let her walk away time and time again, nursed my miserable wounds and then, like I always do, picked myself up and kept on going, burying any emotion I didn't want to deal with.

I never felt worthy of anything good or special. I knew I'd get hurt if I made a real play and frankly, I'd run through all the hurt I could take. Plus, I always felt like I owed it to Dillon on some level to keep my relationship with Fallon what it was.

But seeing her in the café and feeling despondent over knowing she was gone from me for good, going through this incredible career high of releasing my best, most successful album to date, and then crashing into an insurmountable creative drought was eating me alive, morsel by morsel from the inside out.

It was as if her phone call snapped me out of the fog I'd been living in these past six months.

I had to act. I had no choice.

My mind was made up without thinking through the repercussions.

Nothing ventured, nothing gained, and for the first time since losing Suzie, I was willing to risk it all for this second chance at getting it right.

Climbing out of bed I snatch my phone off the nightstand, ripping it from the charging cable, and head into the bathroom. I've had a million nightmares over the years. I either relive the night I put my friend in a wheelchair or I relive the day Suzie died. I'll never forget the call from Zax. His frantic voice. The way he was begging and pleading with me to come and help do

CPR on Suzie because he couldn't get her heart going again on his own and the ambulance wasn't there yet.

I shudder as I close the lid on the toilet and sit down, elbows on my thighs, body bent forward, face staring at my screen. It's late in DC where Dillon lives, the middle of the night here, but that doesn't matter. I've sent this text hundreds of times over the years. I send it with every nightmare I have about him.

> Me: I'm sorry.

Dillon never replies, but he's never blocked my number either, so I keep sending them. I don't actually want his reply and the apology does little to assuage my unrelenting guilt, but that doesn't stop me from sending it either. Part of me wonders if I should tell Fall about what we were arguing about that night.

But tonight...

> Me: I still love her. That hasn't changed nor will it.

My phone rings in my hand, startling me so badly I nearly drop it. I stare at his name as it lights up my screen. Shocked beyond words, I slide my finger against my screen and bring it up to my ear, not even able to say his name.

"Are you with her?" is all he says.

I clear my throat, scrubbing my hand across my forehead. "Do you mean in the geographical or biblical sense?"

He hisses. "Just tell me."

"I'm pleading the fifth for her sake."

"Who else knows you're with her?"

I squint, thrown off by that question. "Why?"

"What are you doing, Greyson? Astley and my parents

know she's in Italy. What they don't know is that you're with her. Don't be stupid. Send her home."

Actually she's not in Italy anymore, but I don't mention that tidbit. She's not using her credit cards or ID anywhere. She wasn't happy about it, but everything tonight I paid for including her gambling money. But the truth is, if I'm seen in France, that's fine because I'm playing Sunday at the festival in Paris. Only now Dillon knows she's with me so that cover is blown a bit too.

I likely shouldn't have answered. Or sent the second text.

"Why on earth would I send her home? He's a piece of shit, Dill. Do you know the things he said about her? Motherfucker referred to her as a dog with the right pedigree, admitted he was all but marrying her to get himself in the White House, and called her fat. Oh, and he was talking about how he's going to fuck another woman the first chance he gets. How can you want that for her, man? She's your sister. Your twin."

"Don't presume you know anything about my relationship with my sister. She needs to come home and deal with this."

I laugh caustically. "You nearly strangled me to death when I told you I was in love with her and yet you want her to return home to that guy? What is it about me that's so awful that you'd rather have her with him and not me? Why is it so important she ends up with him and not me?"

"Greyson, believe it or not, this isn't about you. She's a Lark."

I snort derisively at that. "Wow, Dill. That's the most impressive shit I've ever heard. You know, you're right. She's a Lark. My bad, man. Mind blown. That answer just changed everything. I'll send her home right now."

"You will if you know what's good for you."

"Are you trying to threaten me? You won't. You're not the only ones with power and something you refuse to lose. I have more money than the church and am smarter than you ever gave me credit for. Not to mention, I know people like me a hell of a lot more than they like your father or you for that matter. This isn't about any of that nonsense. Tell me what's actually going on?"

A silent beat. "That is what's going on."

Only I can't help but feel as though I'm missing something. Something vital. Something about all this isn't fully adding up for me.

I release an exacerbated breath, sitting up a little straighter and twisting my back until some of the stress in it cracks away with my spine. "She doesn't want to marry him. And when all this went down with him, she called me and not you. Think about that. What the fuck kind of brother have you been to her that she calls me instead of you? All this time I thought you were being protective of her. That night, I always thought that's what that was. Some misguided brother bullshit, but it wasn't. It was about your family and its name, but what good has that done for either of you? You want her to have that kind of life? That sort of misery? For what? Seriously, tell me because I can't figure it out."

"Again, this isn't about you. This is business, Greyson. Politics."

"You sound tired, Dill. Maybe you should take a vacation. Get away. Clear your head. Think of someone else besides yourself while you do that."

"Fuck you."

"No, brother. Fuck you. Because for years, I've felt nothing but guilt over what happened that night. Years I maybe could have tried to be with her and I didn't. Because of you. Because I felt less than. Because of the control your family had over her. So listen and listen good. I love her. I will take care of her. I will make her happy because I will make it my life's mission to. What I will not do is bring her home to marry some asshole she doesn't love or want to marry simply because it's business and politics. None of you have her best interest at heart, but I do. Your perfect princess is finally mine and I'll fight like hell to keep her that way."

I hit end on my phone and stand up, a weight that had been moored in my chest finally gone. It's time I forgive myself. It's time I put that guilt aside. I can't change the past. I can only work on my future. And my future is waiting for me in bed.

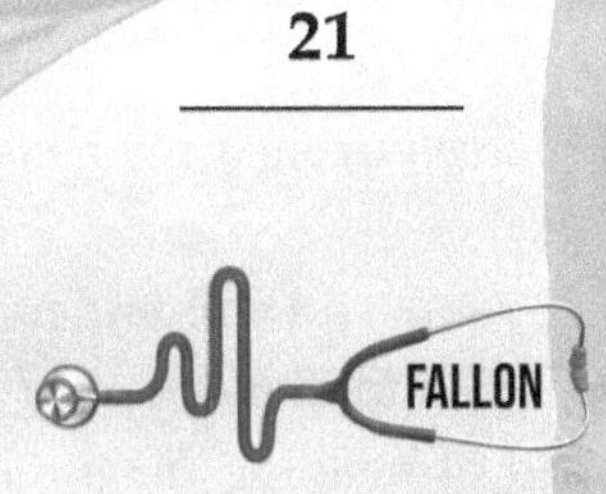

I wake early and with Grey still passed out in bed, I am once again relieved for the time alone. Even as I roll over and stare at his sleeping form, a smile curls over my lips as I mentally replay our night. No! I cannot think about the things he said to me or the way he undressed me or how marvelous his hands and tongue and—

Ah! Stop, Fallon!

I roll back over onto my back, breathing out a silent breath and covering my face with my hands.

Look what you let happen.

Yet I don't regret it. Not a second of it. Hell, I all but initiated last night. Nothing should feel different from any of that.

But it does.

Everything with him practically has from the moment he got on the plane. I can't even put my finger on the pulse point of it, but something is different, and I have a sneaking suspicion the thing that is different is me.

All the things he said to me. Sigh. Swoon! *Don't overthink them, Fallon!*

Dammit, Grey! We weren't supposed to do that because

now I seriously want to do it again. And again! Stupid guy and his stupidly awesome mouth and penis. Does he have to be so sexy and perfect and good at everything? I could handle the looks and maybe I could handle the sweet things, but paring both with a man who knows how to fuck and likes pleasuring me is simply cruel.

Ahhh! SHUT UP! I need to clear my head. Get out for a few minutes.

I channel my inner ninja and slip undetected from the bed, don my workout clothes, and sneak out of the room without him waking up. Instead of heading for the beach, I take a left out of the hotel and head up the streets that snake up into the hills of Monaco. It will test and punish my every muscle and hopefully either quiet my mind or help me make sense of it.

But naturally, because this is the kind of week I'm having, when I step out into the cool early morning, the sun captured in a thin layer of fog that will hopefully burn off by midday and set up my phone to my earbuds, I find a text from Dillon.

Dillon: Call me when you get this.

That's it and it looks like he sent it around three in the morning my time. I don't bother responding right now and I'm not in the mood for a chat. It'll have to wait.

None of my family has asked how I'm doing. Why I ran away to freaking Europe. They don't care about the how or the why, only that I come home and marry Bacchus. How am I related to these people? Argh! I shake my head and then start blasting music in my ears. *Not* Greyson Monroe or Central Square music either.

I set off on the sidewalk and instantly remember why I hate running. And while I do try to exercise with some regularity, I don't run marathons and I don't run up freaking mountains. So simply put, this sucks. But I keep going, determination propelling me through every pant, wheeze, and painful step to get myself back on track.

It doesn't take long. Thank God!

One thing I've come to learn and appreciate about myself through all this is that I'm a lot stronger than I've given myself credit for in the past. I walked away from a jerk of a fiancé. I abandoned a family that doesn't care about me. I said fuck you to a toxic life pattern that had to go. I'm a good doctor—no, an excellent doctor. I'm smart and successful and capable. I have a best friend who is here with me, doing all he can to help me move on from the past.

Simple as that.

I'm covered in sweat, my leg muscles are crying, and my glutes feels like they're on fire. I'm tempted to go down to the beach and walk along the waves, but instead I head back into the hotel, up to our second-floor balcony where the pool and Jacuzzi are and when I get there, I find Grey chilling on a lounger with his guitar, wearing a well-fitted black T-shirt that clings to every sinuous brick of muscle, slow-slung dark jeans, and a smile. His dark hair is in wild disarray, like he didn't bother taming it when he woke up.

Sex hair.

The man has sex hair and is smiling at me with eyes that promise a thousand dirty delights and I want to kick him for all of it. Or fuck him. And all my *it's just sex and I can deal with the aftermath when I get home* bravado evaporates in a puff of air. My days of deluding myself are over. If I continue this, it won't end well.

"Mornin'," he drawls, sipping his coffee. "Have a good run?"

I flip him off and he laughs. "Be nice or I won't share my coffee with you."

I grumble something unintelligible but snatch the coffee from his hands anyway and take a sip. It has cream and sugar in it, which is how I like it and not how he likes it. Ugh. Perfect, perfect bastard.

"Do you always have to be this perfect?" I lament at him.

He bops me on the nose with the tip of his finger. "Right back atcha. I was thinking today we could go skydiving and then get you a tattoo."

I choke on the coffee, sputtering and spitting a little and definitely drooling most of it. "Awesome. Thanks for that." I wipe my chin with the back of my hand.

He removes his guitar from around his neck and takes me in his arms, wrapping them around my waist and pulling my back to his chest. He props his chin on my shoulder and it's annoying how right and easy this feels with him.

"So that's a no then? Because the rule was that you have to do what I say."

"The rules were also separate bedrooms and no sex."

"But my rule was better than your rules from the start," he counters.

I grumble.

"You okay with last night?"

Am I okay with last night? Being held by him like this is tripping up my head worse.

I try for casual, turning in his arms and killing him with a smile I'm positive he can see through. "Nothing we haven't done before, right?"

Hurt flashes across his features, there and gone in a nanosecond. He's silent for a beat and then clears his throat. "True. I guess."

"Argh!" I run my hands over my face, my forehead falling to his chest. "I'm sorry. I'm saying and doing everything wrong. I have no regrets about last night. Last night was incredible. You're incredible. Best sex of my life. Your soldier outperformed himself with all the orgasms he delivered."

His chuckle rumbles into the top of my head where he's planted his lips. "I love it when you talk dirty."

I sigh. "It's new for me."

"I know, but you're staggeringly good at it so don't stop." He kisses my neck, inhaling my skin and I close my eyes, attempting to suppress the shudder my body is desperate to unleash. "If you want, I'll take you downstairs and do it again now. Or... anything else you want me to do."

His tongue snakes out and licks at my sweat, groaning like I'm the best thing he's ever tasted. My teeth slam into my bottom lip so hard I taste blood and my eyes close in defeat at the wicked pleasure of his mouth on me. It's so easy to get lost in him, I'm just worried I'll never be found again.

I need him. I can't lose him. Not again. These last three and a half years without him have been hell. A piece of myself missing.

"A tattoo, you say?"

I feel his smile against my neck. "You'd rather get a tattoo than fuck around in bed with me?"

NO! "Feels safer than jumping out of a plane. Less death-defying."

"Are you equating sex with me to death?"

"I have no idea at this point what I'm equating with anything. But a tattoo sounds fun."

He cups my face and tilts my chin up to meet his eyes, studying me the way only he can. He sees it. And it breaks me. I want him, but where does desire end and other things begin?

He gives me an absent nod and I see as something wash over his expression. "The only person I'd ever let ink your beautiful body is Lenox and he's not here."

My heart sinks, but I keep this going. "Is it weird that Lenox is freakishly good at everything?"

"Except conversing."

I laugh. "True." I finish off the mug of coffee and set it down on the table. I take his pinkies and loop them through mine. "You good?" I ask hesitantly, brokenly. Unsure what I want his answer to be.

"I'm good."

Of course he is. When is Greyson Monroe ever not? Whether it's real or fake. I'm clueless as to what I should do or not do next with this man. There needs to be a guidebook. How to screw around with your hot best friend without falling head over heels in love with him.

"Wanna walk along the beach before we head to our next destination?"

I squeeze his pinkies. "I thought you'd never ask."

WE WALKED on the beach for an hour and then got back in the car and drove up and into Provence. It took us about four hours and that was only after I made us go through Eze with its cacti and succulents and famous botanical gardens.

Along the way, Grey—or better yet his assistant—rented us a small house in Avignon for the night thinking that would be cozier and more intimate. But then he also mentioned how we should take the TGV or bullet train up to Paris tomorrow since it will already be Wednesday, and Gray has to be at the festival grounds on Friday.

We're running out of time.

Already.

I could spend a week in Paris alone, but as it is, I'll have to settle for Wednesday and Thursday.

The ticking of the clock is making me antsy as every day we drive closer to the end of this voyage. I don't want it to end, and yet I also do. I feel split. Divided between adventure and responsibility. I can be this woman here, the one throwing caution to the wind and living in the moment, but at the end of the day, I'm still me.

I like things settled. I like things orderly. I don't thrive well in chaos or uncertainty.

I could go off after it and do my own thing after the festival. I could give myself another week and do it alone if I so desire.

But I'm also anxious to get home.

To find a new place to live and settle into this new version of my regular life as this new self. My old boss from the clinic, Jonah Hughes emailed me just as we got in the car and told me that I'm welcome to come back to my job there any time, and with that email, I felt the tug of reality pulling at me. I haven't heard back from my attending at Children's and that's gnawing at me, but at least I have something for now.

It's this tug coupled with all the uncertainty that has me quiet as we ride with the top down, breathing in the fresh French air, passing fields of lavender and sunflowers that are not yet in bloom. Grey too is a little quiet and it's not like him to be. There's a shift in the air between us. Last night did something to both of us and we haven't fully talked about it.

It's my fault. I know it is. And I need to fix it. But I'm plagued.

I want to say something, but I'm unsure of what. I've become a mistress of mixed signals and head fuckery, and it isn't how I traditionally operate. I rejected him again this morning after saying yes last night.

Did I hurt him?

That thought makes me sick. I was quick to brush all this off as being old habits and him being emotionally absent when it comes to feelings, but was I wrong in that assumption or is he simply quiet because he's enjoying the ride and I'm way over-thinking all of this?

I hate this feeling. It's like ants are crawling over my skin and I'm squirmy and itchy.

I glance over at him, and something clenches inside me. Something foreign that oddly doesn't feel foreign at all when I take in his profile, though I'm positive I've never experienced it before. It riffles through me, jostling me about. Oddly comforting.

Just as I open my mouth to say... something, my phone rings in my purse. Grey and I both tense. Me especially after my morning text.

"Should I answer it?"

"At least see who it is."

He has a point. I set my purse on my lap and pull out my phone and smile so damn big as I swipe to answer it. "Hey!" I say and Grey's head swivels in my direction, his eyebrows pinched. "Wait. Hold on a second."

"Sure," Oliver says in my ear.

I hit mute. "It's Oliver Fritz," I say to Grey. "We used to work together at Hughes Healthcare."

"I know Oliver."

Right. Makes sense since I think Oliver does some modeling for Monroe Fashion and billionaires seem to always know other billionaires.

I unmute my phone. "Sorry about that," I apologize to Oliver. "How are you? I'm shocked you're calling me."

"Are you though?" Oliver replies.

"I don't know. I'm assuming you spoke to Jonah."

"I spoke to Jonah," he confirms. "But what he didn't tell me was what's going on. You're no longer moving to Philadelphia?"

"I'm no longer moving to Philadelphia," I confirm, shifting in my seat and staring out the window. "I'm no longer getting married either."

"Hmmm. Are we happy about that?"

"Depends on who you ask. I am though, for reference. You never liked him, and you were always right in that."

"I'm sorry to hear that," he says genuinely. "I wish I could say I'm surprised, but I'm not. You'll have to fill me in on the details. I haven't heard anything about this though. In fact, if Jonah hadn't told me, I would have still been planning to attend your wedding in a week and a half. What's going on with that?"

"I'm not entirely sure to be honest. My parents and Bacchus are dragging their heels with making it public."

"Interesting. And a bit concerning. Let me know if there is anything the family or I can do to help. We're team Fallon all the way. But hey, I can't talk long since I'm heading to work. But before we hang up, I wanted to mention something to you. I know Jonah offered you your two days a week back at the clinic, but what about your job at Children's?"

"Are you a mind reader, Oliver? I was just doing mental gymnastics over this. I haven't heard back from my old attending there yet. It's likely too late though."

"Great," he exclaims. "Because one of my partners at MGH is retiring and I'd like to offer you his job."

"What?" I gasp, shooting forward, my hand planting on the dash.

"Can you put this on speaker or something?" Grey asks, concern creasing his brow. "You're freaking me out here."

"Who's that?" Oliver questions.

I glance at Grey and then switch it to speakerphone. "You'll never believe this, Oliver, but I'm in the car in France with Greyson Monroe."

Oliver is silent. "Uh. I'm sorry, what?"

"Hey Oliver," Grey says, raising his voice so Oliver can hear him. He smirks at me. "How's it going man?"

"You two know each other?" Oliver is flummoxed. "How did I not know this?"

"Lifelong best friends and former neighbors," Grey answers. "But our friendship was always sort of a secret if you get my meaning. So what did you say to make my girl gasp just now?"

Oliver's silent for a beat. "I offered *your girl* a job at MGH."

The way he says that, and Grey's expression makes me feel like I'm missing something.

"And I accept! But wait, you work in a family medicine practice there. I'm pedi only."

"This partner was a pediatrician. We have family, pediatric, and adult providers. You'll be perfect here."

Oh my God. I could cry with happiness. "This is amazing. Oliver, thank you." My hand lands on my chest even though he can't see my gratitude. "I owe you so big for this."

"Truly, it's nothing at all. Email me your résumé when you get a chance and when you get home from France with your best friend there, give me a call and we'll hammer out the details."

"Will do. Sounds great."

"And Grey? Take care of your girl for me."

"I plan on it."

I disconnect the call, squealing. "Oh my gosh! I'm so relieved." I collapse back against the seat, brushing my hair back from my face and laughing like a madwoman. "I know Oliver's practice. It'll be great."

"One stressor down. Now we just have to get you to chill out about—" A crack of thunder explodes through the air, startling both of us and cutting off his words.

"Shit. We should close the roof."

I nod in agreement just as rain starts to pelt down on us in fat wet globs. "Ah!" I scream, holding my hands over my head like that will do anything to prevent me from getting wet. Grey pulls over in a flash, pressing a button and the roof slowly comes up and then latches into place.

"You okay?"

I laugh, shaking my hair out a bit. "Yeah. Not too bad off. You?"

Another crash of thunder has both of us peering out the windshield at the darkening sky as rain slides down the glass in rivers. "There goes our tour of medieval architecture."

I snicker. "You were taking me on a tour of medieval architecture."

"Seemed boring. Thought you'd like it."

I smack him, making him laugh. "Actually I was planning to take us to the Verdon Gorge and hike for a while there. Jacob says it's very cool. Then I thought it would be fun to get lost and drink our way through a vineyard."

"Both of those sound way too exciting for me. I'm glad we're not going to be able to do either of those now."

He smirks at me just as a bolt of lightning flashes brilliantly across the sky like a jagged knife quickly followed by a boom of thunder that rattles the car. The rain starts to come down harder and we both look at each other.

"What are we going to do now?" I ask.

"There's only one thing left to do."

"What's that?"

"Drink."

Grey's not kidding either. He drives us into Avignon and after we drop our things off in the house—which is ancient and cozy and adorable—and we realize there is no food or alcohol here since his assistant arranged it so last minute, we run down the street into the center of this medieval town until we find a restaurant with a bar.

Both of us soaked, we slide into a quiet corner booth and Grey takes the menu while I scroll through my emails and missed texts. My mother has been all up my ass as I knew she would be, but I haven't heard a peep from my father. Not one word. It makes me question if he knows I left Bacchus or if my mother has been hiding it from him and if she has, why?

Grey is talking with our waiter, and while he's doing that, I fire off a quick text asking this very question. Even if I'm not sure I want to know the answer.

The waiter leaves us, and I tuck my phone back in my purse. Grey twists to face me and then a grin sprawls across his face.

"What?" I ask since he's staring at me in obvious amusement.

"Nothing. You just have a little..." He reaches up and wipes at my face, pulling back his thumbs to reveal thick black streaks.

"Oh." I blush lightly. "I'm going to run to the ladies' room to clean up."

He leans in and gives me a kiss on the cheek, lingering there for a moment. "When you come back, I think we should talk."

My stomach plummets at his suddenly serious tone and expression. "O-okay," I stutter and then slide out of the booth, heading for the bathroom in the back. The heavy door opens, and I lock myself inside, wincing at my reflection. Frizzy, wind and rain swept hair and smears of mascara stain the skin beneath my eyes and down my cheeks.

Turning on the faucet to warm, I lather my hand with soap and wash my face, scrubbing at it until all remnants of makeup are gone. I suck in a deep breath, drying my face and staring at myself in the mirror. I don't know what Grey is going to say to me and I've been mentally hemming and hawing all day about everything to the point where I'm annoying myself. Again.

He's right. We do need to talk.

I'm just not sure what I want to say nor am I sure what I want to hear.

Exiting the bathroom, I wind my way back through the stone-walled restaurant only to abruptly stop before I reach our table. Someone is sitting in my seat. A female someone at that with long red hair. Her back is to me, but Grey's face is in my direct sightline, and I can see he's not the least bit put off by her presence.

No, he's smiling. Laughing. Talking. *Flirting* with her in a way I've never seen him with another woman before. I've seen him around fans plenty. He's sweet and polite but keeps a visible distance and barrier between himself and them.

That's not happening now.

He's clearly interested in her. They're sitting close, their heads angled, his dark eyes on her. All over her. She says something and he touches her arm, lingering there for a beat and then she shifts and... hands him something. A card.

A card that looks suspiciously like a hotel room key.

A dark, helpless feeling rises over me like a flash flood, instantly drowning me in grief. My arms wrap around myself as my heart chills, icing over so quickly I'm wrecked with horrific shivers and brutal pain. My diaphragm convulses and the backs of my eyes burn as I watch him take the card from her hand and slide it into his pocket and I want to die. Because at this moment, with excruciating clarity that crashes into me with the subtlety of a train wreck, I realize I'm in love with Greyson Monroe.

I'm pretty positive I always have been.

From the moment I saw him sitting on his rooftop playing his guitar and singing along all the way through these years to now. It's why I wanted him to have my virginity. It's why I stayed in touch and randomly traveled—sometimes thousands of miles—to see him whenever I could. It's why I walked away— dying a thousand deaths when I left him that note—when I got into a relationship with Bacchus because no man could ever stand a chance of owning my heart with Greyson Monroe still in my life. It's why I listened to his music on repeat whenever we were apart and thought of him a hundred different times a day. It's why I set the rules of no sex and why I couldn't keep away from him despite them.

I'm in love with him.

And I told myself that could never be. I deluded myself for years into believing my feelings for him were simply those entrenched in friendship. Yet I felt the shift the moment he stepped on the plane. I felt my walls start to crumble and whispers of this sneak through my cracks.

I haven't been a mess about Bacchus.

I've been a mess about Grey.

All this time. All my mental back and forth and confusion and questioning. It's all been about him because it's always *been* him.

Now what do I do?

I've ruined us so many times over the years. So many times on this trip *alone*. Me. I have no one to blame but myself for that. My head. My insecurities with how Bacchus never truly wanted me. My fear that everything with Greyson was purely physical and nothing else.

Maybe he's finally fed up.

Or maybe sex *was* the only thing driving him all this time. I refused him this morning and now he's gone on to find it with her. The girl he's kissing the cheek of right this moment.

My hand clamps over my mouth to stifle my sob, and I spin on my heels and run, desperate to be anywhere other than here. I shouldn't have agreed to this trip through Europe with him. Because look where it's gotten me now.

22

GREYSON

Me: I'm going to tell her.

Zax: No. It's too soon. She's not ready yet.

Callan: Agreed.

Asher: You're all a bunch of pussies. Tell her, Grey. Go bold or go home. Be in it to win it. You've got this.

Lenox: Life's short. Tell her.

Me: There's a chance I might be flat out tomorrow when she rejects me.

Again. But I'm done. I was done last night, and I was done this morning and while I gave her a reprieve to freak out, I'm done with that too. Not telling her has been killing me. Every time we're together I'm spun up in her, needing more, anxious for the next time, unable to stop thinking about her for a second.

Callan: Then we'll meet you in Paris on Friday
and help you lick your wounds.

Me: What are you talking about?

Zax: We're coming to the festival. Well, Aurelia
decided we were going, and we agreed. So it's
happening. Flights booked. Hotel rooms
rented. No arguing.

Shit. I scrub my jaw and smile to myself, my chest expanding. But having everyone there with me this weekend, hopefully with Fall as well, it's everything and once again, I'm reminded how grateful I am that these are my people.

Asher: Remember that time I lost that bet and
you fuckers made me strip naked under the
Eiffel Tower and that group of teenage
girls saw.

I snicker, because yes, I do remember that. It was awesome.

Zax: As I remember those girls died with
laughter when they saw how little your
equipment was.

Asher: For the hundredth time, it was cold out.
He's not little. He's mammoth. Just ask my
teammates.

Callan: Uh, something you want to tell us,
brother? You know we'll love you no matter
who you love.

Asher: Fuck you. You know what I meant. They
see me in the locker room.

Lenox: Uh huh.

I decide to save Asher since he's on my side with this.

> Me: A group of nuns caught me accidentally groping Fallon's tits the other day.

> Zax: How do you accidentally grope someone's tits?

I type out the abbreviated version of what happened in Rome and just as I hit send, a figure drops down beside me. My head pops up, thinking it's Fall, only to be completely side-swiped by the vision before me.

"No fucking way!"

A tinkling giggle. "Fucking way."

"Should you be saying that with the bun growing in your oven? I read once that they can hear you from inside the womb."

Vivian O'Connor rolls her green eyes at me. "That hasn't stopped me from swearing yet and it certainly hasn't stopped me from doing the actual fuck—"

I plug my ears. "La, la, la."

"Oh, knock it off. Like you don't do plenty of that." She smacks my shoulder and I laugh, reaching out and hugging her to me. Vivian O'Connor is married to Cian O'Connor, another artist and good friend of mine. A hundred years ago when Central Square was at its peak, Cian and his band were our opening act. He toured with us during our third album tour when I was nineteen or so, about a year before Suzie died. Cian is my age and we hit it off instantly. He's a headlining artist now, rocking the top of the charts like I am.

Over Christmas last year, he met and fell in love with the fiery redhead before me and he's never looked back. Or happier.

"The last thing I want is the visual image of you and Cian," I tease. "Speaking of, where is he? I can't believe you're here." I search around what I can see of the restaurant but come up empty.

She flips her red hair over her shoulder. "We decided to spend some time in Provence before the festival in Paris. Not sure when we'll be able to have much alone time after our little man comes this fall. Cian ran out to get the car and is meeting me in the back, so I don't get soaked. I was on my way out to meet him when I saw you. Such a small world."

"No joke. How long are you staying around here?"

"Until Friday. You should hang out with us later though. Cian and I were just about to head out to check out the interactive impressionist museum that's not too far from here. The rain sort of spoiled our plans for other things. Are you here with the Central Square guys or solo?"

"No, I'm here with... my... friend."

Her eyes sparkle with mirth, and she gives me a knowing grin. "Oh, your *friend*."

I reach out and touch her shoulder, leaning in so my voice doesn't carry. "Between you and me, I'm hoping by the time we reach Paris she's more than that."

"I'm sure she will be considering it's you and what woman, other than myself, could say no to you?" She gives me a playful wink. "We'd love to meet her, and I know Cian would love to see you. If you're up for dinner or drinks or whatever, come to our hotel around seven. We should be back and ready by then." She reaches into her pocket, retrieving a white plastic card. "Here's an extra key card so you don't have to go to the front desk or make your presence known. We're in room five-twenty-six. I didn't want to deal with security since we're supposed to be having a romantic getaway, so we're flying a bit under the radar."

"Me too, so this is perfect." I take the card and put it in my pocket. "Not sure what our plans are, but I'll talk to Fallon. I know she'd love to at least meet up for a drink."

"Great!"

I lean in and kiss her cheek. "See ya later. Tell Cian I say hi."

"Will do." She bounces out of the seat with a wave, and I watch her go toward the back only to catch what looks like Fallon running out of the front of the restaurant into the pouring rain. What the hell?

In a flash, I race out of the booth, knocking into the table and rattling some of the dishes in my urgency. By the time I make it through the door, the sky is dark, and rain is coming down so hard it instantly soaks me and makes it difficult to see. My head whips around and I find her running back toward the house.

"Fallon!" I cry, cupping my hands around my mouth so my voice will carry over the pounding of the rain and thunder. She doesn't slow down or stop. If anything, she speeds up and I sprint after her, my heart hammering, wondering what could have happened to her.

Thankfully Fallon is short and I'm tall, so for every two strides she takes I only need one and I catch up to her quickly. My hand shoots out, grabbing her shoulder and spinning her around, our momentum slamming our bodies together and nearly taking us to the ground.

"What are you doing? Are you okay?" I yell, wiping water from her face as I look her over. "What happened?"

She brushes off my touch, her face casting down to the ground. We're in the middle of a cobblestone street, the weather bad enough to keep everyone indoors and cars off the street. "It's nothing. I just... this was stupid. I need to go."

"Fall, tell me what had you running from the restaurant into the rain without even informing me you were going."

Her hands go through her hair, pushing the sodden strands back from her face and then her hands meet her hips. Slowly her eyes rise to mine, a little broken and a touch angry. It has me reaching out to grab her arm in concern, but she shrugs me off once again.

"I didn't mean for you to chase after me. You should go back to the restaurant. I'm sure that woman is missing you. Or did you just arrange to meet her in her hotel room?"

"What?"

"I saw you with that woman. That redhead." Her voice rises as she points over my shoulder back in the direction of the restaurant before returning her hand to her hip and blowing out a harsh breath.

"You mean Vivian?"

"Vivian?" She scoffs. "Lovely."

I shake my head, bemused. "Yes, Vivian. That was Vivian O'Connor, Cian O'Connor's wife. He's playing at the festival this weekend and she just happened to be in the same restaurant we were. She came over and said hi while he was pulling the car around for her. I've known Cian for years, since my Central Square days. Actually, you might know of Vivian since she's a famous romance author."

She swallows and looks away, nodding as she gnaws on her lip and shifts her stance. "Oh. I didn't realize you actually knew her. Or that she's married."

"And pregnant," I add only to pause, searching her expression, replaying her words. Then it hits me and hits me, hard and beautifully. "You're jealous," I accuse, smiling at her.

She shoves me, likely misinterpreting my smile though it's anything but teasing. "Yes. I'm fucking jealous. It sucks. I don't want to be jealous when I see you with another woman. I have enough in my head right now and then last night happened and now I'm feeling all this." Her hands wave wildly in the air around her. "This is why I wanted separate bedrooms. This is why I said no sex. I'm going to get my heart broken." Another frustrated shove to my chest, but I don't budge. Not an inch. "Why did we have to cross this line? Why couldn't we have stayed best friends? I never would have realized any of this."

I lick my wet lips and step into her, grasping her shoulders and forcing her to see me. "Because you were always more than a best friend to me. *Always*," I emphasize. "Do you know why I dropped everything and ran to the airport?"

She shakes her head, strands of black hair sticking to her face and neck, her eyes wide. Fearful.

"For you. So I could win you. So I wouldn't let this chance go again. I've let you walk in and out of my life because I never felt like I deserved you. Because part of me knew I'd lose if I fought for you. You weren't ready and I guess I wasn't either, and I know I let you believe I was indifferent, but I'm here fighting for you now. Because I'm anything but indifferent. I deserve you, Fallon. Me. Not him. Not some other asshole. You are meant for me. I am your one."

Her breath hitches and a strangled sob clings to her throat. She's shaking. From the cold, from the rain, from my words, I don't know. All I know is I can't stop now.

She has me breathless, craving, obsessed, and desperate for more.

I cup her wet jaw in my hand and hold her against me as I soften my voice. "I'm not going to break your heart. It's us, Fall. It was, has, always, and forever been us. Tell me what I have to do. Tell me how to win you once and for all. Tell me how to make you as crazy and twisted up over me as I am over you."

"Grey—"

"Don't say no. Don't say you're a mess or that it's too soon or you just got out of a relationship or you're scared or unsure or anything else you can think of. Don't doubt this. It's real and I know you know that. Somewhere deep inside of you, I know you know that."

"I think I've always known that. I just didn't get it until now." Before I can process what she's saying, she grabs my face and drags my mouth down to hers.

I react instantly. One hand on the nape of her neck, my other fisting her hair, my lips parting hers. She gasps when she feels my tongue, how voracious my hunger is, and it sets something off inside her.

This is what we do so well. What we've pretended didn't exist. What we stole and then attempted to forget. The fire that burns between us. The flames that stroke along our bodies, thriving on our mixed breaths, impervious to the rain. My blood pulses with adrenaline as sparks dance across my skin. I pick her up and wrap her legs around my waist.

I kiss her like this. Starved for her even though I had her just last night. This is different. This is everything.

Lightning flashes overhead. Thunder shakes the earth. Pressing her tighter against me and not giving a shit if the world is watching or the rain drowns us, I walk us up the street without removing my mouth from hers. Not even to catch my breath or as I fumble with the ancient door that requires a stupid skeleton-looking key.

Fallon is attacking me. Nails raking along my scalp and across my neck. Kissing me, grinding against me, a force of nature more powerful than the storm. It's as if a switch has been turned on inside of her. In me too. This isn't one night. This isn't something that will die the moment we come or the sun comes up.

It's the hello and not the goodbye and we both feel it.

"You know our friendship is ruined now, right?" she murmurs to me.

I grin against her lips, nipping at her bottom one. "I was only in it for the pussy."

She giggles. "Such a Greyson Monroe response. What the hell do I see in you?"

"Your future." And fuck do I mean it.

I slam her against the wall with a bit more gusto than I intend—plus the walls are made of stone—but Fall Girl doesn't seem to notice as she whips off her soaked blouse and tosses it over my shoulder.

"More Grey," she pants. "I need to feel you against me."

Greedily she starts to tug on my ruined leather jacket, but I'm more interested in her breasts. I hike her up my body, unhooking her bra at the back. She squirms out of it and before that can hit the floor, I have her tits in my mouth.

Lost in my need, I suck and bite, my tongue swirling around her hard peaks, one and then the other. Her eyes fall closed, her head back against the wall. My jacket is forgotten as her hand dives up into my hair, holding me there. A shudder takes over, goose bumps erupting across her skin, and she moans softly.

I want to take her upstairs. I want to lay her on a bed and take my time licking, touching, tasting, fucking. But I'm too impatient, so instead, I twirl us around and bring her down on the soft oriental rug lining the front of the cottage. I rip my jacket from my shoulders, my shirt following and then her hands are on me, her nails scraping down my chest, catching my nipple and making me hiss out a breath.

Shoes get kicked off and flung, her hands hastily fumbling with my belt as mine tear at her jeans. We're awkward and wet and it's impossible to remove wet denim from wet skin without a lot of tugging and tearing. We don't make it more than a few seconds without our mouths connecting and it's a mash of teeth and lips and curses and frustrated laughs until finally, we're both only in our wet underwear. Then I'm back over her, needing the contact she begged me for.

She arches under me, her cold, damp flesh against mine making me shiver. Or maybe that's the woman doing that. With my body in between her spread thighs, I swivel my hips, hitting her pussy at just the right spot and making her cry out. There are too many things I want to do to her and for the first time, I realize I'll be able to do them all.

I don't have to rush this. I don't have to try to bend time.

We haven't talked beyond the hasty words I threw at her

outside in the rain and she hasn't said much other than she wants me too, but that's all semantics to me now. I'm no longer trying to win her, but I'd be a fool to believe everything will go smoothly from here on out for us. I will have to fight for her, and I'll have to be ruthless in that.

I swivel again, a surge of possessiveness taking hold, and my face falls into her neck where I groan, licking her skin. "Fuck you feel good. I almost want to make you come like this."

"I'm not far off." She sighs as I keep doing it, grinding and dry humping her like a teenager.

It's not enough though. I have to see and feel all of her. The level of desperation she evokes in me is borderline madness. I slide down her body, devouring her breasts and the valley between them on my descent. I spread her thighs wider and bury my nose in the wet satin of her panties, taking a deep inhale of her. I groan because fuck, that's good, my cock so hard it hurts.

Her back shoots off the rug, her hands ripping at my hair as my nose finds her clit through them and rubs it. "Ah! Grey."

"Shush, woman. I'm worshiping my pussy."

I rip at the thin string on the side of her pretty thong, and it tears away. Her grip on my hair tightens and then instead of shoving me away as I almost expect her to, she's pulling my face in deeper. I smirk at my assertive girl and give her exactly what she's asking for. A long, slow lick from her ass up to her clit.

I slide my hand under her hips, lifting her to me. My other hand snags on one full tit, and then I feast like a man on death row. I kiss her mound, and then start to make out with her pretty cunt. A word I know makes her blush, so I tell her how good it tastes just to watch that flush spread across her fair skin.

Her hips jerk, the sensation of my mouth and the dirty words from my lips unraveling her at the seams. This has always been one of my favorite parts of her. How she's so prim and proper on the outside, a perfect Lark princess, but on the inside, she craves every dirty deed I'm desperate to lavish on her.

She likes my control. She craves how I own her body. She needs my focused possession.

And fuck if I don't love giving my girl everything she wants and more.

My teeth graze along her clit before I suck it between my lips while my finger circles her hole. She whimpers, her head drawn back, her face screwed up in pleasure and concentration. My tongue starts circling her clit, matching my finger's movements, and something about this drives her wild. Her hips shoot off the ground, grinding, seeking.

Sweet Jesus, her legs fly up, her thighs clamping against the sides of my head.

"Oh. Oh fuck, Grey. I need to come so bad."

"You taste so good, Fall. Come for me. Make me taste all that sweet cum you're so desperate to give me." I hump and rock into the floor, desperate for friction as I taste her. If only that were possible. If only I could lick her and fuck her at the same time.

With her hand holding me in place against her clit as she fucks my mouth and face, I plunge two fingers deep inside her, crooking them until I feel that spot against her front wall. It sets her off. Hurricane-force winds plow through her as she takes pleasure on my tongue and my fingers, as they start fucking her the way I plan to fuck her with my cock.

I glance up just as her eyes spring open and her chin tilts. Our eyes collide and I growl at the dark, hazy, lust-drunk expression on her face. With that she screams, yanking my hair and grinding up, bucking into my mouth over and over again while I continue to wring every ounce of pleasure from her body for as long as she'll take it.

She's stunning like this. So open and exposed and bare to me.

It's just us. The way we were always meant to be. The way we should have always been. Me giving her pleasure, burying my face in her most intimate place.

She is my goddess.

My salvation.

The one I'll battle the fires of hell for and won't rest until I conquer.

She sags and I rise up, kissing her pussy that trembles and spasms before turning the same affection on each inner thigh. She looks so beautiful like this. Dark eyelashes fanned across flushed porcelain skin. The large, heavy swell of her breasts with her rose-colored nipples. The soft slope of her belly and the voluptuous curve of her hips.

"You're exquisite," I murmur reverently because, by God, she is.

"Come here," she demands, and I gladly obey, climbing up her body and resting my weight on top of her. My elbows plant into the rug and I prop myself up so I can take in her face.

"Hey, Fall Girl."

A lazy smile. "Hey, Grey."

"You good?"

"I'm good. You good?"

"I'm the best."

Her fingers glide through my hair and she drags my forehead to hers. "Prove it."

Fuck yeah! Without warning I scoop her up in my arms and run us up the stairs, planning to prove I'm the best to her all night.

23

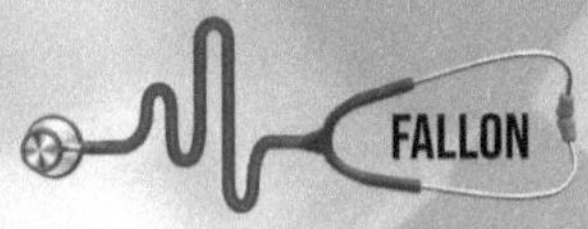

Grey's hazy eyes hold mine as he carries me up the stairs. He's so hard, pressed between us, and my mouth waters while my empty core clenches. Thankfully the cottage is small, and he carries me into the master bedroom, the need for separate spaces more than over. With that thought, my face plants on his neck, and my lips kiss his tender skin as I band him tighter against my chest.

I regret so much when it comes to him. To us.

Never again.

Greyson Monroe is my end game and I'll do whatever it takes for us to reach the finish line together.

The soft bed welcomes me, and I sink into the plush white duvet, staring up at the man before me. He shucks off his wet briefs, standing boldly naked before me, his hand going to his cock almost absentmindedly. His hand plants on the bed by the side of my head and then he kisses me, splitting my lips and twisting his tongue with mine for only a moment before he pushes off and stands once more.

With his eyes on me, his trembling hand cups my jaw. "I need you."

That's all he says, but the dark primal look in his eyes tells me just how much. My expression must match his because before I can steal my next breath, he grabs my ankle, slides me to the edge of the bed, and spreads my thighs wide for him. His hooded eyes lock on my dripping center and he licks his lips, tasting me on them. His finger circles my hole, his eyes glued to the motion, and I prop myself up, just as enraptured by the sight.

"That feel good?" he rasps, his voice shredded in desire.

I can only nod, words stuck in my throat until he coaxes a moan from me.

"Do you know what my favorite part of fucking you is?"

I gasp as he pushes that finger inside me as he says the word fucking.

"What?" I pant, my body flushed from head to toe as arousal surges through me, curling my toes.

"The way you stare into my eyes the first moment I enter you. The twist of your face in both pleasure and pain as if my cock is just a little too big for you but you can't get enough of it."

"Do you know what my favorite part of fucking you is?" I throw his question back at him.

"What?" He starts to jerk his cock to the same rhythm he fingers me and it's blowing my mind how hot that is.

"How every time you get close, no matter the position, you grab me and whisper my name in my ear over and over again."

He gives me a lopsided grin. "I do that?"

"Yes." My fingers slide down my belly and rub my clit as he continues to finger me. His eyes smolder as he watches both of our hands. "After I'd leave you and return to my life, I'd close my eyes and rub myself exactly like this thinking about that until I came."

His breath catches high in his throat. He slides his finger out of me and paints my lips with my arousal right before his lips slam down on mine tasting me and forcing me to do the same. Our tongues thrash, fitful and edgy, our lips consuming until right when I feel the head of his large cock at my entrance. Then he pulls away, and just as he said, stares into my eyes.

"I'm not wearing anything."

"I'm good," I promise him. I re-upped my birth control in anticipation of getting married, going on my honeymoon, and moving states, but whatever.

He gives me a jerky nod. "I'm clean too. I haven't been with anyone before you in a while, and I always get tested after, and I... I haven't ever been bare with anyone."

A rush of delicious heat shoots through my veins and I cup the side of his face, almost pleading when I say, "Fuck me, Grey. I want to feel all of you. Nothing between us."

His eyes close and his nostrils flare as he blows out a silent breath. And when his eyes reopen, they're liquid fire. As black and bright as midnight under the full moon.

"Show me, Fall Girl. Show me how my cock just barely fits in your tight cunt."

I angle my hips up, so crazy with the need to feel him inside of me like this I can barely catch my breath. He starts to push in, and I whimper, because yes, he does just barely fit, and yes, it does border on the line between pleasure and pain.

"Fuck, you're tight. Too tight. And fuck this feels good. Too good."

Another inch and then another and I push up, meeting him, desperate and impatient. Grey's black eyes search my face, watching me intently, and with a strong exhale he thrusts all the way inside me, making my back arch and my eyes snap closed with how full I feel.

"Open your eyes so I know you're with me."

My eyes flash open and the rawness of his cracks something inside me open. Something beautiful and alive and brand-new.

"Fuck me," I tell him again. "Fuck me hard. Don't hold back.

Don't check in on me. Just take me how you've always wanted to take me."

A savage growl sears the air and then his hands grip my hips, and he starts to fuck me like a man possessed. His body comes down on mine, his knee climbing up onto the bed, his chest a hairbreadth from contact with mine, but he angles himself so not only are his thrusts deeper and longer, but he can still watch as he slides in and out of me.

My hand fists at his hair, my nails scrape down his back, and my teeth latch on to his shoulder.

"That's it, Fall. All mine, baby."

His hand squeezes my breast, holding it in a vicelike grip and he watches as the overspill bounces. Sweat gleams on his forehead and shoulders as he continues to pump in and out of me without slowing. My legs wind around his hips, rucking up higher, needing him deeper and in doing so, the head of his cock hits the front wall inside me while his pelvis grinds against my clit.

Stars burst behind my eyes, and I cry out a garbled version of a moan and a whimper. Every nerve ending in my body is firing, that deep, delicious warm ache growing from the inside out, spreading like a disease that has only one cure. The bed moves with the pummeling force of his fucks, slamming into the wall each time he thrusts into me.

My arms encircle his neck and I drag his face to mine, needing to hold him—*feel* him—as close as I can. All of him, all over me. His other knee comes on the bed, and he shifts my legs so they're up over his shoulders.

Then his hips pound. Fierce. Unapologetic and primal as he drags ragged sounds from both of us. His balls slap my ass and I want him in there too. I've never done that before, but I want to do everything with Greyson Monroe.

He tumbles forward, his face pinched tight in concentration. "More?"

"More," I breathe because that's all I can do. Breathe.

His hands take mine, intertwining our fingers and moving them over my head, pressing them into the bed. With my legs on his shoulders and my hands like this, he starts undulating his hips, making his pushes and pulls deeper, hitting every space inside me he can. His eyes glue themselves to mine, watching what this does to me and it's so much.

"So beautiful," he groans. "You're so beautiful, Fall. So beautiful like this, with me inside you."

"I'm so close." He releases my hands, clasping my wrists in position with one hand and using his other to start working my clit and it drags me right to the precipice.

"I know, baby. I'm dying to feel you come on me. I can't hold off much longer. You feel too good."

"Then come, Grey." My back arches. "Yes. Ah! Right there. Don't stop."

"Fall, Fall, Fall." He collapses against me, chanting in my ear. "Fuck, Fallon. You're going to come for me. I feel it."

My eyes screw up, my fists clenching, unable to do much else as his body commands and controls mine. Until it bursts. The dam breaks open in hot, exquisite, almost painful waves. I seize up, shrieking as my orgasm barrels through me and then goes on and on, my name breathed harshly in my ear, his and God's shouted out in tandem from me.

He's so deep inside me and I feel him as he starts to come.

His body goes rigid, his grip on me crushing, and then his hot, hard cock grows even bigger as he pulses. I moan at the feel of him shooting inside me, unable to fully catch my breath as he dives himself in deeper. His mouth captures mine in a scorching kiss as he groans and growls and grunts and curses until we both sag, utterly spent.

His fingers uncoil from my wrist, but I'm too boneless to move my arms just yet.

He lingers in me, on top of me, kissing my lips, my cheeks,

my neck, inhaling my skin as he murmurs words I can't fully make out. Whatever they are, they're gritty and real. His hands grope me everywhere and I already feel his cock starting to stir.

All that soft perfection hidden beneath his gruff, broken, filthy-mouthed exterior is my ultimate kryptonite.

"Already?" I tease only for the sound to grow breathy as he pumps into me.

"I love how your pussy feels. It's my happiest of happy places. I forgot how dangerous it is."

"Dangerous?"

His head pops up and he's smiling so bright it dazzles away all the gloom outside. "You're mine now, Fall Girl. That means you're mine."

"I sorta got that when you said I was yours."

A hard smack of a kiss on my lips. "No. I don't think you do. Because now that you're mine and I've had you like this, you're mine anytime I want you. And since your pussy is my happiest of happy places, that will be dangerous. For both of us."

"Dangerous as in we'll need fluid resuscitation and oxygen?"

"That too. I meant more in line with I won't be able to stop fucking you and we'll likely never leave this bed again."

"What happens when we start to require basic necessities?"

"I'll get you them for us. Thankfully we'll never have to buy condoms again. I wonder how fast I could get you pregnant."

I choke on a laugh, and he groans as my pussy clenches with the action.

"I'm on the pill."

"Shame. I was sort of enjoying that idea. Think of how pretty your belly will look growing our kid in it one day."

My heart flutters and I drag his forehead down to mine. "You're serious with all of this? Knowing everything I come with and what it means to take someone like me on?"

His nose brushes along mine. "I love you. I'm in love with

you. You're the love of my life. You don't care that I'm Greyson Monroe and I don't care that you're Fallon Lark. That's how we work. All this extra stuff around us doesn't matter. Only what's right here between us does." He slides his hand between our chests, pressing his palm against my racing heart.

Tears threaten.

"Ah, Fall Girl. Don't look at me like that. It's breaking my heart."

"It's just... no one has ever loved me like this, and I wasted a thousand years of my life with the wrong guy, living the wrong life for all the wrong reasons. I hate that it took me so long to get here. That I didn't know what was in front of me all along. I hurt you and I wasn't there for you or with you and I hate it. All of it."

"You're here now. That's what's important." He kisses my lips softly. "I've been in love with you my whole life. Since I was a kid. I'm already figuring out if it's too soon to ask you to move in with me. It's not, so that's me officially asking."

I giggle lightly, my hands running up and down his back and through his hair in a continuous motion. "I love you too. It feels so weird to say that, right? I mean, it's like we're saying all the things we couldn't before. I didn't understand what this was until today. Until like a jealous fool I turned into a green-eyed monster when I saw you with that girl and it was like it all came together at once."

"Vivian," he corrects.

"Vivian. Her."

"Listen, babe. You need to understand something. Women will always come up to me. They will hug me and kiss my cheeks and ask me to sign random places on their bodies and yes, some might proposition me." His hand cups my jaw and he stares straight into my eyes. "I will always say no. Do you know why?"

I shake my head against him.

"Because they are not *you*. I won't care about them because I care about *you*. I won't touch them because I'll *only* touch *you*. I won't love them because I fucking love *you*. I want this, Fall. I want all of it. I want you to wake up in the morning in my arms and fall asleep in the exact same place. I want you to come home from saving tiny human lives and I'll have dinner waiting for you and you'll tell me about your day, and I'll tell you about mine. I want the dream and I want it with you."

"You are the most extraordinary man I've ever met. I don't care about anything else. Nothing else matters to me anymore. Not the past. Not my family. None of it. It's you and me." I roll my hips up, sending that message home. We had that entire talk with him inside of me and now that we both know what this is, I want him again and again.

In seconds he's kissing me and touching me, rolling us so I'm on top and he can stare into my eyes from this angle.

"I'm going to come inside you again, Fall Girl. Deeply. Ride me, baby. Give me those eyes as you do." He thrusts up at the same time he drives my hips down. Blood pounds through me, and my insides quivering as we bounce and rock and grind and breathe and touch and kiss.

Our bodies are one.

We've fucked before. But this is different, and we both feel it. I'm living out the fantasy in my mind with a man I never imagined I could live it with.

He pumps inside me, holding me close and singing lyrics in my ear. Lyrics to the song we listened to in the car a few days ago. And when we both reach the edge, clinging to each other and panting for our lives, he whispers, "Yours," in my ear.

All I know is I never want to wake up from this dream. And I pray I never have to.

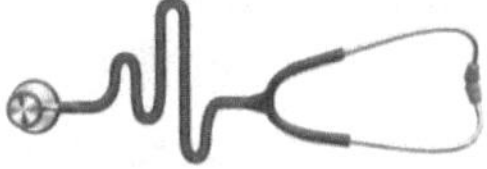

THE SUN WAKES us at some unknown time the next day. It took us forever last night to discover that the power in the cottage was out because we hadn't left the bed or even so much as turned on a light for hours. The grumbling of our stomachs finally pulled us away from each other and even then we had trouble because most of the town was also without power.

We settled for pasta I purchased from a store about to close that we made over the gas stove. We ate not wearing a whole lot. Any time I put something back on, he'd just as quickly peel it back off, and I much preferred him without a shirt to wearing one.

Grey's still asleep as I stretch out my limbs like a cat, sore in all the best places. Grey already informed me were going to be returning the car today and taking the TGV up to Paris. It's nearing the end of our trip, but I no longer dread it the way I was yesterday. All that panic and uncertainty and angst is settled.

I don't care if we go home tomorrow because we'll go home together.

We talked more about his job and mine. About the times he has to be in LA to record and what that looks like. It won't be easy. But I don't care about any of that either. I trust him.

I was living with a man for three years who I never fully trusted. I never allowed myself to unwind around him. No cozy pajama days on the couch without makeup on. No using the bathroom if he was anywhere in the house where he could catch me. No talking back or picking fights, even when he did shit that drove me crazy or irritated the fuck out of me. No displaying any of my quirks or bad habits.

I was a doll.

A façade. Trained and forced to be so outwardly perfect I believed if I was anything less he wouldn't want me anymore. That's been my worth. I don't even know what I like anymore. What I don't like.

I ate breakfast food because it was his favorite meal—he had no clue I originally despised it, and after a while, I told myself it wasn't so bad. For the most part, I ate what he ate with certain caveats of my own. I exercised how he liked to exercise. I enjoyed the things he enjoyed. And anything I didn't feel comfortable sharing with him, I hid.

The worst part of it—it was seamless. Unconscious. I was invisible ink, barely leaving my indelible impression behind. I was a robot. Programmed.

Bacchus was right about one thing. That version of Fallon Lark was boring.

But Grey knows exactly who I am.

Quirks, weird food things, morning breath, makeup-less face, fat ass, drunk, sober, silly, wild, reserved, uncertain, vulnerable, scared, happy, adventurous, whatever. He knows me. He sees me. And he loves me.

With him, I don't have to be perfect and with me, he doesn't either. We're perfect for each other and we're perfect together.

We shower together, taking turns washing each other while he tells me all about the festival. We can't seem to manage distance or stop touching each other. It carries over as we return the car and then kill an hour walking through a lavender field near the train station. No purple flowers are blooming yet and this bothers Grey to no end.

"I wanted a picture of you against the lavender," he says, our arms stretched between us as we hold hands each walking up our own aisle with a row of bushes between us. "Your eyes and dark hair would have looked wild."

"Next time."

His head dips and then swivels in my direction with a smirk that sets off a million butterflies in my stomach. "We could get married here, you know. This summer when they're in full bloom."

I blink about ten thousand times at him. "Are you proposing?"

A half shrug. "Maybe. Does that scare you?"

"Um," I laugh the word. "Maybe," I throw back at him. "A little, yeah. Last week at this time I was engaged to another man. Feels a bit... I don't know... impromptu. Outlandish. Wrong to be engaged to someone else."

"He was the wrong man."

"True."

"I'm the right one."

"Agreed."

"So not so... outlandish. Possibly still impromptu."

"Grey—"

"I'm the impulsive one in this relationship. Remember?"

Now I laugh outright. "How could I forget?"

"Think about it. For real." He squeezes my hand and with it, my heart. "Just keep it tucked in the back of your mind and after we go home to Boston and everything is completely settled with your family and all that, we can talk about it again."

My head and my heart are spinning, making me dizzy. "Okay," I promise, because that thought, the thought of marrying him does things to me that being engaged to Bacchus never did. But there's that niggling in the back of my mind where he wants me to keep the thought of marrying him tucked safely away. The thought that nothing *is* yet settled with my family. Not from their perspective anyway.

The world still thinks I'm engaged to Bacchus Astley and here I am with Greyson Monroe. And we're in love. No business arrangement. No back-end deals. It's just us. But how long can that last before my family and Bacchus try to tear it all apart?

24

The last place I was looking forward to reaching on this trip was Paris. But that's exactly where we're headed now. Come Friday it's going to be a lot of business. Meet and greets and interviews and privately sponsored events. I'm not set to perform until Sunday night, but that doesn't mean I won't be working the whole time before that.

My alone time with Fallon is almost up. With the world of press and paparazzi descending on this event like sharks out for gossip blood, things could get tricky for us.

"What if I just email everyone on our guest list and announce that the wedding is off?" Fallon says as she snuggles into my side on the seat in our private cabin on the train. There are only two private cabins on this train and it's pretty full from what the attendant told us. We were lucky to get it.

My fingers pause on the keyboard of my phone. We never ended up meeting up with Cian and Vivian, but I've been texting with him, and making plans to meet up on Friday at the festival.

"Can you do that?"

She chews on her lip. "I don't know. I mean, yes, I can do

that. But it's starting a war, right? I want this to be amicable, not a bloodbath."

"Maybe we should wait to do anything drastic until we fly home. You should meet with your mother. And likely Buttass since he has a lot of your stuff still."

"He keeps texting me and I keep not responding."

I jut my chin toward the phone in her hand. "What has he said?"

She unlocks her phone, pulls up their text stream, and hands it to me. It's a bunch of one-sided texts saying a thousand different things. Things from I do love you, please believe me to I'm sorry, to come home, to why won't you reply, to I won't allow you to make me look like a fool, to this wedding is happening whether you want it to or not. It goes on and on, some spouting love and others threats.

One thing is clear by the sheer number of texts and times at which they come in, he's desperate. And desperate men do desperate things when they think they're about to lose everything.

Either way, I won't let him get to her and I won't let him hurt her in any way.

But for now, it's just us and I don't want to think about anything else at the moment.

"Come here," I say, taking our phones and setting them down on the small table beside our seats.

"What are you doing?" She laughs, but the sound is strangled and shocked as I haul her against me and press my lips to hers. A private cabin is a relative term on the TGV, at least for this train. We have our own room, but the door is an open space, and anyone can walk past us at any time.

I'm wearing my standard Boston Rebels cap that I flip around on my head and dive back in for a kiss, showing her exactly what I'm doing. I'd love to fuck her, but I doubt we could get away with it in here. There's another cabin right on the other side of the aisle from us and it's filled with four German women. They're loud, laughing and clucking at the top of their lungs, so maybe they won't hear Fallon when I make her come.

With one hand on her jaw holding her mouth to mine, my other hand slides from her shoulder to her breast where I start squeezing and kneading her over her blouse. She hums into me, a little uncertain, but not stopping me either. My thumb brushes back and forth over her nipple, making it harder and me more desperate to see and feel it without the barrier of her clothes.

She has the prettiest tits, the prettiest nipples, and I want one in my mouth so badly I'm moaning into her mouth at the thought.

"Grey," she murmurs into me as my hand finds the base of her blouse and pulls it free from her leggings.

"Yes, baby." My hands slide up her silky skin and then I shove the cup of her bra down, getting to second base on the train as we speed up the French countryside toward Paris.

"We shouldn't do this here."

I smile against her lips, sucking on her bottom lip. "Ah, my little rule follower, but you can't question me."

"What if we get caught?"

"I promise you'll finish before that happens."

She emits a strangled sort of hiccup, but still, she doesn't push me away and I continue to make out with her like a teenage boy, playing with her sweet tits as I do.

"I love you," she murmurs into me, pressing deeper against me and my heart gives a happy lurch. I'll never grow tired of hearing her say that to me.

"Love you." I kiss a trail down her neck, inhaling her skin at my favorite spot—the crevice right between her neck and shoulder—and then work my way back up, sucking on her ear.

"Do you think I can suck you off in here without anyone

seeing?" she pants as my fingers pinch and roll her nipples and just like that, I start seeing double.

"Fall Girl, the world could see you do that, and I wouldn't care."

She laughs and then goes for my zipper, but this won't work well, so I have us flip positions so I'm closest to the open door and her ass is facing the window as she curls up on the two-person seat. I angle my hips in her direction, giving my back to the door, and if anyone were to walk by, it would likely look like she was resting her head on my lap. Or sucking my cock. Either way, the proof wouldn't be so obvious, and my face certainly won't be visible like this.

I twist my hat back around and allow her to unzip me. She reaches in, pulling my hard cock out and stroking it lovingly, rubbing the drop of precum on the head around with the pad of her thumb. I might die from that alone. That's how good it feels.

She thinks she's being naughty and getting away with something here as she gives me a coy smirk right before she takes my most of my cock in her mouth. I see stars and for a moment do nothing but enjoy the erotic bliss of Fallon's wet, hot mouth on my cock. She bobs on me, undoing my button and opening me up more so she can grip me.

I get a flutter of her eyelashes and I smirk, ready to show her how dirty I can be too when my hand slides into the back of her leggings, finding the damp crotch of her panties over her slit. A shocked hum vibrates past her lips, and I swallow my groan and need to thrust up into her mouth.

Because holy *fuck* that was *good*.

I tell her so and she hums again, this time in appreciation. But also, because I'm rubbing her pussy over her panties, making sure she's nice and wet and ready for my fingers to start fucking her. With the crook of my finger, fighting the stretch of her leggings, I slide her panties to the side and run my finger up and down her wetness, skating over her clit with each pass.

She makes a hungry noise, her hand squeezing the base of my cock, her other one shoved in between the teeth of my zipper, cupping my balls.

I wasn't lying when I said Fallon Lark has a wicked mouth and likes to play dirty because she does. I've made her crawl to me on all fours before to suck me off and she did so willingly and with a soaked pussy that she made come as she swallowed me down her throat.

That memory makes a loud groan tear unrestrained from my throat and both she and I freeze, her eyes growing wide. She peers past me toward the door and when the sound of the women in the other car doesn't pause or even drop, she keeps going, moving herself so she's more on top of my cock and can take it deeper while opening up her lower half more to me, giving me better access.

"Filthy girl," I tell her, using my free hand to grip her hair. I won't push her down on me—hell, the way she's taking me into her mouth and working my cock, I don't need to—but I love making her think about it. "You like sucking my cock while I finger you?"

"Mmmm." She goes down deeper, drool dripping from her lips, making me wetter. She slides down as deep as she can, gagging and then swallowing and *hell*. If she keeps that up, I won't last long.

I reward my little vixen by rubbing her clit as her arousal leaks from her opening, lubing everything up nicely. Finger fucking her will be difficult with the angle and restriction of her leggings, but her clit I have unfettered access to, and I can make her come with that alone.

Fallon squeezes my cock, bobbing up and down with my hand in her hair. It's the hottest sight, watching my wet cock disappear inside that mouth. I shudder, my balls already drawing up especially when she starts moaning and wiggling her ass and grinding against my hand as she too gets closer.

"That's it, baby." I start petting her hair as her movements grow jerky, her eyes watering and tearing as she continues to suck me while getting played with. "You're so good at that. So beautiful when you take my cock down your throat." I pick up the pace of my fingers, rubbing her in earnest now, circling around and around and increasing the pressure.

She pulls back, gasps for air, moans, and then dives back down, and I swear I'm about to lose it in her hot little mouth any second. It's almost punishing how good this feels. My legs tense the second I feel her body begin to quiver. Her clit grows firmer against my finger, and I pinch it, twisting it back and forth, and she cries out around me.

That does it. That vibration and siren-wail from her lips that are sucking me off. I curse under my breath, my grip in her hair tightens, my hips shoot up, and I come in hot spurts into her mouth. She swallows me down, sucking and slurping and choking and gagging and the second she's done, I massage her clit until she's nuzzling her face in my thigh to muffle her sounds as she comes all over my fingers and hand.

I hate that I can't see it. I hate that I can't taste it or properly feel it on my fingers, but it's so fucking hot knowing that any second someone could walk by and watch as I make Fallon come. I murmur that to her, and it makes her spasm again, her hand gripping the hell out of my thigh, her nails digging into the denim.

She sighs and slumps, and I slip my fingers from her, licking them clean, and then tucking myself back in and zipping and buttoning up. She adjusts her bra and leggings and then once we're both back to a presentable state, I move her so she's sitting sideways on my lap, her head tucked against me. My hand on her chin, I tilt her face up and kiss her lips.

"Hi, baby."

"Hi." A contented sigh. "That was fun."

"It was."

She's quiet for a moment and so am I. My thoughts are taking me everywhere. Her breathing evens out within a few minutes, her body heavier against me as she falls asleep. It doesn't take long before I succumb too only to have us both wake up in Paris.

WHEN WE ARRIVE IN PARIS, and I turn on my phone, I'm greeted by a text.

> Jacob: I'm not fucking around. You have thirty-six hours to have your fun and then the games begin, and we follow our schedule. A handler will meet you in Paris at the train station and take your things to your hotel. You're under the name Scott Fitzgerald because as Lamar would say, it's Paris, bitch. I did NOT make you any dining reservations because as much as you can, you should stay away from tourist traps if you don't want to be recognized or photographed. You've been lucky thus far. Don't fuck it up!

"Well then," I say, handing my phone to Fallon who yawns and then snorts out a laugh when she reads it.

"I like him. He's a drill sergeant with excellent taste."

"He's definitely that," I tell her as we step off the train only to be immediately intercepted by a woman who is about my height and size with blond hair and a no bullshit expression.

"Mr. Fitzgerald?"

"That's me."

"Excellent." No smile. Not even a crack in her armor. She's also American. "I'm Adira Rainey. Your assistant Jacob asked that I meet you and your companion here. I will take your luggage and make sure everything in your suite is arranged for you. Here are your key cards. You are already checked in and have access to the hotel's private entrance and elevator. Should you change your mind and decide you require security, our staff is discreet and available twenty-four-seven. I am your personal valet while you are in Paris. My number is on the back of the card."

She hands me a cardboard room key jacket with the name of our hotel and her information on it. The keys are tucked inside, and I quickly slide it into my pocket.

"Thank you, Ms. Rainey." I reach out and shake her hand and immediately regret it. The woman makes The Rock look like a tiny kitten, and she has the grip to match.

She gives a curt nod and then she's gone, taking our suitcases with her and another man who is equally austere.

"Yeesh. Think we'll ever see those again?"

"Are you kidding? A woman like that, she'll probably have everything dry cleaned and hung up by the time we get back to the..." I slip out the card out of my pocket. "George V."

"Oh." Fallon's eyebrows bounce suggestively. "Swanky, swanky. Do you always travel in such luxury, Mr. Fitzgerald?"

We start walking through the train station, keeping a bit of distance between us. I have my hat on, but I doubt it matters. We're in Paris and I'll be the first to admit, it's the most pathetic of disguises ever. Usually, I get by unrecognized because people don't expect you to be where they are. If that makes sense.

"Not usually. Ninety percent of my life is spent in Boston at my place or one of the guys' places, or my LA place, or on a tour bus."

"Phew." She sighs dramatically. "I was worried I'd have to start dressing and acting like a Kardashian or one of those Real Housewives chicks in order to keep up with you."

I roll my eyes at her. "Please, you act like you're not rolling in money."

She makes a show of rolling her eyes back at me. "I'm a doctor. I lived the life of a med student and after that a resident. Ninety percent of my time is spent in scrubs with some form of child goo on me."

My nose scrunches up and once again, I partially vomit in my mouth. "Child goo? And no, I'm not asking for you to elaborate on that."

She gives an exaggerated shudder. "I wouldn't. Lucky for me, nothing grosses me out except food."

"Right. That." I give her a wicked sideways grin. "I was thinking about that."

She shakes her head adamantly as we step out into the early evening sun, and both put on our shades over our eyes. "Don't even think about it."

"But this is Paris." I pan my hand out to the city in front of us and holy hell, Paris. Gives you a flutter in your chest every time. "If ever there was a place to get over your phobia of food-borne illnesses, it's here."

"No thanks."

Now that we're out of the train station, I grab her hand and we start walking without any real agenda. "You do know you can get salmonella and botulism and whatever else from non-meat and fish items, right?"

"Shush it, Monroe. Not helping."

"That's *Fitzgerald*. And careful or I'll start referring to you as Mrs. Fitzgerald."

She frowns. "Right now, it's all a step above Lark."

My head swivels in her direction, her dark tone throwing me. "Huh?"

She shakes her head, brushing me off. "Nothing. I like this game we've started. The one where we're different people living a different life and reality is the mean popular girl everyone totally hates and secretly tells to fuck off."

"Do I need to question this? How long was I asleep on that train?"

I get a hard, wet smack on my cheek. "Buy me dinner, Mr. Fitzgerald since I am not allowed to use any of my own funds and then take me to bed or lose me forever."

I bump my hip into her as we meander along. "For the record, I love it when you talk *Top Gun* to me."

"Then you understand my meaning."

I smirk, twirling her into my chest until her neck cranes up at me and her eyes are locked on mine. "You ready to do Paris with me, Fall Girl?"

"Let's go see what trouble we can get into."

I plan to. Even as part of me still wonders if there's something she's not telling me.

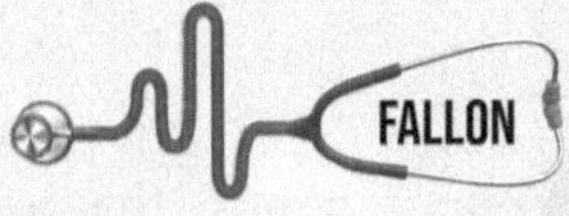

25

My phone was blowing up like a steady stream of grenades for the last hour of the train ride. Grey slept through it, and I haven't mentioned anything to him yet. Not because I'm trying to keep something from him. It's that I'm not sure what I plan to do with the information I got.

Maybe something. Possibly nothing. I don't know.

When I talked to my mother in Rome that day, it became all too clear to me—business.

That was the word repeated to me over and over again. Business.

Lark business. Astley business. Business that had me as the unwitting centerpiece. It stirred in my head like a witch's brew, the truth a poison to my soul. Bacchus can lie and proclaim love all he likes, but I know the truth.

It took a bit to push it aside along with an Oscar-worthy performance not to alert Grey to my inner dismay. Eventually, I focused on the guy and the place and that did the trick.

Grey and I ended up walking for hours, talking, holding hands, exploring, and getting lost. Yesterday at this time, everything was so uncertain between us. Now it all feels like it's coming together and while I can't help but relish in that, there's a large part of me that worries about it.

Not because it's too easy.

Not because we both want it and something this good invariably feels like it's meant to fail.

Not even because it's completely changed everything, going from best friends one minute to a couple in love the next.

But because there are so many who want to see it fail and are willing to go to extremes to make that happen.

For tonight though, nothing outside can touch us. It's freaking Paris, which is arguably one of the most romantic cities in the world. The sun is just starting to set, the air growing cooler with it. Our feet ache. Our bones are weary. And my stomach is officially no longer able to be ignored when it lets out a loud growl.

Grey snorts out a chuckle, his head swiveling in my direction with an amused smirk on his lips. "Hungry?"

I poke his side at his teasing lilt. "Aren't you?"

"Yes, but I couldn't decide where we should eat. Every restaurant on this street looks incredible."

It's true. We're in the Marais or 4th arrondissement and if I spoke the language and could work here as a doctor, I might consider moving. That's how cool and beautiful and amazing this place is.

"What about that one?" I ask, pointing to an adorable smaller café with outdoor seating and gas lanterns. It looks a little less formal than a few of these places, but still has that bistro, French chic feel to it.

"Let's go scope out the menu."

"Good call."

Crossing the cobblestone street, he quickly glances over the menu and Grey is all smiles. "Yes. This one for sure. It's crowded in there, which is always a good sign, and it smells amazing."

Without allowing me to properly peruse the menu, he drags me in, requesting a table, preferably one in the back. I'd be tempted to eat outside, but we're not exactly dressed for it. Grey's leather jacket didn't quite bounce back the way he'd hoped after our fight in the rain and I'm only wearing a sweater and a light jacket.

The restaurant is dark, the only lighting coming from small overhead pendant lights that look more like stars than lights and votive candles on the tables. We end up sitting side by side in a corner booth of sorts, but it gives us a perfect vantage to look out and people watch, which has been my favorite activity of the day.

I settle in next to him, slowly looking over the menu that is completely in French. "Do you want me to order for you?" he offers. His French is much better than mine. In general, his knowledge of languages is better than mine. He seems to have the basics down for several and I know that's come from all the touring he's done.

"Uh. Maybe," I say as I try to figure out what each word is. "It'll take me forever to Google Translate everything otherwise."

"All right. I'll get us a bunch of things to try."

I give him a raised eyebrow because I know this devious man.

"What?" He's the picture of innocence. "Don't you trust me?"

Oh boy.

"Um. I think I do."

His hand covers his chest. "I'm hurt, babe. Truly."

I roll my eyes. "Fine. But please remember I'm hungry and would like to eat the food that you order."

"I'll be good."

"Don't make me regret taking Chinese in high school." Though I was never very good at it. I only took it because my father told me it would be a better language to know, but I struggled terribly with it. I'm a math and science girl and honestly, working at the clinic, I wish I spoke Spanish or Vietnamese since many of my patients there do.

"You're very cute when you're nervous." He leans in and kisses my lips. Then he smiles. "Do you know how good it feels to finally be able to do that? Just lean in and kiss you without having to think or worry about it?"

"I still can't believe you've felt this way all these years and never told me."

He frowns, looking down at the table "Would it have changed anything between us?"

"I don't know," I tell him honestly. "I've been asking myself that question a lot since last night. It's so hard to figure out an answer. My family hates yours. My mother using your father as a revenge piece against my father was like the ultimate betrayal to him. I'm not sure my parents have said five words to each other since. Plus, it's not exactly as if our lives ever lined up all that well until now."

"True. But that never changed anything for me."

Guilt hits me like a sucker punch. "I had just started seeing Bacchus and somehow instinctively I knew I could never give him a real chance if you were still in my life." My hand cups his jaw, running my thumb back and forth. "I don't think I'll ever forgive myself for that though."

He leans in and kisses me again, softer this time. Sweeter. Forgiving. Our foreheads press together, and we stare into each other's eyes. "The saddest goodbyes happen when you want to hold on, but you know you can't. It just wasn't the right time for us then, Fall Girl. But it is now."

"It is now. I love you." The words flow past my tongue like water off a cliff. Effortlessly.

Our waiter picks this moment to come over and Grey ends up ordering us a bottle of red wine—that I understood—and a bunch of other things I couldn't pronounce let alone figure out what they were. It isn't until our first two dishes arrive that I decide to take back every word of love, adoration, and praise I've ever said about him.

"What in the absolute motherfuck is that?" I point to the plate before me. The other one is a salad, but the plate in front of me looks like...

"Frog legs."

I glare at him. And it isn't just any glare. It's a glare that I learned from my mother so simply put, it should make his balls shrivel up into raisins. But Greyson isn't a normal human. He's fucking Greyson Monroe and his smile is proud and unwavering.

"I'm not eating that."

"Sure you are," he asserts. "You're going to try one of everything I ordered."

"Um. No, I'm not."

"Um. Yes, you are."

"Greyson."

"Fallon," he mocks, and I'm a half-beat from strangling the life from him. If he's lucky, I'll resuscitate him, though he should be warned, I work on children and not adults so results may vary.

"I'm not doing it."

He rolls his eyes at me, picks up one of the multi-jointed, scrawny, white legs that appear to be coated in what I'm assuming are herbs and takes a bite. I legit almost throw up and nothing—I repeat nothing—makes my stomach roll. I won't go into details, but as a doctor, you see the grossest things on the planet. Humans, by nature, are disgusting.

This is worse.

"You're eating Kermit," I deadpan, and he chokes on his bite, washing it down with a sip of his wine.

"He tastes like chicken."

My hands fly. "Oh, come on! You can't use that cliché."

"It does." He laughs, wiping his mouth with his napkin and putting the now meatless bones—*hurl*—down on the plate. "I swear it. It tastes like chicken. At the very least, it's cooked and won't make you sick."

I shake my head. "I seriously cannot do it. I'll throw up."

He gives me his most disappointed frown. "Where's the adventure girl who got on a plane alone to fly to Rome?"

"She was drunk!"

He slides my wine at me. "Drink up then."

"You can't make me."

"I'll give you five orgasms tonight," he promises, picking up the frog leg and dangling it at me, and holy shit, it freaking moves like the damn thing is swimming.

"Please stop that."

"Come on, Fall. It's not as gross or as scary as you're making it seem. You can totally do this. One bite for five orgasms."

I gnaw on my lip, watching him eat it. "They better be the best orgasms ever."

A wolfish grin spears his lips. "Any way you want me to deliver them, I will."

I groan and reach for my wine, downing the entire glass in three large gulps. He tops me off, but I can't do it. I just can't! I take a bite of the other thing because that's a salad and it's safe and it's really good.

Grey meanwhile finishes off the leg, and I watch as he chews on the thing like it's the best thing he's ever eaten. I can't tell if he's putting on a show for me or not. All I know is there isn't enough wine or promises of orgasms to get me through this.

"I can't touch it. I'm too afraid."

"Just open your mouth and I'll put it in."

I snicker. "It sounds like we're teenagers talking about a blow job."

"Yes, only this time using your teeth is encouraged."

I down my second glass of wine, lick my lips, and then pinch my eyes shut. My heart is thrashing in my chest, and I swear, a cold sweat breaks out across my forehead.

"Open for me."

My head flies back and forth and I scoot away from him. "Oh my God! I can't. I can't!"

"You can. Stop overthinking this. Open for me."

"Ah!" My eyes scrunch so tight I see bursts of light, and I open my mouth, gripping the edge of the table. I feel it against my lips first. Warm. A little slimy, but I think that's just the sauce it's in. It tastes like fresh herbs and butter and when it hits my teeth, I force myself to take the tiniest of bites and not throw up all over Greyson or the restaurant.

Once the meat hits my tongue, I shove Grey away and swallow whatever I bit in one gulp, grateful it wasn't bigger, and I didn't choke on it. My eyes spring open and I go for my wine, chasing it down.

Grey tsks at me. "That was pathetic."

"Don't care. It counts. Now please, nothing else."

The rest of dinner is relatively uneventful. The other dishes are all stews and cassoulets and things that require hours of cooking and aren't things like snails or even bunnies or goats, and yes, those were evidently on the menu.

It's all delicious and after finishing off the bottle of wine, we find ourselves walking again along the streets, curled into each other through a fine mist of rain. The street lamps glow against the hazy air and with the wine flowing through our veins, it doesn't feel cold or wet, it feels magical.

He's telling me about some of his adventures touring both

with the guys and solo and before I know how the words escape, I blurt out, "I want to move in with you."

He freezes in the middle of the sidewalk and turns to face me, taking my other hand in his. "You're serious?"

I swallow and nod, staring up into his deep, dark eyes brimming with hope. God, this man, he gives me butterflies like nothing else.

"You're not just saying that because you're technically homeless and possibly a little buzzed from the wine?"

"Well, that's certainly part of it."

"Fall—"

"I'm kidding. That's not why I'm saying it. I could go home and get myself a place, but I think I'd always be at your place, or you'd always be at mine and we'd always be together anyway."

"We would," he agrees. "Whenever I'm in Boston, I'd be with you."

"You realize we've only been together a day."

"I'm not saying it'll be easy. I've never lived with anyone before other than the guys or my band when we're touring, but that's very different. Still, I don't care."

"I'll have to get my stuff from Bacchus. It'll be messy. He might make it difficult."

"All of this is going to be messy and difficult. Especially for you and I know that. I'm not making light of it. I know what being with me means for you and your life up until now. But I'll do anything I can to help and support you. If you choose this with me, I'll spend forever making sure you never regret it."

I take our joined fingers and slide them up to my shoulders before I release his hands, leaving them to slide around my neck, and then I do the same with him. "If I didn't choose you, I'd always regret it. Not the other way around."

Leaning up on my tiptoes, I kiss him.

In the middle of the sidewalk.

In the middle of Paris.

In the middle of a misting rain.

We kiss and kiss and kiss. Sweeps of his tongue and whispers in his ear and smiles along my jaw and nips up his neck. It's kissing for the sake of kissing. It's kissing because we can and any separation in this moment feels strange and unwelcome. It's not kissing with an end goal of sex or orgasms.

It's kissing like lovers.

It's kissing that takes us into dark corners and against walls and eventually into the back of an Uber and up into our hotel suite. It's kissing that has clothes stripped and breaths growing heavier. It's kissing that takes us deep into the night.

Eventually, I collapse, sated and exhausted on the bed while Grey goes to the living room with his guitar. I fall asleep listening to the sound of his voice and the strings of music he's plucking. I have no idea how late or early he ends up working. All I know is that he's rediscovering his muse and I love to believe I have everything to do with that.

By the time I wake to the morning sun, Grey is completely out beside me. I do everything I can not to wake him as I quickly get dressed and head out into the Parisian morning, desperate for authentic French baked goods for breakfast.

The concierge informs me there's a patisserie around the corner and when I walk in there, inhaling the scent of freshly baked breads and drooling over the sight of the different home-made jellies and jams they have, I know I'm in the right place.

I order us a baguette, a plain and chocolate croissant, an apple torte thing, some salted butter, a selection of jams and return to the hotel, only to realize I forgot coffee. Which feels like the ultimate crime. Arms loaded with warm bags—drool— I enter the café downstairs and they tell me they'll deliver up coffee service for us.

By the time I step back on the elevator, I realize I haven't stopped smiling.

We have all day to explore Paris and then tomorrow we're

traveling to the festival, which I'm growing more and more excited for. All the different bands and artists who will be there and the fact that I'll have VIP, backstage access to all of it—I can't wait!

Grey told me his brother and friends are flying in and I keep flip-flopping back and forth between nervous and excited about that. I haven't seen those guys in so many years and I can only hope they'll be okay with what's going on between me and Grey.

The door to our suite clicks softly behind me and I go into the dining room—another ridiculously over-the-top suite— and set everything down on the table, just as there's a knock on the door. I don't hear any sound, so I assume Grey's still sleeping, and I pad softly toward the door, shocked that the coffee is already here.

Only when I open the door, I realize it isn't the coffee. Bacchus is here.

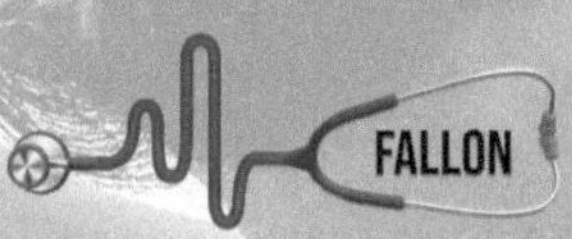

26

I'll be honest, the last person I expect on the other side of the hotel room door is Bacchus. At the same time, I'm also strangely relieved he's here. We talked that one time on the phone and since then it's been all one-sided texts. Having it out in person after everything that's gone down, after all the information I received yesterday feels right.

But first things first.

"How did you find me?"

He scowls at my less than warm reception, plowing past me into the suite though I didn't invite him in.

"I knew you were headed to Paris," he tells me spinning around. "Dillon told me that."

Dillon. That sniveling twin of mine gave me up. And here I thought he was one of my buddies in crime.

"The rest was luck," he continues. "As it happens, I'm staying here as well and saw you walk into the restaurant I was dining in."

Damn. All because I forgot the coffee. Interesting though because somehow, I don't think he knows I'm here with Greyson. He's not looking around. No, his bright blue eyes are locked on me. His entire focus on every inch of me and nowhere else.

With any luck, I can kick him to the curb and end this all before Greyson wakes up.

In a flash, he's on me, hands on my shoulders, eyes boring into mine. "Fuck, Fallon. I've missed you. Jesus, I've missed you." He blows out a heavy breath. "I love you, Dumpling. I love you and I will never be unfaithful to you or ever speak down about you again. Please, I'm so sorry. You have to forgive me."

"You actually expect me to believe that?" I'm beyond incredulous. The man has been an actor for three and a half years and had clearly reached his end with it. That's what I heard when he was on the phone with Tommy.

He's sorry he got caught.

That he slipped up and I happened to be there to overhear it.

Not to mention the name Dumpling makes me want to strangle him. Clearly it's because he thinks I'm fat. Who calls another person a dumpling?

A harsh sigh. "I flew all the way to Paris for you and you're still questioning my love for you?"

"You didn't fly to Paris because you love me, and we both know it."

He's growing more agitated by the second. "What are you doing, Fallon? You hear me blowing off steam, saying shit I didn't mean on a call with a friend, and you chuck your ring at me, pack a bag, and hop a flight? We've been together almost four years, and this is how you do this?"

When he puts it like that, it makes me sound irrational. Possibly wrong in my actions.

I'll be honest, I've asked myself that question too. But part of me also realizes that he's a gaslighter. A masterful one at that. Because there was so much more to this than me simply flying off the handle at hearing him talk down about me. That alone was a red flag and I'm glad I followed my instinct because fuck him with that.

It's amazing to me now the things I took and accepted while I was with him, only to realize how toxic and sick they were now that I'm in a good relationship. I suppose when you're in it, you make excuses and overlook it without even realizing it sometimes. It isn't until we're confronted with something positive and healthy and *loving* that we come to understand all that we deserve and should have had from the start.

I laugh. It's bitter. For a lot of reasons. "Soooo, you talk about fucking another woman, how boring I am in and out of bed, that you're only marrying me for my pedigree, and that I'm fat, and you expect grace, composure, and considerations?"

I'm genuinely curious so I wait him out. He doesn't like my question though. It annoys him to no end.

"I already explained what all of that was."

"Oh. Right. Blowing off steam. I know, it must suck getting into an arranged marriage with a woman you don't like and aren't all that attracted to simply to please daddy and become the next president."

He blanches but covers it in the blink of an eye. "I don't know what you're talking about or where you got that—"

"So, not so funny thing. When we spoke in Rome, you hinted at business. My mother mentioned something similar, and though I've heard you all say that a thousand times before, how us getting married is also good for business and politics and never gave it much thought before, this time I did. I overheard you accept a bribe from Tommy who is a federal prosecutor and that also got me thinking. So I did some digging."

"And?" His voice is cooler than ice.

I push him away from me, keeping my voice even and my expression severe. "And I know everything. I know the pressure your father has been putting on you for years. I know how you bought off grades in law school and how you barely passed the bar. I know how you blackmailed your boss in Boston to gain a partnership. I know you've been accepting bribes and shuffling the money around to dummy accounts that you thought wouldn't trace back to you. I know my mother and you arranged for us to meet years before we ever did and paid you to make it happen with the contingency that you'd have to pay her back if that didn't happen. I know you've also worked out a deal with my father. I also believe your father doesn't know about any of this. Then again, he's always had more scruples than my parents. I was the centerpiece of this scheme. The perfect woman to make you look wholesome and likable. The pathetic part? I tried to love you. I gave up the most important parts of me for you and for them."

"How could you know any of that?" Vitriol drips from his every word.

"I'm a Lark," I tell him since I'll never let him know I contacted Lenox who found way too many things on Bacchus's home computer and in his email. "We're resourceful and I learned from the best." I pause here, glaring at him, my ire creeping back up. "Are you going to lie to me now? Give me some Hollywood line like, 'It might have started out that way, but I fell for you in spite of it?'"

He puffs out a breath, spins in a small circle, and then comes back to me. His body sags, his face falling toward the floor as his hands meet his narrow hips. "I don't know what to say except I'm sorry. Yes, my father's expectations were always more than I could meet. Yes, I cut corners and did what I had to do to get where I needed to be. Yes, you were the middle person and yes, your parents and I engineered it that way. You didn't deserve that from me or from them." His eyes meet mine again, beseeching. "Don't let this ruin us though. We're perfect together and I promise to be faithful and doting. You think I don't love you, but I wouldn't have been faithful to you all this time if I didn't. Please." Hands on my shoulders, desperation pours off him in waves. "*Please,* Fallon. In one week we're getting married and it's going to be everything you've ever dreamed of. Everyone wins with this. We're going to have the life both of us have always wanted. Us. Together, Fallon, because there is no way that happens with us apart."

That last part is the truth. This life, the one he and our parents have envisioned only happens with us together. Still, he's lying. I know he is. He'll say whatever he has to say because he's painted into a corner.

I shove him off me for a second time, creeping closer to the door. I want him gone. I want him gone now and before Grey wakes up.

"It doesn't matter because I don't care about that life. I'm not sure I ever did, which is why I went along with it. All I've ever done is follow the rules and do what everyone told me I should. But that's all finished now. I don't want that life. I don't want Philadelphia. I don't want politics. Most importantly, I don't want you. It's over, Bacchus. All of this is. It was over the second I chucked my ring and our dinner at you. It's about fucking time you and my mother get that."

At that he grows mean, his expression a visual growl, and before I know what's happening, his hand grasps my upper arm. He spins us around and slams me into the wall by the door. Not hard, but enough to rattle me and cause a choked cry to past my lips.

"You think you have a choice in that," he seethes, his face inches from mine. "Think again, sweetheart. You're going to be Mrs. Astley, and you will stand by my side as a beautiful and obedient wife."

"Let go of me."

"Not a chance. Not until you agree to have this become part of our past and not our future. I'm not going to let you ruin me,

Fallon. I'm not going to let you ruin any of the plans we've had for years."

"No. It's too late. It's over."

He squeezes my arm tighter when I try to pry him away and I cry out in pain. "Don't be fucking stupid, Fallon. No way this is over. I wouldn't test me on that."

The way he has me pinned, I can barely move. My knee can't come up to strike. My free hand plants into his chest, pressing him back with everything I've got, but he catches it, circling my wrist with a bruising grip, his gaze fierce and unwavering. Except in the next second, he's pried away from me by the back of his hair as Greyson yanks on it by the roots. Bacchus lets out a pained cry, releasing me as he's dragged over to the door.

"Open that up for me, would you, Fall Girl? Your ex-fiancé was just leaving."

"What the fuck?" Bacchus yells as I scramble for the door. I get it open, but Bacchus kicks it shut, slamming it right in my face and making me jump back so I don't get hit with it. He twists in Greyson's arms, swinging wildly and landing a punch to Greyson's flank.

Grey oomphs, releasing Bacchus who staggers to the side, both of them breathing hard. Grey is fully dressed, his hair wet. He must have been in the shower all this time, which is why he didn't hear us.

Bacchus points, first at me and then at Greyson. "Him? You called him?" He laughs cruelly. "You're angry with me for wanting to cheat when you're already doing the same? Fucking whore."

Greyson's fist flies, slamming straight into Bacchus's gut. He doubles over, splinting his stomach with his forearm and spitting out a slew of curses and threats. Only Greyson isn't letting that ride. He grabs Bacchus's shirt, balling the fabric up in his fists and straightening him until they're nose to nose.

Greyson snarls at him. "Call her a whore again. I fucking dare you because it will be all the provocation I need. Don't imagine for a second that I'm not restraining myself right now for her sake. It would be a pleasure to end you right here, but I don't want to hurt my hands. Sorta need them to play, which is why I went for your gut. But I will break every bone in my hands along with every bone in your body if that's what it takes to get you away from Fallon. She told you she's done with you. She told you it's over. That's final."

He shoves Bacchus who stumbles back, falling against the door.

"You think I don't know about you?" Bacchus spits, his face ruddy, his hair a disheveled mess. "I know all about you two. I was watching Fallon for years before I made her mine. I knew she snuck off to be with you. I knew you two were fucking each other. I also know she walked away and left your loser ass behind for me. You think when she comes to her senses with this, when her family gets their hands on her that she won't do it again? She'll be sucking my dick again in no time."

Grey goes after him, the two colliding, the sound like thunder. Grey's shoulder smashes into Bacchus's chest, but Bacchus hits Grey in the face, making his head snap back. I scream, my hands covering my mouth, unsure what to do or how to stop them.

Grey recovers quickly and comes at Bacchus again, the two barreling into the wall and then onto the floor, rolling as they hit and punch and curse each other. Bacchus gains the upper hand for a second, pinning Grey down, but Grey is bigger and strong and manages to land an uppercut into Bacchus's jaw. The blow knocks Bacchus back, momentarily stunning him.

I shoot over, taking the opportunity to drag a fuming Greyson away before he does actually break his hand. As it is, he's got a split lip.

"Fucking coward," Bacchus snarls. "I will ruin your fucking

life, Monroe. Watch out, asshole, because you fucked with the wrong guy. I'll make you wish you were never born—"

"Shut up!" I bellow, holding Grey back when he tries to go around me to get at Bacchus again. Stepping directly in front of Bacchus, I stare straight at him. "Enough. This is done. If you don't make the announcement by tonight at five p.m. Paris time that the wedding is off, I will make one myself by six. If you so much as attempt to do something backhanded, I'll go to your father with the information I have. If you mention Greyson in anything, forget your father, I will go to the press. If you paint the breakup or me in a negative light, I will go to the press. After that, if you still want to play dirty, I will give everything I have over to the Boston DA and let them sort it out. And since you're a lawyer, I know you're aware that many of the things I have on you are illegal."

Bacchus straightens, the fires of hell burning his eyes, his fists clenching and unclenching. He wipes blood from his mouth with the back of his hand. "Your mother is involved financially. Your father made a deal too. You'd never publicly shame them like that. You'd never potentially cost your father his seat in the Senate and destroy your family name and legacy. We were giving you this. Me coming here and playing nice. You think your family will let this go? Don't be fucking stupid, Fallon. This only ends one way. With us getting married."

"I wouldn't test me on this. I'm not bluffing," I promise him. "I don't care about my father or my mother or my family name and legacy. They made their bed, and I won't allow them to use me ever again. Don't be fucking stupid, Bacchus," I mock, throwing his words back at him. "You know the kind of physical evidence I have on you. Don't do as I say and you're looking at prison. I'm not making a deal. I'm making a real and genuine threat. An amicable split and simple announcement is a gift to all of you."

Bacchus glowers at me good, long, and hard. I've painted

him into a corner, and he doesn't like it. Years of scheming being washed away before his eyes and a man with his level of ego won't take that well. Sucks for him, he doesn't have a choice.

Without another word, he spins around, opens the door, and leaves with a loud bang.

I hear him storm off and I sag in relief, my eyes closing as I take in a deep breath. Greyson spins me around and immediately pulls me into his chest, holding me close, his hand running down my hair, my face over his pounding heart.

"Are you okay? Did he hurt you?" His voice is frazzled, urgent.

"No. I'm okay." I think. I'm shaking like a leaf. "Are you okay?"

"Oh, I'm great. I only wish I had gotten another good hit on him."

"Men," I grumble, inwardly rolling my eyes. "Thank you for stepping in."

I'm not sure what Bacchus would have done. He's never been physical with me before. But in that moment, I wouldn't have put anything past him.

His lips press into my hair, and he holds me tighter. "I'm sorry. I should have been there to protect you from him. I was in the shower and had the bathroom door closed. I didn't hear you until I got back into the bedroom."

"I handled him."

He chuckles, cupping my face in his hand and dragging my gaze up to his. "I'll say. What the hell was all that? You've been holding out on me."

I wipe the drop of blood from his lip with my thumb and he sucks the digit and the blood into his mouth before kissing the pad of my thumb. "Your friend Lenox is very resourceful."

"Lenox," he wheezes out, eyes bursting open wide. "The fuck? You called Lenox and didn't tell me?"

"Sorry," I say, running my fingers along his jaw. "It was just a bunch of stuff my mom and Bacchus said that got me thinking and I needed it confirmed before I said anything to you about it. Well, that and I needed to sort through it all in my head and figure out what I was going to do with that information too. The truth wasn't exactly the easiest pill to swallow."

He kisses my cheeks, running his hands through my hair. "One thing to think it and another to know it?"

"Yes. Exactly that. I had heard Bacchus accept a bribe and do so in a way that made me believe it wasn't the first time he had done that. Turns out my parents and he had made a deal. A lot of money was sent to Bacchus as part of it. Years before we even met. The deal was, I'd marry Bacchus, he'd take over his father's senatorial seat, he'd serve a term, and then run for president with my father as his VP. A perfect political move. Only Bacchus has a big mouth and for a lawyer keeps emails and things on his computer that he should know better than to keep."

"Wow," Grey utters flummoxed.

As for me, it feels like a weight has been lifted from my chest. I'm sad too. Sad that it came to this. Sad that my family put me in this position in the first place. Sad that their own twisted greed and ambition was more important to them than their own daughter. The worst part? I wasn't surprised when Lenox sent all of this to me yesterday.

"I owe your friend a hug," I tell Grey.

"I think I do too. And maybe a punch for keeping this from me."

"No more punching, Mr. Monroe. You said it yourself, you need your hands for playing."

A beaming smile breaks free across his face. "Speaking of, I was up almost all night last night and I finished the song I had been working on and most of another."

My smile matches his. "Really? That's fantastic. I can't wait to hear it."

"Not yet," he says. "Soon though. When I'm positive it's ready."

"Okay."

"You ready to go out and see Paris?"

I laugh. Paris. Right. It's been a busy morning. Just then there's a knock at the door and both Grey and I freeze until the guy says, "Room service," in a very French accent.

We sag in unison. "I ordered coffee and went out early and got us breakfast."

A kiss to my lips. "Fantastic. Let's eat. Then Paris. Something tells me this might be the last chance we get to take it easy. It's going to be a busy few days and I'm not simply talking about the festival."

No kidding. But first, I have to make a call I'm not looking forward to at all.

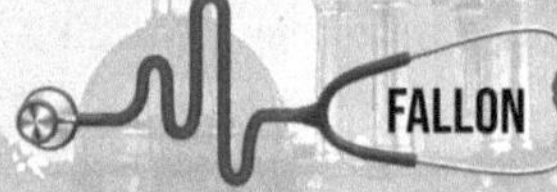

27

I've been avoiding my mother all week. I told her I didn't want to be her and was not going to marry Bacchus and ended it there. The smartest thing I did this entire week was listening to Grey and Lenox when they told me not to use my passport or my credit cards if I could avoid it.

For the most part, other than a quick flash of a passport here and there without anyone documenting my name, I've stuck hard and fast to that. It's how no one in my family knew I was with Grey. It's kept him safe and protected from them. If they had known I was with him at any point on this trip, they would have done what they could to destroy him.

All the things we were so anxious about—the pictures in Rome, the risk of people recognizing him whenever we were out, those dress people in Monte Carlo stealing pics or posting something about Greyson with a woman—never happened.

No. In the end, it was my brother.

Dillon gave up that I was in Paris—I had never told him I was with Greyson so he didn't know that either—and the time to ask him why, especially when I felt we had struck up an alliance of sorts, will come. When I called him in the middle of the night and told him we needed to talk, he was more receptive than I thought he would be.

I told him what Bacchus said about me. Told him my suspicions about me being the center ring of some sort of master plan—I didn't know any of the finer details of until yesterday—and that I couldn't be part of it or them. He shocked me when he told me he'd support me in whatever decision I made. I thought he'd forever be on my parents' side.

But it seems now that he was. Only pretending to be on my side to garner my whereabouts. A wolf in sheep's clothing, I'm grateful I didn't tell him anything I discovered from Lenox.

It hurts, but I can't focus on that right now.

Grey and I devour breakfast—which was out of this world incredible—and then I take to pacing the suite.

"You don't have to do this now," Grey says, watching me with sympathetic eyes. "We can go out and enjoy Paris."

I flip around. "And if someone sees us today? Last night was different and you know it. Today the risk is everywhere with the festival starting tomorrow. Plus, look where we are. The most elite part of town and out that window is bright sunshine that will make us visible to the world."

Grey walks over to me, stopping my rant with a hug. "Any storm willing to find us, we'll meet head-on. Together."

"You're entirely too lovable. This is your fault."

He laughs lightly, rocking me from side to side. "Actually, I think that it's reversed. If you weren't too lovable, I'd never have taken on the risk of a society lady like yourself."

I grin stupidly, propping my chin on his chest and gazing up at the tall bastard. "I'm the lady of breeding and you're the bad boy I can't stay away from who wants to steal me away from it all? Is that it?"

"I think that pretty much sums us up."

"I always did like a good forbidden romance."

His lips meld to mine, kissing me slowly, but deep as hell,

rendering me breathless within seconds. Calloused fingers start to slide up beneath my shirt and cup my breast and if I don't stop this now, I'll never call my mother and unfortunately, I have to.

She has to know my threats are real, because I know she won't naturally believe me to be capable and if she talks to Bacchus, they could come up with an alternate plan.

"I have to call my mother."

He groans and it's not a happy groan. "Nothing kills my erection faster than mentioning your mother."

"I'll make it up to you later. Promise."

His expression grows serious. "Listen, I know you're determined with this, but don't do something you can't undo for me. I can take care of myself and whatever comes at us, we'll manage. I'm not so worried about it. There is very little they can do to me."

"Other than ruin your name publicly, you mean?" I cock an eyebrow.

"Babe, I could take out a fleet of baby ducks waddling across the street looking insanely adorable and I'd still be okay. As strange as it is, the public has a way of forgiving artists faster than almost anyone. Likely because they expect us to fuck up and when we do, there is very little shock in it, and they get over it faster because of that."

"That scarily makes a ton of sense and oddly seems so true. Plus, you're hot. Isn't that what they say? That juries tend to acquit good-looking people far more than ugly ones."

"Another valid point," he quips with a half smirk. "So you see, I'll be fine."

"So modest." I roll my eyes.

His knuckles brush my cheek. "I'm serious though. I appreciate it. I do. But I love you and I don't want to see you hurt any more than you already are."

"I know. Thank you. I'm hoping it never comes to any of

that and if the government or the police or whomever ever find out their secrets, it won't be from me."

"Me too. Go call your mother." A kiss to my lips and he releases me, taking my hand and spinning me in the direction of my phone. "Do you want me here or do you want space?"

Good question. "Maybe don't go far."

"You got it. After you've handled Cruella Lark, we'll go get lost in Paris."

Another kiss and then he's heading back toward the bedroom with his guitar—I swear, now that he's in a groove, that thing isn't far from his hands. I sit on the sofa only to think better of it and stand. Sitting feels too relaxed. Standing is the equivalent of my power suit, and it gives me more confidence.

I dial her up and she picks up on the first ring. No shocker there. I have to imagine she's already spoken with Bacchus.

"Fallon," she answers, her tone hiding none of her displeasure. "I'm shocked to finally hear from you. I have to say, by this point, I would have thought you'd have come to your proper senses. You were always a much smarter girl than how you're behaving now."

I walk slowly over to the window, taking in the view of the Eiffel Tower in the distance. My heart that had been beating wildly with nerves when I dialed her number slows. I don't fear this woman and she no longer has any power over me.

I suck in a deep breath. "I'm not going to ask why you did everything you did. The answer is obvious. But I do want you to know that if Bacchus or you don't make the announcement by five Paris time, I will. If for any reason, any of you play dirty or try to hurt me or Greyson in any way, I will go to the press with evidence of your financial indiscretions and the deal Dad made."

"After all we've done for you, all the sacrifices we made for you, you dare to threaten us? What kind of daughter does that?"

"Consider it insurance that Greyson stays safe and out of this. I won't risk him. Or myself."

"You've completely destroyed this family. I hope you're happy."

Nice try, but it's not going to work this time. "No, Mother. You did. You and Dad both. The only people you've ever cared about are yourselves. Your narcissism knew no limits and you didn't care who you trampled along the way as long as you came out on top in the end. But you weren't as careful as you thought you were. I don't want this to turn uglier than it already has."

"The one to make it ugly was you," she yells, all her Lark polish and refinement gone. "You set all this in motion by running off to Europe instead of acting like a Lark and putting your family first!" She lets out a heavy sigh and she reins herself back in, calming her tone. "Fallon, please think about this. All you have to do is marry Bacchus. He cares about you. He's a good man who will treat you well."

I snort at that. "You can stop trying to sell him to me. I know exactly what kind of man he is and I'm not buying."

"Why are you doing this to us?" Her voice rises again with each word. "For the Monroe boy? He's a loser. Their whole family is a bunch of losers. Womanizing creeps who have no qualms about breaking up happy homes and families."

I want to point out the fact that one, we were never happy, and two, she's the one who went next door and seduced Mr. Monroe after physically catching my father with his latest mistress, but that's simply semantics right now.

"You want to screw around with him, fine," she continues. "You can. Just marry Bacchus. Everyone wins. You get to keep your... *friend*, and we get what we need."

Is she kidding me with that? Sadly, she's not.

I grip the edge of the French door that leads out onto the massive balcony. The side of my head falls to the glass. She doesn't get it and she never will. She's too self-absorbed to see anything beyond herself. For years they knew I'd never want that sort of relationship or life. It's why Bacchus went to such extremes to play the part of the somewhat loving partner. I can continue to go around in circles with this, but I have much better ways to spend my energy and time.

What's the definition of insanity? Doing the same thing over and over and expecting different results? Well, I'm done with allowing their manipulation and my own adolescent notion of family and love to continue making me insane.

I straighten and clear my throat, turning around and walking into the bedroom. Grey is sitting on a chair in the corner by the window, loosely strumming on his guitar, but pauses and sets it down when he sees me enter.

I reach my hand out to him and he stands, taking it, holding it, his eyes unwavering from mine.

I smile and give him a wink. "I'm not marrying Bacchus," I tell my mother even as I look at Grey. "And I won't live that sort of life. That's final and unchanging. I'm in love with Greyson. I'm *with* Greyson and that won't change either. You need to tell Dad since I know you've kept him in the dark all this week. If you don't, he's my next call, but since I haven't spoken to my father on the phone in what I think might actually be years, I'm not sure how well that will go down. Either way, I'll anticipate the announcement at five or you'll have mine by six. And remember what will happen if you dare try anything else."

I disconnect the call and toss my phone on the bed.

"Ready to go see Paris?" I ask Grey without skipping a beat.

"I am, actually. Did you have anything in mind?"

"I'm dying to go to that museum where Monet's Water Lilies are, and I think there's a very pretty park not far from there we can walk in. Oh, maybe we can have a picnic!"

He steps into me, holding me against him, smiling down at me with so much love my bones ache with it.

"Let's do it," he says. "Incidentally, I've hired that security team for the day. They'll be discreet, and hopefully we won't need them, but I'd also rather not take any chances."

"No, I think that's wise. Especially with that five o'clock deadline looming."

If they don't follow through with it, I'm going to have to start making good on my threats.

28

The announcement didn't come at five. It came at five-thirty, and I know that was purely a manipulative power play designed to make Fallon sweat. Fuckers. My girl was ready though. She was armed and prepared and didn't even bat an eyelash when she told me she would make her own announcement at six if still nothing had been reported.

For a girl who has lived her life following someone else's rules, she's come a long way and I couldn't be prouder of her.

It almost felt too easy. Something Fallon said and I acknowledged once she read it aloud to me.

Boston Landing Special Announcement:

Boston Landing has just picked up an exclusive announcement that will break all Bostonian's hearts. We truly regret to inform you that Bacchus Astley and Fallon Lark have officially called off their relationship one week before they were set to walk down the aisle to wedded bliss.

This is the joint statement the couple released exclusively to us.

"After a lot of consideration, prayer, and love, we've made the difficult decision to call off our engagement. We both genuinely care and respect one another and look forward to maintaining our friendship for decades to come. We kindly request privacy during this tough time and are so grateful for your everlasting love and support."

STILL, I know it hurts her. I know all of this does. She's essentially turned her back on her family. A family who betrayed her to the highest, best suitor, but still. There hasn't been a peep from her father, and I know that's weighing on all of us. She doesn't trust that they're going to take this easy, and I appreciate that.

Speaking as a guy who might have killed his mother and had a father who hated his guts his entire life, I can say, it isn't easy being an orphan. I have my family—Zax plus our found family, and as we walked through the Tuileries on the way to the museum, I told her that she may be letting go of her family, but now that she's mine, she's part of the Central Square crew and we take care of our own.

Clearly, since Lenox broke about fifty federal and state laws to help her out.

When I texted him about this, his reply was, **Never underestimate the power of leverage and love.**

Words to live by. Especially from a guy who doesn't speak much.

Fallon read it with a smile glued to her face and a light in her eyes that spoke of freedom. It was sexy as hell, and I fucked her silly all night until she passed out in my arms, and I went after my guitar. My Aurora. She and I have finally been talking a lot to each other. Other than Fallon, she is my greatest love.

My art.

The thing that pumps blood through my veins and coaxes my heart into rhythm.

But I only found her again once I forced myself to realize that it's okay if I don't top my previous album. It's okay if the charts don't love this new one as much as the last. My goal is my fans. And if I can reach just a few of them with my words and my sound, then that's enough for me. Not an easy mantra to accept when we live in a consumer-driven, money-requiring, make-it-or-break-it world.

I think the best art comes from letting go and in letting go Fallon and I found each other. In letting go, we both realized perfection is an illusion and fear should never hold you back from chasing your passions.

In embracing that, I am writing my best words.

My best songs.

Songs that I will forever be proud of, even if they don't end up as my greatest hits.

The sun rises at the perfect hour in Paris, but the truth is, time waits for no man as my assistant Jacob proves right this minute. The front door to our suite thrums with a pernicious pounding and I groan, rolling over and dragging Fallon's sweet body against mine.

"If that's your parents or your ex..." I let that one hang because I'm not sure how to finish that.

"Not them. Bacchus is back in the US, no doubt accepting loving hugs and snuggles from women who learned he's available and believe I broke his heart, and my parents hate me too much."

"That only means they could be pounding down the door vigilante style."

"Have you met the Larks?"

She has a point.

Bang. Bang. Bang. "Open the door, bitch. My man made me come with him and that means I need coffee, a croissant, and an amazing day of shopping."

I groan. Lamar. I should have known it was Lamar.

"We should get that," Fallon murmurs without opening her eyes or moving her body.

"Fallon Lark," Lamar continues to yell. "Open the door. We have things we have to do, woman."

"Ugh!" she moans.

"I heard that. Move your pretty ass!"

"He didn't actually hear that, right?"

"I doubt it," I tell her. "That's just Lamar."

"Ugh!" she groans again and then we both peel ourselves up and out of the bed, throwing on the first things we come by since we're both naked.

I swing the door open and Lamar gasps, his dark eyes wide behind his clear-framed glasses, his dark-skinned hand covering his pink lips. "Honey. I'm all for rough sex, but at least have the decency to run a brush through your hair and a makeup remover wipe across your eyes before you open the door to total strangers."

She snickers, sticking out her hand to him. "Hi. I'm Fallon. You must be Lamar."

He grins. "Baby girl, I'm your fairy godmother today. If my understanding is correct, you're amiable to other people dressing you. Was I misled?"

She glances at me and then back at him. "You weren't. But I'm a doctor."

He rolls his eyes. "Like I care? Don't give me that humble, woman of the children and people nonsense. I have Monroe Paris and Babas Salon opening early for us. Oh and—"

"Where is she? Let me at her."

"Aurelia," Lamar finishes just as Aurelia comes flying into

the suite, slamming into Fallon and practically knocking her over as she crushes her with a hug.

"Hi," Aurelia says, laughing in a slightly self-deprecating way as she pulls back. "Sorry, Lamar cut me out of the elevator in order to get to you first and I had to wait for the next one. I hope this isn't weird. I'm a total hugger and am so excited to see you. I don't know if you remember me—"

"Of course I remember you. And I'm totally great with hugging."

"Missed you too, Reils," I deadpan.

She waves me away over Fall's shoulder. "I'll get to you in a minute. I've had to deal with the sausage fest that is these guys for far too long and now you bring me not just any woman, but Fallon."

"It's great to see you again," Fall tells her sweetly. "It's been an insanely long time—"

"Since you've seen any of us." Zax walks in closely followed by Lenox, Asher, and Callan. The door shuts behind them and what in the world is going on? "True. But it's also been an insanely long time since I've seen my brother look this happy and mean it." Zax gives me a fist pound and then immediately goes over and hugs Fallon. Not something I saw coming, but he's far more in touch with his softer side than he used to be. He releases her and then stands beside Aurelia, his arm wrapped around her.

"Fall! Girl." Asher comes in and swoops Fallon up and off her feet in a huge swinging hug. "Weird. Now I know why Grey calls you that. Anyway, for the record, I always knew you'd come back to our guy. And Asher is an awesome name for a kid."

Fallon smacks his shoulder making him laugh as he sets her down, giving her a big wet kiss on her cheek and winking at me after he does. I don't even bother reacting.

"Doctor," Callan greets her with a hug. "It's great to see you. I've heard amazing things."

"Oh! Me too! And I'll soon be working at MGH in Oliver Fritz's practice."

Callan beams. "That's awesome. I'll be able to give you all the—"

"No one cares about your medical stuff," Lamar cuts him off. "What I need is for Fallon to go and pack up her shit, possibly shower, and then come with me and Aurelia."

"I wasn't expecting to open the door to all of you while I'm dressed like this." Fallon glances at me, her face bright red.

"Honey, that's what I was trying to tell you with the hair and makeup. Incidentally, I was totally lying. You don't have makeup all over your face. Actually, you look fucking fabulous, but if I didn't come up with a drama, Jacob would have never given me a girls' day to shop and spa. He was all, *work, work, work*," Lamar mocks Jacob as he rolls his eyes dismissively.

"Right. Well. Good to know about the makeup." Fallon takes a step back toward the bedroom. "Did you know about this?" she murmurs in my direction.

"No," I tell her, taking her hand and tugging her into my side. "It was my understanding that we were going to meet everyone this afternoon at the festival grounds."

"Change of plans," Jacob declares. "We all took the Monroe jet to get here. Fallon ending her engagement is all anyone in Boston is talking about right now and there are a ton of rumors and speculations with it."

"Great," she grumbles.

"Well, Grey might not care so much, but his PR team didn't feel like putting out any fires before the festival. We came here to separate you two." He holds up his hand to me when I open my mouth to argue that. "Only until this afternoon. Press isn't allowed in the artists' hotel so you can be together there as openly as you want and there are plenty of regular people who have full VIP backstage access for the shows. But for today, for Paris, please don't fight this. Besides, you owe me something while they're out shopping and going to the spa."

I get a meaningful look from Jacob and yeah, I owe him something. Something I've been sending him snippets of that he's chomping at the bit to get the rest of.

"Yes," Fallon asserts, glancing at me and then back at him. "I think you're right. The last thing I want to do is be the cause of anything unnecessary. Let me go pack up my stuff and get myself together. Since I totally haven't brushed my teeth, or clearly my hair and obviously forgot to wash my face last night before falling asleep, how about you all give me twenty minutes and then we can go shopping and to the spa?"

"Honestly, I think you look hot," Asher drawls, giving Fallon a big flirtatious once-over and then shooting me with a smirk this time. Bastard.

"Thank you. Because that doesn't make me feel any more awkward than I was two seconds ago."

"Sex hair is sexy," Asher tells her. "Own it. Grey certainly is. He looks like he's been electrocuted."

I flip him off.

"All of you go wait in the living room. Order room service or something. Fallon and I are going to shower."

"Are you actually going to shower or is that a euphemism for something else and we'll end up stuck out here for an hour?" Callan questions.

"An hour?" Asher snorts. "Dude, you're giving Grey way too much credit there."

"Oh, I wouldn't talk about performance," I tease, kissing the top of Fallon's head.

Asher's huge arms fly all around. "Fuck you! It was one time, and I had an excuse, okay."

"Uh-huh." That's Lenox and it's the most he's said since he's gotten here. No shocker there though.

"Wait. What is all this?"

Asher points at Fallon. "Nothing. Absolutely nothing." That finger swings at all of us. "Bro code of silence, gentlemen. Bro code of silence."

"Next time keep blue pills in your pocket and you won't need us to say silent," Callan drops and all of us break out into laughter. After Asher won the Super Bowl last year, he had an unfortunate mishap with a woman that needless to say left her unsatisfied and challenged his manhood and reputation. He also hasn't been able to stop obsessing over her since.

"Yeah. Ha. So funny. Just wait. I'll find that chick and rock her world."

"Until that never in a million years chance happens, I am going to order room service because I'm starving," Aurelia says. "Gentlemen, follow me. Let them go"—she pans a hand toward both of us—"do whatever it is they're going to do."

"Order something for us too, but not eggs for Fall Girl."

"I plan to order all the bread and pastries. Does that work for you?" Aurelia checks with Fall who eagerly nods.

Before they get very far, Fall grabs Lenox and drags him in for a hug, whispering things in his ear that I can't hear but that have him nodding and even smiling and I swear, blushing slightly. She gives him a kiss on the cheek and then I drag her into the bedroom, shutting and locking the door behind us, barely managing to shut out the sound of Lamar and Aurelia fighting over something.

"So that happened," I deadpan.

Fallon starts cracking up. "It sure did. Are they always like that?"

"Worse," I tell her taking off my shirt and going for my pants next. "They were contained since you haven't seen most of them since we were all teenagers."

She shakes her head. "I take it back. I'm so sorry, Grey, but I don't think we can be together anymore."

"Oh yeah?" I take a prowling step toward her.

Her hands jut protectively out in front of her as if that will stop me. "Yes. You were fun and all, but now that the trip is coming to an end and I was forced to meet your family again, no thanks."

In the blink of an eye I spring, tackling her to the bed. She lets out a loud shriek and I quickly cover her mouth with my hand to stifle it. "Shhh. You want them to come in here?"

"No!" she murmurs behind my hand, her eyes round and wide.

"Then you're going to have to be quiet while I eat you out."

Her body instantly warms against me, and all that terrified shock turns dark and hooded. "You wouldn't," she challenges, and I slip my hand away from her lips and slide it down her body until I'm cupping her pussy over her leggings.

"Ready to find out?"

29

FALLON

"**Y**our family is in the other room ordering room service," I hiss.

"Then you're going to have to be quiet," Grey says as he grinds his cock into the V of my spread thighs. "Can you do that for me, Fallon? Can you be my perfect princess and stay quiet while I eat your pretty cunt?"

Jesus. He's so filthy. And I'm so here for it, it's ridiculous.

I nod because words fail me. As it is, I'm not even sure I'm breathing.

"That's my good girl. Flip over."

Oh hell. It's a big suite and they're all loud, talking over each other. I'm sure they won't hear me. Or know what's happening in here.

I flip over onto my belly and before I can catch my breath, Grey is pulling my hips up into the air. With a firm yank, my leggings band around my knees and then fall away completely and I'm totally exposed to him. It tugs another gasp from my lips, but before I can make sense of much, a pillow is shoved in my face and then Grey is spreading my ass cheeks and licking me from my asshole down to my clit.

Holy mother Christmas! I bite into the pillow, my incisors tearing at the silky fabric as I try not to scream.

I get a smack to my ass that makes me moan. "Have to be quieter, babe."

Is he kidding me?

"Come on, Fall Girl. Spread these thighs for me and show me your paradise."

I do. I spread my legs indecently wide on the bed and allow him to use his hand to spear me open even wider. It's beyond lewd and nothing of me is left to the imagination as the stunning Paris sun gleams in through the floor-to-ceiling windows.

His tongue thrusts straight into my pussy and I arch, grappling at linens and I'm gone. Totally gone. His hot mouth on me and his hands groping and squeezing the globes of my ass and the naughtiness of people in the other room who could hear us or come in at any moment.

It's bliss. Pure bliss.

His tongue is a wicked instrument, thrumming and playing me to artful perfection. One hand spreads my ass cheeks wider, the other plunges two fingers inside me and I'm so open and exposed and he can see *everything*. It makes him feral. A savage animal. Hungry and desperate and not to be deprived.

He shoves my face deeper into the pillow and then he starts pounding my pussy with his fingers as he twists his head so his tongue and lips and even teeth can feast on my clit. It's beyond anything we've done. This angle. All this light. The way he's eating me.

I'm barely breathing.

It's so much.

The most delicious kind of obsession and I can't get enough of how it, how *he* consumes me.

He's grunting and groaning into me, the sound vibrating straight into my clit.

"Oh my God," I breathe, the sound swallowed by the pillow.

Only maybe not enough because I get a hard smack to my ass that has me moaning more, writhing myself against his stubbled jaw that feels nothing short of incredible against my sensitive skin.

"Quiet, Fallon, or I stop."

Fallon. The man never uses my full name unless he wants my full attention and right now, he has it. I press my lips together and bury my face as deep into the pillow as it will go. I don't even care if I suffocate.

His mouth is so warm, and his fingers are hitting me just right and the thumb on his other hand dips into my pussy and then "Oh fuck!" I cry out when he swirls my arousal around the tight ring of muscles in the back. He thrusts the wet digit into my ass as he holds my cheeks open with that hand and I am losing my fucking mind right now.

I squirm against him, fisting the pillow tighter against my face as the flames deep inside my core start to build and grow and multiply until I'm feeling nothing but toe-curling pleasure. I don't even know who I am right now. The woman allowing this to happen when there is literally a roomful of people here waiting on us.

But my need is too great to be denied and Greyson doesn't seem to care about anything other than what he's doing to me right now.

And that thought swirls my mind and pushes me into the greatest depths of that fiery inferno that is now exploding within me. I'm burning from the inside out and it's never-ending as Greyson continues to pump and suck and press deeper into my ass.

I can't speak.

I have no words.

I don't even know if I'm making sounds or breathing. It's everything. My body convulses, my clit throbs, my pussy contracts, and just as I'm about to black out, I feel him adjust me and then his cock slams into me.

"Oh!" Because his thumb is still in me. And now he's slamming into me and I'm gasping for air. It's brutal and exquisite. I feel him everywhere. In the deepest depths of me.

His chest falls to my back, and he starts murmuring things in my ear. Things like I taste so good, and he loves tasting my cum as he fucks me, and that he barely fits, and it's almost too tight, and it feels too good, and that he loves me. He loves me. He loves me.

And on the third time he says it, he snarls in frustration and before I know what the hell is happening, he pulls out of me. I whimper in protest, feeling cold and empty, only to have him lift me in his arms and walk me into the bathroom. He kicks the door shut with a loud bang and then he's pressing me into the wall, looping my legs around him.

His eyes ensnare mine and he lines himself up with me and then slides back in. His lips part on a silent moan and every ounce of savagery from just seconds before is gone. The hand he's not using to hold me up roams over me.

My breasts, my face, my neck.

All I can do is pant in response because if I thought I was exposed to him out there, that has nothing on us now. His eyes are shredding me apart, holding me prisoner, and refusing to let me go.

"Love you," I mouth, and he does the same in return. Sweat clings to his brow, his lips still glisten with me, and I lean forward and lick from them. Tasting myself. It makes him groan as he continues to thrust up and into me.

My hands glide up from his biceps to loop around his neck and I drag him tighter against me as he uses his powerful thigh muscles to hold me as he fucks into me.

"Yes," I moan. "That. There. That."

"What, baby? Tell me." His lips eat at mine, slopping and wet and all smiles.

"You're hitting that spot," I manage. "That spot inside me, Grey, and your pubic symphysis is hitting my clit."

He chokes on a half laugh. "My what?"

I shake my head, fighting my own amusement, but I can't focus on it or my use of medical terminology instead of sexy words because I'm *so* close again. Because yeah, he's fucking me at the perfect angle and yeah, he's hitting my clit with every goddamn perfect thrust.

Grey's forehead falls to mine, his eyes still open and wide, his lips parted with the force of his breaths. He's getting close too and the look on his face is not something I want to miss a second of.

"Fall, Fall," he pants, increasing the speed of his pumps.

That's all it takes.

The way he says my name like that never fails to throw me into orgasmic bliss. My thighs clamp tighter around him as my orgasm barrels through me, deeper waves than the explosion earlier. My orgasm triggers his own, his face twisting and tensing as he gives me three more jerky thrusts and comes on a deep, resonating groan I feel marrow deep in my bones.

He presses me deeper into the wall, panting by my ear, his cock still inside me as aftershocks skate through both of us.

"Now we can shower," he announces, kissing my neck as he carries us across the expansive bathroom. He opens the shower door and walks us in, pressing me into the cold tile wall that has me squealing out. "Sorry," he murmurs as he turns on the water, letting it come up to temperature before he pulls out of me and sets me down on my feet.

I step under the spray, tilting my face up to it and sighing at how good that feels. Grey steps in behind me, his arms wrap around my belly, and his chin lands on my shoulder.

"You okay?" I ask when he doesn't move or let me move to start washing up.

"Honestly? I've never been better or happier in my life. It sort of hit me all at once and I needed a moment."

I twist in his arms and hug him to me.

"You know, Jacob may separate us today, but at some point very soon, you and I will be spotted together. I don't know how good I'll be at keeping my distance or pretending we're not together. Especially with you moving in. People in Boston are used to me, but you're Fallon Lark and that will naturally cause buzz and likely press."

I squeeze myself against his chest, planting a kiss there, then release him as I go for the shampoo. "I know. I've already considered that."

"And?" he asks when I don't follow that up.

I shrug as I start to lather my hair only for him to take over. He has a thing for my hair, I've come to realize. And my eyes. And every other part of me.

"And at some point, you'll likely have to announce our relationship or allow people to see what they'll see since you're right that we won't be able to hide it. The timing is what's bad. Not us. It'll look like I left Bacchus for you. People will speculate I cheated on him with you. He'll come out looking like an angel and I'll come out looking like the slutty villain. Eventually people will get over it, but I have no illusions that's how it could go if we're spotted together too soon."

I rinse the shampoo out of my hair and go for the conditioner as Grey starts in with his own hair, quiet and contemplative. He doesn't like that and neither do I, but what the hell can I do about it? Public perception is just that and I don't feel the need to explain my personal life to others. I never have. My mother loves the public eye and my father is always in it, but I did my best to keep a low profile as often as I could.

It was easier when I left for college and then was in medical school. Even when Bacchus and I were dating, I never wanted the press on us.

He did.

He was all about that, which clearly now I know why, but the only interview I ever did was our engagement interview. But there is nothing low profile about the man in the shower with me despite what he says about people being used to him in Boston.

Anytime he was in the city, I knew about it. Boston is obsessed with their Central Square crew, and other than Callan who is like me and keeps a low profile, and Lenox who lives in a secluded part of Maine and only comes into Boston to be with his friends and rarely goes out, their faces are everywhere. They're always photographed. I knew Zax was with Aurelia way before Grey ever mentioned it because I saw their photos and heard the buzz about their relationship.

"I don't like that, Fall."

"I know." I plant my lips into the center of his chest and then peek up at him. "I don't either, but it is how it is, and it'll be what it'll be." I shrug. "I know how to duck and avoid the press. I know how to smile and ignore." Another kiss. "If we can hold off for a while on being seen together, a month or so at least, it should be fine. Come on. Let's finish up. Everyone is waiting."

He shakes his head but lets it drop as we finish up and get dressed and pack up all our stuff. By the time we make it out to the dining room, the food is here, and everyone is eating.

The second we walk into the room Asher's arms shoot straight up in the air in victory. "Ha! Look at her. I totally called it. You owe me a grand." He points a finger around the table.

"What?" I squawk and Grey groans in a slightly amused but mostly annoyed way that suggests he understands what Asher is talking about.

"You're blushing," Asher explains. "Zax said that you wouldn't be able to meet our eyes. Callan said that Grey would walk in with a smug smirk. Jacob and Lamar bet Grey would be smiling like a lovesick schoolboy. Aurelia didn't bet because she only bets in poker when she's positive she can clean house and Lenox didn't bet because Lenox didn't care enough to weigh in."

"I'm sorry. I'm not following."

"They know we had sex and were betting on what our tell would be," Grey clarifies for me. "You were blushing when we walked in here, babe. I don't even think it was conscious, but you were."

"Couldn't I just have been flushed from the shower?"

"No," everyone says at once and my face falls into my hands.

"A grand?" I cry, beyond mortified, but also laughing. "Who bets a thousand dollars on something like that?"

"Rich assholes," Aurelia supplies. "But it's still pretty funny."

Reluctantly I acknowledge that it is and decide to get over it. My hands drop and I treat Grey to a big kiss on the cheek. "Well, I worked up an appetite so bring on the pastries."

I've managed to stun Greyson and a few of the other guys so now my morning is complete. I take a seat beside Aurelia and gush over the gown I wore in Monte Carlo that she designed. We all eat and then it's time to go because Lamar is hot to trot on getting to the spa.

"I'll have her back sometime before midnight," he promises Grey. "And don't worry, her Cinderella slippers will be crystal and Monroe."

"Of that, I have no doubt." Grey kisses me. "Good luck. I'm thinking you might need it."

"Thanks," I grumble, only it's fake and he knows it. I'm honestly looking forward to another spa and shopping day. This time with my own money.

"I'll see you at the festival grounds," he promises, but there's something in his expression. Something that makes my brows furrow and my stomach sink ever so slightly with worry.

30

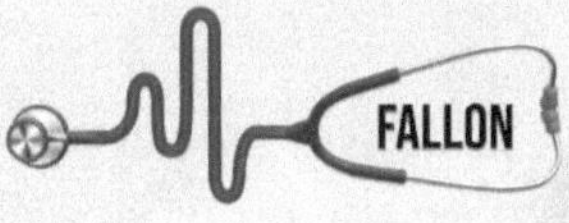

Aurelia, Lamar, and I spent hours doing all things spa and fashion. Not my typical bag, but it is for Aurelia and Lamar and truthfully, it's just fun being with them. I don't have a ton of people who know my story and situation and none who have instantly embraced me as their own while protecting me.

That's what happened this morning.

They teased and laughed and definitely teased some more, but under all that was a trust and bond that was forged in fire and solidified with love and is wholly unbreakable. And because I'm Grey's, I'm theirs. That's it. No questions asked.

I have people now.

It's incredible how lonely I was without realizing it, but now, hanging out with them, I don't feel lonely. I'm relaxed and laughing my ass off at the way Lamar and Aurelia speak to each other. I allow them to pick out clothes for the festival for me and don't complain a bit when they have me add on a bunch of other items I evidently have to have.

Nails, hair, facials, makeup.

For the second time in a week, I'm preened and primped and feeling like a zillion bucks.

By the time we make our way up to the festival grounds, flash our ID badges, and get through to the VIP area, I'm buzzing with excitement. Aurelia is too, her hand on my arm as both of us vibrate overseeing all these artists in one place. Grey told me there was a welcome reception for the artists and people who pay handsomely to attend, but I had no clue it would be like this.

The whole space is tented, the main stage of the festival directly behind us, and on the other side are open fields as far as the eye can see. There are propane heaters set up along the periphery making the inside warm and comfortable against the cool spring night. An enormous spread of hors d'oeuvres along with waiters carrying various canapés, not to mention an enormous bar, adds an exclusive and elegant vibe.

The first concert begins at eight, each band or artist playing an hour set, the last one ending at midnight, and you can faintly make out the sound of last-minute sound checks being done on the stage.

I don't spot Grey or the guys anywhere, but when I pull out my phone to text him, one immediately comes in.

> Grey: Turn around and look straight in front of you.

Immediately I do and lock in on Grey who is on the other side of the tented space from where I am. He's holding a drink in his hand and is talking with—

"Oh my God! That's Cian O'Connor and Jasper Diamond!"

All I can do is nod at Aurelia because I'm in a total fan-girl state. Jasper Diamond is the lead singer of Wild Minds which was my absolute favorite band—other than Central Square of course—growing up. When Central Square opened for them when they were first starting out, I was only sixteen and there was no way my parents would let me go to Grey's concert, so I never got to see them live.

"Should we go say hi?"

Aurelia laughs at the obvious jitters in my voice. "Um. Yeah. Hell yeah!"

"Sorry," I add. "It's weird though, right? I mean, I've seen Grey play live shows to seventy thousand screaming fans, but then it was always just us. I never see this side of him. Not really."

"No, I get it. Before Zax and I got together I was out in a bar with friends one night, and they were playing Central Square songs. It was wild. I was like, wow, he's my hot boss. And an asshole, because he totally was."

"Well, I for one am going to say hi because I've been crushing on Jasper Diamond since you bitches were in diapers," Lamar informs us.

I snort. "I don't think they were playing back then."

"Whatever. I'm just hoping to see Henry Gauthier. The quiet ones always get me hard."

Aurelia laughs. "Don't let Lenox hear you say that."

Lamar gives her a cheeky look. "You think I haven't already told him that? Bitch, please. It's like you don't even know me."

My phone vibrates in my hand.

> Grey: Stop gawking at my friends and get your ass over here so I can introduce you as my woman.

With a wry smirk, I tuck my phone back in my purse and we make our way through the hordes of A-list celebrities all the while trying not to pass out at the sight of them. It's nearly impossible to play it cool though. Aurelia is way better at the been there done that thing than I am. Then again, she was a model and is likely used to mingling with celebrities.

I've met sitting presidents and world leaders and never so

much as batted an eye. Here, I feel like a virgin on prom night, nervous, excited, and having no idea what to do when faced with the situation at hand while praying I don't make a fool out of myself.

Finally, we reach them and by the time we do, Zax and the other guys are there along with a tall blonde woman I recognize as Viola Diamond, Jasper's wife, and the redhead I freaked out over from the restaurant. I'm mortified to see Cian's wife, Vivian, given the way I acted last time, but she has no clue about any of that.

Grey immediately takes me into his side, wrapping his arm around me, and Vivian beams a smile at both of us. Even as I step out of his arms and create some distance between us. There are eyes everywhere.

"I see you were successful at making her yours," Vivian exalts after introductions are made.

My head swivels to Grey, my expression questioning. He kisses the tip of my nose. "I told Vivian when I ran into her in the restaurant that I was there with a friend I hoped would be more than that by the time we made it here."

"Aw, that's so romantic," Viola says, her hazel eyes glittering before she reaches out and touches her husband's shoulder. "I knew Jas and the guys growing up too, so we have that in common. Actually, I dated his brother Gus for years and Jas hated my guts so our story is a bit different from yours."

"I only hated your guts because I secretly loved them. Even when you were with my brother." Jasper smiles, his eyes all over his wife and sparkling with so much love and adoration I can't help but swoon with it.

My mouth hits the floor. "Seriously?"

They both nod and I turn to Zax. "Something I should know about you?"

He winks at me and Aurelia bursts out laughing along with everyone else.

Cian tells us about how he met his wife at the airport right before Christmas and then met her family as her fake boyfriend. I'm dying at that one. Plus I could listen to his Irish brogue all night. They got married last month and are pregnant with their first baby. They're so adorable together.

I tell Vivian that I've read so many of her books and that I'm a huge fan. She's the sweetest person ever and promises to send me some signed copies and that the next time they're up in Boston or I'm out in LA, we should get together.

These people want to get together with me!

I know, I know! I'm being ridiculous but come on! What would you do if you were me and in a room with your favorite all-time artists and they not only talked to you but wanted to chill with you? I'm a mess and Grey thinks it's nothing but adorable. He's laughing. Trying to keep a distance between us for the sake of the press that is lingering around, but he's struggling. I see it. I feel it.

He wants to touch me and look at me and kiss me, and I'm right there with him. We manage though. Other than that one kiss on the nose, we've been just two people talking in a crowd.

He doesn't like it. I know he doesn't, but right now, it's a necessary evil.

That is until later that night when everything goes bad.

AURELIA and the guys are staying in a hotel down the road and after we part ways with them, Grey and I can't keep our hands off each other. High on the energy of watching the opening acts perform and on each other, we stumble off the elevator, laughing and sloppy as we kiss and tear at our clothes.

Grey gets the door to our room open, and we tumble inside, the door closing with a heavy click and then he's got me pressed up against it. His mouth trails down my neck, sucking, kissing, tasting. I moan, my head back against the door as his hands and mouth work magic on my neck.

My hands grasp Grey's hair ready to drag his mouth back up to mine when something flickers behind my closed eyes. It happens again and my eyes snap open at the same second Grey shoots off me and spins around. Immediately his body protectively covers mine, and I can't get a clear sight line at the flashing lights, but somehow, I know what it is even before Grey starts yelling.

"What the fuck?!" he bellows. "Who the hell are you and how did you get in here?"

More flashes go off and then I hear a woman say, "I was hoping you'd fuck me, but it seems I'm too late."

In the blink of an eye, she bolts through the open door that connects to the room beside ours.

"Shit. Stay here." Grey goes chasing after her through the neighboring room that one of his band members is staying in. I spin around in a circle, my hands planting onto the door, debating what I should do. My heart hammers in my chest and I call Lenox.

"Fallon?" he answers, immediately knowing something is wrong.

"Lenox. Oh my God!" My hand hits the top of my head and I start pacing in a circle. "Grey and I just got back to the room and we were kissing by the door and there were flashes of light and there was a woman in Grey's hotel room taking pictures of us. She fled and Grey is giving chase, but I don't know what he can do about it even if he catches her."

"How did she get in his room?"

"No clue!" I cry. "She said she was waiting for him to fuck her."

The door to the room bangs open, nearly knocking into me, and Grey comes storming in, his face a montage of murderous rage.

"She got away. By the time I hit the stairwell, she wasn't there anymore. I went down to the floor below, but I didn't see her anywhere. Who are you talking to?"

"Lenox."

He snatches the phone from my hand and puts it on speaker. "Can you do anything with this?"

"I don't know," Lenox answers. "I can get the hotel surveillance footage easily enough, but so can you after this. Fallon, call hotel security immediately."

I race over to the room phone and dial the front desk, telling them we need security up here immediately and that there was an intruder in our room. I have no idea if she stole anything or what's going on. I hang up quickly, anxious to listen to Grey and Lenox.

"Hacking a cell phone isn't all that easy, Grey. They take time to infiltrate. You can hack apps. You can hack systems. But phones are tricky and damn near impossible if you don't have the number or are within thirty feet of the person to access their Bluetooth."

"Fuck!"

Grey is pacing around, and I flip on the lamp on the bedside table, looking around the room. None of our stuff is touched. None of the furniture is moved. The connecting door is open, but his drummer Freddy isn't back yet. We saw him and a couple of the other band members and stage crew hitting up the after-party we decided not to attend.

"If that woman was here simply to fuck you, she wouldn't

have gone through Freddy's door to get in here and she wouldn't have kept it open while she waited. This was a setup."

"Could be," Lenox agrees.

"Your parents?" Grey asks me and I shake my head no.

"They wouldn't do that. It would tarnish their name and reputation to have their daughter photographed in that way with you. They want to keep all of this as quiet as possible."

"I'm checking Bacchus's systems but he knows you gained access to him before so if this was him, and he's smart enough to learn from his mistakes, he won't use his regular stuff."

Bacchus. Could this have been him?

I knew it felt too easy when the announcement came.

"This could be random. A fan sneaking into a celebrity's room to try to seduce them isn't a new phenomenon." But even as Greyson says the words, his tone and expression aren't selling it.

We leave it there. Not much else we can do but work on it and wait it out.

And by the time we wake up the next morning, the pictures are out there. They're on Boston Landing's website with the caption:

Boston's premier princess and our local rock star bad boy. Fallon Lark caught having secret affair with Greyson Monroe.

By noon Paris time, they've swept around the world, across every tabloid, magazine, online entertainment site, and even Boston's morning news stations.

My parents are furious. Texts start streaming in from them starting at 5:00 a.m. Boston time. It's the first I've heard from my father in all this, and he's not shy on making his wrath known.

Intertainment, a celebrity rag has footage of Bacchus

looking devastated and saying, "No comment." Not to mention, Lenox hasn't turned anything up that says it was done by him.

But I know it was him.

This thing reeks of a set up.

And if I were spiteful, I'd release some of what I have on him to the press. Except when they start digging, they'll quickly uncover my mother's involvement in his financials—five million dollars to be exact—and while I don't like my parents all that much right now, I also don't want to see them dragged through the mud at this particular point in time.

All we were able to get from hotel security is that an unknown woman managed to gain access to the artist's hotel. A woman with the right kind of ID badge who should not have that badge at all.

No one stopped her as she entered the building.

No one checked her name, and there are no cameras in the hallways, so we don't even know how she got into Freddy's room.

Lenox is working on it but isn't all that optimistic we'll ever figure out who the woman is.

The press here are all over us. Grey's PR people have been begging us to make a statement, but what can we say? As far as the world is concerned, Bacchus and I broke up on Thursday and by the next night, I'm screwing around in Paris with Greyson Monroe.

It's taken over the festival. Grey had to cancel every interview he was scheduled to do. With every meet and greet with fans it's there, hanging like a shadow over his head.

I feel awful. Grey certainly didn't need this, and I have no idea what this sort of bad publicity will do to me when I return home. What parent is going to want to bring their child to see a doctor who is in pictures like that? I'd be shocked if I'm not fired from the clinic and discharged before I even officially start at the MGH practice.

Grey's been holding my hand through all of this. By my side and feeling just as miserable for me as I feel for him. With no way to fix this, all we can do is weather the storm that when you're stuck in the swell of it, feels like it will never end.

31

GREYSON

In this life, there will always be people out there who will hurt you. Their reasons aren't necessarily important. Sometimes they're people who have so much of their own strife that they have to spread some of it around in order to function. Some people are just assholes who don't give a shit about anyone but themselves. And some people have egos that are too big for them to handle.

We don't know with one hundred percent certainty that this was Bacchus.

But come the fuck on.

Since Saturday, Bacchus has wiped his entire system and phone. Lenox isn't a fool and we have backups of everything, but Bacchus is cleaning house.

The one thing we were able to find was a wire transfer of five thousand dollars from one of Bacchus's off-the-radar dummy accounts to a numbered account in Switzerland. I consider this a smoking gun but that's not much to go on. When Fallon texted him, his response was *if you don't want to get caught maybe you should be more careful about who you fuck.*

We assumed something would happen when we returned

home. That we'd be seen together, and speculations would arise. We never considered we'd be photographed with my mouth fused to Fallon's neck and her face twisted in erotic bliss with her hands in my hair. Or the following picture that perfectly nailed both of our faces.

"Good luck, brother. Break a leg out there," Jasper says as he passes me, slapping a hand on my shoulder. I nod to him in gratitude, same with the other guys who wish me luck as they pass.

"This could be rough," Jacob says as I stand in the shadows watching as the stage crew clear away the set of Wild Minds who performed before me and ready it for mine.

"I doubt it." Unfortunately, I do doubt it. Fans don't care if I'm fucking someone. They expect that from someone like me. It's all ironic. They call me a bad boy because as a teen I got into a little bit of trouble here or there. But for the last eight or so years since Suzie died, there hasn't been much on me and never anything with women.

As much as I hate to say it, my album sales have gone up since yesterday morning. The saying that there is no such thing as bad PR works well for people like me. Not so much for people like Fallon and that's what has me bleeding internally.

I need to fix this for her and that's not so easily done.

Fallon squeezes my hand. She's been silent pretty much all day and wasn't even going to come with me to see my set. I told her at this stage there is no point in hiding us. If anything, people seeing us as a couple and not just a fling will help.

The stage crew finishes up and I turn to Fallon as my band goes out there and gets set up in the dark. "I love you," I tell her simply, and lean in and kiss her lips.

"Love you," she says back against mine and that's that. They can try to hurt us or tear us apart, but we know what we have and we're stronger than all that. Not even a week of being together and I know that because this isn't a new relationship. This isn't something we have to figure out and learn.

It's sixteen years in the making and nothing will break that.

"You're on Monroe." The head stage attendant pats my back and I pull away from Fall Girl.

"I'll see you after."

A wan smile strikes her lips. "See you after."

I race out onto the stage just as my drummer starts the beat for my first song. I immediately launch into it and the crowd responds in kind. They're here for the music and while they no doubt love the gossip, when you're in this groove, everything else is secondary. I go full tilt for fifty solid minutes.

No breaks. No banter. No chit-chat. Not even a greeting.

Wild Minds was set to end the show but after talking last night with Jasper who mentioned something to me, a piece of advice that evidently worked for him when he and Viola were forced to once face a media storm, I asked if we could switch places and he graciously agreed. The event planner agreed, shockingly, but I didn't say much about it. Not to Fall or to Jacob. The only person I said anything to was Zax and he told me to fucking go for it.

So I am.

Fall Girl may or may not love me for this, but I can't, *I won't*, sit by and do nothing while my girl gets raked over the coals.

White stage lights swirl and then focus in on me as I wipe the sweat from my brow with the hem of my shirt. I get a slew of whistles and cheers for that that have me chuckling. My band is expecting me to go into our last song of the night, one we've been practicing during our downtime of canceled interviews.

But that will come in a minute.

"Bonsoir tous la monde!" I yell into my microphone and everyone cheers, clapping and stomping their feet. It's late, already dark and phone flashlights dance and sway, illuminating the massive size of the audience. "Thank you all for being here and thank you to the event coordinators for having me. My set isn't quite done yet. But first, I wanted to have a small chat with you. I hope you'll forgive my English."

More shouts and cries that make me smile, even as I motion for everyone to quiet down.

"So, by now I'm sure you've heard I have a girlfriend."

The crowd goes insane at that. Like raging, roaring insane. I can't blame them either since I've never in all the years of being asked about love interests and girlfriends ever admitted to one. I give them a few moments and then I quiet them once more since I'm on the clock.

"I'd like to tell you all a little story if I may. It'll be quick and then I'm going to play something brand-new. Something you'll be the first to hear."

It's like thunder shaking the earth and I walk over to the edge of the stage, casually strumming the opening chords as I do.

"When I was fourteen, I met a girl. You see, I didn't have the happiest of childhoods. Before I left with my older brother Zax and the guys as Central Square, I'd spend a lot of time on my roof playing my guitar as a way to escape a bit. One summer night, the most beautiful girl I had ever seen climbed up on my roof and sat beside me. We spent that entire night talking and I knew. I just knew. The way Romeo knew about Juliet. Turned out she lived next door, and I became friends with her brother. But this girl, she was a special kind of girl, and her family didn't want her to have much to do with me."

Everyone boos and I can't help but chuckle a little at that. I run my hand through my damp hair, brushing the strands back from my forehead as I peer out into the captive audience. The stage lights are brutal and hot, but not anything I'm not used to, so I press on.

"This girl and I stayed friends in secret for years and years.

In many ways, she was my best friend, and I was hers. So when things went bad with her current relationship, she called me. What happened next is I hopped on a flight with her to Rome. She was looking to escape, and I was looking to make her fall in love with me."

That's when everyone explodes again and I glance to my right, straight at Fall Girl who is standing in the wings, staring at me with her hands knotted and in front of her mouth and her eyes shining with unshed tears.

"I never stopped loving her," I explain to the audience while I look at my girl. "Never. All these years, she was the one who owned my heart. She didn't realize it until this week as I had never told her. And in return, she hadn't come to realize she had feelings for me too. I think it was something she always fought because she was trying to be the good girl for her family and make everyone happy. She was trying to be with this guy, her ex, who was all wrong for her but everything she was supposed to marry."

I turn back to the crowd as I start to lightly strum again.

"Here's the honest truth about all you've read and seen in the tabloids. Fallon Lark is my girlfriend. The love of my life. And we were *not* having a secret affair. She ended things with her ex-fiancé more than a week ago, which may not seem like all that much time in between, but it is what it is, and we can't change that. She never set out to be with me. That sort of just happened because when something is right and meant to be, it's inevitable and fate takes over. But on Friday night, someone broke into our hotel room and photographed us during an inti-mate moment. Whether that someone was hired to do that or simply in the wrong place at the right time, we don't know. So that's the truth. There is nothing sinister going on between us. No clandestine affair. We're simply two people in love and insanely happy with each other."

I extend my arm, holding my hand out to her, begging for

her to come and join me on stage. Her eyes burst open wider than Fenway Park and she adamantly shakes her head no.

"Come on Fall Girl."

"No," she says, but her voice catches in the microphone and then the crowd gets in on it. Cheering Fall Girl, Fall Girl, Fall Girl over and over again. I join their chant, clapping my hands along to that beat and I know she's going to be pissed at me, but hopefully what I'm about to do next will fix that.

Finally someone gives her a shove—my money is on Asher or Lamar—and she stumbles onto the edge of the stage. The second the audience gets a glimpse of her the whistles and cheers and claps take over and reluctantly she walks over to greet me, glaring daggers at me that have me smiling like a bastard.

"Hey, babe." I give her a kiss right on the lips when she reaches me, and you can guess what that does to the audience. "We're just about out of time for the night, so I wanted to play a song for all our friends."

"And you needed me out here for that?"

I can't stop smiling as I tell her, "I do actually. Because I wrote this song for you this week. You helped me snap out of the fog I've been stuck in for the last six or so months. So while this is the first time I'm playing it for them, it's also the first time I'm playing it for you."

Her lavender eyes are brimming with tears, her lips and chin trembling. I kiss her knuckles to my lips and then release her and immediately start playing the new song on my acoustic. Fall heard me strum this a bit. She may have even caught a few of the lyrics. But she hasn't heard this the way it is now and her face as I start to sing about falling in love with the most irresistibly perfect girl at the wrong time is priceless.

The song is our journey, from beginning to now, and our eyes are locked as I serenade her. Well, her and the roughly one hundred thousand fans and press that are here. I have no doubt that by the end of this song, everything I did tonight will be viral. The only thing I care about is that her name is cleared of anything scandalous.

I've been losing sleep
while I dream of things I can't keep.
I've been losing time
while we pretend this love is a crime.
Here we are once again
as you tell me I'm just your friend.
Here I go this time
robbing, thieving, stealing what was mine.
Stars come out tonight
burning down what we can no longer fight.
Because baby this love isn't simple
it's right and wrong and fucking irresistible.
So here we are once again
only now I'm no longer your friend.
And I'm not so afraid to sleep
when love is the word we both speak.
There is no more losing time
when every second with you is my lifeline.
I don't care what people have to say
their words can no longer harm or betray.
With every touch our world starts
forever fixing every piece of our torn and battered hearts.

The song ends and for a moment, there is nothing but silence. The sort of silence that has chills racing up my spine and raising the hairs on my arms. Fallon is standing here, staring at me, her face painted in her tears.

"Take off your guitar," she tells me, and I blink. That's not what I was expecting her to say after all that, but I do as she asks and the second I set Aurora down on the stage, Fallon launches herself at me. Her arms wrap around my neck, her legs around my waist, and she kisses me like she's never kissed me before.

I hold her tight, kissing her back. Swallowing down her words of love and gratitude and awe for the song. I carry her off stage, throwing a sideways wave to the crowd, louder than I've ever experienced a crowd to be.

I can only hope it was enough to fix everything.

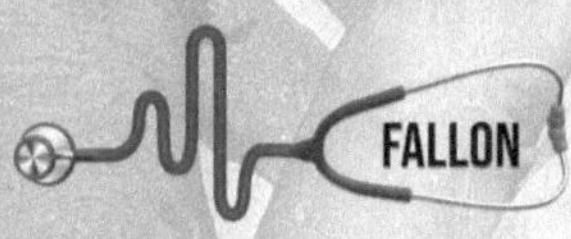

32

We left Paris before the sun was up. Grey carried me off stage and I couldn't stop telling him how much I love him. All the ways I love him. How I'm going to love him like this for the rest of our lives.

The man went on stage last night and told the world all about us.

And after he did that, he sang a song he wrote for me.

The world could catch fire, but as long as I have him, it can burn around us and we'll never feel its heat. But catch fire it did. The madness ensued almost immediately. Forgetting the hundred thousand or so fans that were there and likely recording, there were dozens and dozens of members of the press there.

Grey said nothing about it, but I think that was all part of his plan.

Asher was having the best time with it. Tracking all the places the video had been uploaded and how many hits it was getting. Grey broke the internet and his song, that beautiful song, will do amazing things for him. He doesn't seem to care so much about that either. All that wariness and anxiety and writer's block are gone.

He's peaceful and content and it's the sexiest look on him. Seeing Grey happy is the sexiest thing in the world and I plan to keep that hint of a smile on his lips from now on.

Neither Grey nor I slept much on the plane. We were too wired as was everyone else.

But I also hadn't turned on my phone since Saturday and when we touch down in Boston, and we're back to reality, reluctantly, I turn it back on.

It's flooded. Texts, missed calls, emails.

I start with the texts.

> Dillon: When you get home to Boston, call me.
> It's important.

I haven't talked to Dillon since I learned he's the one who told Bacchus I was in Paris. I have a lot to say to my brother and none of it is good.

> Dad: I don't know what to say to you. You ruined my run at the White House. But I also think you might have unwittingly saved me.

I blink at that, confused.

> Dad: I won't pretend I'm happy because I'm not. But if he loves you like that, I'll learn to live with him.

I stare at my phone, reading that over and over again. My father and I haven't talked much over the years. I'd see him sporadically, mostly at forced family holidays that were never a happy affair. Honestly, my father checked out on us a long time ago. Right around the time of Dillon's accident maybe. I'm honestly not sure. It was slow and subtle.

So for him to extend this type of olive branch? I'm floored.

And touched. I hope he means it. I hope there can be something here. Something salvageable. There aren't any texts from my mother, but that doesn't surprise me. Not after the way we left things on Saturday when she told me I was the disgrace of her life—that hurt.

But my dad coming around?

We'll see.

After the plane lands, we say goodbye to everyone. Aurelia and I have plans to get lunch this week and the guys are always in touch with each other. I thank Lenox again for everything he did for me. For everything he's done for Grey too. I hug Zax and he tells me quite candidly how he wasn't sure about me when Grey ran out to catch the plane with me, but now that he's seen us together, he feels like he finally has a little sister.

I might have gotten so choked up I couldn't speak.

But now it's just me and Grey in the car, exhausted, quiet, as we stare out the windows at the early Boston morning. "How are you going to get your stuff back from Bacchus?" he asks as we get close to his place.

"I'm honestly not sure. A third party maybe. I don't want to be in the same room as him ever again."

"No. I don't want you to be either and I think if I do it, I'll kill him and that's never a good thing. My PR people are already ripping their hair out over the last forty-eight hours."

The car stops and this is why we flew home so early. No one is waiting outside of Greyson's place, but I have to imagine it won't stay quiet like this for long. He unlocks the front of his building and then I gasp out a breath.

"What?" He turns and looks at me over his shoulder.

"You live here? In this entire building?"

He shrugs. "It was a warehouse that had gone into foreclosure. I bought it and renovated it." He's smiling at me. Likely because my jaw has unhinged itself and is now resting on the cement floor.

"Greyson! It's enormous."

He shrugs. "I told you I have too much money. There's a lap pool and a sports pavilion with a basketball court and full gym I added on a couple of years ago that I let the neighborhood kids and a few children's charities use. So if you ever hear shit talking or kids yelling behind that wall, that's all that is." He points to the far wall where there's a large, bolted door. "But they only use it between two and six in the afternoon on weekdays, so we'll have it to ourselves the rest of the time. I work out in the gym and do laps in the pool almost every morning."

Oh my God! He's the cutest man on the planet.

"You built a pool and a sports pavilion for neighborhood kids?"

He shrugs like it's no big thing. "A lot of kids need some place to go after school or a place where they can feel safe and connected. That's all that is."

That's *all* that is. Right. "How have I never heard about this?"

"Because it's not something I want publicized. I don't do it for press. I do it for the kids."

I stare at him, my chest clenching painfully tight as it tries to accommodate how full my heart is. "That's so unfair. I didn't think it was possible to love you any more than I already do and here you go and prove me wrong." I kiss his cheeks and then his lips, my hand cupping his face as I gaze adoringly into his brown eyes. "You are the most incredible man I've ever known. And so is this place. Hell." I pan my hands around. "You have three floors of a warehouse."

"The upper two floors are my space. The first floor is street level and I like my privacy, so I haven't done much down here yet. If you want to take it over, you can. We can renovate it into anything you want." He points over to the side where there are walls, but it's mostly open space. "Come on. Let me show you home."

He takes my hand and leads me over to a very cool, indus-trial winding staircase that separates the first floor, and sure enough, this part is lived in. It's also the size of half a Boston city block, but it feels more like a home. A huge kitchen and family room and offices and bedrooms and bathrooms spread out over the second and third floors.

But it's what's waiting for us in the massive great room that has us both freezing in our place.

"How did you get in here?" Grey asks.

"You have a ramp and an elevator."

Grey rolls his eyes at my brother. "Yes, Dillon. I'm aware I have a ramp and an elevator. I had a best friend in a wheelchair and fully understand the necessity behind such things. But how the fuck did you get into my house. I have security. Cameras. An alarm. Shit that chimes and goes off when someone breaks in."

"You might want to have someone check that out for you. I'm sure Lenox could be helpful."

Grey frowns, folding his arms. "Careful, Dill. Careful. Are you a mind reader? Did you know I was going to tell her right when we got home?"

I feel like a ping-pong ball, my head snapping back and forth between them.

"I had a hunch, but that isn't why I'm here."

"She has a right to know."

"And I told you it's not her business. You promised me."

"I'm done keeping that promise. It's a shitty promise."

"The truth will hurt her."

"It's a secret I don't want to keep from her."

"Will both of you shut up and tell me what the fuck is going on?!" I cry, interrupting their back and forth that's giving me whiplash. I point at my brother. "You betrayed me to Bacchus. I called you in the middle of the night and we talked, and you told me you were on my side. You told me you couldn't believe the lengths Mom and Bacchus went to with this. That I did deserve better and that you were glad I left him and was doing some soul-searching." I jab my finger in the air at him. "Then you told my ex-fiancé how to find me."

"I knew you were with Greyson."

I shake my head at my brother and close some of the distance between us. He's sitting on the couch and his chair is nearby, but I don't want to make him get up and get back into it. "How did you know that? I never told you."

"I did," Grey says, coming over to me and taking my hand. He guides us to the opposite facing couch and drags me down. "I texted Dillon the night we were in Monte Carlo. I have a tendency to do that every time I dream about the night he was hurt. He's never responded in all these years, so this time I told him I loved you."

"I called him," Dillon interjects, his purple eyes on me. We look a lot alike and it's not because we're twins, obviously. But sometimes it's like looking at the male version of me and it makes staying angry with him difficult.

"That night?"

"Yes," Dillon replies. "You and I had already talked and worked some stuff out and then Grey sent that message." Dillon sighs, sitting back against the couch and throwing his arm over the back of it. "I told Bacchus where you were because I wanted you to deal with him before the festival. I was worried you two would be seen together with all the press there and I didn't want you painted in an ugly light. I didn't know he'd go and hire some woman to get pictures of you, though maybe I should have. He's never played by the rules."

"How do you know it was him who hired someone?" I ask, leaning forward and dropping my elbows to my thighs. Grey starts rubbing soothing circles on my back, trying to calm me down, but I'm not sure how calm I can be.

Dillon smirks, swiping at his jaw and lips to hide it. "Your friend Lenox isn't the only one with skills. I work for Congress and know people. People who are part of certain special investigations. Special investigations that involve federal prosecutors."

"What does that even mean?" Grey queries, utterly flummoxed.

"After you and I talked, Fallon, I did some digging. I can't say anything else, but you'll know more soon enough."

"So you did all this to help me?" I press because I'm not sure who or what to believe anymore.

"Yes. I did that to help you and I'm still doing stuff to help you now."

"Her, right? Not me?" Grey questions, almost sarcastically. His hand runs through his hair, his agitation flowing from him.

My brother's sharp gaze cuts to him. "Both of you, actually."

Grey squints at my brother. "Bullshit," he spits.

"Not bullshit," Dillon responds calmly. "That's why I'm here. I knew you were going to tell her. You texted me you wanted to and when you get an idea in your head, you're impulsive. I didn't trust you to wait or not listen to the promise you made me. I'm just glad you did and I'm able to say my part of it first."

"What are you both hiding from me?" I'm growing so flustered with all of this.

"That the accident was my fault and not Greyson's."

That's when everything stops. Grey's hand stops moving on my back, and he turns to stone. I freeze in place and forget how to breathe. Finally I manage to utter, "What?"

Dillon sighs and sits up, using his hands to shift his position so he's facing us fully. "I was angry. I was also drunk and a little too high that night which didn't help. He was my best friend, and I knew he liked you. I'd see the way he'd look at you or try to get you alone or even just talk to you. I'd see how you'd react to him too. Blushes and smiles. It pissed me off. I knew if you two got together eventually it would end since we were teenagers, and then our friendship would be ruined. I didn't have a lot of friends. I wasn't the nicest of kids, and I knew it, but Grey never seemed to care about my shitty attitude."

"What happened that night?"

"It'll hurt you, Fallon," my brother warns me. "It was about you, and it will hurt."

"I don't care. I want to know anyway."

Dillon runs his hands down his thighs. "I caught Greyson humming with a dopey smile on his face. I called him out on it, and he told me he loved you. Just like that. Love. We were fifteen and he was throwing that word out. I didn't realize his feelings were like that and it set me off. Somehow him loving you felt worse. It felt like I had already lost his friendship. That he was only friends with me for you. Then he told me you'd been sneaking into his room, and I lost my mind. I wanted to kill him. It doesn't even sound rational to me now, but at the time I was enraged, and I attacked him. Greyson reacted and defended himself."

Greyson stands up and paces over to the large windows, his hand gripping the exposed brick on the other side of it. He's breathing heavily. Unable to manage what my brother just tossed out at him.

"You fought over me and ended up paralyzed?"

Dillon looks away, swallows, and then says, "Yes."

I nod, trying to absorb what he just told me only there is no absorbing that. "That's why you pulled away from me," I accuse. "Why you wouldn't look at me and any time I tried to talk to you, you were withdrawn or mean."

"Yes. It's also why I never told anyone what happened that night. Not the police. Not our parents. No one. I was to blame, but I was so angry about my injury, and I hated everyone. I hated everyone, but I hated myself most of all and I didn't know how to cope with that other than to be hateful and angry with everyone else. Mom and Dad couldn't stand the sight of me after that. You tried to be perfect, Fallon. Perfect for all of us while keeping our family intact. I didn't realize to what extent until you told me about everything that went down with Bacchus. And Greyson hit it big and got to go off and become a fucking rock star of all things. But the truth is, I owed you. I owed you both and when you called me, I finally saw that as my chance to stop being a coward and act."

"How?" Grey rasps out, still at the window.

"I talked to my dad. He and I both live in DC and believe it or not, have grown close. You should have heard from him by now, Fallon. I told him the truth about everything. Mom is... well, she kept Dad in the dark about everything. The only deal Dad made was that after you married Bacchus and he eventually became a senator, when Bacchus made a presidential run, Dad would be his running mate. There's a lot that will likely happen between Mom and Dad. Maybe. Who knows with them. Bacchus will pay. That I can promise you. And..."

Dillon clears his throat, wiping at the emotion that's there, and stares into Greyson's back.

"I'm sorry, Greyson. It's not nearly enough. I know that. I know you've been torturing yourself for a long time and I let you do that. I was wrong. It was my fault, not yours, and I'm sorry."

Jesus. I can't breathe. I'm choking on sobs. Greyson too as he starts to fall apart, trembling uncontrollably at the window. That night—the one that changed our lives—Greyson told Dillon he loved me, and they fought over me and yet still, Greyson never gave up on me or Dillon. He has a ramp in his home, and I doubt he was even aware of why he put it in, but knowing Greyson, he was hoping, praying this moment would come.

His heart is so big.

A point he proves when he spins around, crosses the room, and envelopes Dillon in a huge hug, knocking him back into the couch. Both of them break down and I do too. Dillon's actions that night had a lot of far-reaching repercussions. For everyone involved. I get up and go over and hug both of them.

The guys forgive each other. And I forgive Dillon.

It's not all fixed. There's a lot of history involved, but I don't think Grey cares about any of that anymore. This isn't him brushing things off. This isn't him thwarting things he shouldn't thwart. This is different.

This is him feeling and him forgiving and him moving forward.

Dillon ends up staying for a while. He won't tell us anything about Bacchus, but frankly, I don't care. Everything is out in the open. Grey and I are together. Dillon and Greyson are friends again. I have my brother back and possibly my father.

And my new family.

My found family.

I'm not sure what else there is to need beyond that.

Grey and I fall asleep tangled in sheets, sweaty and exhausted but so content. And when we wake up the next morning there's a surprise waiting for us downstairs in Greyson's building just inside the back door by his garage.

My stuff. There's also a note stuck to one of the boxes.

"Get your security fixed. - D"

I snort out a laugh. "He has a point."

Grey gives me a sideways glance and then he's on me, his lips all over me. "Come on Mrs. Grant. Let's go move you in. Because from now on, this is where you live. With me. And nothing, I repeat nothing, will ever keep us apart again."

EPILOGUE 1

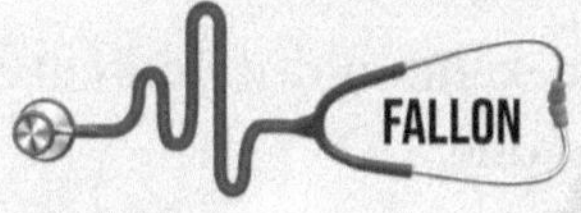

"**A**ny big plans for the long weekend?" Oliver Fritz asks while staring at his phone and typing something at the same time.

"Not really," I admit, trying not to show my level of disappointment with that admission. I was supposed to fly out to LA to see Grey, but he ended up canceling on me, telling me he was going to be stuck in the studio all weekend as he wanted to finish the album in double time. "I thought about going to DC to hang out with Dillon, but the idea of being in DC over the Fourth of July isn't all that appealing."

Oliver's head pops up, his green eyes curious. "Why? Because of all the tourists?"

I tap my nose and then point at him. "Precisely."

"You should come over then," he tells me. "We're having a big barbeque with my family. Food. Alcohol. Swimming. Kids running around like mad. Sounds good, doesn't it?" He bounces his eyebrows suggestively.

"Tempting. I haven't seen your girls in..." I check my watch. "Oh, two hours since I gave them their physicals."

"Keegan and Kenna are the least of it. Wait till they get together with their cousins. We're talking more than a dozen children under the age of nine."

"Yeah, hard pass. I see enough children here."

He chuckles. "Just wait. Soon enough you and Greyson Monroe will have babies."

"Ha. You're very funny. I have one more patient and then I'm out of here."

"Have a good weekend and if you change your mind, just come over. Sunday at one."

"Sounds good." I walk backward toward my next patient's room. "Thank you for the invite. Give Amelia a hug for me and tell her I'll shoot her a text to meet up for lunch or something soon."

He gives me a wave and then I enter my patient's room. A six-year-old with a positive strep test. I give him a quick exam, write him a prescription for some Amoxicillin, and wish the family well. Poor kiddo is miserable with it.

By the time I finish documenting all my patients and close up for the day, I'm exhausted. And a little sad. Greyson has been in LA recording his fifth solo album for the last six weeks. Once we got home from Paris, he set straight to work and wrote a total of fifteen new songs for it including the one he sang to me in Paris. Speaking of that song, it set all kinds of internet records for most watches.

We were bombarded a lot by both press and fans when we got back. That lasted about a week only to pick up again about two weeks ago.

Three things have happened in the three months since we got home from Paris. One, Bacchus along with a hundred and thirty other attorneys, including sixty-three federal and state prosecutors, are being investigated by a special congressional council for giving and receiving illegal bribes. Two, I have not heard a peep from my mother since our last phone conversation. And three, my father and I have had dinner together on two separate occasions.

Bacchus came at me when he first got wind of the indictment, sending nasty texts that accused me of doing this to him. I didn't even bother replying and then proceeded to block his number. He's got more important things to focus on right now since he's the one who accepted bribes, not me.

When the news of that broke, I did call Dillon immediately. He told me he still couldn't say anything but is on the committee running the investigation and promised that they had more than sufficient evidence to keep my name out of it. I won't have to testify on what I overheard unless absolutely necessary. That was a relief.

My phone rings in the pocket of my scrub pants as I exit the hospital heading toward Cambridge Street and the redline T stop. "Hey!" I answer with an unstoppable smile when I see it's Grey. "How's it going out there?"

"Hey, babe. It's going well actually. We're flying through these songs and I should be done in the next week or so."

"Great," I exclaim, but I'm not sure my voice is selling it. I miss him. I miss him terribly. In the weeks he's been out there, he was only able to travel home once and I haven't managed any time out there because I have no vacation days as a new employee and it's a six-hour flight to California, one way, with a three-hour time difference.

Not so easy to manage and then he went and canceled this weekend on me. I know he wants to finish up so he can get home sooner, but ugh.

"Yeah, so, I was thinking..." he trails off and I pull my phone away from my ear to make sure the call is still connected.

"Grey? You there?"

"I am, but..."

"But what?"

"Look to your right."

"Huh?"

"Stop walking, Fallon, and look to your right."

"What?" I do as he says and find Zax's car, and his driver Ashley parked right in front of me.

"Um."

"Good evening, Fallon. If you will." Ashley opens the back door for me.

"Grey?"

"Well, don't leave the man waiting."

"What's going on?"

"See you soon, Fall Girl." Grey hangs up.

"What's going on?" I pose the question to Ashley this time as I slide into the deliciously air-conditioned SUV.

"I'm taking you to the airport. Your flight leaves in an hour."

He goes to shut the car door and I stick out my hands, stopping him. "Wait! What?" I shake my head, beyond confused. "Grey canceled our weekend, and I don't have any of my stuff."

"Aurelia and Lamar packed your bag, and I have strict instructions to tell you that you're not allowed to complain. As for your weekend plans, well, I believe this was Greyson's plan all along." I get a wink and then he shuts the door and we're flying through Friday night holiday traffic to the airport. Ashley weaves us around to the private terminal and then I'm boarding the Monroe jet.

The flight attendant greets me with a glass of champagne and then we're taking off. Just like that. I haven't looked in the bag that was packed for me. I haven't made another call. I just texted Grey and told him that he was crazy, but that I couldn't wait to see him.

I don't have to be back in Boston until Tuesday morning and I'm excited to go to LA and hang out a bit.

Only when we land, we're not in LA.

We're in Sonoma.

A fact I'm only aware of as the flight attendant says, "Welcome to Sonoma."

Because... what the *fuck*?! "Sonoma?" My eyebrows hitch up to my hairline and I stand only to bend to peer out the small oval window. Sure enough, we are most definitely not in LA.

"Sonoma." That's how she replies as if the answer is that simple. I decide, much like everything else tonight, not to question it. Grey obviously has a plan and I'd be lying if I said I didn't love his surprises. Well, I usually love his surprises. But so far, this is turning into a good one.

The plane door opens, the stairs along with it, and as I climb down them, I find Greyson standing there in the waning sun, leaning against a cherry red convertible as he smiles at me. I changed out of my scrubs on the plane, and even showered, so I don't hesitate as I race down the stairs and across the tarmac directly into his waiting arms.

He catches me effortlessly, instantly crashing his lips down onto mine. "Fuck I missed you," he breathes against me, stealing more kisses as if he can't stop himself.

"Me too." I cling to him, my face planting in his neck so I can breathe him in. "What are we doing in Sonoma and why was this all a surprise?"

"You'll see." A kiss to my neck. "Come on."

He sets me down and then opens the door for me to get in the passenger's side. I slide along the sleek, smooth leather and smirk. This man has a thing for expensive convertibles. We race off into the hills, vineyards on either side as we wind our way along. The sun is just starting to set in the west, the air is warm and fragrant and lovely.

All of this is.

I can't stop touching Grey either. I'm angled across the console, running my fingers through the back of his hair as the strands on top tussle about. My head is on his shoulder as he drives us. I went from living without him for so long, which only makes me greedier now that I have him. I don't want any more distance or time between us.

He turns off the main road, leading us down a rocky path until we pull into a driveway of sorts. On the left is an endless field of purple.

Lavender.

I should have known.

On the right is a beautiful home all lit up inside.

I smirk, raising a challenging brow. Instead of answering my obvious question, he pops out of the car, opens my side for me, and extends his hand for me to take.

"Walk with me?" He gives me the sweetest smile.

"Did you rent all this for us?"

"I did," he tells me as he loops our pinkies together, walking us away from the house and into the field. "You didn't think I'd actually go this entire long weekend without spending it with you, did you? I just didn't want to do it in LA. LA for me is work. This is relaxing. This is a holiday."

"You could have told me."

I get a sideways glance, his mouth twisted to the side in a crooked grin. "Ah, but what would the fun in that be? Incidentally, I'm flying home with you Monday night." His eyes meet mine. "I finished the album."

"You did?" I practically squeal in delight. "Wow. So quickly?"

"Lyric, Eden, and I flew through it. I didn't want to stop once I got started and the band was there with me on it. Lyric and Eden took turns with the production end of it." He snickers. "Lyric told me she's never produced an album that fast before, and I believe it. It was insane. And intense. But…" He pauses and twists to face me, taking my other hand. "I love it. I don't know if it will be my biggest success, but I think it's the album

I'm most proud of. The songs are the most authentic to me and I can only hope my fans will come on this journey with me."

"They will," I assure him, squeezing his hands. "When do I get to hear it?"

"Now?"

I jump up and down. "For real? Now?"

"Look behind you."

I release one of his hands and twist around to find a picnic set up two rows over in between the lavender bushes. A blanket. Flameless lanterns. A basket of what I'm hoping is food since I only snacked on the plane. A bottle of champagne and that makes me laugh.

"What?"

"You hate champagne."

"But you love it."

I turn back to him. "I love you."

"Good thing because I have bourbon in the basket for me."

I laugh, leaning up onto the balls of my feet so I can press my lips to his. "This is amazing. You're amazing."

Suddenly I'm so overwhelmed. He mentioned when we were in Provence that he wanted to get married in the lavender fields there. That he wanted pictures of my eyes by the flowering bushes. That he wanted his babies growing in my belly.

"Hey, Grey?"

"Yeah?"

"Will you marry me?" I propose against his lips.

He freezes, his body going unnaturally still. "Are you serious?"

Am I?

"Yes. Will you marry me?"

I wrap my arms around his neck, but he slips out of them, staring straight into my eyes.

"No."

Well, that's not the answer I was expecting to get. Flustered, I look away, feeling my face heating to nuclear decibels.

"Um. Okay—"

He grabs my jaw and drags it back to him as he forces me to hold his gaze while he drops down onto one knee. The sun is setting behind him, casting the earth in an endless glow across the lavender that perfumes the air.

"Fall Girl, I can't accept your proposal before I give you mine. I wasn't actually going to do this here. I thought for sure you'd figure it out all too quickly and I wanted the element of surprise. I was going to make love to you and then when you were drunk on orgasms, I was going to pull out this ring"—he pulls a box from his pocket and opens it up to reveal a huge oval diamond—"and make you say yes that way. But as always with you, you sort of beat me to the punch."

His hand holds mine, staring at my fingers as he plays with them for a moment before his eyes, so dark and full of love and hope and promises, plead with me.

"Love me as I swear to do with you. Give us babies and happily ever afters and challenge me and drive me crazy and know, beyond a shadow of a doubt, that I will crawl through fire beyond the ends of the earth every day for us. It will always be us, Fall Girl. Always. Forever." He licks his lips, swallowing hard. "Marry me? Be mine?"

My knees hit the dirt, my hands finding his face in the same movement, and then I'm kissing him. Romantic bastard never stops outdoing himself.

"Yes," I breathe between his parted lips. "But for the record, I asked first."

He chuckles against me, his chest vibrating. We smile, lips connected, hearts one, souls intertwined. It's always been us. From the moment I climbed out my window and up onto his roof, it's always been us.

And from this moment on, that will never change.

. . .

THE END.

Want more of Grey and Fallon HEA? Check out their bonus epilogue HERE. Excited for more from the Irresistibly Yours world? Turn the page for an exclusive excerpt of Irresistibly Wild!

IRRESISTIBLY WILD

C allan

"It's like something out of a horror film out there," the hostess says to me as I step inside the restaurant, shaking excess rainwater from my hair and shirt. Another flash of lightning streaks across the sky immediately followed by a loud crack of thunder. She jumps, stifling her loud gasp with her hand. "Sorry," she apologizes, her face flushing in embarrassment. "I hate thunderstorms."

The lights flicker and she tenses. So do half the people sitting at their tables and in the bar.

Today has been an epically shitful day and this thunderstorm is the coup de grâce.

"Any chance at a table for one?" I ask.

"Your usual table is taken, Dr. Barrows. Are you okay with one more in the center of the room?"

She gives me a contrite smile and all I can do is sigh and nod. A table in the open isn't my favorite thing and if I had the buffer of my friends with me, I wouldn't care so much—they garner far more attention than I ever do—but right now, all I want is my favorite sushi, a couple of glasses of something alcoholic, and a quiet moment to sort through my thoughts.

With any hope, I won't be recognized, but that's not how this day seems to be going for me so far.

"Thank you," I say as I take my menu that I don't particularly require and sit down, dropping my napkin onto my lap. The hostess walks off and immediately my water glass is filled by a busboy just as the lights flicker again. Thunder rumbles loud and aggressively enough to be heard over the din of Friday night diners who were brave enough to say fuck you to the storm.

That's not what I am.

I'm a man on the edge of his sanity.

I wasn't in any state to be around my friends who offered to come and join me or have me over for dinner, or even to go home alone and drown myself in a bottle of bourbon. Today is not just an insane summer storm. Today is also the summer solstice and with it, I desperately tried to save a group of doomsday cultists who took a crap load of cyanide before feeding it to their children.

Out of all fifteen who came through my emergency room doors, I was able to save two children who are now up in the ICU fighting for their lives.

As if that wasn't tragic or disturbing enough, I received a call that my Harvard Medical School mentor dropped dead today. It was a standing joke that Dr. Lawrence would die in his classroom and that's exactly what he did. He's the reason I got into Harvard, as he was my neighbor growing up. One of the reasons I wanted to become a doctor in the first place.

Even when I was off touring the world with my best friends as the drummer for our band, Central Square, my dream was to become a doctor, not a rockstar.

But his death came with a huge request from the medical school administration. One I can't say no to because I feel as though I owe Dr. Lawrence. The last thing I ever wanted to do was teach medical school, but now it looks as though that's happening. Starting on Monday.

So yeah, crappy fucking day.

My eyes scroll along the menu just as movement captures my attention along with the scent of something sweet. Cherries and almonds. My gaze climbs up my menu, latching onto a pair of vibrant blue eyes that appear a little manic.

"Hi. Are you sitting here alone?"

"Pardon?" I blink at her.

She puffs out an exasperated breath, her long golden-blonde bangs flying up along with it. "Sorry. Dumb question, as clearly, you're alone at the present time. What I'm asking is are you alone, alone? As in dining solo? As in not expecting a friend or lover or significant other or date to arrive in the next few minutes?"

"Why?" I hedge because she wouldn't be the first pretty woman to approach me after recognizing me.

She shifts her weight to her right foot as her head flies over her shoulder, catches on something that makes her grimace, and then she turns back to me. "No time to explain. Just play along and I'll pay for your dinner as a thank-you."

"What?" My eyebrows scrunch together. The pretty thing isn't making a whole lot of sense, and I'm in no mood to decipher whatever the hell she's trying to say.

"You're all about the one-word answers and I like that in a man since I talk enough for everyone, but if you could just smile and pretend you adore me, that would be—"

"There you are," a guy says, half-out of breath as if he's just sprinted here. "Why did you leave? Our food just arrived."

The blonde gives him a withering glare. "I never ordered any food with you."

"Yes, you did. I sat down and we started talking. I ordered you another drink and a round of appetizers."

"Um. No. That's not what happened at all."

"Sure, it is," the guy protests, moving in closer to her.

The woman's hands fly out protectively, stopping him. "Uh, not so much there, Sweaty Joe. I was having a drink and you started talking to me. I told you I was here to meet someone using the universally polite way to blow someone off, but you decided to order me a drink even though I declined it and then a round of appetizers."

He shakes his head, growing agitated. "No. You told me the person you were meeting wasn't here yet. I took that to mean he stood you up and his loss was going to be my gain."

She pans her hand in my direction. "Well, here he is so you can go back to the bar now."

"Uh-uh. I bought you a drink and food. That entitles me to something."

"*Entitles you to something?*" The woman is incredulous and frankly, so am I.

"Yes. I don't buy drinks and food for every woman. It's called quid pro quo, honey, and I expect something in return for my generosity." He looks her up and down lasciviously. "Besides, you wanted me. I could tell. You were flirting back."

The woman's face flushes with rage as if she's about to eviscerate him right here in the middle of the restaurant. "You're crazy! I was definitely not—"

I stand, having seen enough. "She was not flirting with you because she's here to meet me." I walk over to her and wrap my arm around her waist, pulling her into my side. Maybe that's a bold move and maybe it isn't, but my protective instincts are firing on all cylinders, and I don't want this guy near her. She comes easily enough, so I don't overthink it.

The guy's dark eyes swirl, almost looping in opposite directions. He's short. Stalky. Sweaty. And his pupils are blown out. He's on something and my guess is cocaine judging by the white powder crusted beneath his nostril.

He ignores me completely in favor of her. "Forget this asshole. Come back to the bar with me and have the drink I bought you."

"She told you no, and now I'm telling you to fuck. Off."

"Listen, man. I don't know what—"

I remove my hand from her waist and get right up in his face, no longer caring if we're making a scene and people are watching us. I grip him by his shirt and haul him up until he's forced to stand on his tiptoes. "When a woman says no, or that she's not interested, or asks you to back off, you listen. It's not a negotiation. Get out of here before I change my mind about rearranging your face." I give him a small shove, making him stumble into an empty chair, then I tug the woman back into my side. "She's mine."

He glances around the restaurant, noting all the curious eyes on him, and then he straightens himself. "Whatever. Trashy bitch wasn't worth it anyway."

He stalks off, back toward the bar, only to be intercepted by the manager before he can get there. Frank meets my eyes, and I give him a nod. They'll kick him out and he'll never be allowed back in here again.

I release her immediately and retake my seat, running my hand through my slightly too-long-on-top hair.

"Wow. That was not what I was expecting at all." She takes the seat opposite me and reaches for my water, downing half of it. I watch, slightly amused by that.

She's a firecracker.

She blows out a heavy breath as she sets my glass down and

wipes at her lips. "Can you believe him?" She pans her hand in the direction he went. "The guy was so pushy at the bar and normally I would have tossed the drink he bought me in his face and told him where he could stick the food he ordered, but it hasn't been my best day, and I was a bit flustered." She softens, her eyes meeting mine. "Thank you for coming to my rescue like that. I'm obviously not meeting anyone here tonight. I figured once he saw you that would be that, but I guess one should never underestimate the power of cocaine and the madness it breeds."

She sits up straight, folding her forearms on the table, settling in like she has no plans to go anywhere else, and for the first time, I get a good look at her. I know how incredible her body feels against mine and I know how delicious she smells, but seeing her up close like this is a sucker punch I'm not prepared for.

Huge doe-like blue eyes, lighter and more luminescent than mine. Oval face framed by long, flowy blonde hair, the color of honeycomb. A petite nose that turns up slightly on the end and boasts a tiny diamond stud on the right side and full, pillowy pink lips.

She looks like a young Scarlett Johansen.

Fucking hot—and definitely sexy—even though she's not wearing anything all that sexy. Just a plain black crop T-shirt that hits her waist and ripped baggy jeans.

"Anyway." She clears her throat a little self-consciously and I realize it's because I haven't said anything yet. I've been too mesmerized by her face. "Thanks again. Your dinner is most definitely on me."

She moves to stand, and I reach out, circling her wrist with my hand to stop her. I didn't even do it consciously, but that small point of contact warms my hand and makes my skin buzz.

"Or you could stay and join me," I offer, not even sure that's what I want. I wanted to be alone, but I also can't deny that I want to talk to her more if for no other reason than it affords me the opportunity to look at her. "I haven't had my best day either, so I'm not sure what sort of company I'll be, but after that guy, I'd rather not send you back to the bar by yourself or even out in the storm alone."

She licks her lips, the hint of a barbell in her tongue peeking out as she does, and then after a moment of deliberation, she sits back down. I remove my hand from her skin.

"Today sucked," she starts without any preamble. "All I wanted was to eat some sushi, have a big, fat drink, and unwind my mind, and then that asshole came in and killed all my chill."

A smirk hits my lips, and I can safely say it's the first smile I've had all day. "Well, I was in the same boat until some beautiful, crazy woman came over and asked me to be her fake date."

"Actually, I prefer crazy beautiful. It's all in the phrasing, don't you find?" She rests her chin on her hands. "And I don't know what you're complaining about. Asking to be someone's fake date sounds like the start of a great night to me."

I lean forward, angling my head. "You think so?" I challenge, my smirk growing into a devilish grin because I can't drag myself away from the way her blue eyes heat and sparkle. We went from strained and a bit tense and awkward to fun and flirty in a nanosecond, and I'm digging the hell out of it.

Maybe this is what I needed to drag me out of today. Her.

"I think we'll find out after we order." She bobs her head to the left, indicating our waiter who now stands over us. "But I'll tell you this, choose our sushi wisely or this thing is over before it even begins."

"Who says I want it to begin?"

A coy smile curls up the corner of her lips as she rims the empty wine glass of her place setting with the tip of her finger.

"Oh, I think we both know you do." She sits back and waves a hand toward me. "Order away. I'm into everything."

Hell.

I order us a massive boat of several different kinds of sushi, some edamame, and then I pause. "Gyoza?" I pose to her.

"Pork and pan-fried?" she counters.

I give her a look. "Is there any other kind?"

"Not for me there isn't."

I look back up at the waiter. "We'll have an order of that and two doubles of Don Julio 1942. One large ice cube in each, and keep those coming, please."

The waiter leaves and my pretty companion wiggles in her seat and then drops her elbows onto the table. "Tequila?"

"You've never had it with sushi?"

She shakes her head.

"I hate sake."

"Same. But I usually go with white wine instead."

"Then tonight, it seems, you're living a bit on the wild side."

The lights flicker once again as a massive rumble of thunder shakes the restaurant, making our empty place settings and water glasses rattle. It doesn't appear to bother her in the slightest.

She runs a delicate manicured finger along her chin, her nails black and shiny. "You should be warned, that's not just tonight. I always live my life a bit on the wild side if I can help it, and I promise that's not an exaggeration. I'm a lot. Just ask the last guy who fell in love with me after I warned him not to."

Something darkens her features at that, but I don't bother exploring it.

"Hmmm." I tap my lip, my gaze dancing about her face. "I can tell you're younger than me. He was a boy, right?" I shrug indifferently. "I'm not worried about it."

But even as I say the words, something odd hits me. A

twinge. A warning. Like I'm calling myself a liar, which is ridiculous.

She studies me, liking this game we're playing just as much as I am. Not only is she beautiful, she's exciting. Different. Intelligent. Quick-witted. Just sitting here, I have to fight through the pheromones she's putting off.

I'm helplessly fucking magnetized.

"No," she says as if she's come to some conclusion. "I imagine you have the reverse problem. Gorgeous. A bit mysterious. Not afraid to dine alone, threaten a man, and call a woman you've never met before yours." She's delighting in this now, giving me a long once over, sticking on my chest and arms, before dragging her gaze back up to my face. "Oh yes. I can see it all now. You have women falling at your feet. Am I right?"

"You don't expect me to answer that do you?"

She laughs, the sound light and sweet like spun sugar. "Definitely not. It was one hundred percent rhetorical since I already know the answer is yes." She laces her fingers together and rests her chin on them once more. "So tell me, stranger, are you a one-night-only sort of guy?"

"Depends. Are you a one-night-only sort of girl?"

"I am now," she declares with a scrunch of her nose that makes the tiny stud glint against the light. "Who has time for love and relationships?"

Unfortunately, not me. At least that's how it's been since I started med school, and before that, it was random groupies after random shows we played. I was eighteen when Central Square started touring and twenty-two when we fell apart. But now that two of my best friends have found love and are happy and I'm in my thirties, I can't help but start to want that for myself.

But that's for another night, and certainly not with this woman.

"What's your name?" Because I swear, she's familiar even if I can't place her. Could be from the emergency department with the number of people I see coming in and out of there.

"Are we doing names?"

I laugh. "I didn't realize we weren't."

"We weren't, but now I'm curious. I'm Layla. No last name."

"I'm Callan. Also no last name."

She squints at me, and I regret pressing the whole names thing. People in Boston know me as Callan Barrows from the band Central Square. We were one of the biggest pop/rock bands of our time until our manager, Suzie, dropped dead of a stroke in the shower at the age of twenty-two. We were five guys —plus Suzie—who all grew up in Central Square, Cambridge, and Suzie was the girlfriend of Zax, our bassist, and the twin sister of Lenox, our pianist.

After that, we couldn't find it in us to go on, but in truth, I was done before that. I did college entirely online, premed college at that, which wasn't easy. I had to find lab time in between tours.

I wanted Harvard Medical School, and I had an in for it with Dr. Lawrence and the money I was willing to pay. I had mentioned to Greyson—our frontman and Zax's younger brother—that I was thinking of leaving the band. Suzie died two weeks later, and I felt more guilty for wanting to leave the band than I ever had before. That all happened eight years ago, but this is Boston and we're still among their favorite celebrities.

She continues to scrutinize me, but our tequila is delivered, and she doesn't press it further, and I'm grateful.

Whether she recognizes me or not now, I don't think she initially did, and I like that about her. I'm not Dr. Barrows or Callan Barrows, drummer for Central Square to her. I'm just a guy who saved her from a dickhead and is now having dinner with her.

I raise my glass and she does the same.

"What are we toasting to?" she asks, swirling the clear liquid around the block of ice.

"To an unexpected turn of events?" I suggest.

"I'll say." She holds her glass out to mine and we tap them together before she tosses back every drop of tequila.

I choke out a laugh. "That's sipping tequila."

She runs a hand through her hair, flipping the long strands over to the other side of her neck. "Is that what that was?" Her lips smack. "Who knew? I'll sip the next one, I promise. You have no idea how badly I needed that."

"Actually, I do." I toss down mine the same way she did and signal our waiter for our next round. "I had a bad day too, remember?"

"I know we shared names, but I don't feel like sharing my woes."

I wipe away the excess tequila from my lips. "Good thing, because I had no intention of sharing mine."

She beams at me. "Awesome. You're that kind of guy. Hot and broody."

A gust of breath hits the air as she takes me completely off-guard. "I've never been called broody." If anything, I've always been the easygoing guy. The dependable one.

"No? Only hot?"

"Is that what you're calling me? Because I can safely say, I've never wanted a woman to think I'm hot more in my life than right now with you."

"Gorgeous? Hot? You're everything in between for sure. That dimple in your cheek is doing crazy things to my insides, but you didn't hear that from me." She gives me a wink before turning a little serious. "But for real, are you not normally this broody?"

"No," I admit. "I'm normally considered the nice guy."

"The nice guy," she parrots as if testing the words on her

tongue. "I can work with that. I don't necessarily need broody to get off."

I guffaw just as the gyoza and edamame are set before us.

I raise my eyes to hers, unabashed lust in my gaze as I stare directly at her. "Then what do you need to get off?"

Can't wait to find out what happens next with Callan and Layla? Grab your copy of Irresistibly Wild today! Interested in who Oliver Fritz is? Turn the page to read chapter one of Doctor Scandalous!

DOCTOR SCANDALOUS

Oliver

I'm walking toward the gates of hell. And they charge for admission.

"Oh, Oliver..." Christa Foreman greets me with a slow once-over, her pastel-pink lips curling up into an impish grin. She's aptly named, because our senior class president was no joke when it came to strong-arming and manipulating her fellow classmates into getting what she wanted. "It's so good to see you. Wow. I mean, I see your pictures in magazines and on social media every now and then because I follow you, but you're way better looking in person than I remember from high school."

"Um. Thank you?" It comes out as a question, my head tilting in her direction.

"Sure. No problem." She licks her lips, her long, fake eyelashes batting faster than a butterfly's wings at me. "Are you here alone tonight?" She giggles as a flush creeps up her cheeks. She's married. Can we just say that? "I'm only asking because I need to know how much to charge you. I got stuck collecting money until the event coordinator can get her shit together." She huffs out a flustered breath, rolling her eyes derisively. "Anyway, it's a hundred per person. Should I put you down for one or two?"

And this is where I hesitate. Not over the money. The money is not an issue.

"Just give me a second."

Christa stares longingly at me, licking her lips. "Sure. I'll give you all night."

"Right." Because I have no idea what else to say to that. I don't remember Christa being so overtly interested in me when we were in high school. Then again, that was ten years ago, and I was most definitely taken. Which is both the main reason I don't want to be here and the main reason I came. But now I'm starting to reconsider everything.

I have nothing to prove by being here.

Not to *her*, her douchebag husband—my former friend—or anyone else.

I should just go. Maybe meet up with Carter, who I already know is going to our favorite bar, and get lost in a night of fun. Nothing about this hellhole will be fun. And in truth, I could really use a drink. A quiet one. It's been a shitful week. Too many patients. Not enough time. Oh, and finding out that your mom's cancer is back is always a winner.

I slip my phone from my pocket and shoot off a text to my best friend, Grace.

Me: Sorry, babe. Not gonna be able to make it.

The message bubble instantly dances along my screen.
Grace: It's not a choice, honey pie. Everyone is already asking when you're going to get here. Everyone.

And instantly I'm tempted to ask if *she's* asking. In fact, my thumbs, who seem to have a mind of their own, start to type that very question until I tamp them down and rein them under control. Of course, she's asking. That's what she does.

She continues to hunt me down with terrorist-level determination, even all these years later.

She's likely giddy at the prospect of rubbing her picture-perfect life in my face without even caring that she's the last person on the planet I want to see tonight or any other night. Hence why now is the perfect time to leave.

Me: Don't care.

Grace: Yes, you do. Come on. I know you're already dressed for tonight. Carter sent me a text.

Carter. My traitorous brother.

Grace: Just come inside the hotel. Come up to the reunion. Have a drink with me. See the people you haven't seen since high school who will fall at your feet the way they did back in the day. Oh wait, they still do.

Me: You're doing a shitty job of selling it there, sweetums.

Grace: Everyone will think you're a pussy if you don't come.

Me: Nice gauntlet drop.

Grace: I thought so. Now get your ass over here!

I growl out a slew of curses under my breath, still seriously contemplating fleeing for the sake of my sanity, when I catch sight of a short, curvy redhead in a tight, backless black dress, higher than high heels, and fuck-me red lips that match her hair walking up to Christa. She's as late as I am, and before I know what I'm doing, a smile cracks clear across my face.

I know her instantly.

Even if it's been ten years since I've seen her. A guy never forgets the girl who gave him his first boner. A first-ever boner in class, I might add. We were twelve and she bent over to retrieve her fallen pencil when a flash of her training bra caught my eye. Instant erection.

I was pretty smitten after that moment, as you might imagine.

"Amelia," Christa greets her, her face now lacking any of the warmth it had when she was talking to me. "I had no idea you were coming."

What the fuck? You'd think in the ten years since we graduated from our annoyingly prestigious prep school that the rich girls would get over the self-created, mean-girl bullshit they had with the scholarship kids.

Amelia turns redder than her hair, and she takes a small step back before straightening her frame and squaring her shoulders. "Well, I'm here. Graduated same year as you. I even received the invitation in the mail. Must have been an error on your part," she finishes sarcastically.

"Uh-huh. It's a hundred-dollar entrance fee," Christa snaps, taking far too much pleasure in announcing that sum as she purses her lips off to the side, giving Amelia a nasty-girl slow once-over.

"A hundred dollars?" Amelia asks, though it comes out in a deflated, breathy whisper.

"Yup. Sorry," Christa sneers with a sorry-not-sorry saccharine sweet voice. "No exceptions. Not even for the kids who were on scholarship."

And that's it. Before Christa can say anything else that will make me want to throttle her, I walk over to Amelia, wrapping my hand around her waist. "Sweetheart," I exclaim. "You made it. I was starting to get worried."

Amelia jolts in my arms, her breath catching high in her throat as she twists to face me. Then she looks up and up a bit more because she's about a foot shorter than I am even in her heels. Suddenly, two sparkling gray eyes blink rapidly at me, and my heart starts to pound in time with the flutter of her lashes, my mouth dry like I've been eating sand all night.

"I'm sorry," she says, confused, her parted lips hanging just a bit too open for us to be selling this. "I think you must—"

I lean in, my nose brushing against her silky red hair that

smells like honeysuckle or something sweet and I breathe into her ear, "Just go with it."

She swallows audibly as I pull back, staring into her eyes and wondering how a color like that is even possible when she smiles and robs me of my breath. *Whoa.* That's unexpected.

"I didn't mean to worry you..." She trips up, biting into her lip like she's searching for a suitable term of endearment. Or maybe my name? I guess it is possible she has no idea who I am. We didn't exactly run in the same circles, and I just came up to her and wrapped my arm around her. "Oli," she finishes with, and I blow out the breath I didn't even realize I was holding.

"It's fine. I just didn't want to go in without the most beautiful woman in the world on my arm."

Amelia gives me that stunning smile again, this time with a blush staining her cheeks, and I marvel at how it makes her eyes glow to a smoky charcoal. Goddamn, she's fucking sexy.

"Wait," Christa interrupts. "You're with her?" She points at Amelia.

"I sure am," I declare without removing my eyes from Amelia's because those eyes, man. They're just too pretty not to stare at. "I'm a lucky bastard, right?"

"You're with him?" She turns that finger on me.

"So it seems," Amelia replies, her tone a bit bewildered, though there is a hint of amusement in there, too.

"But. You're. You. No. You're Oliver Fritz," Christa sputters incredulously. "And she's Amelia—" Her words cut off when I throw her my most menacing glare, already knowing the exact nasty nickname she's about to throw out. Why certain women feel the need to degrade and belittle other women, I'll never understand.

I slip two one-hundred-dollar bills from my wallet and toss them at Christa. "Have a good night," I say instead of what I'm really thinking. My fingers intertwine with Amelia's, and then

I'm dragging her past Christa, down the long corridor with the paisley rug and gold walls, toward the ballroom.

I guess I'm going to my high school reunion after all.

The second we're out of sight of Christa, Amelia yanks her hand from mine, stopping in the middle of the hall and turning to stare up at me. "You remember me?" she asks and then shakes her head like that's not what she meant to say.

"Amelia Atkins. You were in most of my classes from the time we were in sixth grade or so, on."

"Right. What I meant to say is, thank you for stepping in back there, but it really wasn't necessary."

"Maybe not. I'm sure you can handle yourself with women like Christa. But it felt wrong to stand there and watch that go down, doing nothing. I can't stand women who feel the need to hurt others just to make themselves look and feel better."

She folds her arms over her chest, giving me a raised eyebrow. "And yet you dated a woman who did exactly that all through high school."

Touché. A bark of a laugh slips out my lungs. "Can't argue with that. Hell, I dated that same vicious woman through college too. Adolescent mistake. What can I say?"

Still, at the mention of that particular woman, an old flair hits me straight in the chest. My fingers find my pocket, toying with the large diamond solitaire set in a diamond and platinum band I stuck in there tonight. It's *the* ring. The one I nearly gave to said woman who was screwing around on me with my friend, Rob. A lesson in betrayal I've never forgotten. It's why on certain occasions, I carry it with me.

A reminder to never get too close again.

"Sorry," Amelia says, withering before my eyes. "That was insanely rude of me. I don't even know why I said that. Christa got my hackles all fired up, and I just took them out on you instead of her, like I should have. Damn, some women seriously suck, right?" I can't stop my chuckle, though I think she was being serious. She stares down at the rug, shifting her stance until she's leaning back against the wall opposite the closed doors where the reunion is taking place. "Look, I wish you hadn't paid for me. Money and I aren't exactly on speaking terms at the moment. It's going to take me a while to pay you back. But I *will* pay you back. I just don't have that kind of—"

My fingers latch on to her chin, tilting her head back up until our eyes meet. "I don't care about the money. And I don't want you to pay me back." She opens her mouth as if to argue with me, and I shake my head, cutting her off again. "I mean it."

She huffs out a breath. "Well, thank you. That's very generous. But if this is how this night is already starting off, I'm thinking maybe I should just go. Hell, I shouldn't even have come here in the first place. I don't know what I was thinking. My sister talked me into it, and I thought..." She shakes her head. "Never mind. It's stupid."

I prop my shoulder against the wall so I'm facing her, folding my arms while I stare at her because I can't seem to help myself. "Why is it stupid?"

"You really want to know?"

"I really want to know."

Those big eyes slay through me, slightly glassy with emotion. "Because no one in there wants me there. You heard Christa. I was fooling myself into thinking that I could waltz in here ten years later and everyone who treated me like garbage growing up would finally see me for me. That they'd finally realize we're all on an even playing field now that high school is over. It was going to be like putting all my old bully nightmares to rest once and for all. Only, nothing has changed. I'm still the girl wearing thrift store digs who couldn't even afford to pay the entrance fee."

Wow. That's...

"Can I tell you something?" I ask.

Her hands meet her hips. "You mean something to rival the

way too personal verbal diarrhea I just spouted at a man I haven't seen in a decade?"

She's trying for brave and strong, and even sarcastic. But she's sad. I can see it in her eyes that bounce around my face, almost as if she's not sure she wants to know what I'm about to say. No one wants to be slammed back into their high school nightmare. She wanted to walk in there and make all those assholes eat their words.

I want that for her too.

I like Amelia. I always have. There was something about her that just got to me on a weird level I never quite understood. She was sweet and nerdy and quiet and reserved. So understatedly beautiful. Her hair was all wild with red curls. Her glasses a touch too big for her face. Her body small with her ample curves hidden beneath her ill-fitting prep school uniform.

And looking at her now, after hearing what Christa was saying to her...

In truth, I do remember people being that nasty. Though now I'm positive it was a lot worse than I knew about if Christa's reaction to her tonight is anything to go by. I only heard comments here and there that I didn't pay much attention to, nor did anything to stop. Even if I never directly contributed to it, by not stopping it, I was part of the problem.

That's on me. And it's not okay. I should have done more to protect her. I should have said something.

"Something like that. You told me yours. Now I'll tell you mine."

"Alright."

I step into her, bending down like I'm about to tell her a secret when really, I just want to be closer to her. Smell her shampoo that makes my cock jump in my slacks. Feel the heat of her body as she starts to blush from my proximity.

"I don't want to be here either. I got talked into it by my friend, Grace, and now here I am."

Her eyebrows knit together. "Why wouldn't you want to be here? You're a doctor. You were the most popular guy in our class. Captain of the football team. Everyone loved you. Still do, if the tabloids are anything to go by."

I suck in a deep breath, ready to tell her something only my family and Grace know. "My ex is not only in there with her husband, my former friend, but she's pregnant. Likely going to be delivered by either my brother or my best friend since she sought them out to be her OB. How's that for irony?" I roll my eyes. "The only saving grace I have when it comes to Nora is that she never knew I was about to propose. I had the ring in my pocket, ready to drop down onto one knee, but before I could do anything, she told me she was in love with Rob and that we were over."

Amelia sucks in a rush of air, her eyes flashing. Her hand shoots up, covering her parted lips as she stares at me with a combination of shock and sympathy. "God. That's awful."

"The real kicker of all that is I had made a lot of sacrifices for her. A lot. Nearly everything I wanted I had given up for her with the exception of medicine. But I chose NYU to be with her instead of playing ball at Michigan. I finished college in three years instead of four because she said the sooner I can complete med school and residency, the better. Then, on the fucking day I got into Columbia for med school and was set to propose, she informed me she had been cheating on me for the better half of six months."

Six. Fucking. Months!

"Jesus, Oliver. I'm so sorry. I never heard anything about that."

"That's because no one knows, so if you wouldn't mind keeping that to yourself, I'd appreciate it. The last thing I want is for that to hit the press next."

She reaches out her hand, touching my arm and giving me a squeeze. "Of course. I'll never tell anyone. I don't blame you for not wanting to go in there. It seems we both felt like we had something to prove by showing up tonight."

That's not the reason I came tonight. But Nora is the main reason I didn't want to go in. I've successfully avoided seeing her for years. In truth, I've been over her for a long time, just not over what she did to me. Most of my bitterness and resentment is on me. I should never have made those sacrifices for her.

I gave up pieces of myself I can never get back.

But Amelia deserves more. She always has, and she never got it. She deserves to have people look at her and treat her with the respect they never did. They owe it to her. Hell, I owe it to her. I don't want her to leave tonight the way she is now.

"I only wish it had turned out better for us," she continues. "But I think my carriage has officially turned back into a pumpkin and I should just cut my losses and head home. Tonight can't possibly end the way I had envisioned it."

Like a bolt of electricity flowing through me, suddenly I'm giddy with an idea that is quite possibly the most ridiculous idea in the history of ideas. Christa nearly swallowed her tongue when she thought Amelia was my date. So maybe everyone else will react the same way if that's what they see. Bonus for me—I'll have a hot as hell woman on my arm and maybe Nora will leave me alone.

More than that, I *want* to go in there with Amelia. I want to spend more time with her tonight. And if they don't like it or think less of me for it, well, I don't give a shit.

But Amelia being my date isn't enough. Not with my reputation. They'll just assume I'm using her, because ever since Nora and I split up... I've been somewhat of a player. A fact the media loves to report on. Hell, my face is splashed across the internet every other week, showing me with a different woman each time. Not in the last few months or so, but it's been the standard of my life since Nora. It's the way I keep from getting hurt again.

And the media reporting on it all? Well, that's the standard of all my brothers' lives. It comes with being a Fritz and living in Boston. We own this city. We're royalty. For better or worse, that's how it is.

But if Amelia and I really want to make an impact tonight... if I really want to make all those assholes who hurt Amelia choke, and Nora—who still calls me to tell me *all* her 'happy' news—realize that I've finally and officially moved on from her... it needs to be more than just people thinking I'm dating Amelia.

They need to know she's something special. Believe she's something special *to me*.

My fingers dig back into my pocket, locating that ring. Looking at her... plotting this insane idea... I'm hit with the fact that I know it will change everything. Both for her and for me.

A deviously crooked smile curls up at the corner of my lips.

Yeah. I have an idea, alright. And I think I can get Amelia to go for it. It's only for a few hours anyway. What could go wrong?

Doctor Scandalous is FREE in Kindle Unlimited!

END OF BOOK NOTE

Thank you lovely reader for taking the time to get lost in Greyson and Fallon's story. I hope you loved read it as much as I loved writing. I fell so hard for this couple and their journey. It was hard-won, but I don't think it's possible not to love Greyson Monroe. He is my love letter to every romance-loving person out there. Not perfect, but all heart and so fierce with his love for Fallon.

Some books are easier to write than others and I struggled with this one simply because there is SO much backstory to each of them. I could have kept writing this couple and never stopped.

I also want to say, and this will be news to everyone because I haven't shared it before, but when I was a teenager, the world lost an incredible guy by the name of Grayson. Yes, the spelling is different. Out of respect for him and his family, I won't go into any specifics, but his loss shook me to my core. He had the best smile and the kindest heart and this was my tribute to him.

Gone, but never forgotten.

I want to thank #teamJulie for their constant help and my gorgeous beta readers, Patricia, Danielle, and Kelly. You ladies are incredible and I couldn't do any of this without you. I also want to than Nina for taking the time to read this book and help me make the changes I needed to make.

I also want to thank my incredible husband and kids. Your endless love and patience and support and confidence is what drives me and makes everything I do possible.

And thank you, lovely reader, for helping to make my dreams come true. I am eternally grateful! XO

- J. Saman